HIM

L.J. DIVA

HIM

★ Royal Star Publishing ★

Chances is an imprint of Royal Star Publishing
www.royalstarpublishing.com.au

First edition paperback published in 2025
All Rights Reserved, Copyright ©L.J. Diva 2025

Trade Paperback ISBN: 978-1-922307-89-7
Large Print Paperback ISBN: 978-1-922307-90-3
Dust Jacket Hardcover ISBN: 978-1-922307-91-0
E-book ISBN: 978-1-922307-88-0
A catalogue record for this book is available from the National
Library of Australia.

Cover design: Royal Star Publishing and ©Designed with Grace
Cover photos: Male silhouette: IconicPrototype/shutterstock.com
Cityscape: 4LUCK/shutterstock.com
Typesetting in Minion Pro by Royal Star Publishing

DEDICATION

This series is dedicated to the crime fighting Reagan family, especially Sean. Sometimes, *Blood* is not thicker and definitely not *Blue*, and the truly wrong will always pay for their sins.

PART ONE

Chapter 1

He turned along the road, the freezing rain pelting his back, and pulling his collar higher around his neck, glanced up and saw it just ahead. Not long now and he'd be shucking off his soggy clothing and getting warm in front of the fireplace he knew would be roaring merrily in its place.

He arrived at the fence, and with two hands on the top, pushed his right foot into it and hauled himself over, landing with a dull thud. His backpack fell to the ground beside him, and he pulled his hood back over his rain covered face before picking it up. Hurrying across the yard to the house, he dug into his right jacket pocket for the keys. He had his own set; had for some time.

He slung his backpack over his shoulder, rushed down the stairs to the basement door, and turned on the small flashlight attached to the ring of keys. He inserted the first key into the first lock and turned it. After pulling it out, he selected the second key and unlocked the second deadbolt, and with the third key, he inserted it into the third lock but heard a click louder than the one at his hand.

"Hold it right there. Let me see your hands."

The man slowly raised his hands. His heart pounded under his ribcage, but his lips slid into a sly smile. Turning around, he blinked at the flashlights the two officers were aiming at him. "And what can I do for you this fine night, officers?"

The female officer spoke into her radio. "This is Officer Biedermeier. We've got a prowler on a break and enter in progress on the Upper East Side."

"Prowler on a break and enter?" the man mocked. "I'm neither. I have keys and permission to be here. In fact, my key is still in the lock." He turned sideways and pointed to the door. "Three deadbolts, three keys. She keeps the basement locked up tight."

Hesitating, the young officer lowered his weapon. "We're taking you in. You jumped the fence and now you're trying to break in. Do you live here?"

"No, I don't," the man said confidently. "But I know who does and she's waiting for me."

"Prove you've got the right keys," Biedermeier said. "Open the door."

He looked at her but only smiled.

"Go on, young man." Biedermeier approached him slowly. "Finish unlocking the door. If you can open it, we'll chat to the owner. If you can't, we'll take you in."

Smiling, the man cockily turned back to the door, removed his key and turned the handle.

The door wouldn't budge.

He frowned. "What?" Trying again, he turned the knob and leant against the door. "She must have the metal bars in place. I know I opened the locks."

"Clearly not," Biedermeier said. "You'll have to come with us."

Puzzled, the man retrieved his key and turned. "I'm still not breaking and entering. She probably hasn't removed the bars yet. I'm going to call her." As he reached into his jacket pocket, the two officers raised their guns. "Whoa, easy." He raised his hands. "It's just the phone, see." Waving his right hand, he added, "Just let me call her and if she doesn't answer, I'll come peacefully."

Biedermeier nodded, and watched him make the call, but saw his brows furrowing that the call wasn't going through.

"Are you home? I'm trying to get in, but the bars are down, and I've got two cops in my face wanting to arrest me. Are you home?" Sighing, he ended the call. "Looks like she's not home, so I guess I'll come peacefully." He slid his phone into his pocket and tightened the collar of his coat. "Lead the way, officers."

With one in front and one behind, they hurried to the back fence and deftly vaulted over.

"Couldn't we've just opened the gate," the male officer complained.

"You can't. She keeps it padlocked," the man replied, stopping at the back door of the police cruiser while Biedermeier opened it and waved him in. "This'll be fun." The man grinned and climbed in. On the way to the station, he tried to engage them in conversation. "So, how long have the two of you been on the job? Do you like it? I considered becoming a cop once."

Biedermeier's gaze flickered to the rearview to glance

at him, but she remained silent.

The young male officer, however, took the bait. "Breaking into houses is a hobby, then, or did you consider breaking and entering at the same time you considered becoming a cop?"

"Good question," the man said. "But I wasn't breaking and entering. I have keys, and I have permission to be there."

"Yet you can't even get the homeowner on the phone to tell her you're waiting for her. And if those so-called metals bars were in place, she clearly didn't want you there." Biedermeier turned into a parking space out the front of the precinct. "And now we get to take you in and charge you." She alighted and opened the back door.

"With what?" the man asked, sliding out of the car. "You haven't even cuffed me, so have you even arrested me?"

She rolled her eyes. "Oh, such a moral dilemma." Gripping his arm, she escorted him inside and led him to a cell. There was only one other occupied with a passed out drunk. Quiet for that time of night.

"Biedermeier, Vasquez. What's his name?" the booking clerk asked them. "And why's he still got his bag?"

"Hey, kid, what's your name?" Biedermeier turned around to see him lay his coat over the bench next to his bag, and noticed he was tall and slim.

He smoothed his short brown wavy hair and blue jumper before facing them and sliding his hands into his pockets. "Sean. Sean Ryan."

The three officers stared at him before the woman

spun back to the booking clerk. "I didn't know that was the PC's grandson. What do we do?"

"Do I need to use my courtesy card? My *grandfather's* courtesy card?" he called.

They looked at him and saw the shit-eating grin on his lips, and the sapphire blue eyes that radiated across the room.

"What do I do?" she asked the clerk again.

"What's the charge?" he asked.

"Break and enter, trespassing," Officer Vasquez supplied.

"Except, he said he had permission to be there, and he had keys to the basement door." Biedermeier sighed. "I do not want to be on the wrong side of the commissioner."

A door banged open, and Declan Ryan hauled a perp through the inner door, yelling at the top of his voice. "I wouldn't have to haul your ass in if you didn't keep crapping on the streets." He opened a cell door and pushed the man in. "You stink. We're gonna have to hose you down and I need my car detailed to get rid of the stench." He slammed the door shut and shook himself off. "Ugh, I'm gonna stink of crap now."

"Nothing new for you," Sean said, looking at his old man.

"I don't want no smart mouth…" Declan paused long enough to look from his son to the officers and clerk. "Why the hell is my son in a cell?"

"We caught him trespassing on a property and trying to gain access via the basement door," Biedermeier explained. "There'd been reports of prowlers."

"Did he go onto any other property?" Declan asked.

"Not that we know of. We came down the road to check on the call and found him hurrying along. We then saw him jump a fence, and we went after him and found him trying to get into the basement door."

"With keys," Sean added.

"Whose house was it?" Declan asked all of them.

The officers shook their heads, but Sean said, "Sydney's."

Stunned, Declan glared at his son. "You were trying to get into Sydney's—"

"Not that you haven't done the same," Sean cut in.

"Why the hell would you try and break into Sydney's house?" Declan yelled. "After everything you did—"

"What *I* did?" Sean retaliated. "*You* accused her of being a paedophile rapist and then years later fucked her. Uncle Connor slapped her and fucked her, and Ethan just fucked her. But I could say a lot more about that *and* him. So don't act so high and mighty. Sydney and I resolved our issues and had become friendly. She gave me keys and permission to be there, whereas you, Connor, and Ethan just kept turning up whenever you needed to plant your dicks in her."

"You little asswipe." Declan slammed against the bars, thrusting both hands through them to get to his son. "You little bastard. Sydney wouldn't give you anything."

"No? She gave it to you," Sean mocked, enjoying the heated conflict. Years of working out and martial arts had given him a lean muscular figure and he had a good head in height on his father.

"Open the goddamn door so I can kill the little punk," Declan yelled, spit flying from his mouth. "Open the goddamn door."

"Detective!" The booming voice quieted the room and Declan spun towards it. "What the hell are you doing? Get yourself together and stop behaving like an animal."

Declan straightened his jacket and looked down. "Yes, boss."

"Now what's all this about?" Lieutenant Loutin moved towards the cell. "Young Sean Ryan. You've got your father riled up. What are you in for?"

"B&E and being a prowler, apparently." Sean greeted the six-five, robust lieutenant calmly. "I was visiting a friend, who's given me the keys to her door and permission to be on her property. I came in of my own volition, but I'm yet to be arrested or charged."

Loutin turned to the officers. "Is this true?"

"He does have keys, sir," Biedermeier said. "A key was in the lock when we found him. But he couldn't open the door, and the homeowner wouldn't pick up when he called."

"Her basement door has three deadbolts with three keys, which I have copies of, and three interior metal bars for protection. She obviously hadn't moved them yet. She also has the back gate padlocked most of the time, which is why I jumped the fence. The basement door is right next to the locked door of the sex room that my dad, Uncle Connor, and Cousin Ethan know all too well."

Declan lunged at him. "You little—"

"Detective!" Loutin yelled. "Get out of here and get back to work."

Declan shrugged, fixed his jacket, and pointed at Sean. "I'm warning you, kid. I'm warning you. You'll get yours."

"I got mine all through childhood except I'm not a child anymore and you don't get to dictate what I do or who I see. Any more than Mom got to dictate what you did all those nights you didn't come home." He glared pointedly at his father.

Shaken by the comment, Declan backed away until he reached the doorway and hurried through it, slamming the door behind him.

Sighing, Loutin turned to Sean. "You seem to know the law, but considering who your family is…"

Sean smirked. "I also graduated at the top of my class at *Harvard* Law. Only took me two years. I took to law like a duck to water."

"But why do you enter through the basement if you know her?" Vasquez asked.

"In the rain, it's easier to leave my muddy shoes and sopping clothes in the basement bathroom so I don't traipse mud or water through the house," Sean replied.

"And who's the homeowner?" Loutin asked.

"Sydney Kingston," Sean said. "The *author.*"

"Of the Cassandra Kingsley thrillers?" Loutin asked. "I love those."

"So does my grandfather. So did my pop before he passed. My grandfather's engaged to Sydney's best friend, Emerson Lake, the writer, director, and producer of the true crime series, *Twisted Minds.* She also directs and produces the movies from Sydney's books. Sydney mentored me in writing four years ago, and it led to my career as a young adult author. A *best-selling* young adult author." He loved to bring out the big guns every now and then to let people know who he was and who he was related to. And it always worked.

Loutin nodded. "Well, as your family knows Sydney—"

"Some do, intimately," Sean replied, hiding his mocking tone.

"Yes," Loutin muttered in embarrassment. "Then there's no point keeping you here. Officer, release Sean without charge." He motioned at the clerk to open the cell and waited while Sean gathered his coat and bag. "My daughter loved your novels; you captured the YA market brilliantly." He shook his hand. "You're quite a writer."

"Thank you, I appreciate that." Sean slid into his coat and pulled out his phone. "Do you mind me waiting for an Uber?"

"No, no, there's no need for that. My officers will drive you home." He clicked his fingers at Biedermeier and Vasquez. "Please take Mr Ryan home and then get on with the rest of the shift."

"Sir." Biedermeier nodded, but her furrowed brows showed displeasure.

When Loutin had walked away, they escorted Sean back outside and into the car.

"Don't think we're your personal taxi service." Biedermeier swiped a strand of wet red hair out of her eyes.

"Just for tonight, since you picked me up," Sean replied, keeping his manner friendly. "You can drop me off at 42 Rochester Street."

Biedermeier rolled her eyes and drove off into the rain that slammed the car with a ferocity stronger than when they'd come in. "I hope we don't get washed away in this," she muttered, hunching over the wheel and peering out the windscreen.

They were silent after that, except for her odd muttering, and finally made it to Rochester.

"Thank you for the lift." Sean picked up his bag and waited for Vasquez to get out and open the back door. "I hope the rest of your night goes well." He heard a sigh from the front, grinned, and alighted from the cruiser. "Officer Biedermeier," he said, and hurried up the path to the front door where the doorman greeted him warmly.

"Let me know when they're gone," Sean told him and walked away from the front door. He pulled out his cell phone and booked an Uber, seeing he had at least ten minutes to wait.

"They've moved on," the doorman called, warming the backs of his legs against the small bar heater near his desk.

Ten minutes later, Sean handed him a twenty and ran out to the car. His home was in an entirely different suburb, not that he wanted anyone to know that.

The doorman didn't mind. He was earning extra pocket money every month from Sean's manoeuvrings. What the tax man didn't know and all that...

Sean was dropped off at his condo and hurried inside.

He had a story to write and that look on his father's face… That was a classic he needed to get into words. But that would happen after he called Sydney.

*****

One week later, a woman in a sharp black skirt suit and white blouse, a single strand of white pearls at her neck, black matte leather heels, and a matching roller briefcase, walked into the office of Police Commissioner Ryan.

"Commissioner, so nice of you to meet me on short notice." She stood at his desk and shook his hand, taking in the greying hair and moustache.

"When you said it had to do with my grandson, I figured we'd better have the conversation sooner, rather than later. Please, take a seat." He motioned to the chairs at her back and waited for her to sit. "Tell me, which grandson do I have to worry about." He seated himself and tapped his desk. "As I'm the commissioner, I suppose it has to be Ethan."

"No, commissioner. It's Sean." Mariel Strasinsky, from law firm Strasinsky and Rowe, opened her briefcase and pulled out a hefty file. She placed it in front of him and then pulled out a second, placed that in front of him, and then pulled out a third. She laid her hands on the pile in front of him. "All of these concern Sean." Sitting down, she waited, watching him frown, lean back in his seat, cough, and lean forward. "I know your son Alec is the DA and Kieran is a lawyer. I also know Sean's father, Declan, is a hothead, but this information could not be ignored when it came to light."

"And what information would that be?" Cormac heaved a sigh and opened the top file.

"The information about the stalking and harassment of Sydney Kingston."

Cormac looked up sharply. "What!"

"It seems that no one knew," Mariel said. "Two weeks ago, Ms Kingston left for her home country of Australia. During the packing stage, many hidden cameras were found in her brownstone. Landon Security did a sweep, checked for fingerprints, but found only one. They suspected the cameras were planted by one of her previous stalkers; maybe they'd broken in after all. Or it could have been by Lennie Cuzco to check up on his then living girlfriend, Nora, who was housesitting a couple of years ago. We don't know when they were planted, but we do have the proof of who planted them, who stole Ms Kingston's underwear, entered her house when she wasn't home, slept in her bed, etcetera."

"And what makes you think it's Sean?" Cormac picked up an 8x10 photograph of the wall in Sean's condo. It displayed photos of Sydney in all sizes.

Mariel breathed in. "Did you know your grandson is the author known as Bryan Jamison?"

Cormac glanced up under his deeply furrowed brows. "Sean writes young adult books under his own name."

"And psychological crime thrillers as Bryan Jamison." Mariel slid back in her seat. "When Ms Kingston spent the night with Mr Jamison, she had Landon follow him home. She suspected something was wrong, had a sense that she knew him, but couldn't put her finger on it. Landon sent a PI to follow Bryan from Sydney's house and watched him walk into a condominium. He followed him in and found the apartment he entered. An extensive search found that your grandson, Sean, owns the condo, with the one beside it, under a company he set up. We discovered a bank account worth millions in his name and that's when we found out he was the hotshot new thriller writer Bryan Jamison. We wondered if Sean could've been the one who planted the cameras, and Landon gained entrance to both of Sean's condos. That's when they found that the second was used for an office, and two walls were covered in photos of Ms Kingston."

She pointed at the photos in Cormac's hand. "That's the wall opposite his desk, so he can look at her every time he writes. We also found the video footage from the cameras. He's been watching her sleep, shower, dress, and entertain men."

Cormac placed the photo to the side and slowly shuffled through the pile. Images of Sean installing the cameras, sniffing her underwear, and sleeping in her bed. He pushed the photos back into a pile and closed the folder on them. A deep heaving sigh of despair ensued. "And the other two folders?"

"One contains the company and house information. The third contains his actions for the last two weeks." She paused a moment and crossed her legs. "You know he was found trying to break into Ms Kingston's brownstone a week ago? He jumped the back fence and tried to gain access with keys to the deadbolts on the basement door. Fortunately, the house was locked up tight and the three metal safety bars were in place. Ms

Kingston did not give keys to Sean, nor give him permission to be on or in her property. We understand two officers took him in, but a lieutenant let him go. The two officers were directed to take him home and dropped him off at 42 Rochester. It's an apartment building in which he owns an apartment. The doorman says he drops in from time to time, but he isn't there all the time."

"And why have you brought this to my attention, Ms Strasinsky?" Cormac pushed the files away and leaned wearily in his chair. "He's not an officer. I don't get to reprimand him, *or* fire him from the NYPD. Sean's an adult. What do you expect me to do?"

"Ms Kingston felt that you should know. She didn't want to bring this to the attention of the press, or have it get out. The public embarrassment and humiliation is something she doesn't want, and as a sign of respect to you and your family, she felt you should know and be given the chance to deal with it. Just as you dealt with it *last* time."

Cormac's thick brows rose, and he nodded. "Sydney was right then; he got out of hand. But we thought we'd fixed it. He received therapy and we ordered him to stay away from her. Which, for the most part, he did. And he made great strides in his emotional progress." He sighed and turned his chair to the window. "What am I supposed to do with this now? How do I take care of this?"

"Quietly," Mariel said. "Ms Kingston wasn't a fan of pressing charges, but she felt that some punishment should happen. Quietly."

"And what punishment would that be unless we go through legal channels and arrest him? There are so many crimes he could be charged with." He waved a thick hand at the files. "Do we keep him out of jail? Put him in detention?"

"Home detention," Mariel suggested. "Family appointed, with the threat of going public with arrest. Ankle monitor, home monitoring. If he steps out of line, charge him."

"I need to speak to my son." Cormac heaved himself up and over to the window. Nearing seventy-five, he was soon for retirement and didn't want to deal with this again. With Sean again. He'd thought that was over.

"Declan?" Mariel stepped over to him. "That's going to cause even more trouble for your grandson, and possibly Ms Kingston. I understand he had a rather unfortunate blow up with her several years ago concerning his son."

Cormac gave a nod. "He did. But it will get out in the family, what Sean has done."

"Unless you keep it quiet. Come down on him like a tonne of bricks, threaten his life in a familial way."

Another sigh left Cormac. "The son I meant is Alec. As the district attorney he can offer some advice and guidance and maybe help out without letting it out to the rest of the family."

"Ms Kingston didn't want to send Sean to jail, but she did want him to face the consequences for his actions. She doesn't want press or publicity and was shocked and dismayed by what he'd done."

Cormac looked sharply at her. "And what should I do

about her sleeping with my grandson?" Mariel frowned and went to speak, but Cormac cut her off. "You told me that Sean is passing as this Bryan Jamison character. I've read his books; they're just as good as Sydney's, but Sean's only twenty-one and you said that Ms Kingston spent the night with him. She slept with my grandson."

"And she didn't know it was Sean when it happened, which is why she felt something was wrong. Like everyone else, people believed Bryan Jamison was a forty-something college professor who'd written books. She was shocked to find out he wasn't. And even more shocked to find out he wore a disguise as Bryan. Ms Kingston is sickened by what's happened and wishes she could take back that night, but she can't. And legally, Sean *is* an adult, even though he's much younger than her. He ran a con, commissioner. On Ms Kingston, on his career, his life, his family. He's not the first author to use a pen name, or change their look for it, but his con has lasted quite some time."

"How long?"

"We're not sure. From the footage we did find it was about three months."

"But it could have gone on for longer?"

"Considering the time stamps on the photos, and dates of the articles he has on the wall, probably years."

A low growl came from Cormac's throat. "Since Sydney first turned up in our lives and Sean first became obsessed. I thought I'd taken care of it, and he'd come good with therapy and getting out of his parents' house."

"Apparently not good enough," Mariel said. "Or it was all an act. Just as all of it has been an act. Is this act two? The first being the obsession, the second this persona."

"An act that will come to a close with the threat of arrest, embarrassment, and being outed to the public, and him being shunned and cancelled."

She studied his morose expression. "That means embarrassment for you and your family."

Cormac nodded in thought. "I know. But let's hope it doesn't come to that. Let's hope he has enough sense to finish this obsession."

Mariel agreed. "And that there's no act three."

*****

Cormac spent several days consulting with Alec about Sean. They decided to not tell Declan, as he'd just explode and want his son thrown in jail. And Kieran was kept out of it. On the fourth day, Sean was asked into the office.

"Hey, Grandpa." Sean stopped when he saw his uncle standing next to his grandfather behind the desk. "Uncle Alec." He closed the door and stepped tentatively towards the desk. "What's going on?"

"Something important." Cormac's smile was grim as he motioned at the chair. "Take a seat, Sean. We need to talk."

Sean glanced from his grandfather to Alec and back, and he knew in his blood that something was very wrong. He chose to not remove his messenger bag from his shoulder, but sat in one of the chairs and steeled himself. "What's this about?"

"It's about your obsession with Sydney Kingston," Cormac told him, clasping his hands together and tapping them on the desk as he studied his grandson.

Sean sighed in a bored manner. "I don't have an obsession, Grandpa. I had therapy for that, and it was just because she showed me some attention during a really screwed up time in my life." He breathed as evenly as he could so his heart would stop trembling. "It's long over and far away."

"Apparently not." Cormac sighed and leant back. "You were found trying to break into Sydney's brownstone—"

"I have keys," Sean snapped. "I wasn't breaking into it."

Cormac held up an authoritative hand. "Stop. Just stop lying, Sean. We know all about it. You planted cameras in Sydney's house, you stole her underwear, and you slept in her bed. You have thousands of pictures of her on the living room wall of a second condo in your company's name—and we didn't know you even owned the first one, or that you'd set up a company to protect your money and assets you make as author Bryan Jamison. Another thing you didn't tell us about." He saw Sean's eyes narrow and his nostrils flair. "We know, Sean." Pushing the photos across the desk, he waited for the explosion.

Sean picked up the photos on the top of the pile. There was one of the wall opposite his desk. He stared at it before shuffling through the others to see what they had. He could play it one of two ways. Inhaling, he casually threw the photos onto the pile. "Yeah, so? How do you think I get inspiration for all of those novels I wrote? Some people obsess over singers, actors, I take inspiration from Sydney Kingston. My one-time author mentor that my family abused and accused of heinous crimes. Dad yelled down her doorstep and Connor slapped her."

"So did you," Cormac yelled. "That's why I got you help, Sean. Because your obsession with Sydney got out of control. That's why I ordered the family to stay away from her and for you to go to therapy. Which I thought had worked."

"It did," Sean spat. "I got over my obsession, but two of your sons certainly didn't. Neither did your eldest grandson, and yet all the attention was on me because I was the youngest." He huffed, removed his bag from over his head, and dumped it on the other chair, stalking over to the floor-to-ceiling window and looking over the city. "My so-called obsession was *and is* nothing compared to Ethan's. And my dad's. God." He rolled his eyes. "If only you knew what I do about him. But no, it all gets dumped on me."

"Sean, we've seen the footage of you in her house. We've seen the photos on your wall. But I gotta say, your contracts are first class." Alec walked over to him. "I'm not to be let off when it comes to Sydney, either. I went to her house and gave her an inquisition, but I didn't do any of *that.* You worked so hard to deal with it. Were you faking it?"

"The same way you fake being a good DA? Or Dad faked being a great father and husband?" Sean mocked and glared at him. "The only decent one left in this family is Kieran, but we'll see how long he lasts."

"You're a cynical little bastard," Alec spat. "Just like your father—"

"Like father like son," Sean replied. "Apple doesn't fall."

Cormac heard that last sentence and flashed back to when he was standing outside Sydney's door, after Sean and Connor's assaults. He'd asked who left the bruise, and she'd said, apple doesn't fall. His eyes narrowed. "Sean, you have one of two choices. You take your punishment and move on with your life, or you have this made public and embarrass your family and get yourself cancelled."

Sean laughed. "Yeah, Grandpa, because Sydney would really want this out in the open, and believe me when I say this…" He moved over to the desk and placed his hands on it, leaning towards Cormac. "I know things about members of this family that they would pay *dearly* to keep quiet. So no, this won't go public, and as for consequences, there won't be any. Sydney gave me the keys to her basement door so I could arrive unseen. I've made amends for what I did, and she allowed me to use her brownstone to gain inspiration about madams and sex rooms. She's not the only one who can write a book or two about Madam X."

"Then why didn't you know she'd left New York almost two weeks ago?" Cormac asked. "Why didn't you know when you tried to get into her house that night that she wasn't there? That she had left the week before? The day after you slept with her?"

Sean reeled back in shock. "What?" His breath left him and he stared hard at Cormac. "How did you…"

"How did I what?" Cormac heaved himself up and around his desk towards Sean who stepped back. "How did I know you dressed up as a forty-something year old man and named yourself Bryan Jamison only to get Sydney into bed? You're twenty-one, Sean. She's fifty-one. That's a thirty-year age gap. Did she know?"

Swallowing the awkward lump in his throat, he mumbled, "Know what?"

"That *you*, Sean Ryan, was, *are*, Bryan Jamison. The author."

Sean shook his head and inhaled a shaky breath. "No, not that I know of."

"She does now. Now she knows that the author became her lover. That a twenty-one-year-old boy was her lover for the night." Cormac stepped closer and his voice grew quieter. "We have all the proof. Sydney knows all the facts. And now, you need all the help."

"I'm an adult," Sean muttered through clenched teeth. "It's not illegal."

"But putting hidden cameras in someone's house is." Alec walked up to his side. "Putting pictures of someone on a wall isn't but stalking them is. Using them as inspiration isn't but stealing from them is. If we arrest you, you could serve five to ten minimum. Sydney wants you to be punished, but not to go to jail."

"And how do you know that?" Sean glared daggers at his uncle.

"Because her lawyer said so," Cormac told him and saw a look of surprise slide over Sean's face. "She came to see me four days ago and gave me the three files on you that Landon had put together after Sydney left. They found out who Bryan Jamison is, and that you own a company that owns multiple homes. They found your cameras; found the proof."

"They illegally entered my home?" Sean said, anger brewing inside. "And yet *I'm* the one being punished?"

"You're the one who committed the crimes," Alec reminded him. "Be lucky your father doesn't know."

"Oh, please. With all the crimes he's committed he's the one who should be in jail." Sean walked back to the window, arms crossed, breath shallow. He knew he was stuck and couldn't get out of it. Even his legal skills wouldn't get him out of it.

Alec and Cormac exchanged puzzled glances before Alec spoke. "Sean, this is your only chance. I have a way we can keep it out of the press, but you have one of two options. Six months in detention, or one month detention and five months home detention. You'll have mandatory therapy for six months to try and get rid of this obsession you have."

"I don't have an obsession," Sean growled. "She's my inspiration. She always has been."

"Whatever you want to call it," Alec argued. "This is the only way. This is all you've got, Sean. The only way out of an embarrassment you'll never get over. You'll be a convicted criminal. Your publisher won't want you—"

Sean huffed. "My publisher will love me even more because I'll have more books out of this experience."

"You'll lose your followers," Alec went on.

"I'll get even more," Sean countered.

"Sadly, you probably will," Cormac said, looking at his watch. "What will it be, Sean? The consequences start from today."

"What!" Sean spun around, his fists clenched by his sides. "Are you kidding me? You want me sent to jail today?"

"You have a choice of six months or one month plus five in home detention. And it's detention, not jail. Your crime, while serious, doesn't need to send you to the big house."

"Yes, Alec," Sean snapped. "I graduated Harvard Law in two years at the top of my class. I know the law just as well as you do. If not better."

Surprised at that information, Alec snapped back. "Then why the hell did you break it?"

Seething, Sean breathed hard and stared even harder at his uncle. "Because, like you, I could. And how, pray tell, will I be treated? Since I'm a Ryan with everything that comes with?"

"You'll be away from the others, unless you can think of a better way to behave and be treated," Alec said. "You need to pick."

Sean shook his head. "I'm obviously picking the easiest option. But I need at least an hour to sort things out."

"And what do you need to sort out?" Cormac asked, his disappointment over his grandson weighing heavily.

"Oh, I don't know, Cormac," Sean sneered. "Telling my publisher I'll be gone for a month. The super in my building, locking up my valuables in case I'm broken into while I'm gone. Letting my lawyer know what's happening, and my manager, you know, important people."

Alec checked his watch. "You can have one hour. I'll drive you to your place, you can make your calls on the way and then I'll take you there, once you have a change of clothes."

"How nice," Sean spat. "Guess we'd better get on with it then." He grabbed his messenger bag from the chair and glared at the photos on Cormac's desk. "Destroy those while I'm gone. You have no need for them."

"I'll do what's right," Cormac said, watching Sean barge out the door.

Alec glanced at his father and followed.

Cormac sighed heavily, made his way around the desk and sat down. He pulled the file closer, wondering where the hell they all went wrong.

*****

On the way to his condo, Sean made multiple calls; to his manager, his lawyer, who he talked to in great detail, his publisher, and his agent. Finally, he held up his phone and hit the video record button.

"Hey, everyone, Sean here. I have a secret rendezvous to go to and it's going to last at least a month. So, you won't see me on social for the next four to five weeks. I'm going undercover for research. I'm not sure if it will be in a novel—it could be a side project, or something completely different, but I won't be around. So, don't freak out, just hang on because it could create something amazing that will come your way in the future. Okay peeps, see you in a month. Peace out." He made a peace sign and ended the recording.

"Did you really need to send that out?" Alec pulled to a stop in front of the condominium complex.

"I have over a million followers, so yes, I did." Sean hit send on TikTok and quickly went to X, Facebook, and Instagram.

"What did you mean about your father? With all the crimes he's committed he's the one who should be in jail?" Alec asked quietly.

"Don't worry, Alec." Sean grabbed his bag and opened to door. "You'll find out one day. You'll all find out one day."

Chapter 2

Sean walked out of the correctional facility one month later, wearing the clothes he'd worn the day Alec had taken him in. While not jail in the adult sense, and much more than juvie, the facility was for lightweight criminals who'd done a bit of stealing, a bit of dealing, and a little bit of conning people in the general public.

He had a monitor strapped to his ankle, his bag slung over his shoulder, and his phone in his hand. But he stopped scrolling for a number when his grandfather's car rolled to a stop in front of him. He heaved a sigh as Cormac emerged.

"Sean. Get in the car, I'm taking you home."

"And which home would that be?" Sean hadn't wanted to see his family. He had wanted his lawyer to come and pick him up.

"Yours. Get in." Cormac's smile was dead as he motioned to the car.

Reluctantly, Sean climbed in and pulled on his seatbelt, heard the click of his grandfather's, and heard no engine as the car moved on. "What's this about?"

"I wanted to talk to you about your stay. I didn't keep

tabs, although I was to be alerted if anything happened to you. Which it didn't, luckily."

"Yeah, lucky me," Sean snarked and looked out the window.

"I was told by Alec that you used your time wisely and helped out the other inmates. You taught them the law."

"The basics. What to say and do if stopped by the pigs. What to say or do to not be charged with a crime by the pigs. How to behave in court."

"Like victims," Cormac muttered. "When they're not."

"They were fun lessons," Sean said. "They found out who I was pretty quickly, but when I explained I have a black belt in martial arts and am a seasoned best-selling author, and a lawyer, they backed off. Especially when I told them I would teach them the basics of law and English."

"The basics on how to get away with crimes," Cormac argued. "Your therapist was pissed off that you didn't want to do therapy, but said he learned a lot just from watching you teach the other inmates, and actually admired the way you helped them. He says you don't seem like the bad apple; you probably have some leftover issues from last time, or they've re emerged."

"I did notice him sitting off to the side. He didn't like the not wanting to talk bit, but I saw him scribbling notes."

"The therapy is mandatory, so you'll be going to it whether you talk or not." Cormac sighed as his car pulled up to the condo. "You know you can only go to the designated areas."

"My publisher, my therapist, my grandfather's house. Although…don't bet on that." Sean pushed the door open and stepped out. "Since I'm confined to home, I've hired an assistant to help me out and I'll be having a very long chat with my lawyer." He slammed the door and walked around the back of the car.

Cormac opened his door and alighted. "You do that. Meanwhile, I'm escorting you in and Alec is waiting to give you instructions."

Sean's head dropped back, and he growled. "I don't need you breathing down my neck."

"You do." Cormac followed him inside and up to the second floor where they found Alec waiting in the condo.

"How did you get into my apartment!" Sean demanded and dropped his bag on the kitchen counter.

"The same way we got into your second apartment," Alec said and pointed to the secret door. "Follow me."

Fear spread through Sean, and he glanced from Alec's back to Cormac's face.

"Go on." Cormac waved a hand at Alec. "Go."

Clearing his throat, Sean followed and found Alec standing in the middle of the living room. "Why do you…" He froze, but his gaze darted from wall to wall. "You took my…why did you…when did you…" He lurched forward, steaming with anger. "How dare you take my photographs? They were my inspiration. When did you come in? How dare you enter my home without my permission!" He lunged at Alec, his hands in front of him ready to strangle his uncle.

Alec knew a thing or two about defending oneself. He threw his hands up between Sean's and flung them away, then landed a swift punch to the face.

Sean stumbled back in shock, his hands flying to his face. "You asshole."

"Enough," Cormac roared. "We came in here and cleaned this place out. Every last photo, poster, cut-out is gone. Burned into ash along with your Bryan Jamison disguise."

"What!" Sean yelled. "I need that for interviews. It's how I look."

"Tough!" Cormac told him. "We cleaned out the apartment, and we expect it to stay this way. We'll be checking once a week to make sure you keep to it."

"And you'll have to deal with not being Bryan Jamison for a while since you can't go out anywhere besides what's on the list," Alec said.

"I have an assistant," Sean spat. "He can get more for me."

Alec frowned and shook his head.

"There was nothing in our agreement about me giving up my writing career or Bryan Jamison." Sean stepped closer. "You have no right to dictate how that part of my life works."

"You're right. There wasn't, but if you want to keep that secret, you'd better play along for the next five months, or you will be outed," Alec warned.

Sean scoffed and turned away. "You can leave now. I want to take a shower and need to make some calls." Crossing his arms, he wandered over to the expansive floor-to-ceiling window. At twenty feet high, it allowed a lot of natural light for writing.

"We'll be checking on you this time every week and

monitoring your whereabouts. If we see one photo, one poster, one anything, you'll be back in detention," Alec said, and followed Cormac out the door.

Sean waited until he saw his uncle and grandfather get in their cars and leave before doubling over, fists balled, and a deep guttural growl came out of him. "Damn you, Sydney, damn you to hell. I'm gonna make you pay for this. And damn you, Alec, I'll make you pay, too." He gave another growl and walked into the first condo and locked the door. He called his lawyer to bring his things from his safety deposit box, and rang his assistant to stock the fridge before going upstairs for a shower. He luxuriated in it, having been deprived of privacy for the last month. He'd had to watch his back, and his front, for the first week, but quickly gained respect and privacy when he'd started teaching the law.

He finished up, dressed, and made it downstairs as his lawyer buzzed in. He unlocked the downstairs security door, and opened his, waiting for what he needed.

"Sean?" Maxwell Pierce entered the apartment. "Sean?"

"Coffee?" Sean called from the kitchen.

"Absolutely." Maxwell closed the door and hurried to the dining table. "I brought everything. Your laptop, hard drives, and an extra disguise."

"Excellent." Sean poured boiling water into two cups filled with crushed coffee beans. "Do you know what's happened?"

"I got the paperwork from Alec." Maxwell picked up his cup. "And he showed me everything."

"Most of that was legal, like setting up a business, my money and homes, it's not illegal to have photos on the walls and to wear a disguise," Sean countered.

Maxwell swallowed his boiling hot coffee and said, "Sean, stalking, breaking and entering, putting hidden cameras in the house you broke into, all of that's illegal. Sydney's incredibly generous on not sending you to jail. So are your uncle and grandfather."

Sean sighed, took a sip, and set his cup down. "There's only two people who know the truth and we're keeping it that way. Look, while I was in detention, I was allowed three hours of computer time a day. I used it to write more of the novel I started before I was hijacked. I'm hoping it will be the next massive bestseller, but, as you know, I'm limited to my publisher, my therapist, and my grandfather's which will not be happening. Are you on the list? Or can you be added to the list, or will you just come here?"

"I'll come here, but the first thing I'd do is get this place checked for bugs and cameras."

"Think my family's doing to me what I did to Sydney?"

"Wouldn't put it past them. Why did you do it to Sydney?"

"Long story and only two people will ever know. Know anyone who can check for bugs and cameras?"

"Don't you know how to?" Maxwell asked and whipped out his phone. One call later, he shoved his phone back into his pocket. "Here in an hour."

The intercom buzzed, and Sean let his assistant in downstairs, and then opened the door. "Do you think they'd do it? To see what I get up to. The calls I make, whether I put any photos back up, oh, Alec said they're checking on me same time next week to see if I do, so yeah, I guess they would."

Astro rushed in the door laden with ten bags in each hand. "Jesus, Sean. Why do you need so much?" He dumped them on the floor in front of the fridge and sighed in relief. "You want me to unpack them, too?"

"No, I'll do that, it'll give me something to do while I wait. Thanks, Astro."

"Okay, if you need anything else, give me a call. Toodles." He waved his fingers and dashed out the door.

Sean closed the door and chuckled before heaving several bags onto the counter. "What do I do?"

"Take the next five months to write as many novels as possible. See the therapist when you need to, and then move on with your life. You know the law as well as I do, you've been given a lifeline. Take it."

Sean placed more bags on the counter. "Yeah, I guess I have. Thanks."

"I'll be off then." Maxwell drained his cup and gave Sean a slap on the back. "Call me when the crew are done."

"I will." Sean watched him leave and then placed groceries in the fridge. He was organising things when the crew arrived. "Hey, I need to know if there are bugs, listening devices, or cameras in the house."

The team got to work, with Sean working around them. Once they finished in a room, he re-organised the furniture for a fresh start, a fresh vibe. When apartment one was finished, they moved into apartment two, but after four hours they came up with nothing.

"Thanks anyway. It makes me feel a lot safer." Sean shook their hands as they left and bolted the door. He sighed, and leaned his forehead against the cool metal, closing his eyes. He could either see this as a living hell, or make the most out of it, and that was what he needed to do.

After a late lunch, he walked into apartment two with his laptop, hard drives, and Bryan Jamison disguise. He put the foam head with the wig on the kitchen counter, and the laptop on the desk and booted it up. He plugged in the drive before logging into his publisher's email address to collect the chapters he'd written every day in detention.

Sighing, he got up and walked into the kitchen, opened the bottom cabinet door, and flicked the small switch hidden up in the corner. He watched the wall next to it pop forward and slide back in sections. On the wall beneath were all the photos and posters and magazine cut-outs of Sydney that he'd collected. The ones destroyed by his uncle and grandfather were copies and he'd be damned if he'd lose Sydney over a wall full of images.

He sat down at his computer and got to work.

PART TWO

Chapter 3

The man walked into his office and stopped. "Sean! I'm surprised to see you here. You refused to talk to me in detention. I wasn't sure if you'd even show up."

"Dr Levinworth." Sean stood at the window staring out at the cityscape, hands in pockets, defiant at being there.

The doctor closed the door. "Why don't you have a seat and we can get started." He sat down in an easy chair and opened Sean's file.

"I'll stand, thank you. You should remember from last time I like to walk around and stare out the window."

"Avoid eye contact."

A small grin slid across Sean's lips. "Yeah. Avoid eye contact. But didn't you get more out of me when I wasn't confined to a chair?"

"It's true, I did." Levinworth scanned the file quickly and sighed. "I thought we had dealt with your obsession."

"Can obsessions ever be fully dealt with?"

"They can be if you work hard enough. Which I thought you had."

"I did. But you can't really deal with love at the heart level."

"Are you saying you love her?"

"Then, I most certainly did. First love, first kiss, first everything."

"And now?"

Sean sighed and finally turned from the window. "You've just read the file, doc. I wouldn't say I'm obsessed. I say I find inspiration in."

Levinworth looked up at him. "How? I see you've moved onto writing adult crime thrillers. Are you finished with young adult?"

"I'm not a young adult anymore, so yeah. I moved on to adult."

"I didn't realise the hot new sensation was you. Bestsellers, I hear. Congratulations."

"Thank you." Sean slowly walked around the room. "She inspires a lot. Everything I went through, thought, physical reactions, it was all because of her. So why not use it as inspiration for novels?"

"All perfectly reasonable," Levinworth agreed. "Unless it's still an obsession that's come back or wasn't dealt with in the first place." He watched Sean pick up an arrowhead he'd recently acquired in the hope it inspired him to write a paper on Native American peoples. He knew what Sean was talking about as he'd often gone in search of something to inspire a paper.

"I see your décor hasn't changed much." Sean turned the arrowhead over in his hand, rubbed his thumb over the rock formation and set it in its place before sliding his hands back into his pockets and moving on.

"No. I like my décor; it speaks to me."

"As she speaks to me." Sean stared at a charcoal drawing of a nude on the wall. "You do this?"

"My sister did. Gave it to me as a present. She's very artistic."

"And what inspired her?"

"Everything, anything. Are you trying to make a point?"

"Don't you already get the point?" Sean glanced over his shoulder at him. "Because there is one and it's very simple."

"She's your inspiration, hence all of the photos, cut-outs, posters on the wall." Levinworth stared at the photos of the wall opposite and behind Sean's desk. "Nice place, shame about the décor."

"Why's there shame? Your shame? Or is it supposed to be my shame? Because I'm not ashamed." He stared at the nude and noted her curves weren't as good as Sydney's.

"If you see her purely as inspiration, no, but as she's your obsession…"

Sean sighed and turned from the drawing. "My so-called obsession has made me millions of dollars, bought me two condos, a nice apartment, two cars, and set up a healthy nest egg. I don't believe it needs to stop anytime soon, not while I get so much out of it."

"Why are you here, Sean?"

Another sigh. "Because I was caught trying to enter a brownstone. With keys, I might add." He waved his finger. "No crime was committed. I had permission to be there and to enter when I liked. But the cops who followed me didn't care. They took me in, but their boss let me go. There were no charges to file against me." He moved on to the next wall and stared up at a painting of an ocean, with waves crashing onto rocky outlets and rugged cliffs.

"Why did you have keys to her brownstone?"

"Because she gave them to me so I could come and go as I liked. Which is why I know there are three metal safety bars across the door, and the door next to it leads to the sex room. Which is *very* well-known in my family."

"Your family raided the brownstone when it belonged to Josephine Pompadour, New York's madam to the rich and powerful. Now it belongs to Sydney Kingston, the author who wrote not only a novel, but a biography about her."

"The infamous Madam X; Sydney's highest selling books by the way. She only bought the brownstone because of its history."

"When did she tell you that?"

"At the first family dinner she went to."

"The *only* family dinner she went to."

Sean looked over his shoulder. "No need to be pedantic." He turned his head to the painting. "I feel like this sometimes."

"Like what?"

"Like I'm smashing against the rocks and cliffs, tumbling, turning, head over heels, being sucked out just to be smashed back into the rocks again and again. Rinse and repeat."

"It must be exhausting."

"It is. But then you'd know that as you diagnosed me four years ago with ADHD and mild autism. You said it would feel like that, and sometimes it does."

"You mentioned it was only when you wrote. Do you still feel that way when you write four years later?"

"Yeah. Tumultuous tumbling of thoughts and feelings until I get them in order, write it out, and when I'm done, they smash about until they calm down. I don't get the pain in my head as much anymore."

"Your glasses and meds help?"

"They do. Didn't realise I had vision problems. Thought it was all in my head."

"Is it still in your head, Sean?"

"What?" Sean leaned against the cupboard along the wall.

"Your obsession with Sydney Kingston."

Sean sniggered. "Doc, you have no idea."

Levinworth glanced at the photos of Sean's condo walls. "For many teenagers, it's absolutely normal to cover their walls in photos and posters of their musician, singer, actor crush."

"Was never a crush."

"But you have photos of death threats and stalker notes. You have photos of her out on the street, at functions, book launches. Hell, you even have photos of her in the shower and in bed. Sean." He glanced up. "This *is* an obsession. You set up cameras in her home and filmed her. That's illegal. And you know that. You're from a family of cops and lawyers."

Sean sighed, glanced away and shrugged. "What do you want me to say, doc? I didn't do it. No, I did. I got into the brownstone and planted cameras so I could watch her *and* hear her. And I saw and heard a lot, and it's all made its way into my novels. My *best-selling* novels, that is." He wandered back to the floor-to-ceiling window. The view of New York's rooftops offered a grey and brown dullness, but the blue sky shone down and brightened it all. "I did it. I did all of it and will continue to do all of it in order to *keep* being a best-selling author."

"You'll continue to break the law just for story ideas?" Levinworth glanced through the file. While having photos on the wall wasn't illegal, breaking and entering was. When he received silence, he added, "Sean, clearly your obsession has come back, and clearly you need to talk it through. And having posters and writing about someone isn't illegal, but you have committed a crime."

"Have I, though? Except for the initial break-in to set up the cameras, I haven't broken in since. Once Grandpa forbade the family from seeing her, I saw her on rare occasions. I stayed away. I got help from you. I lived with Grandpa and Pop, and my life straightened out. Mom's death was a curve ball, but I got through it. Threw myself into my writing, wrote as much as I could so I didn't have to think about it. Then Pop's death… But by then, I was already living on my own and releasing my adult thrillers."

"Did your family read them?"

"I introduced the books to them. Grandpa and Pop loved them."

"As much as Cassandra Kingsley's?"

"You mean Sydney Kingston's," Sean corrected.

"Yeah, though Bryan was her rival in crime thriller writers, they liked them too."

"Must've made you proud?"

"Yeah, it did. I revealed my secret to Pop on his death bed."

"It must have hurt, losing him."

"It did. But he wanted to see Sydney before he died. No one knows why."

"He didn't tell anyone? She didn't?"

"No. Neither said anything and he died minutes after seeing her. I don't think even Grandpa knew what he wanted to talk to her about."

"Do you love her, Sean?"

Sean huffed. "Do I love her? What sort of question is that?"

"A straight and to the point one." Levinworth picked up a novel from his side table, opened to the first page and read out loud.

"This is a story that starts when I was seventeen. It's about love, betrayal and obsession. A love that was the first, a betrayal that couldn't be trusted, and an obsession I am yet to let go of and leave with the past. That day, when I was seventeen, the day I fell headlong in love, was sunny with light clouds. It was late in the year, so a chill was still in the air. But it didn't matter. The light clouds didn't matter. The chill didn't matter. The time of year didn't matter. Not even the fact I was only seventeen mattered. Because all that mattered then was when I kissed her I fell down a rabbit hole I've refused to climb out of over the last four years, and one I will continue to refuse to leave for the rest of my life. Because when you

find the one you're meant to love, you grab onto it with both hands and run as fast as you can with it. And that's just what I did. Grabbed onto it with both hands, I mean. I grabbed her and kissed her and when she kissed me back I knew this was it. That she was it. That this was the love people talked about. And I had it. I had it right in my hands and I didn't want to let go. But I had to, for another year I had to let her go until I could be with her again. And that's where the story continues. All I know was, I wanted her. I wanted to fuck her, love her, and possess her. But what the hell does a seventeen-year-old know about that? About any of that?"

He closed the book and noticed Sean's laboured breathing. "That's quite a scene. The cold hard honest truth, isn't it? The way you truly feel about Sydney Kingston. A woman thirty years older than you. A woman who was off limits to you. A woman who, if I read the book right, slept with your uncle, which was her right as an adult. And you hated it. You said so in our sessions four years ago. You became obsessed with a woman old enough to be your mother, and you saw her as a mother figure because your mother didn't care about you at the end. Just cared about her affair with your uncle. And this is your ode to her. The woman you fell in love with." He looked at the cover. "No wonder you called it *Illicit Things*. Everyone was having everything they wanted regardless of who it hurt, so why couldn't you?" He set the book aside. "Are you still in love with her, Sean?"

Sean stared out the window, unmoving. He didn't want to give too much, if anything, away, and was trying to control his raging heart. What the hell was he meant to say? What the hell was he meant to do?

"I'm twenty-one, doc, I don't know much more about love than I did at seventeen."

"Have you had partners in the last four years? Fallen in love with anyone else?"

"Why would I? Why would I fall in love with anyone else? The last four years of my life have been about one woman who possessed every waking thought, every feeling, every change. She shaped my life, my career, my body, my soul, my heart."

"You slept with her as Bryan Jamison. Her report states she sensed something was wrong, something was off, and then she found out who Bryan Jamison really was. You."

"Yeah, I read the report. But there's so much more to it than that." Sean looked at his watch. "Time's up, doc. We'll leave that for another time, shall we? And maybe by the end of my five months you'll have the answer."

"The answer you already have?"

Sean grinned and opened the door. "Maybe, doc. And maybe I'll tell you nothing at all. See you next week."

*****

"So, what are we going to do with you, Sean Ryan? Or should I say, Bryan Jamison?" Vincent Viceroy the third crossed his legs and placed his hands on the blue velvet arms of his high-backed Rococo Revival chair. "Tsk, tsk, you could be trouble."

"You didn't have a problem with who I was when you signed me." Sean sat on the matching velvet sofa in Vincent's office.

Vincent tilted his head. "I know. The fact that we snagged you from Pulsate was a coup for us—"

"Even though no one else knew it," Sean interjected.

"True, but then you have been incredibly profitable and your plan for promotion without showing your face was priceless," Vincent said.

"And it's made both of us wealthy." Sean opened his backpack and pulled out his completed manuscript. "I started writing this a couple of months ago, and I finished it off last week. The new book." He handed it over and sat back, crossed his legs, then got up and walked over to the floor-to-ceiling window view of New York City that every high-rise office building seemed to have. His hands slid into his pockets and he stared out at the skyline; a habit when he talked to people.

"*Her*, by Sean Ryan writing as Bryan Jamison," Vincent murmured, his fingers lightly sliding over the paper. "Roger, get this read as soon as possible. We have a new contract to sign." He handed it to his top agent, Roger Barker, who looked after Sean and four other high-profile authors, and added, "Are there any more like this?"

"Not so much like that, but there are definitely more coming. I'll be spending most of the next five months at home writing them. I'll get a spec of them to you next week. I'm still outlining them, figuring them out. But they're all similar in theme."

"About women," Roger said, turning the first page.

"Considering the title, if the rest are like the first page, we'll be taking them."

"As I said, similar in theme." Sean turned from the window and studied the office as he did every time he came in, which wasn't often. He could count on one hand how often he'd set foot in that room. Usually, he dealt with his agent either at his home, or at Roger's. It kept anonymity and chance for being outed to a minimum.

"Jesus Christ," Roger muttered as he turned to the third page. "I can say we'll definitely be paying for this." He read on.

"How much?" Vincent asked him.

"Five million." Sean wandered over to the wall on the left and stared up at the paintings. "For one book."

"For one book!" Vincent repeated. "You can't be serious?"

"You paid me two apiece for my first three, and the same for the next three and the next six. I want five million for this one."

"I'd say it's worth it." Roger finished off the eighth page and turned it to find a new chapter. "From the pages I've read, it's definitely worth it and I can't stop reading."

"And how much do you expect for the others you have?" Vincent watched Sean studying a Japanese artwork on the side table.

"I expect the same as that one, because after three best-selling books I'd say I've earned more per book."

"The *She Is Mine* books haven't started coming out, and I'm still not sure about naming each book a single word. Whoever heard of a book called *Is?*" Vincent complained.

"Joan Aiken. Mine will be another." Sean moved onto the next piece of artwork. The Viceroys were a wealthy family with many priceless antiques and art pieces that Sean could only dream of owning. Not that he wanted to. He knew how to invest, and it wasn't in art.

"But this new one is called *Her*," Vincent continued. "Won't that confuse people when they realise you have two books called *She* and *Her*?"

"Not really." Sean walked over to the opposite wall to study the paintings. "*She* is clearly stated that it's the first book in a trilogy. It's on the cover, as it will be for *Is* and *Mine*. And you might want to get those out sooner rather than later, because once *Her* comes out, it will blow everyone else's book out of the water. In fact…" He spun around to face his publisher. "Maybe I should do what Sydney Kingston does and keep my electronic and audio rights so I can release more books. With the numbers I'm writing, I want to get them out sooner rather than later. I don't want to wait for *She Is Mine* to come out before releasing *Her*. I want that out as soon as possible."

"How soon?" Vincent's gaze flicked from Sean to Roger.

"When Sydney Kingston's new book is released. September nineteenth."

Roger glanced up in surprise. "You want to go head-to-head with Sydney? You've never beaten that one-horse race. The only way you had a hit before her was because we released the book at the beginning of

September and then she knocked you out of the park when her book came out."

"Except." Sean put up a finger. "I've heard from a little bird that Sydney may not be publishing this year. She's gone back to Australia for a holiday, or permanently, I'm not sure, but she may not release a book this year."

Vincent leaned forward in excitement. "Who did you hear that from? We have to find out if that's true, Roger." He turned to his agent. "Can you find out anything?"

"Probably not, but I do happen to know we have someone who's friends with Pulsate's publicist. Maybe we can get some info from her."

"Excellent." Vincent rubbed his long bony white hands together.

With his dark slicked back hair, pale skin, taut face, and sharp teeth, Sean was reminded of Dracula every time he saw his publishing house boss.

"Are you sure this information is correct?" Vincent asked Sean. "We can start planning the release now."

"I'm not a hundred percent, but she moved back about two months ago, and I heard rumblings from different book launches." He'd tried calling Sydney multiple times since finding out she'd left, not only New York, but *him* high and dry to deal with the consequences of his detention and house arrest. She'd changed her number and wasn't answering emails or DMs on socials. He was being ignored and that he wasn't going to tolerate. He'd sought revenge in his book, which was why it was important it came out on Sydney's publishing date. To get back at her for leaving him.

"We'll definitely be publishing this book, Vincent, and it's definitely worth five million. I've just finished chapter five and it's incredible." Roger let out a rush of breath. He'd acquired the ability to speed-read over the last few decades of editing.

"Thank you, that's why it needs to be released on Sydney's publishing day." Sean picked up his bag from the couch. "I'll get back to you with those specs for the other two novels. They're explosive too, but I have to write them, so I'm off to get a start. Vincent, Roger, I'll see you when I sign that contract."

"Of course, Sean." Vincent gracefully rose from his chair and escorted his star author to the door. "We'll see you soon, my darling boy. We'll see you soon."

Sean took the lift down to the ground floor and caught a taxi for his ride home. There was no point driving into the middle of Manhattan on a weekday with nowhere to park. It would have taken too long to get to each appointment, so taxis and Uber it was.

He arrived home and hurried up to his condo, making sure to lock the door behind him. He made a coffee, hot and strong, and went into the adjoining condo to work. The space, air, and light made writing for long hours a breeze, and with the ideas lurking in his head, he would be working long hours to get them written.

Sean stared at the pictures of Sydney on the wall while his laptop booted up, and opened a file marked *new novel spec.* He read what he'd previously written and added another page of ideas to it. They poured from his mind, through his hands, to the keys and into words in the document. His fingers flew over the keyboard as fast as he thought and he added another page, and another.

He finally stopped and took a deep slow breath, rubbed his hands together, and sat back in his chair. It was perfect, just as perfect as *Her*. As all of his books were. Because all of his books were about Sydney.

Sean left his chair and walked over to the wall opposite. His gaze pored over the photos, studying them. Sydney's face, her eyes, lips, nose, her hair and the way it sat just so, framing her face. Her eyes sparkled in many photos, were worried or overcast in others; the ones he'd taken when he'd followed her. She hadn't known he had, he'd kept his distance, and used a zoom lens, worn a disguise, and pretended to take photos of other people, architecture, and nature.

He unpinned two photocopies of notes he'd made and sent her, and wandered over to the window, staring at them as he remembered the day he'd made the first note.

He'd placed the last of the letters onto the sheet of paper and set it just so. It didn't need to be perfect, just to dry in place.

Gazing upon the three words, a small smile slid across his lips. It would be sent tomorrow, and she'd get it in a few days. If only he could see the look on her face when she ripped open the envelope and pulled it out, reading it, as she would be thinking it was fan mail. As it was. Just not the type she usually received or expected.

No, this fan mail was special. One that would make her blood run cold and drain from her already white face as it contracted in fear. That's what he wanted to see. The fear. He wanted her to fear him and what he would do. Because, by God, he would do it.

About that, he was certain.

"Ow!" He dropped them, and they fell from his hands like molten lava, burning his flesh in the process. He blew on his fingers and stared down at the pages. They weren't lava and weren't on fire. They were simple photocopies of letters.

Sean sighed and muttered, "Why did I make them? God, how could I be so stupid? Why would I do that?" He slowly bent and reached for them. They were cool to the touch, and he picked them up. They were just paper, after all, evidence of his stupidity. His seventeen-year-old stupidity. Stupidity that led to jealousy and hatred and revenge.

The scent of the glue he'd used to attach the letters to the paper wafted into his nostrils. He heard the metal on metal of the scissor blades as he snipped out the letters from the magazine. He felt the powder left on his hands from the gloves he'd worn to leave no prints. The mask, hair net, and goggles he'd worn to leave no accidental evidence behind. He'd gone all out for the preparation. Had learned from his family what criminals did to leave no evidence behind. He'd done it and had left no evidence behind. No one had arrested him. No one had found out that four years ago he sent Sydney death threats. *Die, bitch, die!* was the first one he'd sent. It had taken him hours to think of it. It had to be perfect, and it was. But then he'd done a 180 and insisted his mother invite her old college roommate and her best friend

Sydney Kingston, author extraordinaire, over for lunch. "Why?" he muttered. "Why did I do that? After everything that happened."

He sighed and walked back to the wall, pinned them in place, and slid his hands into his pockets. Staring at the copies, he remembered making them, cutting them, gluing them, and sending them off. The scene played over and over. The scents, the sounds, grew louder and stranger. They bounced around the inside of his head, the walls of his skull, pounding against his eyeballs, the back of his skull, hitting the nerves of his spine at the very top.

"God, stop!" he yelled, clutching his head, bending at the waist, his eyes bulging out of their sockets. Sharp waves of pain shot from the centre of his spine to either side of his skull. "Just stop!" Sean fell to his knees and sobbed. "Stop, just stop." He breathed slowly, remembering the exercises his therapist had taught him four years ago. His breathing slowly regulated, the pain throbbed less until it eased altogether, and he was able to get to his feet.

"What the hell was that?" he gasped, and made his way to the couch, rubbing the back of his head and eyes. "What the hell was that?"

It hadn't happened in three years. The rumbling, tumbling, crashing waves did, before the pain behind his eyes made him focus on writing, but that, that, hadn't happened in years. Why now? Why now? What was going on now that caused that?

He sighed and rested his head on the back of the couch. *Is it because I'm in therapy, or is it karma come back to bite me in the ass? Or am I overreacting? I've dealt with these attacks before. I can deal with them again.* He slowly rose and sat behind his desk, staring at the image of him and Sydney in its frame. He pulled up a new Word doc and began to type.

*****

On Sunday afternoon, a banging at the door roused Sean from his writing. He glanced at the clock, heard another bang, and quickly checked the outside camera on his security tablet. "Shit!"

His family were at his door with lunch. He tapped a green button and said, "Just a minute," and quickly saved his document and closed his laptop. He hurried to the wall opposite and closed it over the photos of Sydney, and rushed through the secret doorway to his front door and flung it open. "What?"

"'Bout damn time!" Declan declared, striding into the condo. "We shouldn't have to wait around for you, Sean."

"Then why are you here?" Sean asked in return, glancing at each family member as they crossed his threshold. "I was busy, *Father*, you caught me in the middle of writing the new book. Not that you know what that is." He closed the door after Sierra and walked into the kitchen area. "Why are you all here?"

"We brought Sunday lunch to you." Cormac removed his glasses and gazed around the room. "It's already cooked; just needs a reheat, and since you have an oven in both condos, we can heat it all up at the same time." He gave Sean a grim-lipped smile. "Don't worry, I know my way into the other condo."

"Feel free." Sean waved a hand. "The kitchen's the same layout as this one." He watched Emerson, Sandy and Sierra, along Alec's partner Diane, start the oven and prepare the food. He sighed, and saw Alec grabbed a couple of trays and followed his father into the second condo.

"There's a dinner set and cutlery in the cupboard," he told them. "Might not be enough, unless you brought them along, too." He sat on an island bench stool and watched. "I had no need to buy a bigger dinner set; it's just me."

"Why didn't we know where you lived?" Declan, hands on his hips, turned around to face Sean. "How the hell can you afford this place?"

"And the one next door?" Alec said, come back through the secret doorway. "He bought both."

Declan frowned at his brother. "And how do you know that?"

Sean's eyes narrowed at his uncle.

"Just a little legal thing I did for my nephew." Alec slid his arm around Sean's shoulders. "Ain't that right, nephew?" He gazed at Sean and raised a brow.

But Sean, not to be outwitted, was prepared. "No, Alec, you actually didn't do anything for me, I did it all myself." He pushed Alec's hand off his shoulder and turned to his father. "I've earned enough from my books to have invested wisely in the housing market. I own these two condos, and an apartment. Plus, I bought myself two cars; a run-around and a sports model. I also set up a company to deal with my writing, finances, and properties." His gaze moved to his uncle then back to his father. "I've made *a lot* of money. So yes, I can afford this place. I also did my own contracts because Alec and Kieran aren't the only lawyers in the family."

Declan's frown deepened. "Whaddya mean by that?"

"Sean graduated from Harvard Law in two years, top of his class." Cormac left his coat over the back of a dining chair and walked past Declan into the living room. "We may have to get the dining table from the other condo. This one's not big enough."

"Wait!" Connor put his hand up and looked at the others. "Sean graduated from law school? When?"

"Last year," Sean said, staring at his grandfather. "And I use next door's dining table as a desk."

"Then you'd better clear it off and bring it in," Cormac told him, relaxing back on the couch as Emerson joined him.

"The food was still close to hot, so it should only take ten to fifteen minutes," she said.

"Better get that table." Alec squeezed Sean's shoulder and wandered over to the couch. He passed an incredulous Declan as he did so. "Ethan, Brandon, help him out."

"Why can't you?" Brandon sniped at his father. They'd recently been having arguments over his current occupation of influencer, but at twenty-five, he was old enough to do what he wanted.

"Because you're a grandkid," Alec reminded him. "Sierra, help them out."

Her hand paused the reapplying of her lip gloss. "Why do I have to? I helped with the food."

"Again," Alec called. "Because you're a grandkid."

Nostrils flaring, Sean let out a slow huff of air and strode into the condo next door. He cleared off his laptop and notes, put them on the side cupboard behind the desk and they all took a side.

"If you can afford these two places, then I guess you don't write crap anymore," Sierra remarked and then grabbed her hand when Sean dropped his side.

"I guess I didn't tell you often enough to go fuck yourself, oh, wait, I didn't tell you at all because I just took your bullying, like I took everyone else's. *Silently,*" he said, staring her down.

"Hey, man." Ethan placed a hand on his arm and noticed the shock on Sierra's face. "There's no need for that. It was a long time ago."

"It was *only* four years," Sean snapped at him.

"Yeah, and I don't like you talking to my sister that way," Brandon added with his fake arrogant bravado.

"Even though that's how you talk to your friends about her?" Sean asked him. "Don't be a hypocrite, Brandon, you've talked even worse about her, and treated her worse on your OnlyFans account. And as for *you,* Ethan…" He turned from their shocked expressions to his. "Remove your hand before I do it for you. Law school wasn't the only thing I graduated from. It was martial arts too. I'm a triple black belt and there are things I know about you that you wouldn't want getting out." He watched Ethan's eyes narrow. "You may be the eldest, but that means nothing when you follow in daddy's footsteps down the wrong path." He leaned closer and lowered his voice. "Sydney."

"Hey, what's taking so long?" Connor strode in and glanced around. "Looks just like the other one. You must be rich, kid."

"I am, and we're bringing in the table now, if only these lazy asses would get moving." He motioned at his cousins who still stood shocked to their cores.

"Come on kids, get a move on. Food's ready and you need to set the table." Connor clapped his hands and watched his son and nephews manoeuvre the table through the narrow doorway and into the dining area.

Sierra had looked at the food instead and brought up the rear. She was shaken that Sean could have spoken to her that way after all these years. *Guess his money and fame has gone to his head*, she thought. *But what was that crack about OnlyFans? Could he know?* "Food's ready. I turned the oven off."

The boys put the two tables together and silently followed Sean to pick up the extra chairs as the women set the table.

"How long do you plan on staying?" Sean asked, placing two chairs under the table. "I have to get back to writing and hope I remember where I left off since you interrupted me."

"It's one now so I think we'll be here for a good couple of hours." Cormac took his place at the head of the table.

Sean rolled his eyes and swore under his breath, taking a seat at the other end of the table.

"You don't get to sit there, kid." Alec laid a hand on his shoulder.

Sean eyed Alec's hand before glaring at his uncle. "In *my* house, *I* do. *My* house, *my* rules. *You* don't get to sit here. You can stop with the power trip in *my* home. It's not working."

Removing his hand, Alec glanced at his father and then took his seat next to Sean.

"Who cares who sits where? I'm starving, let's eat," Cormac said.

Emerson placed the roast beef in front of Cormac to carve, and the rest of the women gathered the vegetables from both ovens, laying the table before sitting.

When everyone was seated they said grace, and passed around the dishes of vegetables while Cormac carved the beef. Once everyone had a full plate, the conversations started. Work topics, such as what they did that week, and how many perps Declan and Connor had caught.

Sean studied each member of his family, even those he wasn't interested in, noticed the always present rivalry between his lookalike father and Uncle Connor, the man who had fucked his brother's wife during their yearlong affair. He noticed Ethan watching them intently from across the table. Ethan the upstart who thought because he was the mini version of his father he could win a woman from him and fuck her the same way. If the rivalry wasn't there between Connor and Declan, it certainly was between Connor and his son.

Sean stabbed a piece of beef and slowly placed it in his mouth. It was juicy and succulent. He knew Emerson had cooked it; she seemed to be cook and maid these days, and he always enjoyed her food. *It's a pity she hasn't directed or produced much lately. Her last movie was based on one of Sydney's books, but since Pop died, she's taken charge and doesn't work anymore. I wonder if she calls Sydney?*

His gaze moved to Sierra, still clearly upset about his comment. He held back a grin. It was about time she got it back in spades. *All I ever got from her was bullying.*

He glanced at Brandon beside her. Both were Alec's kids, but neither looked like him, and they weren't sitting near him. His gaze moved to Diane, Alec's latest flame. Attractive, rich, auburn hair that slithered around her shoulders in silken waves, slim, a gym junkie, and a lawyer with her own firm. Perfect for Alec, the slimy bastard.

His gaze darted to his uncle then back to Ethan.

"I collared ten," Connor boasted.

"So what! I got twelve." Declan waved a hand. "That's nothing."

"I collard fifteen." Ethan jumped into the conversation. His father and uncle stopped competing long enough to look at him.

"Ah, that's nothing, you pipsqueak." Declan waved him away. "Let the real cops talk."

"Come on. I'm as real as you and Dad," Ethan complained. "And I caught more crims this week. I win."

"Ah!" Declan gave him another wave. "Buzz off you buzz kill. Hey, Kieran, how many of our crims did you let off this week? And you, Alec?"

"Too many," Alec declared. "That's all I seem to do all week. Fight to keep crims in jail, but the damn judges let them out."

"This is amazing beef, Emerson," Sean said, cutting up his last slice. "You always do a great job with the food since you took over from Pop."

The buzz died down.

"Thank you, Sean." She smiled warmly. "It's one of my specialities and I don't mind cooking. I kind of missed it when I worked so much on my TV show or Sydney's movies. I seem to be making something every day now. I enjoy it."

"And I enjoyed *Twisted Minds*," Sean said. "Will you be doing another series?"

"Yes, I've been wondering that myself," Cormac said, taking a sip of wine. "How many seasons have you done?"

"Five." She set her cutlery down and dabbed her mouth with her napkin. "I've been working on season six, something set here in New York. I have many people running around finding all sorts of information on crimes so I can put it together. But I've been so busy making Sydney's movies these last few years, I didn't think I'd ever get back to it."

"Sydney's not releasing until next year or the year after, so you'll have plenty of time." Sean sipped his beer and stared directly at Emerson. "How is she? Enjoying being back in her home country?"

Surprised, Emerson glanced at Cormac and Connor before speaking. "She is and she's fine. I was thinking about holidaying there so I can go and see her."

"Have you've spoken to her since she left?" Sean glanced at the family members who were eyeing each other off.

"I have. She's free from stalkers and peeping toms."

"And Ryans constantly turning up on her doorstep," Sean quipped. "Quite a few of us did that. Some more than others. A regular occurrence." He saw Ethan's gaze flick back and forth between his father and Declan. He saw Declan's gaze flick from Ethan to Connor, who glared him down. None of them said anything. "Even Uncles Alec and Kieran and Aunt Sandy. Seems there's only two members of this family who didn't turn up on her doorstep and I don't know about anyone else, but I apologised for turning up so often. Certainly would've been easier if I had keys." His grin was sly. "Bet I wasn't the only one who wished for those." His gaze darted from his father to his uncle, across the table to Ethan, before moving to Cormac and Alec. "Did you ever apologise, Uncle Alec? Or you, Dad? Or you Uncle Connor? You three made quite a disturbance on her doorstep when you turned up."

Alec swallowed and cleared his throat. "No, Sean, I didn't, but I most certainly should have. Considering what you'd told us, I didn't need to go banging down her brownstone making a fool of myself. Emerson..." He looked down the table at her surprised expression. "Since we're in confession time, please apologise to Sydney for me. It's way past due, several years in fact, and I really should have."

Emerson gave a slight nod. "Alec, I'll pass that on, and thank you for doing so. I know several of you didn't apologise for your behaviour—"

"I did." Declan speared a potato. "It was awkward and in the book store where she got paint thrown at her, but I still apologised for my behaviour over what Sean did." He aimed his fork at his son. "That was all your fault."

Sean huffed. "You turning up on her doorstep yelling at her had nothing to do with me. It was all of you acting like the macho assholes you are."

"Hey!" Declan half rose.

"Sit down," Sean growled and watched his father's expression change. "*My* house. I didn't invite you here so you're free to get out, and you being an asshole to Sydney got you demoted by Grandpa. That's on you. Just like Connor slapping her is on him."

"What!" Emerson gasped. "Oh, my God, Cormac, you never told me. Sydney never told me. What the hell is wrong with you people?"

"You know, kid." Connor pointed his finger at his nephew. "I'm not the only one who slapped her, but I did beat the crap outta you for it."

"And I you," Sean retorted and raised his glass at his uncle. "You deserved it."

"So did you," Connor spat.

"Enough," Cormac roared, thumping his hands on the table.

Everyone went quiet and looked down, except for Sean who glared defiantly at his grandfather.

"There will be no more talk of Sydney, and Emerson." He grasped her hand. "I am sorry you didn't know that. I thought Sydney had confided in you."

"No," came out shakily. "No, she kept the whole business about the black eye to herself. Jesus!" She pulled her hand from his and covered her mouth. "*Two of you* assaulted her?"

"Not something I'm proud of," Sean said. "But I have apologised. Of course, I had been completely mindfucked by my parents, so that didn't help. I wasn't in my right mind when it happened."

"Assaulting a woman is never something a man should be proud of," Cormac said gravely, looking at Sean. "Connor, how 'bout you?"

"Ah…" Connor's eyes never left his plate. "No, I don't think I ever did. Sorry 'bout that."

"How could you hit her?" Ethan's brows furrowed deeply. "How could you hit a woman? But most of all, Sydney. She's an incredible, amazing woman and you hit her?" His gaze turned to Sean. "And you? Are you the whole reason we were banned by Grandpa from seeing her? You started this, Sean. Are you the reason?"

"It never stopped you from seeing her, Ethan. You hooked up a year later." Sean's heart did a little tap step as the shock flew over his cousin's face.

"We never hooked up," Ethan replied. "I had a break-in to deal with. Nothing happened."

"Ah-huh." Sean punctured a potato with his fork, the same way his father had. "Just like your father."

"And you're turning out just like yours." Connor glared daggers at him before his gaze turned to Declan beside him. "*Just* like yours."

"Who is Sydney?" Diane asked, unfazed by the family. "I keep hearing her name, but I have no idea who she is. Can someone enlighten me?" She picked up her wine glass.

"Sydney Kingston, author extraordinaire, writes thrillers as Cassandra Kingsley, and is Emerson's best friend. She lived here in New York for four years in Madam X's old brownstone. *Many* members of this family know that place well," Sean gleefully told her. "Madam X used to have a sex room for the rich and powerful men of the city, until Grandpa busted it up and shut it down. Sydney got her most successful books out of the story. That's the novel, *Madam X*, and the accompanying biography. Sold over six million copies each. She used to mentor me as a writer back in the day when I was striking out. She got to know the family quite well. Certain members in particular."

"Oh, I know those books. I didn't connect the name Sydney with Cassandra Kingsley, though." Diane set down her glass. "Did you all read them?"

"Pop and Dad did," Alec supplied. "Pop was a great fan of hers and had first edition hardcovers as collectables. He bought the e-books and paperbacks to read. Wouldn't let anyone touch his hardcovers. Sydney signed many of them."

"Oh, how sweet." Diane glanced at each member. "Did anyone else read them? Even though I'm a lawyer, I don't want to read crime books, but I had a few new clients when *Madam X* came out. They were worried they'd be in it."

"A lot of people were," Sean said. "*A lot* of people."

"I think we should clean up if everyone's finished." Emerson gathered her own and Cormac's plates. "Sean, we'll pop these in the washer for you and leave the leftovers."

"That's very kind of you, Emerson." Sean nodded. "Let me help you." He helped put away the leftovers while Sandy and Diane did the dishes. "Amazing food as always. I've missed your cooking these last months," he told her.

While they were both standing at the fridge with the doors open, Emerson whispered, "Did you really hit Sydney?"

He kept his voice low. "I did, and it was stupid, and I was seventeen and I apologised multiple times and when you call her, tell her again how sorry I am." He closed the door. "That's the food put away, my dinner set, glasses are in the dishwasher, and I just need help setting the table and chairs back next door."

"I'll help," Ethan offered, grabbing two chairs and rushing them next door. He passed Sean as he carried another two, then they picked up the table and carried it back into the condo.

When it was set in Sean's preferred placement, Ethan grabbed his cousin's arm. "Hey, what you said before. What do you know about me and Sydney?"

Sean leaned closer. "Everything."

Panicked, Ethan asked, "How could you possibly? Did she tell you? She wouldn't've told you. How could you know everything? There's nothing to tell."

"Then why is there panic in your eyes?" Sean asked. "I know everything, Ethan. And I *mean* everything. Every moment, every kiss, every fuck that you had. *Everything* including what you did for her." He stared into his cousin's green-blue eyes. "Did you enjoy fucking Sydney? Did you enjoy trying to outman your old man? Did you enjoy being inside of her, just like your old man had been?" His voice dropped and he leaned closer still, his gaze never leaving his cousin's. "Did you enjoy knowing your dick was doing the same thing as your old man's? Fucking her, being inside her sweet, sweet cavern of love, just like your old man?"

"Ethan, let's go," Connor called from the adjoining doorway. "What's taking you so long?"

"Just having a chat," Sean said, watching Ethan swallow hard as the panic whipped around his body.

Ethan's throat was a desert and he swallowed again. "Ah, yeah, be there in a minute." He waited for his father to leave before whispering, "Keep whatever you think you know to yourself, Sean Ryan, because you're dead wrong. None of that happened, and you have no idea what you're talking about." He strode off, leaving Sean and his sly grin alone in the room.

"Oh, don't I?" Sean murmured and followed him. "Thank you again for the food, Emerson." He opened the front door and waved them out. "I very much appreciate it." He gave Ethan a dirty grin, and Sierra a raised eyebrow. "I don't expect this to happen again. In fact, I don't want it to happen again. I just want to be left alone to work."

Cormac stopped at the door with Alec. "Then you'd better get your ass to my house every Sunday or we will be."

Sean wasn't to be turned off. "Or what? You'll put me away? I have a life and a career that keeps me busy. I'd rather work, especially since I won't be doing much else for the next five months. Although, I will be releasing more books, so I'll have to do interviews." He tapped his chin with his finger. "I'll have to set up Zoom and I'm having a gym delivered next week so I can keep working out." He waved them out.

"And how can you afford all of this?" Declan asked

again. "You're living high and mighty for someone writing kids' stuff."

"I'm living quite well, as I said earlier, but thanks for again asking. In fact, I'm living so well I just signed a contract on Friday for five million dollars for my next novel, so I'm doing very well. Bye now." He noted their shocked stares before locking the door, managing to hold it together long enough before he collapsed on the floor in pain.

He gritted his teeth and tried not to make a sound, so they didn't hear, and breathed in and out and counted to ten. When the pain started subsiding, he got to his feet and managed to make it over to the window, watching them get into their cars.

Cormac and Alec stopped conversing and glanced up at the window.

Sean waved and watched them frown.

Finally, all six cars pulled out of the carpark and went their separate ways. Breathing a sigh of relief, Sean clicked the button to close the curtains and found his pills in the cupboard. He swallowed them back with leftover wine and brewed a kettle of water for a strong coffee.

When it was done, he walked into the second condo, closed the curtains, put on his desk light, sorted his items, and opened his laptop. He walked over to the wall and opened it to see Sydney, and pulled down a Ziploc bag with 8x10 photos in it. He flicked through them, seeing Sydney and Ethan fucking in the hallway, the sex room, her bedroom, and the living room. Every room they'd fucked in, he had photos of. He also had photos of

Ethan's extracurricular activities.

His cousin had been a very bad boy indeed, coveting Sydney and a secret stash of photos he'd taken. And he'd found all of this when he'd broken into Ethan's house and taken photos. That's how he'd found the stash, the pairs of Sydney's knickers, a couple of bras, and graphic photos of Sydney naked.

They'd also filmed a sex video and Ethan had taken pictures of his dick inside her, of her breasts and vagina, her tongue as it licked his chest, even his dick as she gave him a blow job.

It had disgusted him, knowing Ethan had violated her so intimately *and* taken photos of the violation, but it had disgusted him more that Sydney had enjoyed it. She was laughing in the photos, shoving her tongue into his mouth or laughing while he shoved his tongue into her most intimate part.

A deep gut-wrenching growl came from him and he ripped the photos apart, slamming them onto the ground where they fluttered and settled. "I'm going to get my revenge on you, Ethan Ryan."

He stormed over to his laptop, opened the book he'd been working on, and got back to writing. Revenge was a dish best served in the pages of a novel for all to see, for all to read. And he'd make sure Ethan knew it was him. Might even dedicate it to him, to give him a clue, because Ethan wasn't as smart as he believed and revenge was coming fast.

Chapter 4

"Let's start at the beginning, so we can refresh our memories. How did you first meet Sydney?"

"Do we really have to do this, doc? I did it four years ago."

"It's just a refresh, Sean. It's not going to kill you. Unlike your father."

Laughter burst from Sean. "Oh, he could have at Sunday lunch. The whole damn family turned up on my doorstep with food and the old man demanded to know how I could afford it. At one point, he thought he could abuse me and started rising from his chair. I told him to sit down, it was my house and he was free to get out."

"How'd he take that?"

"Well, but then he was in shock. My old man doesn't take to being stood up to, especially by me. But at twenty-one, and a good half a head taller, and definitely wider and stronger, I could take him, and I think he realises that. He can't bully me anymore. Just like I said to my cousin when she mentioned that my books can't be crap anymore if I could afford two condos. I told her to go fuck herself, that all she'd done was bully me and I was over it."

"How'd she take that?"

"Not well. She was upset. Brandon, her brother, and our cousin Ethan tried to pull me up, but then I got back at Ethan later by telling him I knew everything about him and Sydney. It freaked him out."

"What about him and Sydney?" Levinworth flicked through his notes.

"They hooked up a year after his dad hooked up with her." Sean stared at the pigeons making a nest on the next building's rooftop. "I don't think he thought anyone knew, but I know a lot. Including what he and Sydney did, and neither of them had a problem with it."

"Neither had a problem with what?"

"With the fact Sydney had slept with Connor the year before, and now she was sleeping with Ethan. And Ethan's not that much older than me, but *my* love for Sydney *is* a problem. Not really following that one."

"You know full well why, Sean. You assaulted her, and she fought back. She—"

"Let's talk about my mother." Sean turned from the window and slowly moved over to the wall of paintings. "Isn't that what you wanted to know about?" He stared up at the painting he'd talked about last time. The one of the rocks and cliffs being pummelled by the waves. "My mother spent her four years in college as the roommate of Emerson Lake. And as a fan of Sydney's, I knew Emerson was turning her books into movies and they were best friends. I'd seen Mom going through her year book and saw them, and after Sydney and Emerson moved to New York, I started telling my mom she should catch up with her old college roommate and that she was best friends with Sydney Kingston. Maybe she should invite them over for lunch as the family were huge fans."

"Was your mom?"

Sean sighed. "She'd read a couple of books, but didn't find them interesting and just insulted Sydney over them. Which I found incredibly rude."

"Why did she insult Sydney over her books?"

"Don't really know, and she never really said. Called them crappy or sloppy romance novels when they were anything but. I did get my books signed and Mom got pissed off her face drunk at lunch.

"Did your mom get drunk often?"

"She did once she took leave from work, and it got worse. To the point she insulted everyone. Hell, Sydney even dished it back, but Mom was so drunk by then she didn't remember."

He flung the door open and started freaking out. "Oh, my God, I can't believe you're here." His hands flapped excitedly in front of him. "I'm such a big fan. Oh, my God. You're Cassandra Kingsley. Oh, my God." He was pulled away from her by his mother, phasing out of what everyone was saying as he only had eyes for Cassandra, and only heard snippets as he watched his mother motion for their guests to go into the living room, and watched them settle down on the sand-coloured couches. He quickly grabbed the three books he wanted her to sign from the sideboard and only came to when Sydney looked over her shoulder at him holding the trilogy of books she'd written. The One Who Loved, The One Who Lied, The One Who Betrayed.

"Oh, you read those? Not exactly for teenagers."

Sean set himself beside Sydney. "Oh, Miss Kingsley, these were the first three I read and I was hooked, so I read all of your others and will you sign them please? They're all first editions." He thrust the books and a black Paper Mate Flair at her.

Hesitating, Sydney glanced at Emerson and Laura and said, "Ah…okay. And it's Ms Kingston. Cassandra Kingsley is just my pen name." She quickly whipped her signature across each half title page and handed them back. "There you go."

Sean looked at the one on top and disappointment rained down. "Oh…you didn't personalise them."

"You didn't ask me to," Sydney said point blank. "You just asked me to sign them."

He brightened and thrust the books and pen back. "Can you add my name to them?"

He watched Sydney take a moment to breathe in and stretch her neck. She quickly added For Sean above her signatures and handed them back. "That's me done." She turned to the others. "Em says you've read some of my books, too."

Sean phased back out and gazed lovingly at Sydney, glad he'd hounded his mother to invite her over. He phased back in when he heard his mother say his name.

"Sean, sweetie, can you get us another bottle from the fridge and then leave us alone to talk."

His head turned to her, and he started protesting. "But, Mom—"

"No buts, Sean. The adults are talking." She waved him off.

Embarrassed, he grumbled under his breath and

headed for the kitchen, coming back with a fresh bottle straight from the fridge.

"Great, now piss off and leave us alone." Laura unwrapped the top and popped it.

Slinking away in shame, unable to look anyone in the eye, especially Sydney, Sean headed upstairs for his bedroom.

"Sydney sympathised about my mom. That meant a lot," he told Levinworth.

"When did she do that?"

"When she came in search of me. She found me moping in my room because Mom had banished me from the lounge room and their party."

"Having a drunk for a mother must suck."

Sean looked up to see Sydney leaning against his bedroom door frame.

"But at least you got three books signed. Your mother told Em that you're into writing."

His sad face brightened at that last word, and he jumped off the bed. "Absolutely. I'm not as good as you, but I've been writing through high school and my teachers say I'm really good." Sean pulled out a drawer in his desk and rustled through some papers. "I saw the picture of you in the paper and hounded Mom to call up Emerson. I was hoping she'd invite you over so I could talk to you about my work. Ah..." He found a notebook and held it up. "Finally. I was hoping you'd have a look at some short stories and give me advice. You're a professional writer. You do it for a living, so you know what editors and publishers want. If I'm good enough, then I might pursue it, but if not..." Sean became glum and held the notebook to his chest. "Then I'll have to find another class to take in college." He watched Sydney looked around the room and sigh before speaking.

"I'll give them a flip through. Don't think I have time to read each one. A page here and there to see the scope of your work. Here." Sydney held out her hand and he eagerly thrust his book into it.

"Oh, my God this is so exciting. Cassandra Kingsley is going to read my work. Oh…" He spun around, looking for a place for her to sit, and grabbed his desk chair. "Here."

"No, I'll stay here in the doorway so no one can say I was in a teenage boy's bedroom."

He watched her lean back against the door frame and flip open the book, reading the first page and quickly finishing off the rest of a ten-page story and then starting another. When she finished that, she flicked through the book and read passages.

Finally, he watched her close the notebook and waited with bated breath.

"They're great. You absolutely need to study writing. You should publish these."

"Really?" Sean bolted up from the bed where he'd been anxiously watching her face. "You mean it? You really mean it? They're great?" He grabbed the notebook from her outstretched hand and bounced up and down.

"Calm down." Sydney put her hands up and he came to a stop. "Yes, they're great. You seem to have a natural storytelling ability and use your words well. You also write tight prose. In fact, it's as if you've already learned it all."

"No, no, I haven't." He shook his head violently. "I haven't taken any courses or classes other than school. But my teacher said I write well, and my stories are great."

"Then I definitely think you should pursue it at college if it's something you want to do. Maybe take a part-time job at a publisher or do some work experience with an editor somewhere. You could even get a mentor to guide you."

"Could you mentor me?" Sean jumped at the chance. "I know on your publisher's website it says that up-and-coming writers can win a chance to be mentored by one of the authors and you're one of the authors."

"Oh, no, no, no." Sydney put her hands up and backed into the hallway. "No. I don't mentor anyone under twenty-one. It's too risky, age-wise, and I don't want complications. Besides, you write sci-fi fantasy, I don't. You'd be better off with mentoring from someone who does."

"What if I change genres?" Sean took an excited step towards her. "I could give romance or thrillers or crime a go. You got a mix of all three in your books." His hands went to his chest. "I'm from a crime family. I know procedures and the call signs for each crime. I hear about crime all the time from my dad and uncles and Grandpa and Pop. I could take notes and craft an outline."

"No." Sydney sighed and shoved her hands into her jeans pockets. "You're underage and I don't write children's stories. I wouldn't be helpful."

"What if I get my mom or dad's permission?" Sean stood in front of her. "Would you do it then? I'm sure Grandpa and Pop would tell them to say yes."

"It's up to the publisher. They have their contracts, not me."

"Okay, so I'll contact them. You can put in a good word for me and I'll get permission."

"I'm agreeing to nothing." Sydney shook her head and walked off.

"And what advice did Sydney give you?"

"The best advice ever. And I knew then that I had to apply for the mentorship with her at Pulsate."

"Is writing something you'd always wanted to do?"

"It was something I did." Sean stared at the painting. Heard the crash and smash of the waves on the rocks. The splish and splash of the broken waves falling back on themselves. "I hadn't thought of it as a career. It was something I did that I was good at. But when Sydney said it was good…" He chuckled. "I couldn't believe it. I couldn't believe that a best-selling author of crime thrillers actually thought my little old stories were good. That I should do something with them, maybe publish them, and get a book deal. Huh." He turned around and stared at the therapist. "Someone finally had confidence in me, *belief in me*. Little old Sean Ryan. That something *I* had done was good. Was publishable. That first conversation with Sydney made everything right. Made everything make sense. That my writing was worth something. That *I* was worth something. That I could make something of myself apart from my family. That I could *be* something *and* someone away from, and apart from, this family."

"Is that important to you?"

"Very. It always was." Sean walked over to the side

buffet and stared at the artworks, but not really seeing them. "My family name is a burden. You know it is. I think it was to Mom, too, even though she didn't take it. She became a doctor in her own name and wanted to keep it for continuity. My pop would constantly suggest she change it, and she told him where to get off because she had *her* father's name and was proud of that."

"She didn't mind you having Ryan, though."

"I think I was the sacrifice. The sacrificial first-born." He shrugged. "And I ended up being the only born. Mom didn't want more kids and I don't think Dad ever wanted them or me, but needed the proverbial to hand down the name to."

"How does that make you feel?"

"Sacrificed."

"You did just used variants of the word, so I guess you would." Levinworth made a note in Sean's file. "You didn't really mention this last time."

"Didn't I?" Sean sighed and rubbed his eyes, adjusting his glasses back in place.

"Do you hate your mother?"

"Yes…and no."

"Let's start with no."

"She was attentive when I was little, but still worked. I was in the hospital day care once I was big enough, and saw her through the day. We didn't do much as a family. Dad was always working, so it was Mom and me, or mom and me and Pop. Once I started school…" He gave a shoulder shrug. "I saw them at breakfast and Mom at dinner. And she was attentive and doting, and then she wasn't."

"Why?"

"Why?" Sean glanced at him. "Because I was in high school and getting too big and I wasn't the cutesy baby boy anymore and I could find my own way to and from school or go to Grandpa's and see Pop after school, and then I turned sixteen." He took a shuddering breath. "And things changed."

"Why?"

"Because Dad changed, things changed, and then Mom changed."

"And you?"

Sean's fingers slid slowly along the edge of the buffet. "Doc, you know the answer to that."

"Tell me, in your own words." Levinworth watched Sean's face. He saw him drift off in thought…saw his eyebrows furrow, and his mouth turn down.

"She became a drunk and a whore."

"And?"

"And she didn't love me anymore."

"Did she tell you that?"

"No. Her actions spoke louder than her lack of words."

"Did she ever tell you she loved you?"

"When I was a kid." Sean's fingers slid off the cupboard and he walked to the wall near the door, staring up at the artwork. "As a teenager, no. Once her sabbatical happened, she got drunk and didn't care for me anymore. She was dead two years later. One year after Sydney came into my life."

Levinworth checked his watch and made a note in Sean's folder. "Do you think your mother died loving you?"

"She didn't tell me, so I doubt she did."

"Didn't tell you before she died?"

"No."

"That must have hurt?"

Sean breathed deeply. "It did and it didn't."

"Is that why you hate her?"

"I hate her for a lot of things. Not loving me, not being my mother once I grew up. Not caring about what I wanted or needed."

"Not encouraging you to do anything."

"No. She never did."

"Not even your writing? After Sydney said you were good."

"Not even then." Sean turned from the wall. "Time's up, doc. You really should remember how I feel about my mother, I talked a lot about it four years ago."

"We did. But now you're four years older, doing a lot of stuff, and you lost your mother amongst it all. Moved in with your grandfather, lost your great-grandfather."

"Lost my mentor."

"That was your own fault."

"Don't you think I know that? That's why I got stuck talking to you." Sean glanced at the ticking clock on the wall. "Time's up, doc. Same time next week?"

"Yes." Levinworth showed him out and closed the door before sitting back down to take notes. Sean has a good grasp of it all, just as he had four years ago. Unfortunately, his parents never figured out just how intelligent he was. He stopped and picked up *Illicit Things*, Sean's first adult novel under the pen name of Bryan Jamison.

My fingers slid over her, over her curves. Her skin soft, yet supple. They wanted to do so much more than slide. They wanted to stroke and tweak and feel their way into places too taboo to go. But I didn't believe in taboos. I just believed in love and the love I felt for her surpassed any other emotion I'd ever had. My lips longed to follow my fingers and she allowed them the same freedoms as my fingers. They followed the path of my hand and made her feel things she said she'd never felt.

My tongue tasted every last millimetre of her skin, her body, inside and out. It made her come, made her scream and groan and cry out as she hit the highs of ecstasy. I made her do that. I made her come. I made her arch and writhe and accept me as I was. For who I was. Who I am. And I allowed her the same in return. Watching as her fingers roamed my body, cupped my testicles, her mouth sucking my penis that was yet to make her come. Yet to make her scream and groan. But I did. I groaned and held her head there as she sucked me like an all-day sucker, and I came in her mouth and she took it like I was about to take her. Her body writhed its way up mine, her hands, doing damage to my flesh until she hovered over me like the ethereal goddess she was.

A leg either side of mine, her hair falling in silken waves either side of her face. Her breasts leaning towards me, her nipples inviting me to suck them, teasing me just as her vagina did as it made its way slowly down my erect penis. She enveloped me whole. Her whole body enveloped my whole body and we fused together and became one.

*****

"Hello, my darling boy, how are those specs for your other books coming along?" Vincent asked via Zoom.

"Ah…coming," Sean told him. "I got involved in writing and have been going almost non-stop day and night. Everything's pouring out so fast I can't keep up. I started dictating a lot of it."

"Sounds delicious, I can't wait to see it."

"There's something I want to do, and I know it's short notice, but the books are done and ahead of schedule."

"And what's that?" Vincent delicately sipped his tea.

"I want to release *She* now, *Is* in May, and *Mine* in July so that *Her* can come out in September."

Vincent choked on his tea, spitting it out. He hastily set his cup down and dabbed at his mouth with his silk napkin. "You what?"

Sean suppressed a chuckle. "I want to release the trilogy sooner rather than later. Faster than we'd planned, and they're done, after all. We can release the e-books first if the print books aren't ready. Besides, I have plenty more books, remember, you have a store of my books. You can afford to release four this year."

"But why?" Vincent waved away his assistant who was cleaning up his mess.

"Because I need to, and I need to make money, and I need the stories out there now."

"But how will we explain your house arrest?"

"I broke my ankle falling down the stairs. It will make for a good story for writing more."

"You've clearly thought about it. And how will you do your interviews?"

"Exactly how I'm doing this one now. Via Zoom. Or, I could come into Viceroy and have the camera crew set up."

"But then you could just as easily go into their studio so the excuse won't work."

Sean nodded. "Okay, then I'll say the doctor has me on bed rest, or under house arrest, so I'm not out there irritating it any further."

"You could pretend to have a flu."

"I could, or an infection," Sean said. "Either way, I'll do them via Zoom."

"And when would you want to release them?"

"Nineteenth of March, May, and July. So *Her* can come out on the nineteenth of September."

"Sydney Kingston's publishing date." Vincent turned his cup around three times before picking it up. "Do you really want to try to beat her to the top? Why would we do that?"

"Because, as I said when I was there, Sydney's more than likely not publishing this year."

Vincent's hand paused mid-air, the cup halfway to his lips. "Didn't we have this conversation last week? I think Roger was supposed to find something out."

"We did. And it's just something that was said. She's busy in Australia having a holiday. She wanted a break."

"But do you know *for a fact* she's not publishing on the nineteenth of September?"

Sean shook his head. "No, I don't. But I could maybe find out."

Vincent tapped his chin in thought. "If you could, it would be a coup to get the top spot on her day."

"Not that that's what I'm after," Sean said with a chuckle. "I just want *Her* released on that day."

"It is an exquisite book." Vincent picked up his cup and took another sip of tea. "I've read it and it's your best so far."

"I believe it will outsell *Madam X,* and I want that record."

"I'm sure we can achieve that. Any particular reason why?"

"Just to compete with Pulsate and Sydney's records. I want to break them all."

"To prove you're better?"

"Yes." Sean nodded. "And to prove a point to her."

"And what point do you have to prove to Sydney?"

"Never you mind. Now get publicity onto releasing *She.* I want it out on the nineteenth, so you only have two weeks."

"As you said, everything is ready. We'll send the promo packs out this week and get ads going on socials. We probably can't get ads in magazines, but we'll try."

"Magazines don't matter, just get onto socials, maybe some book bloggers, and whatever we've done for the last three books."

"Okay, my darling boy. We'll do what we can. In the meantime, we'll set up some interviews and get the book out to the bigwigs. Rockefeller and Grant for TV and radio will be at the top of that list."

"Anything I can do from home," Sean said. "And I'll get my disguise ready and keep on writing the next book."

"Don't forget to send the specs, my dear boy."

Sean logged off and closed his eyes, but the banging on the door broke the silence and peace. He rolled his eyes and got up to open the door. "Uncle Alec."

"Sean." Alec walked into the condo and looked around. "Time for your weekly visit. Have you been behaving? You certainly didn't with Sierra."

After another eye roll, he led Alec into the adjacent condo. "One comment after years of bullying and she's the cry baby? Get real."

Alec strode into the living area, looked at each wall and saw the open laptop on the table. "Working on another book?"

"Yes. Happy? You can get out now." Sean waved him on.

"I just need to look upstairs in the bedrooms."

"Go ahead." He watched his uncle hurry upstairs and come back down a moment later.

"You don't use that bedroom?"

"No. I was thinking of cutting through the wall, though, turning it into a bigger room with a bigger closet."

"For all those fancy clothes you wear as Bryan Jamison?" Alec walked back into the first condo and upstairs to check on that bedroom.

Sean leaned against the wall, hands in his pockets and waited for him to come downstairs. "Yes, for all those fancy clothes I wear as Bryan Jamison, not to mention, all the fancy clothes I buy for myself."

"Not that you'll need them for a while, since you can't go anywhere." Alec glanced in the mirror beside the door and adjusted his blue silk tie. It matched his Italian blue suit perfectly.

"I still get to go out to my therapist and my publisher, so I can make all the cash to afford all those clothes," Sean said. "Just like you can afford yours. But I make more money."

"So I heard." Alec smoothed his suit blazer. "I read your contracts. The ones you made up yourself. You've made a lot more on your adult novels than your kids'. Quite a little fortune you got there, Seany."

Sean seethed at that name. "You know I hate that name. You always were as bad as Sierra. I can tell you to go fuck yourself, too, if you want."

Alec grabbed him by his top and rammed him against the wall. "You little punk-ass piece of shit. You don't get to talk to my daughter that way."

Sean shoved his arms up between Alec's and flung them outward to break his uncle's hold. He then shoved him sideways, spinning him around into a choke hold. "And if you ever assault me again I'll have you arrested," he murmured in Alec's ear as he struggled. "And don't think I won't. This place has cameras from every angle for my protection and they just recorded you assaulting me and me defending myself."

He shoved him away and watched him straighten his suit. "Get out, Alec. I don't want you here. Sierra gets her bad behaviour from you. Her mother, she doesn't care; she helped you raise a spoilt brat who thought it was perfectly okay to bully me for years because I was the youngest. So did Brandon. They're both arrogant assholes like their father. But when I got a publishing deal, because someone outside the family believed in me, she started sucking up like she'd always been my champion."

Sean advanced on his uncle. "But she wasn't. She's just a user, like her father, and wanted to use me, like the rest of the family to get stuff out of me. Money, invitations to author book launches or onto TV shows that I did interviews on. Yeah, that's right, you all wanted to use me for more fame and what you could get out of me as my family. You're just money grubbing assholes and the apple doesn't fall far."

"And you're just like Declan," Alec sniped. "An asshole who thinks he's entitled to do what he wants when he wants and that he's going to get away with it. You haven't, Sean. You were found out and put in detention for it. You're being punished with house arrest for five months, and that's the basic punishment that Sydney wanted because she still feels sorry for you." He smoothed his suit and steeled himself as he did when he was about to strike in court. "You're nothing but an asswipe like your father, and this punishment can be gone with the drop of a hat." He clicked his fingers in Sean's face. "I can take all of this way from you in an instant, Seany."

Sean slapped his hand away. "Think again, asshole. Do you seriously think I didn't have another lawyer look over my contracts and company? Do you seriously think I didn't have enough brain to also set up a will and conservatorship if everything went ass-shaped because of my family?" He stepped closer. "Because you'd also know, Alec, that you can't do a damn thing about my contracts, or my company, or my estate. You can't get your dirty little paws on it any easier than my father or grandfather. None of you can. And believe me when I say, I know just how dirty your paws are, Alec. The whole family does."

He noted his uncle's surprised expression. "And don't think that you'll keep getting away with it. Hell, I'm surprised that a woman of Diane's ilk would even want to date you. Do you make her suck your cock too?" Sean's head spun with the crack of Alec's hand and his fingers went to his cheek. "One more thing I can have you charged with, Alec. One more assault. Keep going and it will be the start of your downfall."

"You are a punk-ass piece of shit," Alec sneered. "At least your father knows how to fight back."

"Yeah." Sean wiped his bloody lip. "Dad's good at beating up people; Mom, me, the prostitutes he fucks."

Alec rammed his forefinger into Sean's face. "You watch your mouth. You have no proof that he's done any of that."

Sean's laugh was hollow. "Proof? Proof? I have plenty. The x-rays of broken bones, Mom's split lip and bruised cheeks. Why do you think I wet the bed until I was twelve? Because my old man was an abusive cunt that none of you did anything about." Sean's blue eyes glared into Alec's matching ones. It was a Ryan trait along with the brown wavy hair. "You're the DA, Kieran's a lawyer, Connor a detective, and Grandpa, the fucking PC, and yet none of you did anything to help Mom or me by stopping Dad from dealing out the abuse. *Nothing!* You just turned a blind eye like you do all the damn time for each other. You want proof, asshole, I got plenty of it and if you, or Dad, or Connor so much as make a move to destroy my life, I will ruin you. *All of you.* Do you understand me?"

Alec swallowed the lump in his throat and blinked. There was no way Sean had any proof of anything either he or Declan had done. He'd made sure of it. "Oh, I understand, little boy. I understand that you are no man, and never will be, and that you have nothing that we want or need." He straightened his suit for the third time and strode for the door. "Your grandfather wants you at lunch on Sunday. Be there."

"Or what? You'll arrest me for not leaving my house while I'm under house arrest," Sean mocked. "Go to hell, Alec. You and Dad and Connor don't scare me anymore, so tell Grandpa I won't be there."

"You're going to regret that, kid." Alec paused in the open doorway. "I'll make sure of it."

Sean's lips turned into a sneer. "And you have no idea what I can do to you."

Breathing in, Alec pulled the door shut behind him and worried. What did Sean have on them, on him, that could bring them down?

Chapter 5

"Let's go back to the lunch when you first met Sydney. How did you feel after meeting her?" Levinworth asked.

"Felt like I was floating on air." Sean stood in his usual position by the window.

"It must've. Your favourite author was showering you with attention. What happened after the lunch, when Sydney left?"

"Ah…" came out in a sigh. "It wasn't great."

"Your mother?"

"Pissed off her face as usual. She had drunk the majority of the six bottles of champagne. She certainly couldn't hold her liquor."

"And how was she in that state?"

"Angry. Crying. Miserable. Happy. She was an out-of-control pendulum."

"Was she verbally abusive?"

"Very. I wondered, towards the end, if she loved me. Did we talk about that last time? It didn't seem like she did." He frowned at the memories. "She treated me better when she was sober, and she treated me badly when she was plastered. I was glad when Grandpa moved me into his place. I got away from it *and* Dad."

"Do you want to talk about your father?"

"No." His hands clenched in his pants pockets. "I had to clean up after that lunch…"

Sean watched Emerson's car back out of the driveway and roll on down the road. A whimsical sigh left him, and he turned from the window. "How was your lunch?" He walked over to the coffee table and started collecting glasses and bottles.

"No, no, leave that one." Laura waved him away. "Just clean up everything else."

"That's what I'm doing," he mumbled under his breath. He dropped the bottles off in the laundry and put the glasses on the sink. His father hated seeing his wife plastered, so he knew he needed to clean up before Declan came home. If he came home. He gathered the plates of food, threw out most of it, and dropped the crockery into the sink.

"Can you get me another bottle of champagne, hon," Laura called.

"There isn't any," he told her, standing in the doorway. "You've drunk it all."

"No, I haven't," Laura whined. "I had several crates dropped off yesterday." She tumbled off the couch and into the kitchen, rummaging for another bottle.

Sean picked up the bowls of food, the scraps from the floor, and the last empty bottle, and found his mother in the pantry digging for another. He dumped the trash and leaned against the sink. "Mom, you have an alcohol problem. I want you to get help. You're a doctor, and you know better."

Laura emerged from the pantry, ripping off the foil on the bottle. "Don't you fucken tell me I'm an alcoholic. I'm not. I'm having fun. I had friends over that you harassed me into inviting, and when we have a drink, you accuse me of being drunk. Emerson did. What's-her-name drank, too." She popped the cork and sculled it back, swiping at the dribble on her chin.

"Sydney didn't drink any, Mom, and I doubt Emerson had one full glass." He watched her stumble into the living room and collapse on the sofa. "Mom… Mom…"

"I'm not a drunk, Sean. You know what…" She struggled to haul herself up. "If anyone's got a problem, it's you. You're a fat little pig and you need to get on a diet and lose weight. That's far more important than me enjoying a glass or two of champagne."

"That's your seventh bottle," Sean snapped, and stood at the end of the couch. "You're an alcoholic, and you can get help."

"And you're a fat little pig, who's just like his father." She drunkenly leered at him. "I wouldn't be surprised if you turn out to be a cunt just like him." She knocked back a quarter bottle and slid sideways until she was horizontal.

Sean sighed, walked away, and muttered under his breath, "At least I'm not fucking my brother-in-law."

"You already knew?" Levinworth asked, flicking through Sean's file.

"I wouldn't be surprised if the whole family knew. It wasn't hard to see she had an attraction to Connor. She would stare at him a lot at family dinners, more so when she was drinking. She got frisky when she thought no one was looking, but he pushed her away and would then come around when Dad or I weren't home and fuck her every which way."

"And how do you know that?"

"It's in my notes from four years ago, doc. You know exactly how."

Levinworth turned a couple of pages and found it halfway down. "You ended up at home from a school cancellation and they came home and started in the kitchen, you filmed them, and when they went up to your parents' bedroom. They had no idea you were there."

"Nope. I heard Mom sneak him out before the time I was due home. So, I sneaked out and pretended to come home."

"Did either of them ever find out you knew?"

"I told Connor that night at his house."

"Which night?"

"The night I assaulted Sydney and he took me to his house. We got into it, but I talked about that four years ago and don't want to talk about it now. I never told Mom. I don't know if Connor did, so I can't say if she ever knew that I knew."

"You were seventeen then. You had one last year with her."

"Didn't know that then." Sean sighed. "Didn't know the shit was going to hit the fan a few months later."

"Whose fault was that?"

"Yeah, yeah, mine. But Connor didn't help by getting involved with Sydney after dropping my mother like a hot potato. She had no clue why he'd stopped coming around to see her. Didn't answer her texts, her calls, nothing. Just blanked her completely. She hated it and it made her drink more. She became worse."

"What happened after the lunch date with Sydney?"

"Come on, doc. You know this one. Mom was supposed to invite her to lunch, but she didn't do it and Connor told her by accident."

"The full story, Sean."

"Why?"

"To refresh my memory."

"Then read my file if your memory's that bad." Sean flashed back to the lunch.

"But I really want to do the mentorship with Sydney at Pulsate. I've filled in the online form. I just need your permission because I'm under eighteen," Sean told his parents at Sunday lunch.

"I don't know, Sean, you've never wanted to do anything like this before." Laura picked up her glass and drained it. "And if it's online, why do you need our permission?"

"It's not online, it will be in person and it's because I'm under eighteen," Sean repeated. "Anyone under eighteen needs their parents' permission in writing so they can be mentored by an author at Pulsate Publishing. I'm choosing Sydney because I love her books and want to write like her. She can teach me a lot."

"Like how to write," Sierra said from across the table. "'Cause you certainly can't now. Your stories are crap."

"And what would you know about my stories?" Sean asked. "You've never read any of them and none of you even knew I'd written any until I brought this up."

"Where's writing gonna get you?" Declan speared a

potato and cut it in half. "Writing's for chumps, you don't need it. Get yourself a decent job so you can earn decent money and help out around the house." He shoved half of a potato into his mouth and speared the other half.

"Writing is not for chumps. Sydney's a very successful author, as many are," Sean argued. "She's made millions from her Cassandra Kingsley thrillers."

"Cassandra Kingsley." Douglas perked up and jumped into the conversation. "I love her books. How can you get a mentorship with her?"

"And when did you meet her?" Cormac asked from the other end of the table.

"Sydney's pen name is Cassandra Kingsley. Her best friend is Emerson Lake, the writer, director, and producer of your favourite show, Twisted Minds. Emerson was Mom's college roommate. When I found out Sydney had moved here I persuaded Mom to invite her and Emerson for lunch. They came around yesterday."

"You'll have to invite them here," Douglas said. "How about next Sunday? Laura, can you call your friend and invite them here next week?"

Laura's refilled wine glass paused at her lips. "Ah, yeah. Sure. I think I got her number."

"Anyway, Sydney's publisher, Pulsate Publishing, has mentorship programs for up-and-coming authors. It's a three-month stint, once a week, and at the end, if you've improved enough that they want to publish you, they'll give you a contract for your first book."

"But your stories are crap," Sierra repeated. "No one wants to read them."

"*And yet, somehow you seem to've, Sierra. How is that?*" *Sean frowned. "How would you know what my stories are like when you don't even come to our house?"*

Sierra casually shrugged and sipped her water. At nineteen, she wasn't allowed wine, whereas her brother, Brandon, was since he'd turned twenty-one a few months earlier. "I had a look when we came over for that barbeque back a couple of summers ago."

Sean reeled back. "Let me get this straight, you broke into my bedroom and went through my drawers in my desk and God knows what else, just to see and do what?" He shrugged. "Tell on me to Mom and Dad? Grandpa? What? What could possibly be the reason you walked uninvited into my bedroom and raided my personal belongings? You clearly didn't find anything to hold against me, but you read my stories and labelled them as crap? I bet you can't write anything to the same level as I can. My English teacher tells me I'm writing at college level and even passed some of my work along to a college professor friend of his who teaches English and writing. And he says it's college level and better than some of his students. Exactly what are you calling crap, Sierra? Huh?"

"You went uninvited into his bedroom? That's not the Ryan way, young lady," Douglas reprimanded. "Neither is going through his personal belongings. I hope you left everything as you found it, otherwise I'd be very disappointed if you stole from your cousin."

"I didn't, Pop." Sierra looked chastised.

But Sean knew Sierra and her antics, and knew she'd gone for a look for dirt. "I have everything numbered, and a list of those numbers. It was all there."

"Sean, how long have you been writing?" Cormac asked.

Sean shrugged a shoulder. "Since I was a kid. In school, after school. It's just something I did. Like drawing. I like creating things."

"And you really want to do this mentorship?" Cormac's gaze shifted from Sean to his parents. All three sat to his left, with Ethan and Connor. Kieran and his girlfriend Sandy, and Alec and his wife and kids were to his right.

"I do. I've written so many stories I'm thinking of doing writing in college. I'm not sure what else at this stage, but if I can get a mentorship now, it will help before I even get to college. And I'll have real agents and editors helping me craft my stories into something worth publishing."

"I still don't know," Laura said. "How will it happen? When, where?"

"In person at Pulsate Publishing; unless it has to be online. However it can happen. Once a week for three months."

"And if they still think you're stories are crap?" Sierra smirked.

"Enough!" Douglas told her and saw her blush.

"Only you think that Sierra; and you're probably lying just so you can bully me," Sean sniped. "I'm sick of it." He turned to his parents. "I just need you to sign the permission slip. I printed it out and I'll send it in. The rest of the form is online. Please, please," he begged. "Can I do this?"

"I think it would be a wonderful learning experience," Cormac said. *"Let the kid have it."*

"And we'll be meeting Sydney next week, so we can talk to her about it," Douglas added. "I can't wait to meet the author of my favourite crime thrillers."

"And her best friend and Laura's college roommate, Emerson Lake. Everyone on the force has watched her Twisted Minds series. Let Sean have this," Cormac told his son. "You just need to sign the form."

"God, if it will get you all off my back, all right," Declan yelled and downed the rest of his beer. "Just to shut you up."

Laura noticed and sighed. "Yeah, sure. Whatever, Sean. You might not even get it."

"Don't have to be so pessimistic, Mom, I'm keeping everything crossed." On the inside, Sean's blood was singing, on the outside, he played it cool.

"How did that make you feel?"

"What do you mean?" Sean finally left his spot by the window and stood in front of the wave painting that called to him.

"How did you feel knowing you had your grandfather and great-grandfather on your side? That they encouraged you and got your parents to sign."

"I think by that stage, my mom was dejected, and my dad was an even bigger asshole than he'd ever been. When Grandpa gets behind something, he's pretty good at convincing people to do things. And it was just a piece of paper. I was already getting myself to and from school, and anywhere else I needed to go. I could take buses and trains and cabs and I was learning to drive in school. I certainly didn't need either of them to get me around. I could get myself to wherever I needed to go for the mentorship."

Levinworth changed tack. "Sean, you harassed your mother into inviting Emerson and Sydney over; did you already know where they lived? Did your mom know how to get in contact with Emerson?"

Sean's heart hammered to a stop, and his breath left him before he spoke. "Emerson's details were on her website. I made a few calls and emails and found her number and made it easy for Mom to find it to call her."

"It had been what? Twenty years?"

"Thirty," Sean corrected. "Both were fifty-five at the time."

"And Sydney?"

"Thirty years older than me."

"Did you know where she lived before you met her?"

Sean breathed out and his hands clenched. He moved away from the wall and onto the cabinet full of artworks.

"Sean?"

Silence, before he spoke. "It's not that hard, you know. Real estate sales are online if you try hard enough and use the right search words. You find surprising information."

"And you found Sydney's address?"

"I did."

"And what did you do with that information?"

"Looked up the address and found it was the infamous Madam X's old brownstone. Quite intriguing that, considering its history."

"That involved your family, right?"

"It most certainly did." Sean smirked. "My grandfather raided the place with an army of cops, arrested Madam X, pulled apart the house, ripped up floorboards and walls, and confiscated every piece of equipment from the sex room in the basement. They trashed the place looking for Josephine Pompadour's little black book."

"How many members of your family—"

"Too many," came the sharp reply.

"You don't know what the question was."

Sean's head tilted, his ear listening. "No, I don't. I misspoke."

Levinworth made a note. "How many members of your family were in on the raid? It was twenty years ago."

"Fifteen or sixteen years, and I didn't misspeak. Too many. Grandpa, Alec, Connor, my dad. And Pop when he was PC and he turned up for a look on the day because he wanted to see her go down. My cousins and I were kids, and Kieran was in law school, although he learned all about it in his three years at Harvard."

"And how many years of law did you complete?"

"Two. I was damn good. I completed all three years in two. Helps knowing the law inside and out from your family. I was ahead of everyone else, so I was accelerated. The teachers knew my family; had taught Alec and Kieran."

"And where did you come, compared to them?"

"They were in the top ten percent. I was at the very top." Sean moved on to the next wall of paintings. "Is that because of my learning issues?"

"Partly. It means your brain learns a little differently. It takes in more information, remembers more, but that can lead to the overload, hence the drugs."

"Were they supposed to slow me down?" Sean asked.

"They were meant to calm the neurological pathways long enough for your brain to absorb everything properly. But your brain absorbs more regardless."

"No wonder I'm so damn good. Have I mentioned Alec dropped by? The asshole does a weekly check-up to see if I've behaved myself and kept my walls free from photos of Sydney. However, this week, he took it upon himself to assault me. Shoved me against the wall and then punched me."

"I wondered about the bruise." Levinworth wrote that information down. "Are you okay?"

"I'm fine. I fought back and told him I have cameras everywhere for my own safety. It was all being recorded."

"How did he react to that?"

Sean grinned. "Not well. Demanded I be at dinner this week. I told him no."

"How'd he take that?"

"Not well, but then, none of the Ryan men take being told no well. I guess I inherited that from my old man, and his old man, and *his* old man."

"Has he ever beaten you?"

"My old man?"

"Yes."

"Yes. But you know that."

"Before you came to me?"

"He certainly didn't do it after. Knew he'd probably be reported by you. Ironic, considering his wife was a doctor."

"And he beat her too."

"At times."

"Is that why she had the affair with her brother-in-law?"

"More than likely. She wasn't getting anything from her husband, so she turned to the man who could give it to her."

"And when he met Sydney?"

"He lost all interest in her and she lost all interest in life."

"Is that why she killed herself, do you think?"

"I don't think she killed herself."

Levinworth perked up. "I remember you said that last time."

"Still true now. I saw it on the way home after that lunch. When I got permission. My parents had actually driven together, and I was in the backseat like the kid I was, listening to them argue, feeling like I was five again. Not that they argued much back then." His brows furrowed. "They argued about Mom's drinking, my mentorship, and how Grandpa had badgered them into giving permission."

"And how did that make you feel?"

"Like absolute shit. Mom didn't want me to do it, and felt pressured. Dad didn't give a shit as long as he wasn't paying for it. But neither believed in me. I don't think any of them did, outside of Grandpa and Pop."

"But they signed the form."

"I had it with me and made them sign it in front of everyone so they couldn't pull out."

"Smart move."

"It was. Especially since Mom tried to back out and

Dad actually convinced her to let me do it. Which was surprising. I got upstairs as fast as I could and made a scan of it to add to the online form and jammed it into the envelope and sealed it up. I shoved it in my bag to post the next day and sent off the online form that night. It didn't take much."

"What did you need to fill it out?"

"Name, address, scan of the form, and a completed piece to show them I had what it took to be an author."

"And you were accepted."

"By the publishing company. But only after Sydney said yes." Sean brought the subject back around. "That night, they kept arguing long after we'd gone home. Dad finally left, slamming the door behind him at two in the morning."

"You were still awake?"

"I was. I'd been writing a piece about my parents. It was something I showed Sydney weeks later at our second mentoring session. I told her I wanted to write adult fiction."

"Because of her?"

"Pretty much. Her works are amazing, and I wanted to write like her and told her so. She asked why. I said I won't be young for much longer, why can't I graduate from young adult to adult."

"No reason you can't. You're very good."

"I've been told I'm just as good as Sydney." Sean finally turned and slowly walked over to the couch, hiked up his pants at the leg joint, and sat down. "It's a pretty good feeling to be told by publishing professionals that your work is just as good, if not better, than the author you admire most and want to write like."

"That must have been an ego boost?"

"It was. Especially when the dollar signs came out to play."

"A lot?"

"Two million apiece for the first three books. Same for the three that are about to come out, and the same for the next six. But I've jumped to five million for the one I finished in detention."

"That's quite a leap for one book."

"They've sold millions," Sean said. "They've got six books to publish out of me, six more ready to go into production, then the new one, and many more because I can barely stop writing, and the second set are coming out in two-month increments. The world won't know what hit it with me publishing four books this year."

"Is it also your thought to out-publish Sydney?"

Sean thought about it, his hands moving slightly in front of him as he spoke. "I'd like to. I feel like I have a lot of catching up to do. I feel...I feel like I've lost so much time." He touched his chest. "In here. I have to publish more to make up for lost time and when I've written enough then I'll stop. But for now, I can't stop writing and I can't stop telling my story in multiple ways. So many ways." He closed his eyes and deflated on a sigh. Resting his arms on his legs, he let his head drop. "I get overwhelmed with how much I have to write. It's like, I have to keep writing my story until it's done. And it keeps coming out in different ways."

"That means your soul's not done dealing with it."

"Yeah, that makes sense." Checking his watch, he

rose. "Gotta go, doc. I got other things to do. Same time next week?" He left and closed the door behind him.

Levinworth opened Sean's book, *Creeper,* turned to the first page and read the first line. *Nobody was going to stop me from having her.*

*****

On Sunday, Sean strode into his grandfather's house for dinner. Not lunch, as stipulated by Alec, and he had pre-booked it with Cormac. "Hey, Emerson, that smells good. What is it?" He set down the double chocolate sponge cake on the kitchen island bench and sniffed the air. "Chicken?"

Emerson smiled brightly. "Yes, a casserole made with the leftovers from lunch. There were a few." She opened the oven to check on the pot.

"Leftovers?" Sean opened the fridge and removed a light beer. "Did the family not come?" He put the cake on the top shelf and closed the door. "Where's Grandpa?"

"In the sun room watching the news. Your father and Connor didn't turn up. Both are dealing with cases and were needed at crime scenes."

"Nothing new then. Kieran and Sandy? Alec and his brats? Ethan?" He drank several mouthfuls and watched her face as she considered his words.

"They were all here." She wiped her hands on a towel. "Why don't you go see your grandfather and tell him it's nearly ready. We can sit down soon."

"Sure." He wandered through the doorway and stood by his grandfather's chair, watching the presenter on TV talk about the news of the day. "Hey, Grandpa. Why do you watch this stuff when you deal with it all day?"

"Because I need to keep informed." Cormac looked up at his grandson. "Are we going to keep doing Sunday dinners instead of lunches?"

"I told you. If you want me here then it's when the family aren't." Sean slumped onto the nearest chair. "Besides, we used to eat Sunday dinner all the time when I lived here."

"I know." Cormac smiled. "And Pop and I didn't mind dinner every night. It meant we got to spend more time with you and invest in your future."

"And how'd that work out for you?" Sean crossed his left leg over his right and pulled up his pants leg to show off his ankle monitor. "'Cause this thing isn't working for me at all."

Cormac grimaced at the bracelet. "But you did this, and this is your punishment. Be grateful Sydney didn't want to press charges and wanted it kept private and out of the press."

"Would've only been bad press for the rest of the family. I would've had a boost in popularity. By the way, Emerson said dinner's almost ready."

"I heard." Cormac sighed. "Sean, this could have ruined your life."

Sean shrugged a shoulder. "But it didn't. And the family's fine and I'm...I'm nowhere near being fine because I have an ankle bracelet and I'm under house arrest for five months with mandatory therapy and I can't go anywhere or do anything outside of my therapist's office, my publishing house, or my grandfather's house.

Everyone's fine but me."

"And again, you did this to yourself," Cormac repeated. "You know, Sean, what you did…" He shook his head and huffed. "It was beyond illegal. The cameras and everything, it was just damn creepy. But then, maybe you've been telling us what you're really like in your adult novels, especially your last one, *Creeper.* Autobiographical, wouldn't you say?"

Sean's brows rose and he gave another shrug. "Maybe, maybe not. And maybe I just took the experiences that I'd already had and used them as ideas for novels. That's what we authors do." He saw Emerson put the crockery on the table. "I'll do that Emerson." He saw her appreciative smile and walked into the dining room. Three placemats, three plates, three sets of cutlery and glasses.

Emerson carried in the hotpot, her hands in '60s floral print oven mitts that matched her apron, and she set it on the wooden pot holder in the centre of the table in front of Cormac's chair. "Dinner's ready." She dished out the meals as Cormac took his place before seating herself.

Cormac and Sean said grace while she sat silently due to her Jewish faith.

"Smells delicious, as always." Cormac whipped his napkin across his lap and picked up the wine bottle. He popped it open and poured two glasses.

"Keeping the wine away from me?" Sean joked and popped a forkful of chicken into his mouth. "Mmm." His eyes closed and his fingers touched his lips and did a chef's kiss. "Unbelievable, Emerson. I've thoroughly gone over my paperwork, Grandpa. There's nothing in there to say I can't enjoy a drink or two. I'm not a drunk and never have been. That wasn't a rule in my house arrest."

Alarmed, Emerson's eyes widened. "House arrest? What did you do?" Her gaze darted between Sean and her fiancé. "Cormac?"

"I was a stupid young man, Emerson," Sean replied. "I did some stupid things and was punished for them. I was in detention for a month and I'm now under house arrest for five months. I have an ankle bracelet and all."

Emerson was stunned. "Are you serious?"

Sean sighed, set his fork down and took a sip of beer. "Sadly, yes. It seems I fell back into some old ways and did some stupid things. But I'm dealing with the consequences of that and it's house arrest for five months after a month of detention. The good news is, I can still go and see my publisher and being at home has afforded me a lot of time to write. I'm halfway through a novel now, finished off the previous one in detention, and have another one to go, plus, I have novels coming out this year. Starting with next week."

"Novels?" Emerson frowned. "You're still writing young adult? I haven't seen any of your books in a few years. Are you getting back to them?"

Sean glanced from Emerson to his grandfather, whose expression was neutral. "No. I haven't written young adult in years. It was just the five. They were so popular Pulsate published them every six months, until they weren't and they didn't. I'm talking about my thrillers. I mentioned my last one at Sunday lunch at my place. It sold for five million, my publisher loved it that much. I sold the next two for the same based on the specs alone. They're thirteen, fourteen and fifteen for me."

Emerson's brows rose and she gaped. "Fifteen novels on top of your five young adult. Cormac, you have a prolific author on your hands. They must be good for Pulsate to spend so much."

"Oh, I'm not with Pulsate for my adult novels," Sean said. "I'm with Viceroy."

Emerson's fork paused in mid-air. "Viceroy? You didn't stay with Pulsate?"

"No. Pulsate were great for getting me started, but when the sales declined with books four and five, they passed on more, so I passed on them. I subbed to different publishers and Viceroy was the winner." He finished off his beer. "I know Viceroy's a sore spot with Sydney and Pulsate. They're the competition after all." Sliding his chair back, he hurried into the kitchen for another beer. "I know Sydney hates Viceroy authors and has often bad-mouthed them, but some of us are actually pretty cool and big fans of hers." He sat down and went back to eating his casserole.

"She hasn't bad-mouthed *all* Viceroy authors." Emerson took a sip of wine. "Some of them are old friends she made when they were with Pulsate."

"And some of them she hates," Sean reiterated. "Did you pass on my apology? Have you spoken to her since the last lunch?"

"I have and I did. Also passed on Alec's apology, which she laughed at, and remembered your father's half-assed apology in the bookstore. She said she couldn't figure out who it was more painful for. Her or him."

A chuckle came from Sean. "That'd be about right."

Emerson giggled. "Yes. She did laugh about it, but the laughter died when I asked why she hadn't told me that you and Connor had both slapped her. She sighed and said she didn't want to talk about that time in her life and what this family had done to her. I mean," she waved a hand, "I knew a lot of it, and know she'd been involved with Connor, and when Nora was murdered, he and Declan and Ethan all turned up on her doorstep. Poor girl. It was just a horrible time for all of us." She swiped at her mane of black curls back. "But I still don't know the full story. Care to elaborate, Sean?"

Sean gazed up from the remnants of his meal. "I did bad shit back then, Emerson. I hurt Sydney and I regret it deeply, especially after everything she did for me. I was a very screwed up kid and Grandpa got me help. One of the rules was I would never talk about it outside of those in the know. Sydney wanted it kept private because she was hurt and humiliated, and Connor and I and this family did that to her. And I'm incredibly sorry for it, but I won't go into detail. I'm sorry."

"Neither did Sydney," Emerson said. "And she pretty much said the same thing. I guess I have to understand and accept her decision. Did you apologise, Cormac?"

Startled, Cormac stopped eating and glanced at his future wife. "I did. When I went around after Sean's debacle. It concerned the murder of my wife and apologising for my family's behaviour, and I told her she was right when it came to being wary of Sean's behaviour and not wanting to mentor a young man. I got it wrong, and I apologised for that."

"You shouldn't've. The mentoring meant the world to me," Sean told him. "Without it, and Sydney's first few weeks of encouragement, and then insisting I keep it up, even after what I did to her, changed my life for the better. I have an amazing career, I'm set for life, I love what I do and it's all because of her and what she did to help me. I'm incredibly grateful for her support and mentorship."

"Even though you went off the rails?" Cormac asked.

Sean nodded. "Absolutely. Even though I went off the rails. She believed in me enough to encourage me and wanted me to keep going when she could've had me arrested and charged and thrown in jail. She didn't. She told you to keep pushing me because I needed it. And I did. And I'm forever grateful that Sydney and you and Pop kept on at me to keep going with the mentorship and then my publishing and writing. It's led me to my amazing career."

"But you're in trouble again," Emerson said. "Did you not learn?"

A sigh rolled up from Sean's gut and he let it out. "It's only been four years. I had extensive therapy for two of those years and I..." He flung up his hands in disgust. "Guess I still have some fixing to do. What my parents did and said, my mom dying, being published, I guess it's made me backslide a little and I did some more stupid stuff. But I'm getting help again, so let's see what happens."

"Did this time have to do with Sydney?" Emerson asked.

Sean gave a slight nod. "Sort of. But she was already

gone." He changed tack. "Is she still enjoying her time in Australia?"

"She is, very much so. She's taken up surfing, can you believe it. She never did that while we were in L.A., but she's loving it. And she's taken up the Jackie Collins lifestyle of the Gold Coast. Every party she goes to, celebrities, and even mere mortals, tell her all their secrets."

"Is she going to use them in her books? Has she written it all down?" Sean asked, taking a sip of beer.

"She has, but she hasn't been writing much, just notes for potential stories. She thinks she's burnt out."

"That's not good." Sean frowned. "Does that mean we're not getting any Cassandra Kingsley thrillers anytime soon? I love those books. So did Pop."

Emerson's lips curled into a soft smile. "Yes, he did. But no, I don't think so. Unless she has a backlog of unpublished work."

"So, no new thriller this year? That's sad." Sean played with his bottle, waiting.

"Not that I know of, and it kind of is," Emerson agreed. "Speaking of releases, you didn't tell me what genres you're writing as an adult. Are you using your own name? A pen name? What are some of your titles and have I read any?"

Sean glanced from Cormac to Emerson and dropped the bomb. "I write crime thrillers under the name Bryan Jamison."

*****

"Bryan Jamison, Oh, my God. Bomb drop. Mic drop. Bestseller book drop," Rhett Rockefeller, host of his own daytime TV show, Rockefeller, said down the camera via Zoom. "How? Why? When? Oh, my God!"

Bryan chuckled. "Good to know you're shocked, Rhett. So were all of my fans, apparently."

"Ah, yeah!" Rhett said, and he glanced at the audience. "You said last year when you were on with *Creeper*, another bestseller by the way, folks, that your next three books were called *She, Is,* and *Mine*, but we didn't have any release dates and now, oh, my God here we are with *She*, the first book in the trilogy, and you and your publisher, Viceroy Publishing have already announced that *Is* and *Mine* are coming in May and July. Was this already planned with the three books? Was *She* due for release now? Are you getting them out of the way for something else? Are you trying to outdo Sydney Kingston's record of the most number one crime thrillers?" Rhett leaned back in his chair and fanned his reddening face with his note cards. "I'm all worked up here, folks. This book is the bomb and it was *dropped on us* like a bomb. Another bestseller, Bryan. How did you do it? Tell us about it?"

Bryan clasped his hands in front of him and rested his chin on them. "It wasn't that hard, Rhett. The books were written, the books were done, and everything was ready to go. I just felt the need to up the publishing date and get them out there as soon as possible, and Viceroy did an amazing job of bringing the dates forward and releasing *She* now."

"I was sent a copy, as I'm sure a lot of other TV and

radio hosts were, and I was so surprised that this came out of the blue, that I devoured it the night I got it. It clearly says book one in a trilogy on the cover, and in the book. Is that why they're being released every two months?"

"Good question." Bryan nodded at the camera on his laptop. "And yes, it is. The original timeline was going to be every six months again, but I've written an amazing standalone novel that I want published after these books. I said let's move them up and get them out this year. My fans will have four new books this year, all two months apart because I couldn't wait."

"Okay." Rhett held the book up for the camera and did a casual head toss to get the lock of blond hair off his forehead. "The new Bryan Jamison novel is called *She*, and it's book one in the trilogy, followed by *Is* and *Mine*. Tell us about the book and how it came to be. How the series came to be."

"Well, Rhett, one thing I've noticed is that I tend to write in the same theme, the same story told a thousand ways, and this is just one more. We crime authors, thriller authors, suspense authors, all have a niche that we write in. All of us have stories that we tell the same way, and I seem to have a knack for telling my stories a certain way. It's about what all of my other books are about. Unrequited love, obsession, a man who can't have a woman and vows to make her his, hence *She Is Mine*. It's psychological. He's a stalker out to get the woman he loves, but she thwarts him at every turn because she's smarter than him and has seen it all before. He sends her death threats disguised as love letters, and dead rats as gifts. He's quite obsessed, but she plays the same games with him and makes it harder for him to keep his cool, which he loses on more than a few occasions."

"He certainly does." Rhett turned the book over. "It's paperback. Will there be a hardcover?"

"There will be for those who want it, along with the other usual suspects. All formats are important, but I wanted to get the paperback out so more people could enjoy the novels, plus, you have the e-book."

"You do. Now, Bryan." Rhett flicked through the book. "Normally we'd have you here in person. What's happened that we had to organise our interview via Zoom?"

Bryan pushed his silver wire framed glasses up. "It's all rather embarrassing, Rhett, but I'm under arrest."

"What!" Rhett's head shot up. "Arrest? What did you do?"

"I broke my ankle, and my doctor has me under house arrest for a couple of months."

"Oh, no. Are you okay?"

"I am, but it's a nasty break, did it falling down the stairs, can you believe it? My ankle rolled right out from under me when I was walking down. The doctor said I was lucky I didn't break anything else. Although I do have bruises and cuts. I'm all right, just out of commission for a few months."

"It sucks to be you," Rhett said. "Right when you have to promote your book. Will you be in studio for the next one?"

"I don't know, but don't count on it." Bryan smiled.

"You know." Rhett looked around the audience. "I

just realised you have four books this year; you said every two months. The trilogy and a standalone which will be out in September. Are you aiming to take over Sydney Kingston's publishing date? Are you trying to outsmart the queen of crime thrillers?"

"I wish." Bryan chuckled. "I am releasing the standalone in September, but you'll have to wait and see what date."

"So, you want to be reigning crime thriller author?" Rhett asked. "You'll definitely do it with four books this year."

"And that is a title I would love to have one day," Bryan replied. "We can all dream."

"You certainly can, Bryan Jamison. And all the folks in the studio audience and at home can too. *She* by Bryan Jamison is out now in all formats, and the next book *Is,* is coming in two months followed by *Mine* two months after that. If you want to wait until the third book is released so you can read them all together, you only have to wait four more months and another two for a standalone. Do we know the title of the novel coming in September?"

"I do, and my publisher does."

"But you're not going to tell us?"

"No. Not when you have a trilogy coming. You'll just have to wait, Rhett."

Rhett laughed. "Yes, yes. *She* by Bryan Jamison is out now, folks. Thanks for joining us today, Bryan, and hope you're better soon."

"Thanks, Rhett, thanks everyone." Bryan watched Rhett be counted out to the break and saw a producer pop up on the screen.

"Thanks so much for doing this, Bryan. We'll see you again in two months."

"Thank you, goodbye." Bryan turned the Zoom call off and closed his laptop, then receded while Sean came back. "God, what a hassle. But I have six more of these today and more tomorrow." He looked at his manager, Dexter Regas. "And then what? Radio and magazine interviews?"

"Which can be done via phone or Zoom. We have a press kit going out this time with the new author photos they can use; an AI sheet for the book, and a bio for Bryan."

Sean scratched his ankle. The bracelet was making him itch and he'd noticed a slight rash under the band. He finally stood up and checked the time. "Okay, I have time for a leak and a coffee then we'll get on with it." After satisfying himself, he settled back at his desk with his coffee and got on with the next Zoom interview for another TV show.

Once all seven were done, he closed his laptop and pulled off the wig. "Are the radio interviews via phone or Zoom?"

Dexter checked his notes. "All phone, so no need for the getup." He watched Sean remove the brown contacts and beard. "Is all that stuff necessary? Isn't it time to come out?"

Sean looked at him. "I use a pseudonym for a reason."

Dexter nodded. "Your family name. Your family profession. You want to keep that to yourself."

"Unlike my two cousins who milk it for all it's worth," Sean snarked. "Sierra and Brandon think they're social media influencers who had no problem using my fame and newfound success as an author to get what they wanted, and God help me if they didn't." He set the wig on the foam head, and the beard on the face. "I want this for me. To prove I can do it on my own, without the Ryan name. That I can have bestsellers and write crime and win awards and sell millions of copies and make millions of dollars on my own without help from anyone. Least of all my loser cousins."

"What about the cop one, Ethan?" Dexter asked. "I seem to recall he didn't do much."

"He's not an influencer; he's a cop and not big on social media. But regardless of him not using me for any personal gain like my two rat bastard cousins, he's done other things to me that he should suffer for."

"Such as?"

"Such as none of your business, it's a private family issue." Sean motioned for him to go into the next-door condo. "I'll see you tomorrow, I take it you'll be here for the radio interviews."

"I will be, and Sean..." Dexter turned in the doorway and look at his client. "Try not to get into any more trouble than you already are."

"Who? Me?" Sean said as he grasped the door handle.

"Don't act so surprised," Dexter said before the door was closed on him. He shook his head and set off for the lift.

*****

"Hello, Preston, good to be back on your show."

"Hello, Bryan Jamison," Preston Grant, the biggest DJ in radio called down the line. "How come you're not in the studio? We can't have any fun now."

"Broke my ankle and I'll be out for a couple of months unfortunately. But we're still able to talk. How've you been since the last time I saw you?"

"Good, good, thanks for asking. Let's get right into it. *She*, the latest bestseller, dropped on us like a bomb, is number one on all the charts. It's book one in a trilogy, and I read the media kit sent out by your publishers. It's a hell of a book as always, but tell listeners at home what this book, and the trilogy as a whole, is about."

"It's what I always write about," Bryan said softly. "A man obsessed with a woman."

"Seems to be a running theme in your books," Preston said.

"It is, it's my niche, but my women always get the last laugh, revenge, and their day in court. These books are no different. As a trilogy, there is an arc that covers all three. The full mystery is not resolved until book three, but each one is satisfyingly concluded so you're not left completely hanging."

"So, the woman, whom the man is obsessed with, gets revenge?"

"In all of my books, the obsessed man doesn't win all the time. Sometimes, he loses, and you'll just have to wait and see until the third book, *Mine*, to see if he wins or not."

"The titles of all three, *She Is Mine*, suggests he wins."

"Just because it suggests it, doesn't make it so," Bryan said.

"Like all of your other novels, there's a twist ending, as I saw, but obviously there'll be the massive twist in the final book, *Mine*. The title alone suggest he gets the woman in one way or another."

"And you have no idea what the twist is," Bryan said. "People are going to have their minds blown. More so by my standalone that comes out two months later."

"Do we have a title for that?"

"I do, but no one else will know it before it's released."

"And what are the dates for all these novels?"

"March, May, and July nineteenth, and then September nineteenth for the novel."

"So, you're out to win Sydney Kingston's place as reigning crime thriller author?" Preston asked.

"Yes, maybe," Bryan said. "I've heard she may not even be publishing this year, so we'll see. We may have another battle on our hands and then we really will be duelling authors as you and Sydney once joked."

"My God, you remember that?" Hank asked. He was the producer of the show and sat in the studio with Preston every day the show went on.

"I do," Bryan replied. "And I thought it was a great idea."

They talked for another fifteen minutes before ending the call, then Sean went on to make another ten radio interviews via phone before calling it a day. At least he hadn't needed his Bryan disguise.

Chapter 6

"How did your grandfather's fiancée handle finding out you're Bryan Jamison?"

"With a lot of shock." Sean wandered around his therapist's office. "And then I had to explain it all to her. How I came to use the name, when I started writing adult fiction, that I knew Sydney hated me."

"*Does* Sydney hate you?" Levinworth asked. "She kept you out of trouble *and* jail. Both times you landed yourself in trouble."

"Sydney hated Bryan Jamison," Sean corrected. "I don't know why. I guess people talked me up as her arch nemesis in thriller writing. I was her major competition and came out of the blue with three bestsellers within eighteen months."

"But you slept with her as Bryan Jamison before she left. Did she hate him then? Did she know it was you, Sean Ryan, then?"

"Sydney…" Sean paused and stared out the window, contemplating his next words.

"Sean?"

He sighed. "Sydney *seemed* to hate Bryan. We verbally

sparred, a lot, but even I could tell we had a chemistry, *and* other people could tell we did. As for whether or not she knew it was me…"

"You lied to her. You defrauded her."

Sean glanced over his shoulder; brows furrowed. "Defrauded?"

"*You* knew you were Bryan Jamison, Sydney didn't. *You* flirted as a way of pushing her into sleeping with you as Bryan Jamison. She, and many other people, thanks to your outfit as Bryan, thought you were in your forties. You're only twenty-one."

"I don't see that as fraud," Sean said and walked towards the wall. "If you want to talk fraud, let's start with most of my family. Let's continue with Sydney saying she'd be my mentor and then backing out." He stared up at the painting that captivated him every time. "How 'bout *that* fraud?"

"We can talk about your family first, but how does Sydney stopping her mentorship equal fraud?"

"Because she told me she would and went back on her promise." He thought back to the family lunch.

"Is Sydney here? I saw Emerson." Sean stumbled to a stop in the kitchen and saw her. "Oh, my God, you came, you came. We have Sydney Kingston in our house."

"Whose house?" Cormac gave him a clap on the arm in greeting.

"I know, I know, your home. But I can't believe she's here." He bounced in excitement,. "And now we can talk about my mentorship. I got my parents' permission and filled out the online application, so this can happen now."

"And I didn't say I'd do it." Sydney turned back to the stove and put the lids on the pots.

Sean's face fell. "But why not?"

"I told you why not. I don't write in the same genre, so I don't think I'll be of any real help. You'd be better off with someone who does."

Sean didn't get a chance to say anything else as multiple Ryans converged on the kitchen for beer and greeted their guest. He noticed the way his father treated her, and the way she snapped right back. A small grin slid across his lips and he turned away to hide it. When Sydney wandered into the living room, he stood behind her, and keeping his voice low, said, "Sydney. Can we talk in private about it? I really want to do it."

Sydney glanced over her shoulder at him. "I told your grandfather I'd consider it after today."

He gave her a great beaming smile and hovered by her side.

"I'm here. Did I miss lunch?"

"Hey, Ethan, come and meet the author who's going to mentor Seany," Connor called and slung his arm around his son's shoulder.

"I hate being called that," Sean muttered, his face dark with hatred as he watched Sydney greet his cousin. After a brief conversation he phased out of, he followed her back into the kitchen to check on lunch.

"So, are you going to mentor me?" He stood beside her breathing in the aromas of the food. His stomach grumbled and he couldn't wait to taste it, just as he wanted to taste Sydney.

"You actually don't need a mentor, me or otherwise.

You're already good." She stirred the food in the second pot. "What you need is guidance on how to get your material to publishable level and then apply for submissions. In fact, you could probably do that now, and if your English teacher can help you with your writing, all the better."

"But that's part of the mentorship with Pulsate Publishing. A possible contract at the end of it."

"That is true." Sydney placed the lids on the pots. "But we also have sci-fi and young adult authors who mentor, and they would be more appropriate, if not the best ones for you."

"But I don't want any other author to mentor me. I want you." He grabbed Sydney's arm, but she shook free. "I love your books; Grandpa and Pop love your books. I want to write like you and just because I'm writing YA and sci-fi now, doesn't mean I will be in a couple of years, or once I turn twenty-one. I might want to spread my author wings and write in other genres. Adult, instead of young adult." Sydney's gaze darted over Sean's shoulder, but he didn't bother turning around to see what she was looking at.

"Your grandfather mentioned it earlier, I told him, if by the end of the day he thought it was still a good idea, then I'd think about it. But I want you to think about someone else as a mentor." She glanced at the wall clock. "It's nearly lunchtime."

Sean heard Cormac call out. "Kids, time to set the table. That includes you, Ethan." He heard nothing else as he watched Sydney finish off their meal, but helped pull out cutlery, napkins, placemats, and pot holders, and then it became a mad house as everyone found their place at the extended table.

He made a beeline for the seat beside Sydney, with Emerson and Laura to her right, and Declan and Alec to his left. Cormac and Douglas sat at the heads of the table, and everyone else was on the other side. He phased in and out of the conversations, only listening to Sydney's words, only watching Sydney's lips move.

"The beef balls are amazing," he managed around a mouthful of food and then choked as his father slapped him upside the head and heard the words, "Don't talk with your mouth full."

Shocked, he couldn't look at anyone as his face flamed bright red, but he heard Sydney say to his grandfather, "Was that necessary?", and Cormac reply, "What?"

Sean kept his gaze in his bowl of hotpot, unable to look at Sydney for the sheer embarrassment. He heard the back and forth between her and his grandfather, and his grandfather and father, until he looked from Sydney to his grandfather, stunned by what was happening. The rest of the table was quiet. And curious.

He heard his father reply, but the words were drowned out under the crashing waves of pain in his head, so, like everyone else, he just stared back and forth, waiting for the outcome.

Sean vaguely heard Douglas chastise Declan, and the next thing he knew, he was having the back of his head rubbed. He came to and the wave faded into the distance. He pulled away.

"Sorry, Seany. All better now," Declan's tone was patronising as he glanced at Sydney behind Sean's back.

"All better now?"

Sean turned to Sydney and saw her eyes narrow. He heard her words and knew there was more behind them than she meant right then. "Thank you so much *for* showing me what type of person you really *are.*" He watched her turn back to her meal and say, "So, who else has read my average sloppy romances, or seen Em's *Twisted Minds* TV show?"

The conversation went on and became boisterous as lunch was finished and the pies were served, but he didn't listen to most of it. Just bathed in the glow of Sydney until she spoke about her gift.

"I came home from shopping to find a mysterious white gift box wrapped in a white ribbon on the stoop. When I asked Amy, my assistant, if she knew about it, she pushed it with an umbrella, and we saw the blood trail. That's when she called the cops and this one," she waved her fork at Connor, "came screeching along in his muscle car."

"Of course, when I heard the address of the call out, I recognised it and went right over. The owner's name had also come up so I thought I'd go and introduce myself," Connor regaled the family with his story. He was opposite Sean at the table but pointed at Sydney with his beer bottle. "This one here is feisty and put me in my place."

"How'd she do that?" Sean asked, seething inside at the attention his uncle was showing Sydney.

"Slapped my hand away and called me," Connor glanced at her, "what was it, a pathetic shit fucker. Whatever the hell that is."

You certainly are, Sean thought.

"Exactly what it says," Sydney told him and raised a cocky brow. "That's what you were being. I calls 'em how I sees 'em."

"You certainly do," Connor replied. "And for the record, even though I haven't admitted it until now." He glanced around at his family before returning his gaze to Sydney. "I have actually read some of your books and they're actually pretty good."

Laura swigged back her wine. "How can you like them? They're sloppy romances."

Sean cringed at his mother's attack on Sydney. She'd been badmouthing her since their lunch the week before, and now he had to listen to it at family lunch. God, how embarrassing!

"We all know how you feel about Sydney's books, Laura." Emerson looked at her friend. "You've mentioned it quite a few times today. But I'm actually beginning to wonder if you've read them at all because they're not romance novels. They've won multiple awards in the thriller and crime categories and could be considered comedies as a tertiary genre. I've also made five into movies. That's how Sydney and I became best friends."

Laura thrust up and out of her chair. "I need some air," she said, and stormed off through the sun room into the backyard

Sean watched her go, the embarrassment now at full pelt.

"You tell 'em, Em," Connor said. "They're definitely not sloppy romances, otherwise I wouldn't've admitted to reading them."

Light laughter went around the table and they resumed eating their pie. Sean paid close attention to the conversation.

"Have we inspired you for a new novel yet?" Alec asked as he swiped up the last of his pie. "Although, New York is a highly inspirational town."

"It certainly is." Sydney pushed her plate away and picked up her glass of lemon lime spritz.

"Especially your brownstone," Connor butted in. "I recalled that address from a long time ago."

Sydney laughed. "Yeah, yeah. She does have a colourful history and maybe it was that history that led to a rat on my doorstep."

"What's the history of the house?" Cormac asked, refilling his cup with coffee.

"Do you remember the Madam X case?" Connor asked everyone.

Sean's fork paused in his mouth. Oh, this is going to get juicy.

Cormac's eyes widened as he thought. "Josephine Pompadour? Madam to the half of New York who serviced the other half of New York?"

"Yeah." Connor grinned. "That's the one."

"What's that got to do with it?" Cormac turned to Sydney for confirmation.

"I bought the brownstone," she told him, an amused half smile on her lips.

His thickset brows rose. "You bought Madam Josephine Pompadour's brownstone?"

"Technically, it wasn't hers," Sydney reminded him. "It had that colourful history before I bought it from the

last owners. They got it cheap, renovated it, and rented it out. Little did they realise what Josephine Pompadour was or did. Once you lot raided the house and ripped it apart, it was sold off, the couple spent a lot of money renovating it and then rented it out, but a lot of people just came to look and gawp at it, and they finally had to sell it. Once I saw it, and read about the history, I grabbed it."

"I remember that story," Douglas said. "She had a sex room in the basement."

Sydney blushed and everyone turned to her. "What?" She hid behind her glass and took a sip of spritz.

"Is it still there?" Connor asked.

"Is what still there?" she asked innocently.

"The sex room in the basement?" Connor's lips slid into a dirty grin. "Still got it."

"Not that you'll ever see it," Sydney returned.

Sean's gaze darted back and forth between them, noticing the sparks fly. It made his gut clench. He also noticed Ethan's gaze was doing the same thing.

"There were also rumours of hidden money and jewels," Alec added. "I didn't get the case, but I know all about it."

"Maybe that's why the rat." Emerson pulled on her friend's sleeve. "Have you told CC yet? Here I am just finding out today."

Sydney shook her head. "She'll freak out, so why bother. We called the cops, it's now up to Bozo the Clown here," she pointed at Connor, "to actually find the guy and find out why."

"Who you calling Bozo the Clown, sloppy average

romance author," he quipped.

"Oh, so it's like that, is it?" Sydney grinned. "Game on, pathetic shit fucker."

"Back to the brownstone," Kieran interrupted. "Was there anything left behind?"

Sydney shrugged. "Don't know. Whatever you lot took, the owners removed, her girls snagged as they left, who knows. But since being there, everything is dead bolted and triple locked. More so now."

"Tapped on any walls, or pulled up floorboards?" Sean asked, intrigued by the whole tale. "It'd make a great story."

"Yeah," Sydney replied. "It would if it hadn't already been told multiple times."

"Yeah, but you'd make it into a novel, not a non-fiction book about a madam getting arrested," Sean continued, happy that he was contributing to Sydney's writing.

"By this family, mind you." Sydney raised her brows and grinned. "So, what secrets would this family have to hide about Madam Josephine Pompadour, aka, Madam X? You know what, that's actually a really good idea right there. Police Commissioner's family arrest mysterious Madam X, but what do they have to hide?"

"That'd make a great movie," Emerson said. "Or a TV series. What do you say, Cormac," she turned to him, "wanna go on the record?"

He beamed at her and gently laid his hand over hers on the table. "What I say is, let's retire to the living room so the grandkids can do the dishes."

"Oh, man," Sean complained.

Sydney giggled. "Let's retire."

Sean sped through his chores and hurried into the living room, so he didn't miss out on any more time with Sydney. He jumped into the conversation as he heard the last of her words. "Start with your brownstone and the mysterious Madam X," he said and sat beside her.

She waved him back. "Boundaries. You take up too much space, no need to sit on my lap. Is there any way I could get the info you guys have on the case?"

"You can apply via public record, but it won't be everything," Alec said. "She died in jail."

"Oh." Sydney's brows rose in surprise. "I didn't know that. Maybe I'm being haunted by a ghost. Her ghost."

"You could put that in your story," Sean said, and turned to see his mother walk through the French doors. "There's pie in the fridge if you want it."

"I don't need pie. I need wine." Laura moved into the kitchen, and no one said anything until Sydney spoke up.

"So, Madam X is dead. In jail. I could add that in. In fact, I feel the tingle of a new idea now, so I'll probably get some ideas written down when I get home," Sydney said.

"Is that how it starts? With a tingle?" Ethan asked. "Isn't that how love and attraction starts? With a tingle. Is it the same kind, or different?"

Sean's eyes narrowed at Ethan's expression. He was more than love-sick and making googly eyes at Sydney. And he hated it!

Sydney paused before replying. "Most times, yes, that's how it starts. And yes, I guess it can be the same for attraction. It can be a title, a line, a picture, an idea out of the blue, and the ones that cause the tingles are the ones that progress and end up being novels. It's just the way it works. As do the other tingles."

"When I come up with an idea, I just get this driving force in my head to write it down, and I end up writing until it's done. I don't stop. I can't sleep. Is that bad?" Sean asked.

"Why would it be bad? It's different for everyone," Sydney told him.

"Yeah, but it's like a pain or something behind my eyes, or in my brain, and it drives me to write and when I'm done it's all gone."

"Maybe you need an MRI or CT Scan to make sure there are no issues." Sydney frowned.

"All it'll prove is he's got nothing in there," Declan said.

Sean blanched and said nothing, noticing no one else did. They just glared at Declan until Sydney spoke.

"Make you feel good, did it? Make you feel like a big boy? Make you feel big and brave insulting your son?" She glared at his stunned expression. "Why? Why did you feel the need to insult him? He's actually very talented."

"Talented!" Sierra exclaimed. "His stories are crap."

"So's that attitude," Sydney retorted, staring at her until she shrivelled. "And what is it that you've actually read?"

When Sierra couldn't reply, Sydney turned to Sean. "What has she actually read of yours?"

Sean shrugged. "I have no idea, but she loves to say it's crap."

Sydney turned back to Sierra. "Exactly what have you read of Sean's in order to call it crap? Do tell us so we know why you insult your cousin all the time."

Sierra finally spoke up. "It was ah…something about robots from outer space or something, really crappy stuff."

"Robots from outer space?" Sean frowned in thought. "I haven't written about robots from space since elementary school. Oh, my God, is that what you read? And you've been telling everyone my writing is crap because you read something nearly ten years old?"

Sierra gave an embarrassed shrug. "Um, I guess so."

"Well, that's just pathetic," Sydney said. "You read an old story and made the assumption it's current and that gives you the right to bring your cousin down and insult him. Is this what this family's like?" She looked from person to person. "You insult each other and put one another down? That's really incredibly sad." She looked back to Sierra. "His teachers have told him he's very good. I've told him he's very good, and my publisher, from the sample he submitted said he's very good. So, if multiple experts are saying he's very good, then clearly we know what we're talking about. I've read two of his stories and glanced at more, he has a natural story telling ability. But clearly you don't care. You'd rather just insult him. But is that what this family's about?" Again, she looked at each one. "You're so tied up in dealing with crime you'd rather insult and put down instead of encourage and support. That's just pathetic."

Sean watched everyone's stunned faces, amazed that someone was finally standing up for him and ripping his family to shreds. Especially his dad and Sierra.

"I agree," Cormac spoke up. "There's too much nasty behaviour going on out in the real world and no need for insults. You should be encouraging your cousin, not insulting him. Same goes for you, Declan. Stop with the bullshit. Sean deserves a better father than that and that's not the way your mother and I raised you."

"Yeah, yeah." Declan waved him away. "He's my kid."

"Don't yeah, yeah me," Cormac roared. "Stop abusing my grandson!"

No one said a thing and Declan sat straight in his chair and turned bright red.

Sean mentally applauded his grandfather. You asshole, you deserve it, he thought, glaring at his father.

Cormac turned to Sydney. "You said he was good. Could he go all the way?"

Sydney took a beat. "You mean published? Yes, it's a part of the mentorship, but if Pulsate turns down future writings, he should absolutely submit to other publishers. He's very good."

Cormac nodded. "Then this family will support and encourage you all the way, Sean. Sydney, I'd like you to mentor him, help him get on his way, and Sean," he looked at his eager grandson, "I'd like to read some of your current stories if you don't mind."

"Ah..." Sean's mouth dropped, and he glanced at each family member who was all just as shocked as he. "I...guess. I could get some to you. I don't have any on me."

"Well," Cormac gave him an encouraging smile, "when you do, send them. I can print them out if it's easier, and you have them on your computer."

"Ah…yeah. I've been typing some of them. Either I write on my laptop or my notebook, but yeah, I'll email you a file when I get home."

"That's great, thank you, Sean." Cormac glanced at Sydney and Sean saw him nod. Sydney nodded in return.

And that was the moment Sean knew it was done.

"I sent Grandpa a copy of one of my stories when I got home. He printed it out and read it. Pop, too. They both loved it and didn't understand why Sierra had called my writing crap. But then Sydney had called her out on it."

"Did anything about that lunch piss you off?" Levinworth asked.

"A lot. Everything."

"Such as?"

"Do we really have to go back over all of this?" He sighed and rubbed his eyes. "We did it four years ago."

"And we'll do it again to give you a refresh of the situation."

Sean stared at the crashing waves of the painting and heard them deep in his ears. "My mother was already drunk and was pissed off that Connor was showing Sydney attention and I was pissed off at Connor showing Sydney attention, and Sydney showing it in return. Mom hated the fact Connor's attention was on another woman. It made her drink more that day."

"And when you went home?"

"She got blotto, as Sydney would say."

"Blind drunk?"

"Raging drunk is more like it." Sean's hands clenched in his pants pockets. "She raged at my dad the moment we walked in the door, and that was only after giving us the silent treatment on the way home."

"About what?"

"I don't think we knew. She didn't make a lot of sense. Raged about Sydney and Connor, what was going on, how dare Sydney. Dad was confused. I was confused, although had a vague idea. Especially when Connor's name was brought into it. Dad, he just turned around and raged right back. I went upstairs, closed my door, and put my headphones on as I always did."

"Was that usual? Them fighting?"

"Considering they were really only together on Sundays, yeah. Dad worked all week, was out all night. I wrote until late, Mom drank and cried until late every night. We were incredibly dysfunctional and toxic."

"That is true. But then you went to live with your grandfather, and things would have settled down."

"For me, not for Mom. It was still the same old same old until she died."

"And then the two most important people in your life were gone. Is that why you ended up at Sydney's the night of the funeral?"

"You're getting ahead of yourself, doc. Did I mention my publicity tour this week?"

"Not yet. I was very impressed with your Zoom interviews and your reason for not being in the studios. They had no idea you were telling the partial truth."

"None whatsoever." Sean moved to the buffet and stared at an old piece of pottery under a glass display case. "I wanted the books out faster, so many of the interviewers were unprepared. But we got through them."

"How come you upped your publishing schedule?"

"Because the book I finished in detention I want out on September nineteenth."

"Sydney's publishing date."

"So people keep telling me."

"What's it called?"

"*Her.*"

"Why?"

"Why what?"

"Why's it called *Her?* I've read your books. You pick your titles, don't you? They're very telling, so are your stories."

"I aim to please."

"Why's it called *Her?*"

Sean's fingers trailed along the buffet as they did every week. "Because it's always…*her.*" He moved onto the next wall and stared at a painting. "You can't see *her,* you can't have *her,* you can't be with *her,* keep away from *her.* All the fucking same," he spat and his face screwed up in pain. "And yet all I ever wanted *was* her. All I did was *want* her." He gasped, tears prickled his eyes and he quickly wiped them with the back of his hands. "All they did was tell me I couldn't have her. Well, they can't either."

Levinworth made a note. "And the current one. *She?*"

"*Is Mine.* Great titles, I thought. It's just a trilogy, doc. One long story cut into three."

"*Illicit Things* was about your feelings for her, a seventeen-year-old's feelings for a forty-seven-year-old woman. The things you did, you dreamt of; you wanted to do. *Sinister Motives* is about wanting and losing.

Creeper is about wanting and turning tables. *She Is Mine* is about a man doing all of the above, and *Her*, is it like *Illicit Things? Sinister Motives? Creeper?*"

"And you're trying to tell me that I keep repeating the same story in each of my books because they're about unrequited love and hopes and dreams? Don't bother, doc, I got that a long time ago when I wrote the first six books. There's another six books done and two more in the oven. I get it, I have a theme."

"All of your books *do* suggest unrequited love, although some suggest darker undertones. Are the unpublished books of the same ilk?"

"You could bet on that," Sean replied. "Because I know it's true. All of my books are clearly about my feelings for Sydney. Trying to work through them, understand them…"

"Continually relive them."

Sean considered his words and sighed. "It's not like I lived them in real life. How else was I going to do it."

"It's been four years, Sean."

"And it's still fresh and new. Feelings like that don't just go away, Walter. Don't disappear, fly away, dissipate. They hang around in your heart and soul."

"Are you still obsessed with Sydney?"

Sean's eyes closed and he breathed slowly to regulate his heart beat. "I'm not obsessed with Sydney, Walter."

"How did you have the keys to her back door?"

"Does it really matter now?" He checked his watch. "Besides, it's time to go and we are one month down, only four more to go. Yippee. Next week, Walter."

Levinworth watched him close the door and sighed.

Sean was still holding onto a lot of the same feelings for Sydney, even after four years. His verbiage was different, and he danced around the subject, but it was still the same. He was still obsessed, or, in his words, in love with Sydney Kingston.

He picked up *Creeper*, Sean's third book as Bryan Jamison.

She was the most incredible woman. Beautiful, smart, talented, creative, rich, and she was mine and I was all hers. She'd had my heart from the moment I saw her at her very first book launch. A friend had introduced me to her, her books, her world, and I had fallen head first down the rabbit hole of what was about to become reality. Every breath of air I breathed, every moment of time I lived, it was all about her. Her book was the calling card. From the very first to the very last word, it was the invitation to come into her life and be with her in it. To share it. The same air, the same bed, the same love. To be one with her, her body, her mind, and imagining what I was going to do to her, with her, was all well and good, but I needed to make it happen and it did. That look she gave me, the smile, the way her gaze lingered on me as she whipped her signature across the page of my book. It was her telling me she wanted me too. That I had the invitation into her life, her body, her soul, and I was going to take it and make her mine. Down to every last millimetre of her body, heart, and soul. And I knew exactly how I was going to do it. Fifty different ways, and I'd counted them, wrote them down, prepared for them, and I planned on putting her through all fifty. Watching her writhe beneath me as I invaded her body. Hearing her scream my name as I tied her up and took her from behind. All I want is to drive home my love for her, again and again and again. Drive it home inside of her, whether she's willing or not. But after all fifty ways I show her my love, she'll be willing, she'll be more than willing. She'll be screaming my name until her dying breath.

Levinworth closed the book and took a deep breath. Sean's novels were his innermost thoughts and feelings, signified in every paragraph. What he wanted to do to Sydney, how he wanted to love her, possess her, drive his need for her home to make her love him. And he'd done it well; written it all down in a way that would either leave you thinking he'd actually done those things and his books were autobiographical, or, that he'd made them all up because he was sick and twisted. The problem was, Levinworth didn't know which they were.

He clicked the button on his voice recorder and held it close to his mouth. "The first three books are extremely telling. All three talk about illicit things which is the name of the first novel. The story depicts a love that cannot be, an older woman and younger man, he loves her, it's his first love, and while she's reluctant at first, she gives in when she knows she shouldn't, making it illicit. *Sinister Motives* is what seems to be a continuation of love of an older woman, a woman who doesn't give in to the younger man and he rages. *Creeper*, the third book, is about a man who's obsessed with the number one romance author in the world and stalks her. He breaks into her house, sets up cameras in different rooms, namely the bathroom and bedroom, and watches her masturbate, or have sex with men that she enjoys. He steals her underwear and other items, and he takes photos when she's asleep. He even drugs her wine so he can sleep with her, and she doesn't know she's being raped, which is what that is. Has Sean done this and is he writing about it to show the world, using his exploits as inspiration? Or is it all in his head and he's telling the world what he wants to do? That's the question."

*****

Sean walked into his grandfather's house the next day and saw the family there except for Alec, Brandon and Sierra. "What's going on? Why'd Grandpa call a family meeting?"

"No idea," Ethan said, his leg swinging over the side of the easy chair he was sitting in. "But it looks like he called all of us."

"Except for Alec and his brats," Sean muttered and looked out the front window. "Is Grandpa here?"

"Not yet." Declan walked in from the kitchen, an overstuffed sandwich between his hand and mouth.

Connor followed with a beer. "God, what is taking so long and why's Alec running late? Kieran, you know where Alec is?"

Kieran shook his head. "Haven't heard." He slid an arm around Sandy who sat next to him on the couch.

Sean saw his grandfather's car turn into the driveway and watched him alight. "He's here and he's not happy."

They waited until Cormac walked in and shucked his

coat onto the closest chair and looked from son to son to grandson. "Sierra and Brandon were killed last night in a blast that blew apart their car as they were leaving a club. It was caught on hundreds of social media accounts, the club's surveillance, and witnessed by many bystanders. Alec has been at the morgue with their mother all day, dealing with questions and cops and lawyers, and trying to find out what the hell happened."

The room was silent.

Declan had stopped eating, Connor stopped drinking, and Ethan's leg fell off the chair arm as he sat up.

Sean's hands slid into his pockets and clenched. "Wow, I was not expecting that."

"Nor I," Cormac said. "I've been with Alec all night, trying to make sense of it all; watching videos of it happening."

"There was no warning, no nothing?" Ethan asked, his brow deeply furrowed. He'd lost two of his cousins in one hit.

"Nothing. The attendant brought the car around for them and because they were social media influencers with a lot of followers, they were filmed getting into the car, and as they drove off, the car exploded, killing them both instantly, and severely injuring dozens more."

"Do they know why?" Declan asked, looking for a place to set down his sandwich, his appetite long forgotten.

"The CSIs are examining what is left of the car while the medical examiner is examining the remains." Cormac wearily sank into his chair and his head twitched. "I just… don't know what we're going to do. Last year I lost my father, and now I've lost my two middle grandchildren."

"Sierra's car was known to be problematic," Sean ventured. "She's had problems and the maker had issued warnings to return certain vehicles to the dealership."

"Doesn't bring back Brandon and Sierra, though, does it, Sean?" Connor said.

"No." Sean turned and stared out the window. His hands relaxed in his pockets and a small smile fled across his lips. *It doesn't.*

"What happens now?" Kieran pulled Sandy closer. She was three months pregnant, and they were yet to tell the family…something they wouldn't be doing right now.

"I don't know." Cormac deflated. "We wait for the report on the car and wait for the report on the autopsies, and when the bodies are released we bury them."

"With Pop and Grandma?" Ethan was shell-shocked. "They'll look after them."

Cormac's grief-stricken smile was brief. "Yeah, they'll look after them. Your grandma loved all of you grandkids. She'll make sure they're okay when they get there."

"So…do we hang around or get back to work?" Declan asked. "I vote we get back to work."

Connor agreed. "We can come back tonight, if you need us."

"No, not tonight. I need to tell Emerson, and Alec will need time to grieve." Cormac rubbed his hand over his mouth. "I'm home for the rest of the day. You all may as well go."

Silently, they filed out the door one by one, got into their cars, and left.

*****

Sean could go only home, to his publisher, or his therapist, and he'd seen him just two days ago, so he went home and sat staring out the window, trying to imagine his life without his cousins, Sierra the bitch, and Brandon the brat, and found that he was quite happy without them, wouldn't miss them, and had no problem with that. Hell, he'd already written them into a novel as villains, killing both of them off in grisly circumstances.

At dusk, he finally stood, stretched his back, and opened up his wall of Sydney.

There was an A4 sized page in the middle of the wall with a grid of images of his family. He marked those of his cousins off with a red cross on each.

*****

The funeral of Brandon and Sierra Ryan was a simple affair. At least, that's how Alec and his ex-wife Sonja had organised it. The family turned up on a cool spring day to the cemetery after an hour-long service at the cathedral in the city. Their coffins would be laid side by side in the Ryan plot as Sonja's family weren't from New York and weren't buried there.

The coffins, white for Sierra, and black for Brandon, were lined with matching silk. There had been no clothes to dress them in, no jewellery to adorn their burnt mangled bodies.

They watched the coffins being lowered into the graves, and heard the crying and shouting from the thousands of fans who had turned up to film the burial of their favourite influencers. The police held them back.

"Can't even get a goddamn moment of silence for the dead," Ethan muttered, looking over the crowd. "They don't fucking care that we're burying our family."

"No, they don't," Connor agreed, and put his arm around his son's shoulders, pulling him close.

Declan gave the crowds a filthy look and moved over to his wife's grave, a few feet away. He hadn't been there in three years, not since her funeral, and didn't want to be there now. He looked at his brother and nephew, noting the closeness they shared, and then saw Sean standing beside them on his own. Kieran and Sandy were on the other side of Cormac with Alec and Sonja. He looked down at Laura's grave. "Where the hell did we go wrong?" He wandered back to his father who was taking comfort from Emerson.

The priest finished his piece and the family crossed themselves.

Sean glanced at the other people around their graves. A few close friends of his cousins had been invited, and his grandfather's team. As the others slowly moved away, Sean held back, and walked over to his great-grandfather's grave. "Hey, Pop." He kissed his fingers and placed them on the top of the headstone. "How've you been this last year? Sorry I haven't been here lately, but the cemetery is not on my list of places I'm allowed to go. Today, they made an exception." He brushed away a few dead weeds and smoothed the headstone down. "You would get a kick out of what I've been up to these last few months. Would've had a great laugh about it."

His fingers traced the lettering of his great-grandfather's name and birth and death dates. "Beloved son, husband, father, grandfather, and great-grandfather," Sean read. "You certainly were, Pop, you certainly were." He stood up. "Not sure when I'll see you again, probably in four months, so I'll see you then." He slid his fingers over the top of the stone and walked a few feet over to his mother's grave. "Hey Mom." He did the same tidy up of Laura's grave. "Been awhile. Will probably be another while, but as you can see, something pretty bad has happened and it's taking everyone's attention. So, if you don't see me, don't panic, I'll be back eventually." He read her gravestone. "Beloved daughter, wife, and mother. Beloved, not devoted," Sean muttered and stood up. The ankle monitor had dug into his leg and he reached down and rubbed the spot.

"Sean…we're leaving." Cormac's voice drifted over the wind.

"That's my cue to leave," Sean told his mother. "Bye, Mom." He touched the grave before he turned and walked away, passing Alec and Sonja at their children's final resting places, passing the horde of mourning fans taking photos of him, passing the countless headstones until he reached his grandfather's car and climbed in.

They drove back to the house in silence and filed inside in equal silence.

Sean walked over to the back French doors and opened them onto the garden. Even though it was March, and the air was still fresh with chill, it had burnt off with the clouds and the sun was warming the air. The flowers were starting to bloom, the trees starting to grow their green leaves, and the view of New York from the Brooklyn side was magnificent.

He stood in the garden, hands in pockets, breathing deeply. The cemetery's stench of death on him slowly dissipated and was replaced with fresh spring air.

"What do we do now?" he heard Ethan ask. "Will the family dinner be the same?"

"No, it won't be, kid," Connor replied. "No, it won't be."

No, it won't be, Sean thought. *Family dinner hasn't been the same since four and a half years ago when Sydney came into my life. When Mom got dropped by Connor, and then murdered by Dad. Then Pop died. Things haven't been the same. Family dinner hasn't been the same.*

"I want to say a few things," Cormac started, but Sean tuned him out. He tuned all of the family out and walked towards the edge of the garden. He watched the water of the East River lap against the stone walls that held it back from reclaiming what it believed it owned. He watched the boats putt by, and heard the cars pass by on the bridge. He heard the crack and groan of the steel and the wire, and the pounding of the water on the rocks, the pounding of the cars on the asphalt of the bridge, the pounding, the banging, the lapping, the pounding, the pounding, the pounding. He growled, clenched his teeth and grabbed his head.

"Sean."

He gasped and his hands lowered.

"Have you taken your medication? You seem to be suffering." Emerson halted beside him. "Do you need your medication?"

"I've had my medication, thank you, Emerson. It just all got a bit too much for me for a moment." His hands slid into his pockets, and breathed slowly.

"Understandable. I haven't had a chance to offer my condolences. I'm sorry about your cousins; it must be tough losing them both together."

"Yes," Sean murmured. "Tough. Both of them. I don't even know how to begin dealing with it. My therapist, I guess."

"Yes, that is the most convenient place. There's food and drink, and your grandfather's car will take you home when you're ready. Again, my condolences."

"Thank you, Emerson." He heard her walk away and chose to leave, managing to circumvent the house and pull up Cormac's detail to drive him home. Once he was inside and leaning against the door, he sighed in relief. The heavy weight of the funeral and wake lifted, and he strode into his office and over to the cupboard that held his Bryan Jamison clothing. He quickly changed, pulled on his wig, added the contacts, and used a burner phone to call a cab.

He picked up a roll of masking tape and a pin, stuck the pin to the sticky side of the tape and shoved it into the small hole on the top of his ankle bracelet. It popped open while the light stayed green. He stuck the tape down and set the monitor on the bench, picked up the frequency jammer he used to put a glitch in the video surveillance of not only his condos, but the entire building, and quickly grabbed his bag and left. He hurried downstairs and out the back door, crossed the alley into the next condominium block and grabbed the taxi out the front as it pulled up.

Twenty minutes later, it dropped him off on the Upper East Side and he hurried down the street to a brownstone. He stared up at it, remembering all the times he had been there before climbing the stairs.

After opening the vestibule and front doors, and locking them against the world, he dropped his bag and coat by the door. The scent of hot roast chicken soup permeated the air, and his stomach growled as he walked into the living room to warm himself by the crackling fire in the grate.

He breathed deeply.

He was home.

Chapter 7

"I am so incredibly sorry."

"For what?"

Levinworth waited a moment. "The death of your cousins."

"Why would you be? You know how I feel about them. About all of them. It's all there in my file from four years ago."

"And I've read your file multiple times and listened to my recordings. I know how you felt about them then, but I thought now would be different."

Sean was standing in his usual spot by the window, so he didn't have to look at Levinworth, but now, he glanced over his shoulder and studied him. "Why would *now* be different? I hated them then, I hate them now."

Levinworth shrugged a shoulder. "Because you had two years of therapy and have grown, emotionally and physically."

"I might have grown that way, but they certainly hadn't. They went from abusing me to demanding I help them become influencers. They can rot in hell." He turned back to the view.

"And how did that happen? I saw you for two years. I know only what happened in that time."

Sean rolled his eyes and sighed. "When my first book was picked up for publishing I said nothing. But once the book came out and sold over a million copies and I gained over a million followers on social media, and started appearing on TV shows and the like, they were up my backside like starving hyenas. They kept taking selfies of us at family dinner, demanded tickets to places I was going, or to interviews, posted everything they could to social media and tagged me, so everyone knew they were my cousins. They gained hundreds of thousands of followers but never beat me to a million, and they hated that. They hated that they got less than half the followers I did, and that I never liked their posts or followed them. Sierra said I wasn't recognising them, or publicly claiming them as my family. Why the hell would I? They were scabs."

"How long did they do it for?"

"From the moment the press for the first book came out, and pre-sales were starting, and I started gaining followers right up until the final book came out and the publicity wrapped up. When they found out I wouldn't be publishing more books, they only posted about me a third of the time, if that. By then, they had deals with local stores and were earning money flogging products."

"And you? How did all of that make you feel?"

"I was being used, how do you think I felt?" Sean shook his head and moved on to the painting he loved. "Who's this by? Is it for sale?"

"That one isn't, no, but there should be a few

reproductions floating around. I bought it at a Parisian flea market."

"I like it. It looks like the inside of my brain. Sounds like it too."

"How was the funeral?"

"Loud."

"How so?"

"Interrupted by their pissant followers from social media. There was about a thousand at the cemetery, all being held back by the NYPD, all filming and taking pictures. It was sick."

"Did you hate the fact they'd become famous because of you?"

"Of course I did. They had a few thousand followers because they were the brats of DA Alec Ryan, and interior designer to the stars Sonja Molkov, a fake-ass Russian princess who wasn't actually a princess. She claimed to be descended from Tsar Nicholas who was related to Queen Victoria. Turned out, she wasn't, but she already had the ring on the finger and the bun in the oven by the time Alec discovered that. They kept the bullshit going and she turned to interior design for a living. Hit it big with that. All because her husband was a Ryan, of the New York City Ryans. The law enforcement kind. She became a celebrity by marrying Alec and a celebrity interior designer thanks to his money and the family contacts."

Sean turned from the painting. "You know, she decorated Josephine Pompadour's brownstone twenty-five years ago. I found out that fact in Sydney's book on her and found it quite surprising considering my family raided that brownstone. The infamous Madam X paid my aunt to decorate her brothel." He laughed. "But then, Sonja used to be a pro back in the day in Russia. She knew all about the profession and probably all about Madam X. Hell, *Josephine* probably knew all about Sonja." Sean turned back to the painting. "They divorced two years ago, and she was pretty pissed about Sydney's book. From what I can gather, she was scared that her true profession would be in it. I always wondered if she'd been one of Josephine's girls and if that's how she met Alec. He always did like getting his dick sucked, and prostitutes learn how to get what they want from a man. I wouldn't be surprised if that's what happened to Alec."

"Did Sydney put any of that in her biography of Madam X?"

Sean glanced at Levinworth. "Haven't you read it, yet? No, she didn't, but she sure as hell put it in her novel. I always wondered how she came up with those characters. When I read the novel, and then the biography, and found out Sonja was the interior designer, it got me thinking, and I guess it had Sydney thinking too, because she has an up-and-coming DA who marries the hooker he's seeing in Madam X's brownstone who then goes on to being a fashion designer. Not an interior designer, but a designer, nonetheless. Sydney obviously didn't want it to be to specific."

Levinworth's brows rose. "I've read the bio, but not the novel, I'll have to look into that now. Do you think she wrote about the rest of your family in that book?"

"I think there was another member, but I'm not sure who, and everyone else I could only vaguely connect a dot to. I remember Sydney always being cagey in interviews. She never wanted to give it away, who they were, and all of those still alive didn't want anyone to know who they were either. Do you think Sierra and Brandon could be retaliation for Alec or Sonja? Their pasts? Alec puts criminals away. Sonja's an ex-prostitute. Maybe this was retaliation for being put in jail."

"It's all possible," Levinworth said. "But how do you feel about the death of your cousins?"

"Nothing." Sean gazed at the crashing waves in the painting.

"No empathy? Sympathy?"

"It's hard to feel anything for the person who bullied and used you. But then again," he shrugged, "maybe I'm still in shock, walking around not thinking, not feeling. Like the rest of the family. Not saying much, automatic pilot."

"Could be." Levinworth made some notes. "Tell me about your mentorship with Sydney. From your point of view. Start with the first time you met up with her. How were you feeling, and what did you do?"

Sean thought back fondly, and a smile lit up his face.

"Am I late?" he gasped, letting go of the door and striding down the room to where Sydney was standing. *"Am I on time?"*

"Apparently," Sydney said. *"My alarm went off as you arrived. So, let's get on with this, shall we?"* She motioned for him to sit to her left. *"Okay, I have no idea how to help mentor you about your actual writing. You'd probably benefit more from an editor than me on that, and as part of your mentorship you get an hour or*

two with one here at Pulsate. They'll go over your writing and give you advice."

"What type of advice?" Sean gazed adoringly up at her. She was even more beautiful than she had been at the family lunch. Her light pink knit sweater brought a rosy tone to her cheeks and the blue and pink scarf holding her hair back brought out the blue in her eyes. "You already said I was good."

"You are. But an editor will help pinpoint anything that can be improved and tell you what they look for in new authors or new acquisitions. Now..." Sydney glanced at the papers. "These are writing tips and tricks that editors and publishing companies look out for." She handed a stapled stack of paper to him. "All very basic and simple. The editor will go over most of it when you see them."

"Can't you?" he asked, skimming the papers and seeing some good information.

"Yeah...not really my forte, you'll get more out of the editor, and this stack..." She handed him another one. "Is information on writing. If you haven't read books on writing all of this is very helpful. It covers every aspect, and has lists of qualified websites and blogs to read, books to read, and anecdotes from authors." She handed him a third pile of papers. "And this stack, is on publishing itself. The ins and outs, how books are published, what they look for, how it all works. So if you want to submit to others, the info's all in there along with a list of publishing houses and their submission pages. All mentees get the same info along with sessions with an editor, and a tour of Pulsate."

"*Will you take me on the tour?*" Sean piped up eagerly. "*Can we do it today? Or don't we get the tour yet?*"

"*Ah…*" Sydney looked out the glass wall dividing the meeting room from the offices. "*There's no rule to say it can't be done today.*"

"*Great!*" Sean motioned at the paperwork. "*If this is all there is, can we take the tour now and you can tell me about the program while we walk.*" He slid the papers into his bag, stood up, and hiked it over his shoulder.

Sydney picked up her bag and pushed her chair under the table. "*Okay, um, let's go.*" They walked out and started the tour, making their way down to each floor until they came to the first floor of the business. "*And here's everyone else. Junior staff and part-time workers. It's also where you stop, when you come to Pulsate, to check in, and London will do that for you.*"

"*Hey, Sydney.*" London nodded and raised a brow at Sean. "*Your mentee?*"

"*Yes, he is.*" Sydney introduced them. "*London's been here five years and CC says she's the best receptionist she's ever had.*"

London laughed. "*She's lying. She says I'm the worst.*"

Sean eyed her high, offside blonde ponytail with spikes of coloured hair snaking out of it, and her bright *pink lips.* She's attractive, *he thought,* but not beautiful like Sydney. "*How old are you?*"

"*Oh…*" she stuttered and glanced at Sydney. "*Ah… twenty-five.*"

Sean nodded in thought. "*Are there lots of young people working here? Or working in publishing in* general? Is it something I could get into as an intern or something?"

"CC's rule is twenty-one and over," Sydney informed him. "Especially if doing one of the degrees in English or writing. It will help you get your foot in the door."

"And help with college bills," London added. "I'm still paying mine off."

"Is it good money?" Sean asked. "I take it all levels of workers are on different levels of income." He gazed across the room full of junior staff.

Sydney's brows rose in surprise. "Why would you be worrying about that?"

He shrugged his free shoulder. His bag was over his right one and he clung to it like a life raft. "I'm seventeen. I'm not exactly relying on my parents to pay my way through college. Even though Mom's a doctor and earns far more than my dad. And since taking her sabbatical, she's been blowing through money like it's going out of style." He nodded to a private corner of the reception area, and they walked over. "I want to earn a living and will probably have to pay my way. But if my writing is good enough to be published, maybe that'll give me a good chunk of money to pay off my debts. And if I'm good enough for Pulsate to publish me after this mentorship, then I'll choose English and writing courses for college to get that foot in the door you were talking about." He was a good head taller than her and could smell the fresh apple scent of her shampoo.

"How *is your mum?*"

"Well..." He sighed and looked at the framed authors on the wall in front of them. "Drunk most of the time.

Angry, loud; she and Dad are fighting when he's home. She's drunk whether he is or not. But something's changed in the last few days. I don't know what, but she's angrier than she was, and has been drinking more. I'm not relying on her to pay my way, as I said. I think she spends a few thousand a week on alcohol, especially champagne."

"Is she doing drugs, or anything? What about an intervention?"

His head shook slightly. "She's the doctor. Ironic, isn't it. She knows better, but she doesn't care. So, what would an intervention do?"

"What about your grandfather, or your great-grandfather? Aren't they able to do anything?"

Sean finally looked at her. "They're cops. What would they do? What can they do?"

"For the sake of the family's reputation, they could do something. The family has money; your mother would have money. Quietly get her into a facility for the rich or famous who want to keep it quiet. Is there one at the hospital she works for?"

Hysterical laughter burst out of Sean. "Can you imagine my mother's shame and embarrassment if she went to the rehab clinic at her own hospital? She would die before she did that. Besides, I asked her not long ago why she was drinking so much now she'd left work, and you know what she told me?"

Sydney shook her head.

"She told me that if I knew what she knew about my father, I'd be drinking too."

Sydney's left brow rose. "Did she explain what she

meant by that?"

"Nope." He shook his head and gripped the strap of his backpack until his knuckles turned white. "But I questioned her and she told me nothing. So I started thinking, they're clearly having problems, now she's not working and is home more. Dad's angry that's she's there. Angry that she's drinking. Angry that he doesn't have dinner on the table. Angry that she's blowing through money. 'But it's my money,' she screams back. 'I made it with my own two fucking hands on my feet fifteen hours a day, six days a week for three decades. I fucking earned the time off to do everything I couldn't in the last thirty years.'" He took a breath, and tried to shake off the embarrassment making his face red.

"Fucking hell!" Sydney murmured. "Maybe your mum taking time off has brought all the problems to the fore. It's shone a light on them. So to speak."

"Yeah. I reckon that's it. But I never saw problems when Mom was working."

"Maybe they were too exhausted to fight before, but now she has the time and sees how things really are and has the time to fight. Sucks for you, though."

Sean huffed. "Yeah, sucks for me. Not that they give a fuck about me. You saw how they were at lunch. Grandpa and Pop had to talk them into giving me permission because I'm under twenty-one and still in high school. I don't go to college until next year, or unless I excel and move up classes to graduate early. They don't care about me. Mom's a drunk, an alcoholic; Dad's an abusive asshole who uses being a cop to lord it over me. Always has. His only son and only child. I'm going to do what he wants me to or so help me."

"Seriously? I saw what he was like, figured him to be a Grade A Douche, only second to Connor. Kieran and Alec seem to be the sensible ones. But if it's one thing I cannot abide, especially in a family of cops, is abuse. Whether of each other, or of minors. That's why I said something to your grandfather. Emerson and I were guests in his house, and one of his sons was abusing his grandson. That's not on in my book."

"Thanks for defending me," Sean told her. "I appreciated it so much I actually cried that night when I went to bed." A raging blush raced across his cheeks. "Not that I should be admitting that. I'm a grown man after all."

Sydney snorted with laughter. "Oh, little boy, you ain't no grown man, but at least you behave in a more mature manner than your father. And *your* mother. They clearly raised you well before turning into despots."

A small grin lit up his face. "Yeah. That's one thing this family did. Raise me well. Even though I'm still seventeen, I definitely act more mature than my parents. Or *my* cousin. Thank you for standing up for me with her too."

"She's a snarky little thing, isn't she? Is she older?" He gave her a nod. "Yet she behaved so rudely and arrogantly tarred all of your stories with the same brush just because she's read an old story and believed that's what you'd been writing. Quite pompous, really." Sydney turned her nose up. "Maybe you should get yourself published to prove her wrong. To prove your parents wrong. To prove your whole freaking family wrong."

"That sounds like a plan for revenge." Sean was intrigued. "Are you into revenge, Sydney?" He hoped she was.

"I can be if I need to be. I get revenge in my books all the time." She wiggled her brows.

"Ah…that might come in useful." He nodded. "Very useful."

A group of workers stopped at the elevator doors and Sydney glanced at the clock over London's desk. "Damn, it's already after five. Time for you to go. So…ah, same time next week? You can obviously get here after school okay."

"Yeah. I take the subway, so it's pretty quick." Sean hefted his backpack higher on his shoulder. "Same time next week is fine. What will we be doing?"

"I'll hook you up with an editor and they can go over some of your stories. Can you send me some via email and I'll pass them on so they can read before then."

"But I'll need your email." Sean mentally crossed his fingers that he'd get it.

"Ah, send it to me via the pub house and I'll forward it on to the editor. That way it's on the house system." Sydney moved towards the lift. "You'd better get going."

"I guess." He reluctantly hit the button. The glut of workers had already departed.

The lift dinged open, and he entered, hitting the button and facing her. "Bye, Sydney. Same time next week."

"Wednesday at four," she agreed before the doors closed.

"I walked out of there having unburdened, which I

probably shouldn't have, but feeling lighter, happier, than I had in months…yeah."

"Why?"

"Because someone outside of the family believed in me, because someone was encouraging me, because I had scored a mentorship at a publishing house. *Sydney's* publishing house." He sighed in happiness at the memories. "Someone finally believed in me and supported me, and I had a publishing house mentorship with the opportunity to get published and I was only seventeen. I mean, how many seventeen-year-olds get all of that?" He turned back to his therapist. "Tell me, how many teenagers get that?"

"Not many, I'm sure." Levinworth noted the happiness on Sean's face. "Even the memory of it makes you happy, though not much else does. Sydney was very gracious giving you her time and doing the mentorship even though she was wary of helping you."

"Which I didn't know at the time," Sean said, walking back to the window. "I didn't know about the conversation she had with Grandpa, or the decision they'd come to. All I knew was she'd had one."

"Did you feel your life change from that day? When you walked into Pulsate?"

"I did. I knew it was day one of a three-month mentorship, and I had to make the most of it."

"Except you didn't."

Sean glared out the window until he finally said, "The second time was even better. But it's time to go, doc. Same time next week?" He patted Levinworth on the shoulder as he walked past and out the door.

Levinworth waited a few moments, took a deep breath, and read back over his original notes from four years ago when Sean talked about his cousins. He recalled the childlike voice that Sean had spoken in.

"I hate Sierra, she's a bitch, and I know I shouldn't use that word 'cause Mom and Pop said I shouldn't, but she is. She broke into my room one year to read my stuff. Raided my desk and read some of my stories from ten years ago. And then kept telling everyone it was crap. No one cared that she bullied me, no one cared that Brandon used to hit and punch me because I was the youngest. Ethan did when we were younger, 'cause his dad and mine were best friends and so Ethan kinda looked after me when Brandon was around. But when Ethan wasn't, Brandon got away with it."

"Did no one do anything to protect you?"

"Talked a lot. Brandon don't hit your cousin, Brandon don't do that, but no one actually stopped him until Ethan beat the shit out of him when Brandon was fourteen. Ethan was seventeen and my hero. Pity how that turned out."

*****

Sean glanced around the table. Three empty seats. His father was to his right, with Connor next to him. Ethan, Kieran and Sandy sat opposite. Emerson had Douglas's old spot at the opposite end of the table to Cormac. The mood in the room was solemn, thick, suffocating, and he studied each face with interest.

Kieran and Sandy kept glancing at each other, and

Ethan kept sighing and looking forlorn. Cormac had the weight of the world on his shoulders, Connor was quiet, Declan indifferent.

Wouldn't be surprised if Sonja took him for a ride or two being an old pro, and dad loves pros, Sean thought. *Wonder if Connor took her for a spin as well. She and Alec have been divorced a while, not that that would have stopped Connor; he fucked Mom and then Sydney.*

His gaze flicked to Ethan who stared down at his half-eaten meal. *And then he fucked Sydney. The asshole. What did he have that I didn't? He was my hero, my saviour who stopped Brandon from bullying me when I was ten. Just eleven years ago. And then he left me. Stopped coming over, went off and got a life and fucked the woman I love. But then, so did Connor, and so did Dad.*

Sean's brows furrowed deeply, and he side-eyed his father. *Sydney slept with him too, after her house sitter's death. In need of a quick hit of affection and attention I suppose. A hit of pheromones to get them through the death.*

He knew it hadn't lasted, barely a month, and was over by Christmas or New Year. But, it still cut deep that the woman he loved had fucked his father, uncle, and cousin, and not him.

"Do we still have dessert?" Emerson asked.

Cormac looked at each half-eaten plate. "I don't think anyone's up for that today."

Nodding, Emerson stood. "Then I'll start clearing away the plates."

"I'll help," Sandy told her and collected Kieran's and

Ethan's plates and stacked them on her own.

Sean picked up his father's plate, added it to his, and put them on Emerson's. Once the women were in the kitchen, he said, "When will Uncle Alec be back?"

Cormac sighed and leaned back in his seat. "I don't expect him for some time. He may need weeks, or months, to deal with this, and I won't pressure him to come back. It's only Sunday family lunch."

This was something Sean hadn't been to in some time, preferring to have dinner instead after the family had gone home. But now was different.

"I'm surprised we got you here," Declan told his son. "You haven't been in how long?"

"Months," Sean replied, and accepted a cup of coffee from Emerson. "Thank you. Why?"

"Because family lunch is mandatory, but you haven't been here," Connor said.

"Can't be mandatory then," Sean retorted and shrugged. "I've been coming for dinner every couple of weeks instead. I get Grandpa all to myself."

Declan sneered at his son. "Lucky you."

Sean frowned at his father. "What's your problem?"

"What's yours?" Declan returned.

Sean glanced at Cormac and rolled his eyes before shaking his head.

"Declan, grow up," Cormac said, tapping his fingers on the table. "It's not the time or place."

Declan blushed at the scolding and stared into his coffee cup.

"We've been through a tremendous hardship in the last few weeks," Cormac went on. "The loss of anyone, any member of the family, will be hard to deal with. It's hard to move on from, and having lost two at once, after Pop last year, it's going to take some time to grieve and move on. Feel free to not be here on Sundays, but just know that this, Sunday lunch, this house, is your refuge to do so."

Ethan shoved his chair back and strode out of the dining room, along the hall, and into Douglas's room. They hadn't done anything with it after his death, and it still held his valuables and personal possessions, and all of them used it occasionally for a refuge to talk to his spirit.

"Guess he needs to talk to pop," Connor said. "I'll go in, in a few minutes."

"When did you two become so close?" Sean asked. "He lived with his mom during the week so we, and you, only saw him on the weekends and holidays. But since he turned eighteen and joined the police force he became distant, and then once he hit twenty-one you decided to be his pal instead of his father. But lately..." He shrugged. "Things seem different the last few years."

"What's that got to do with you?" Declan sneered.

"It's not like *our* relationship will ever be loving and wonderful," Sean replied tartly. "It's just an observation. They seem closer."

"Yeah." Connor nodded. "I guess we are. And you're right. Once he was twenty-one things changed. He was an adult, and we could do more adult things together."

"Boys' weekends; boozing with the ladies at the bars," Sean suggested.

Puzzled, Connor tilted his head. "Why would you say

that? Although it's true."

Sean shrugged it off. "All the things a boy should do with his dad when he turns twenty-one. But that was six years ago and that seems to have calmed down."

"Yeah." Connor agreed and sipped his coffee. "It has. Even though he's my son, he's an equal. He's an adult. He's not a kid anymore, like Declan." He nudged his younger brother with his elbow. "And things have changed. I don't know what I'd do if I lost him. And in this business, that's a very real threat. What about you, Declan?"

"What about me, Connor?" Declan glared his older brother down.

"We're the only two with kids left. How would you feel if something happened to Sean?"

"He wouldn't feel anything," Sean retorted. "He certainly didn't when Mom died." His hand flew up, grabbing Declan's hand as it flew at him, surprising everyone at his swiftness, especially Declan. "You don't get to do that anymore, *Father.*" He stood up and dropped Declan's hand. "I'm going outside. Connor, go and see your son, because it's not like my father wants to see his."

Sean left their stunned faces behind as he walked through the sun room and out into the back yard. The lap of the water called to him, along with the hum of the motors on the cars and the boats. He stood staring out at the city of New York. Manhattan. Lady Liberty was all the way to his left. Roosevelt Island was all the way to his right.

He breathed and slowly released it into the wild as his head titled back. He loved New York. Loved the humming of the sounds all mixed together, and the scent of the ocean and rivers. Hell, he loved the scent of the snow in winter and the rubbish in the summer. But the smell of hot asphalt when it's hit with summer rain was his absolute favourite. He breathed in.

"Sean."

His breath came out in a sigh. "Grandpa."

Cormac stood beside him, hands in pockets. "Did you do that on purpose?"

"Do what? Ask Connor about his relationship with Ethan? No, I was genuinely curious. They do seem closer than they ever have."

"That seems to be true, I've noticed it myself. I'm talking about your father."

Sean scanned the city. "It's not hard to set him off, you know that. But it's pretty damn obvious he doesn't love me and never will. He's never been nurturing, loving…never hugged me. I'm actually a bit envious of the relationship Ethan has with his dad, and Brandon and Sierra had with their mom and Alec. Pretty much envious of any kid who has a great relationship with their father because I didn't fucking have one."

"And I'm sorry you didn't." Cormac rested his hand on Sean's shoulder. "And maybe I should have stepped in sooner; maybe your grandmother and I should have had a tighter rein on him. But he turned out the way he turned out and I can't change that, nor go back and change it."

Sean's right leg twitched, and he wiped away his tears. "I know. It just really sucks to see Connor be a loving father when mine would beat me and none of you did anything about it." He took a shaky breath and sniffed. "You could have beaten him back, arrested and charged him, demoted or fired him. You didn't do anything." He tore away from his grandfather's grip and faced him. "I love you, Grandpa, but I hate my father and you know exactly why, so you can't be surprised."

Cormac gave a small nod. "I know, Sean. I know. And I wish I could do something about it. I wish I *had* done something about it."

Sean shook his head in resignation. "But you didn't, and you won't. Or can't. None of you will." He stalked off around the side of the house and drove himself home.

*****

Bleary-eyed, Sean walked into the Viceroy office the next day and found his agent, Roger, there as well. "Hey, what's going on?"

"You tell us, you poor boy." Vincent strode towards him, swathed in his usual '60s style velvet pantsuit with frill necked white shirt. He'd been happy when Austin Powers had brought back the style in the movies because his retro clothing was suddenly in fashion again. "Both of your cousins at the same time. Oh, my poor boy." He put his arms around Sean and pulled him close, his hand stroking his hair. "You poor boy."

"Vincent." Sean grasped his arms and pushed him away. "What have I told you about hugging me? It's a no-no."

"Oh, I'm sorry, my darling boy, but you've been through so much. Come, sit." He led Sean to the couch and plumped pillows behind his back. "Tea, coffee, wine?"

"None of the above. Let's talk books. How's *She* going?"

"Number one for the last week and looks like it'll be heading into next week. All on short notice, of course," Roger said.

"Yeah, I know." Sean rubbed his tired eyes. "But at least everything was ready to go and we could pull it all together faster. How many sales, do we know?"

Roger looked through the paperwork. "Heading for half a million. Which is great for short notice, especially since you're not on social media *as* Bryan Jamison."

"Viceroy publicity deals with all of that, that was part of the contract, to keep my real name out of it. Any videos I do are posted through those channels."

"Are you keeping up with your own socials?" Vincent asked. "I know you post on the odd occasion, but you haven't published as Sean Ryan for two years now."

Sean nodded. "Yeah. I post once a week to keep it going. Strangely, I still get sales for those books, and still earn from them each year."

"Your influencer cousins would have given you a boost." Vincent poured himself a cup of tea. "Weren't they posting about you until...oh..." He set the pot down. "I'm sorry, I forgot. Where are my manners?"

"No, you're right. Those assholes still posted about me to keep getting likes and followers. They earned a living from me because companies wanted to milk our name and they were the only two not in law enforcement other than me. In fact, they never worked a day in their lives at a normal job or career; they went straight from high school to using me to gain followers, even though their parents were both well off. Alec is the DA and Sonja the interior designer to the stars after she was the prostitute to the entire law enforcement division."

Vincent's cup stopped at his lips, and Roger looked up from his papers.

"Don't look so surprised. Sydney mentioned it in her book, Madam X, and I made a veiled mention of it in one of mine." He got up and walked over to the window, staring out at the city of Manhattan. "God I love this city, but I don't know how much longer I can do this."

"Do what, my dear boy?" Vincent set his cup and saucer down on the table beside him. "Write? Publish?"

"Live in New York."

"There's nothing to say you can't," Roger told him. "Authors can write anywhere."

"Yeah, I've been thinking I should get out and see the world. Get away from this city, the family, my life, for a while."

"It must be hard, your family is Kennedyesque in that sense, large and cursed," Vincent said.

"Cursed?" Sean frowned. "How?"

"Your great-grandfather died, your mother, and now your cousins, together."

"No, I wouldn't say that it's cursed; we're a big family, so when one dies, it's noticeable—"

Vincent cut him off. "But when three die within a year?"

"Still not a curse, Vincent. Wait a few years and see what happens. My dad, uncle, and cousin are cops; they could go anytime. Grandpa's the PC and nearly seventy-five, and he's retiring in the next year. Alec's the DA, and Kieran a lawyer; they could get shot by a disgruntled client or mob boss. It's a rough life being in law enforcement."

"True," Vincent agreed. "I just hope you don't have to go through all of that at once."

Sean turned from the window. "If Dad and Connor, or Connor and Ethan, are working together, then yeah, two or three could go at once." He pulled a manuscript out of his bag. "Book number two. I've been working on it day and night, but don't have a title yet. Since my books tend to come in threes, with convenient titles to match, this one is sort of a follow on in genre and style, as the next one will be. But I just can't figure out a title. And I'm not really sure the title *Incarcerated* will work, for this or the next." He handed the book to Roger. "Have a read and tell me what you think. I need to head home for a rest."

"Okay, my darling boy, we'll let you know." Vincent blew him a kiss and watched him walk out the door. "He needs more than a rest. It looks as if he needs a transfusion."

Roger glanced up from the manuscript. "Of what?"

Vincent shrugged. "Blood, vitamin B, D, C, love, happiness. Have you ever noticed how he always seems to have the weight of the world on his young shoulders? He always has."

"I have noticed, which is probably why he vents in all of his books. They're autobiographical, you know."

"What?" Vincent sipped his tea. "No, I hadn't realised."

"Oh, yeah, veiled and disguised, but you can pinpoint many things that have happened, and I also noticed some have been replies to Sydney Kingston's books."

Vincent perked up. "How?"

"She'll write and release one, then he'll hand over a masterpiece that's a reply to it. Book reviewers who've read both have noticed and commented on it."

"Mmm." Vincent pursed his thin lips. "No, I still haven't noticed."

"Considering what *Her* was about, let me read this." Roger cleared his throat. "*Little did I know, that cold rainy January night when I tried to enter the brownstone by the back door, that she was already gone and about to dump me in the biggest trouble I'd ever been in in my life. I had keys, but the cops didn't care. Neither did I, because I had the law on my side, and my law degree, and my name. And for what she did, I was going to punish her.*"

Chapter 8

"Do you want to talk about your family more? Your cousins?"

"No."

"What do you want to talk about?"

"Weren't we going to talk about my second mentorship visit? For some reason you wanted to continue talking about those."

"Okay." Levinworth nodded. "When you're ready."

Sean met Sydney in the boardroom at Pulsate.

"You'll be meeting with Victor today. He's an acquisitions editor of young adult and he's looking for new talent. No idea what he thinks of your stories, but we'll find out today," she said. "You seem happy. Good week?"

"Not really, but I've got another hour with you and I'm getting my stories edited with an acquisitions editor. Why wouldn't I be excited?" He'd been nervous for the last week after hitting send on the email to Sydney with five of his stories attached. He'd laboured over which ones to send, and finally decided on which were his best. If they weren't going to get him published at the end of

this mentorship, then nothing would. His heart raced every time he'd thought of Sydney and seeing her again, and now he was standing next to her and there was so much he wanted to say.

Victor Brothers walked into the room. "Hey, Sydney, and you must be Sean." He pulled out a chair and sat at the table. "Take a seat and let's get into this so you guys can chat about it." He settled piles of stapled paper in front of him and laid them out neatly, waiting for Sean and Sydney to take their seats.

"What did you think?" Sydney jumped in. "Good or what?"

"Very," Victor told an eager Sean. "You're actually very good already. Have you studied? Or is it just high school English?"

"High school English and lots of books on writing, lots of courses and videos on writing from and by famous authors." Sean fidgeted in his seat, anxious for the rest of the critique.

"Okay. Well, you have talent and some skill. With some editing advice you'll definitely improve to a point we could publish these at the end of your mentorship."

"What!" Sean's head pulled back in shock, his body rigid. "Wait…what?"

"Isn't that what you wanted?" Sydney asked. "An honest opinion and a published book at the end of the three months?"

He gaped at her blankly. "Ah…yeah…I guess so."

"No guesses about it." Victor slid a pile of paper over to him. "I've written notes on each story, suggesting where to tighten phrases, use different words, or to avoid

more description, but overall, you're far more advanced than most teens your age. Are you acing English?"

"I am." Sean flicked through the pages and saw red pen on a few of them.

"Great. Let me go through each story with you." Victor spent the next forty minutes giving advice to Sean that was invaluable to young or new writers, and something Sean could take forward into future writings.

"And I think that about covers everything." Victor glanced at the clock. "We've got ten minutes left. Anything you want to ask?"

"Ah…" Sean slowly shook his head. "Not off the top of my head. But what if I come up with a question later? Or more than one?"

"Then email them to me via the publishing house and ask. It comes with the mentorship." Victor pushed his chair back and stood. "Sean, Sydney, until next time."

"Thanks, Victor." Sydney watched him leave and sighed. "If that wasn't helpful, I don't know what else will be. You're already so good you might not even need a three-month mentorship."

"What if I started writing adult?" Sean asked, laying each stack of paper on top of the other. "It's all well and good to talk about these stories, and maybe have them published, but what if I start something adult and got a critique for that?"

"Why not work on them for the rest of the month, and then try something else? But…" she dragged out the word. "You're good at YA, why change?"

"Because I'm going to be an adult in a year," he said earnestly. "Why shouldn't I write it?"

"Didn't say you shouldn't, just said you're good at YA, so why not stick with it for now and wait and see what being published gets you. You may end up with a contract for more books. What then?"

He pondered for a moment, biting his bottom lip. "Is that possible? If it is, then I can do that for a couple of years and earn my writing chops. Prove to my parents and cousin that I am good enough. Make some money to pay my way through college, and then when I'm in my twenties give adult a crack." His head bobbed up and down. "I could do a four-year plan. Seventeen to twenty-one, college years, a young adult author popular at college. But wait…" His head spun so he could look at her. "If I'm already good enough to be published, would I even need to get a degree in writing?"

"That would definitely be one for Victor. When do you apply for college?"

"At the end of the year so I have time to find out. It would give me a degree and my first book would be considered by publishing houses as a part of the course. But if I'm already published by Pulsate…"

"What if your book doesn't sell? And is only the one? The one book, the one contract?" Sydney asked. "A degree would be another leg up, another useful link in the resume. You'd be considered above others, but then struggling to get a book picked up."

"True." He made some notes in his notebook before slapping it shut. "Our time's up, but this has been incredibly helpful." He shoved his book and paperwork into his backpack.

Sydney stood and picked up her handbag. "Apart

from getting the normal advice from everyone else, I really have no idea what kind of help I can offer."

"Help me write adult stories." Sean pushed his chair under the table and hefted his bag onto his shoulder. "I've gotten advice about my YA stories, now you can give me advice in adult novels. Stories for kids and teens are one thing, but stories for adults are a completely different animal."

"Not really." Sydney led the way to the elevator bank. "The outline is the same. The acts, the beats, the arcs. Every story is laid out the same. It's how you tell it that makes the magic."

The bell dinged and they stepped into the lift, the doors closing just as the second onslaught of workers leaving for the day reached them.

"Okay. So that's all the same, but what about making it adult? I don't write sex or romance, but I'd have to in adult."

The doors opened and they stepped into the lobby, stopping by the side of the front glass doors.

"It helps if you've had experiences, you can make it authentic that way, but if you don't want to write romance or sex, then go for crime thrillers, psychological or domestic, action adventure, or something else completely. You could just take a story or two you've written and see if you can adultify it. Change the ages, etcetera."

"That's a good idea," he said. "But still not quite adult. And while crime would be a natural move, considering my family and all, maybe a thriller might work."

"Let your deepest, darkest secrets out and see what

happens," Sydney suggested. "Doesn't matter if anyone reads it; just use it as an exercise for trying adult."

"Another good idea," he said. "And this is why this mentorship is a good idea. You have suggestions I wouldn't think of—"

"Then you'd better start thinking of them if you want to write adult when you grow up. Because sometimes when you're stuck for ideas, you have to reach far and wide for something to write. It doesn't matter if it's wacky and too far out there, give it a try and see what sticks." Sydney motioned for them to walk outside, and they stopped on the sidewalk next to the car.

"Another great idea." Sean waved to Amy and turned his attention back to Sydney. "Considering the family I'm in, you'd think I'd be all over crime, but I can't stand it most of the time. Maybe a medical drama, but there's plenty of those on TV."

"Again, reach far and wide and see what ideas stick." Sydney opened the door and dropped her bag on the seat. "We can talk about it more next week."

"If I write something can you read it and let me know if it's good enough?" Sean stepped closer, but Sydney stayed behind the open passenger door, keeping it between them. "I can whip up a few pages, or few thousand words, and have it ready for next Wednesday."

"Think it's that easy, do you?" she mocked. "Just you wait. You said at lunch that you get pain behind your eyes or something and it won't stop until you're finished writing."

"Yeah, it's horrible," he complained. "My eyes throb and my brain pounds."

"Then use that as an indication you've picked the right idea," Sydney suggested. "If an idea does that to you, go with the flow."

"Another great idea." He waved a hand. "I'll do that. Take care, Sydney, see you next week."

"And how did it make you feel, having such an acclaimed editor tell you your stories were good?"

Sean's chest puffed out a little. "Good. Great. Amazing. I not only had Sydney, an award-winning author tell me I was good, but a well-respected editor as well."

"Did you feel vindicated after everything your family had said?"

"Absolutely." Sean nodded. "I got crapped on by Sierra for about two years, and you should have seen her face when Sydney pulled her up at lunch that time. Priceless." He laughed. "She *hated* being admonished by an adult, an acclaimed author, no less, who *had* read some of my stories. She never did it again because she was ripped apart. Except when—"

Levinworth glanced up at the silence. "Except when?"

Sean's shoulders dropped. "Except when I was under house arrest and Grandpa made everyone bring lunch over to my place. We were getting the extra table from my office when she made her dig. I told you about that. They wanted *me* to apologise for saying what I did. I made some comment about bullying and that I wasn't apologising."

"Were they happy?"

"Nope. But I don't care."

"Not even now they're gone?"

"Why would I care? They bullied me. Why would

them dying change my mind about how I feel, or change my feelings?" Frowning, he turned to Levinworth. "Why would them being dead change my feelings about them? It would be like someone not believing in God all their life and then having an accident and suddenly believing in God. Or the prisoners who suddenly find God when they've been thrown in jail. It's hypocritical. Like saying nice things about someone in a eulogy if they were nothing but an asshole. Why would my feelings change because they died?"

Levinworth thought for a moment. "You make a good point. But didn't you feel *anything* when they died? Didn't you have *any* loving feelings for them left?"

Sean moved away from the window, hands steadfastly in his pockets, to stand in front of the crashing wave painting. He'd found a copy online and bought it but was awaiting its arrival. Finally, he said, "Loving no, hateful yes."

Levinworth made a note in Sean's file. "Understandable."

"I loved the mentorship," Sean continued. "Even though I nearly fucked it up after session four. But when I continued, I found it really enjoyable because I had both Victor and Michael helping me perfect my writing; Victor with YA, and Michael with my adult stuff. I guess if anyone is going to know who Bryan Jamison is, it's Michael. The stuff I put in my novels was similar to what I wrote for him. They both taught me a lot over those two months, and it resulted in my YA being published. I only had a small following on social media before that, a couple of hundred followers, mainly kids from school, until everyone found out who I was and that I had a publishing deal."

"Were you in high school or college when the first book was published?" Levinworth flicked through his papers.

"First year of college."

"But you went to Harvard Law."

"Added that to the roster and did it in two years instead of three. My adult books paid for it eventually."

"Did your family find out?"

"My dad wasn't paying for college anyway; said since I was a hotshot author I could pay my own way through. The money that Mom had was divided between Dad and me, and I put that towards my college tuition with the advances from the young adult books, plus I had a few side gigs and hustled a bit to earn extra money."

"Like what?"

"I got a job at a publisher at one point, but that's for another time."

"Why another time?"

"Because I'm telling this story in order, doc. Have you forgotten? You wanted me to start at the beginning as a refresher."

Levinworth nodded. "You're right. What happened after the second mentorship meeting?"

"Went home and wrote more stories and got the ones I had written in order to maybe be published. If I could get all of them edited professionally, I could get published sooner and not have to come up with more. But as it turned out, I couldn't stop writing, even at school. I'd sit in an empty classroom and write, or in the library. I just wanted to be left alone."

"And how did your schoolmates react when you were published?"

Sean grimaced and remembered back to one episode in particular.

"Hey, Duffield, if it's not the loser, Ryan, writing more of his shitty stories because he thinks he's a big publishing star now."

Hunter Dexter flipped Sean's pencil case off the table. "Oops, looks like the loser dropped his pencils, little boy better pick them up before the librarian tells him off."

"If anyone's being told off, Hunter Dexter, it's you," Ms Roylan barked. "Pick up Sean's case and put it back. Now."

Hunter froze, turned bright tomato red, and glared at Sean who raised his brows in amusement. "I'm going to get you, Ryan," he spat and slowly bent to snatch up the case and slam it on the table.

"Dexter, that's one week detention, and Duffield, you can get it too."

"But miss," Barry Duffield complained. "I didn't do anything."

"You stood by while a school bully thought he could get away with bullying," Ms Roylan said. "Both of you, detention. Now."

Sean waved his fingers at Hunter and Barry as they walked away and then did an inconspicuous high-five with Ms Roylan as she passed. He knew that wouldn't be the last he saw of Hunter, because he liked to beat up other college kids off campus, so he didn't get detention. He'd just have to be prepared.

And after school he needed to be.

Sean walked out the front door, down the stairs, and through the car park. Even though he lived part-time on campus, he had places to go and people to meet. His first year in college had proved to be useful in teaching him how to stand up for himself and he'd been taking some self-defence classes at his local YMCA and working out to strengthen his muscles. He'd lost some weight and gained some confidence in return and had no problem punching someone if need-be. That looked to be in about five seconds when he stepped out of the carpark and onto the street.

And in four, three, two, one...

"Fatty boom bah Sean Ryan thinks he's a published author. Who'd want to publish your crap, 'cause no one will want to read it, that's for sure."

Sean kept going. "And yet, you will. That I know for sure. Because you won't to be able to help yourself. You'll just have to read it to see what the fuss is about. But then—" Sean stopped and turned around, pointing a finger at Hunter. "You won't be able to help yourself again, you'll just have to tell everyone who'll bother listening to you that it's crap, and no one will read it, even though by that point, you will have as will everyone else because none of you will be able to help yourselves and will have to read it. And what will I get then? A whole lot of classmates that don't know me or don't care trying to milk their connection with me on social media. Well, fuck you, Hunter, fuck you, Barry, fuck all of you." He flung his arms wide. "Because I won't let you, and I won't care." He turned and kept walking, his hands on the straps of his backpack that sat firmly on his shoulders.

"No, Ryan, fuck you."

Sean felt the tug on his backpack pulling him back. He bent at the waist, took a step forwards, and back kicked Hunter, who gasped and bent over. Sean lashed out with a spin kick and watched Hunter crumple to the ground and Barry back away with his hands up in defeat. "Anyone else?" Sean asked the couple of hundred sticky beaks standing nearby, phones in the air recording. "Anyone else wanna try bullying me? Because I'm ready." He saw shaking heads and kids walking away. "No, aw, too bad." He looked down at Hunter. "Leave me the fuck alone, you cunt. 'Cause you don't know who you're dealing with."

He adjusted his backpack and walked away with the knowledge he could actually fight back.

"I got a lot of crap, as you'd expect. I had through middle and high school anyway thanks to who my father and my grandfather were."

"What about your mother?"

"What about my mother?"

"Did you cop any flak when she died? Had your book been published by then?"

Sean's eye's drifted shut as he exhaled a slow sigh. His shoulders drooped and his hands turned into fists in his pockets. "I copped a lot of flak which is why I'd hide out in the library or a classroom and write. She knew I was going to be published and the first book came out before she died."

"Was she proud? Did she read it?"

"Did you read my file? Because it's in there." Sean's

fingers slid over the canvas of the crashing wave. He'd found the title, upon researching and buying it. It was *Distoria*. Knowing the name made it all make sense. He felt distorted when staring at the painting as if his brain were out of shape, distorted into something else, something it wasn't supposed to be. His hand dropped to his side, and he exhaled. "My mother's a touchy subject. You know that, doc."

"Still? After four years."

"That's just it, doc, it's only three, three and a half. It's not long to deal with the death of a parent."

"What would you do if your father died?"

Sean considered the question, searched for a feeling he might have, and found none. "Nothing. No," he paused, "celebrate. Heave a sigh of relief. Feel the weight of the world dissipate."

"Do you hate your father that much?"

Sean's head spun towards his therapist. "You know full well I do. What a stupid question." He walked back to the window, eyes burning with anger, hands clenched into fists in his pockets.

"Do you love your father?"

"No."

"At all?"

Silence.

"Did you ever?"

"Once upon a time when I was young and naïve and believed my parents loved me." He snorted. "I quickly grew out of that."

"How old were you?"

"Five when I realised my dad didn't love me. Probably

ten or twelve when I realised Mom didn't really care."

"Is that why Sydney's love was so important?"

Sean looked at Levinworth. "Probably. Why?"

Levinworth shrugged a shoulder. "Your father didn't love you, your mother ended up not loving you, your grandmothers were dead…where else were you going to get female attention and love from? Sydney was the woman who showed you attention, told you that you were good at writing, and showered you with encouragement and support. Everything your parents didn't."

"Yeah well, not hard to figure out, doc."

"No, it isn't. You have mother issues, so you looked towards another woman for what yours didn't give you. Love and affection, support and attention."

"So, you don't believe that I could love a woman because she's amazing and incredible?"

"Not at seventeen, no."

"Why not?" Sean turned to him; his curiosity aroused.

"Who the hell knows how they feel about anything at seventeen?" Levinworth said. "Boys have testosterone throbbing through their body thanks to puberty. The body's growing and changing, hair grows, balls drop, along with voices, you grow taller, wider, thicker. What the hell do these testosterone rage machines know about anything? Especially love? And add alcohol and drugs to the mix, you have angry turdburgers who want to fight, rape, murder—"

"Not all of us, doc," Sean chastised.

"Not all of you, but, sadly, many," Levinworth finished. "No one, boy or girl, in their teens and early twenties has any clue about anything thanks to puberty. It completely fucks with the brain, and quite frankly, kids should not go to school during puberty. I think they need to wait until later or be home-schooled."

"And you got all of those diplomas from where?" Sean pointed to the framed certificates on the wall. "A cereal box?"

That got a chuckle out of Levinworth. "My point is, it's well documented that hormones and puberty do not make for mature beings. You have no idea about love, Sean; you stated so in *Illicit Things*."

Sean's mouth opened, but he stayed silent. His brows furrowed as he thought of something to say. He couldn't find a reply to something that was true. He sighed and closed his mouth.

"Exactly." Levinworth nodded. "Exactly *what* did you know about love at seventeen, Sean? What did you know about the notion, the need, the want." He tilted his head. "Sex."

"Ha!" Sean cracked. "That's a conversation for another day, doc. Believe me. I know a lot and you might be surprised by it. But time's up and it's time to go."

"You cop out early," Levinworth said, hearing Sean pause at the door. "Unless your watch is running fast, you always leave early. Do you cop out of everything in your life?"

Fury burned in Sean's chest. "I cop out of nothing. I just walk away from assholes and bad situations."

"Is this a bad situation? Am I an asshole?"

Sean let out his anger in a sigh. "No, *you're* not an asshole, but this isn't a great situation either. I don't want to be here. I don't want to be under house arrest, I don't want this damn ankle bracelet on. I just want to get on with my life."

"Why are you here, Sean?"

"Because I was caught trying to get into Sydney's house with a key."

"No, you're here because you were found to be defrauding Sydney and breaking into her house with keys she says she never gave you. Which means, they were master keys, or you somehow made duplicates. You were also found to have set up cameras and taken photos of her. All of that is illegal, Sean."

"I didn't steal or make duplicates of her keys," he yelled, fists clenched by his sides. "She gave them to me so I could come and go as I pleased."

"That's not what she said," Levinworth said quietly.

Sean stormed back to him and leaned over him. "Just you wait until the real truth comes out. Because the whole world will be shocked to the back teeth." He slammed his way out of the office, leaving Levinworth shaken.

The anger in Sean's eyes had made them a clouded grey; different from their usual sapphire blue, and he'd never seen Sean's eyes change colour in anger, or any emotion for that matter.

He took a few deep breaths to calm his heart and realised Sean could be more disturbed than he first thought. He picked up his pen and made a note. *Subject appears to still be deluded, even four years on. He believes Ms Kingston gave him keys to the back door, and free access to come and go. He also thinks there's nothing wrong with putting cameras in her house to spy on her, although we are yet to get to that. We're currently going over the past in order to refresh his memory of what he did four years ago. What started this off, how his parents affected his mental state, and just refreshing myself with his notes. They affected him greatly, and the after-effects are still very much intact, even though he had greatly improved. Maybe his cousins' deaths have something to do with it.*

He set his pen down and picked up Sean's book *Creeper.* Turning to chapter three, he read, *I knew I needed to set the cameras up sooner rather than later. I needed to capture as much of her as I could until I could capture her in the flesh. The plan was to infiltrate her personal space and learn everything about her until I could infiltrate her, body, mind and soul. I know her schedule. I know when she'll be out. I had keys made to fit the locks on her back door and I'll use them as soon as I can and then she won't see me coming. Even when I watch her sleep at night as I sit by her bedside watching her breathe.*

*****

Since there were only a few places Sean could go, and he desperately wanted to sit by the river to hear the waves, the only place he could go was his grandfather's. He pulled his second-hand runabout up in the driveway and made his way around to the backyard and over to the stone wall keeping the river at bay. The spring weather was a little warmer, the sun a little brighter, and the sky a little bluer. He sat on the wall and dangled his legs over the water, watching it lap against the stones, trying to reach for his boots. The water looked black and deep, even this close to the side. He didn't know how deep, but had often sat on the wall staring into the water, wondering if he could touch the bottom, even if he hung onto the stone jutting out.

He'd tried it once, when he was six. It was summer, and all of the family were over, so the grandkids were too, and he'd been left out of the game Brandon and Ethan were playing. Sierra, at eight, had been playing princess of the ball with everyone, so no one noticed him sitting on his own and feeling alone and unwanted.

He'd slipped into the water to find out how deep it was and found out the moment his head had gone under and smashed against the wall. He'd struggled, flapping his arms like crazy, and Ethan had managed to grab onto one of them and pull him up. Brandon had stood by doing nothing, but his mother and grandfather had rushed over with Pop to help dry him off.

"Sweetie, what'd you do? Did you fall in?" Laura wrapped him in a towel and held him close. "What happened?"

"I wanted to see how deep it was," Sean stuttered in shock. "It didn't look very deep near the wall."

"Oh, sweetie." Laura pushed his wet hair off his face. "It's very deep. Don't go in again, okay?"

"Okay." Sean wiped his nose on the towel. "Efan saved me."

"He did. Have you thanked him yet?"

"No." Sean shook his head and gazed up at his cousin. "Fanks Efan, you're my hero."

Ethan grinned and ruffled his hair. "No worries, kid. Just stay away from the river."

"Sean?"

He glanced up to see Emerson behind him.

"You okay?"

"Yeah." He sighed. "Just reminiscing about being six and Ethan pulling me out of the water when I decided to see how deep it was. He saved me. He was my hero from that day on."

Emerson sat on the wall beside him. "Is he still?"

Sean sadly shook his head. "No. He stopped being my hero when he fucked Sydney. Although, it was probably even before that, when he stopped coming around on weekends once he turned eighteen and joined the force, or maybe when he turned twenty-one and hung out with Connor more and left me behind. Seems to be the way for me. Everyone leaves me behind. Probably because I'm the youngest, the stupidest, the baby." He gazed over the river. "Did you know she fucked Ethan? One year after…"

"No," she said quietly.

"For a best friend, Sydney didn't seem to tell you a lot." He finally looked at her. "Are you still working on the final season of *Twisted Minds?*"

She nodded. "I am. It's going to take a while."

"I'm sure it will. You don't mind if I sit here, do you?"

"Of course not; it's your grandfather's house. Will you be staying for lunch? Dinner?"

"I don't know. I just came from my therapist. I'm worn out. Don't know if I'm hungry."

"How's it going? The therapy."

"Oh, I think people keep forgetting that I'm only twenty-one." A grin slightly lifted the corners of his lips. "I certainly do, considering how old I feel sometimes. And after the conversation with my therapist today…" He shook his head. "I might just be here a while. Might go and talk to Pop, too."

Emerson laid her hand on his arm. "You do that. I'll be cooking all afternoon, making up meals for the rest of the week. If you get hungry, just ask."

"Thank you, Emerson. You've always been kind, and I know Grandpa loves you."

"Yes." She stood up; her face emotionless. "He does."

Sean waited until she was inside before turning back to the river. He sat watching the boats, listened to the cars on the bridge, and remembered memories from days gone by. He was only twenty-one, but had lived a lot of life, and he was sick and tired of having the one he currently had.

When all of this is over, I'm going on a holiday and may never come back to this god forsaken family.

Heaving a worn-out sigh, he swung his legs over the wall and walked inside to his great-grandfather's bedroom and closed the door. "Hey, Pop. Let's get some light and air in here, huh." He flung open the curtains and opened the window. "Ah, that's better." Turning around, he looked at the still intact bedroom and sighed before a small laugh came from him. "I'm sighing a lot these days, Pop. I can't seem to help myself. I have the weight of the world on my shoulders, but then, when didn't I?"

He roamed around the room, stopping at the bookshelves either side of the TV on the wall. Sydney's hardcovers were all lined up in pristine condition. The paperbacks sat on the shelf below. Sean's books were on the shelf below that, along with photos of them when his first book was published.

A smile touched his lips and he picked up the photo, looking at it a moment before turning it over and removing the back. Nothing. He closed it and replaced it on the shelf. He went through every photo frame checking for papers hidden behind photos, pulled each book off the shelf and flicked through the pages looking for anything, something. He went through his books, Sydney's books, and all the other books. He pulled out drawers, felt underneath, opened the closet doors and saw his uniform hanging neatly. He opened the bedside cabinet, slid his hands between the mattresses of the bed, then checked under every layer of sheets and blankets.

"Come on, Pop. If you were going to hide anything, where would it be?" His gaze darted from furniture, to built-in, to window. He looked under the bed, slid his hands across the back of the headboard, and then checked the backs of the bedside cabinets. "Come on, Pop, show me what you've left behind."

He noticed the bible wasn't on the bedside table. "Where did that go? I didn't come across…" He glanced at the bed and picked up the pillows, pulled the mattress aside and saw it down on the floor hidden by the headboard and bed leg. "No wonder I didn't see you, you're hiding." He picked it up and reset the bed before sitting on it. "Now. Why would you have been on the floor? Did Pop hide you there, or did you fall?" He skimmed through the pages ,but found nothing and sighed. "I was so sure I'd found something." He closed the book and sat it on the cupboard staring at the door with his dressing gown hanging neatly on the back. He searched the pockets, found nothing, and sat back down. "Come on, Pop. Where would you hide something?"

His gaze moved back to the bible, and as he reached out to straighten it, he noticed the cover wasn't flat against the pages. His brows furrowed. "Why aren't you…" He picked it up and checked the interior of each cover, his fingers sliding over the end paper and lining. "Is that…" He switched the lamp on and held the book up to the light. The back cover was definitely thicker than the front. Peering at it under the light, he pushed his thumbnail under the endpaper and along the glue line. The paper peeled off with a crackle and out slid a folded chunk of paper.

Sean put the bible down and unfolded the sheets. Names of politicians, lawyers, doctors, athletes, police officers, judges…anyone and everyone in power were written in Douglas's handwriting with seven hundred and fifty-one names crossed off. Including his.

*****

Sean sat at his desk looking at the list of the who's who of New York society. He had an inkling this was the list of men Sydney had mentioned that was in Madam X's little black book. One thousand names, seven hundred and fifty-one dead; not long after Douglas Ryan had died, and his name was crossed out too.

"It can't be." He fingered the paper and looked out

the window, leaning back in his seat to analyse the possibilities. Why would Pop have a list and cross his name out? Did he cross his name out, or did someone else? Was this an exact list from Madam X's book, or a made up one? Where did Pop get it from? Had Sydney given it to him when she came to see him? He died only minutes later. Had he died happy? Had he died happy for a hail Mary into heaven? Had he wanted to vent his soul?

He sighed and turned to his wall of Sydney. Sydney in all shapes and size calling out to him, teasing him, wanting him, calling his name.

"I'm not obsessed." his voice was a whimper as he stared at the wall. A little louder, he said, "I'm not obsessed." At normal voice level, he continued, "I'm not obsessed with Sydney, Walter. I love her and you have no fucking idea what you're talking about."

A loud banging came from his front door, and he checked the security system on his tablet. "Fuck, Alec." He slammed his laptop shut and hurried over to the wall to close it on Sydney, making sure it connected before hurrying into the condo and opening the door. "You don't need to keep banging."

"Sean." Alec glanced at his watch and walked in. "Here for your weekly check-up."

"Go right ahead, although I'm surprised you're here, considering. Thought Grandpa would have checked in." He followed Alec into his office and saw one of his prints on the wall was swinging slightly.

Alec noticed. "Your print isn't straight."

"I know. I'm trying something different." Sean walked

over to the wall and hung the painted canvas on a different angle. "I might hang them all off centre to see what kind of effect I get." He tilted another one on its nail. "Why are you here?"

Alec watched him tip another print towards the others and frowned. "This is my job."

"But considering…"

"Consider this," Alec snapped. "Don't piss me off, Sean. I can put you back in jail with a snap of my fingers." His right hand reached up and his fingers clicked.

"Don't piss you off about what?" Sean turned from a painting. "Asking why are you still doing this when your children died two weeks ago? I thought you'd be taking time off to mourn, and yet you're here pissing *me* off." His brows lowered along with his voice. "And don't talk to me about pissing *you* off because this is pissing *me* off and you can't destroy me, Alec. I have way too much dirt on you. Or did you forget what I told you at the beginning of all this?" His blue eyes glared into those of his uncle. "Go and do your job so I can get on with mine."

Alec simmered and stormed up the stairs to the bedroom and back down. He followed up with the bedroom in the first condo with Sean waiting by the door. Alec buttoned his blazer as he descended the stairs. "Same time next week." He stopped beside Sean who'd opened the front door. "And if you ever threaten me—"

"Fuck off, Alec, that's your forte. I'm just the messenger of doom." Sean smirked. "Adios amigo." He shoved his uncle out the door and slammed it shut on his enraged expression. "Asshole." He locked the door and walked into the kitchen to make himself a strong coffee, and then made his way back into his office. He opened the wall of Sydney, sat behind his desk, and opened his laptop. He saw the list of one thousand names that had been hidden there and picked it up. "What were you up to, Pop? What did this list mean to you?"

With a sigh, he set it down and opened up the new novel's document, reading over what he'd written yesterday. Once he was fully immersed in the story, he began to type.

*****

"That's amazing, Bryan. Your new book *She* has been out for four weeks and you're still at the top of the chart. How does it feel to be number one again?"

"Incredible," Bryan said, pushing his glasses up the bridge of his nose. "And I hope the feeling continues until I release the new one next month."

"Yes," Melody Caldecott of *The Book Review* said. "Why is the new one coming out next month instead of next year?"

"Because I wanted to give fans something to say thank you for making my first three novels bestsellers. They sold over two million each and I didn't want to make them wait for parts two and three in this trilogy."

"But every two months is a quick turnaround. Is there another reason? I believe you mentioned a new standalone coming out in September."

"Yes, Melody, I did. I wrote a fantastic novel that blew me and my publisher away, and I really wanted it to come out as soon as possible, but *She Is Mine* were first in the publishing line up. I asked my publishing team if we could speed up the release dates, and because everything was done, they said yes."

"You've released *She. Is,* which is a weird title for a book, is coming next month in May. And *Mine* is coming in July. Can you tell us the name of the standalone?"

"No, Melody, I cannot. That will remain a secret until it's released."

"And do you think you'll score the top spot in September, or will Sydney Kingston beat you to it as that's her usual publishing date?"

"I've heard that Sydney's not publishing this year, so I'm hoping to score the number one spot away from her with my seventh novel. Seven is seen as a lucky number in some countries. But even if she does publish, we'll just battle it out again and see who comes out the victor."

"How do you know Sydney's not publishing? Has she said? Have you met her yet? I know that was a bone of contention every time your books were released. Everyone asked if you'd met her."

"Yes, I finally got to last year. We were at several book launches and then Rhett Rockefeller's festive celebration parties."

"And what happened? Did the two of you get into a fight? Did you congratulate each other? What?" Melody asked.

"We got along as rivals do. I wanted to have conversations and Sydney would turn her back and walk away. Typical rivalry, I guess. But I've read everything she's released and absolutely loved it all, which is why I use her books as inspiration for my own."

"And how do you do that?"

"Well." Bryan adjusted his glasses that had slipped down his nose. "I read her book and then think about what the answer would be. I think about what the opposite would be, and suddenly ideas start flowing and I write them all down."

"That's an interesting way of using an author as inspiration. Where else do you get your inspiration?"

"From personal life experiences. From fantasies, from watching movies, reading the news, reading other authors. Inspiration is all around us every day."

"That is very true. *She*, by Bryan Jamison, is out now in all good book stores and the follow up, *Is*, will be out next month. We'll see you again, Bryan Jamison. Thanks for zooming in."

"Thank you, Melody, see you next month."

*****

"Bryan Jamison, good to see you. I'm loving this book, your new one, *She*, out now. And even though it's April, and you have another book coming next month, tell us what *She* is about if you can—what all three are about?"

"All three books, *She Is Mine*, was one giant write-fest of an idea. I kept writing and writing, and when I was done, realised I might have to break it into three books. I came up with a title and broke that up as well. That's why my publisher doesn't think *Is* is a good title for a book. But I persuaded them to try things a little differently to normal, after the success of my first three." He shrugged lightly. "They decided to give it a go."

"That's why they're coming out every two months?" Brian Emery of *Let's Talk Books*, a popular cable TV show, asked.

"That wasn't the original plan. But when I had the idea, and told it to my publishers, they decided to try it out. After all, I was the one who suggested not showing my face to begin with when we released *Illicit Things* and *Sinister Motives*. *Creeper* was when I came out of hiding and sales went through the roof for all three. It worked well. We're hoping this will too."

"It definitely gives your fans something to look forward to. When it comes to trilogies, readers want the next one the moment they finish the first, and the third when they finish the second. Now they just have to wait two months in between."

"Or wait four months for all three books and read them all together."

"That's a good idea. Should these books be read together?"

"Ah…" Bryan pursed his lips while thinking. "I did consider re-writing each one *as* a standalone, but it's probably better to read them all together, otherwise as a reader you tend to forget what was in a book you read a year ago."

"That is true," Emery said. "Even I've had that issue. How's your foot, by the way?"

"My what?" Bryan asked.

"Your foot. I heard you broke it."

"Oh, yes, I did." Bryan calmed a little. "I have almost no pain so tend to forget I even broke it. And I've been busy writing."

"Anything you can tell us about?"

"Not at this stage, no."

"Okay, then, Bryan Jamison, thanks for being on *Let's Talk Books.*"

"Thanks for having me."

Sean clicked off Zoom and closed the laptop. "Thank God that's over." He walked over to the kitchen counter, pulled off his wig, and removed the contacts. "When are my next interviews?"

"In May, when you release the next book," Dexter said. "And that's me for the day. I'll head off and see you next month." He started off through the adjoining doorway but stepped back. "Will your foot still be broken then?"

"Probably." Sean chuckled. "And I'll have rehab to deal with and by then I'll be a recluse and not want to do interviews at all."

Dexter considered it a moment. "That's actually not a bad idea, especially if you plan on exiting stage right into a new life at the end of the year."

Sean nodded in agreement. "Good idea. I'll give that some more thought." He locked the door after his manager and finished taking off his Bryan disguise; beard, and clothes. It wasn't fun playing Bryan Jamison anymore, hiding from his family and the world. He wanted to be himself, but himself was cursed up the wazoo and not having the name Ryan would be a blessing. A new name wouldn't be held against him. Wouldn't be *used* against him, and people wouldn't be hounding him on the street. Maybe being anyone other than Sean Ryan would be the better thing to be. No more family curse. No more dictatorship.

Sean sighed and walked over to his wall of Sydney. The light in her eyes, her laughter, her sense of self all thrilled him. She didn't care what critics said. She didn't care what she said about other authors. Sydney was her own woman and did what she wanted, and he wanted her and all the things she could do to him.

"God, I love you, Sydney." He touched a finger to a photo of her fucking Connor. He'd taken them off the video from the hidden cameras. She was wild and free with him, doing it in the hallway, the living room, the bedroom, and the sex room. The sex room hadn't needed his cameras; Sydney had her own, so he'd hacked into them and watched. He'd watched Sydney tie up Connor and whip him all night long. God, how he'd wanted Sydney to do that to him, to show him, teach him, educate him in the ways of sex and love. Instead, she'd shown his uncle, *then* his cousin, *then* his father while he had to contend with prostitutes.

Sean pulled down the photo and tore it into a million little pieces, watching them all fall onto the floor and settle into the position of a full image, mocking him with how they'd fallen. Just right, so he could still see Connor inside Sydney.

He scarpered to the floor and picked them up, then set fire to them in the sink.

Chapter 9

"Who did you think the three men were?" Levinworth asked Monday morning. "You were going to see Sydney after she didn't turn up for your fourth mentorship meeting, and saw the men leave. Do you know who they were? Did you recognise them? Did you know why they were there? And most importantly, why did *you* think you had the right to be there?"

Sean rolled his eyes. "Too many questions, doc. I didn't know who they were. My mind made up wild explanations. The first was that they had come to use the sex room and Sydney had turned into a madam. Then I saw their briefcases and thought they might be businessmen. I quickly took photos of them and their licence plates. I later did a motor vehicle check and found out who they were." He stood by the window, hands in pockets, looking out at the view of Manhattan. It was the first spot he went to upon arriving at his therapist's office.

"How did you do a motor vehicle check?"

"Used my dad's log-in details. But it's amazing what you can find just by googling it."

"So, breaking into Sydney's house and setting up the cameras wasn't the first fraudulent thing you've done." Levinworth added that to his notes.

"Was it really fraudulent, though?" Sean asked. "His computer happened to be open, I used it. He really shouldn't bring work home."

"He managed to make it home?"

"On the odd occasion. Certainly didn't stay there when Grandpa demoted him for abusing Sydney. But I found a way."

"And who were the three men?"

"Antiquities and something experts. They studied old things and told you if they were authentic or not. When I found that out, I wondered what Sydney might have that was so important she'd asked experts around."

"Didn't you just check the cameras you'd set up?"

Sean glanced over his shoulder. "Funny."

Levinworth stared back. "Wasn't meant to be."

Sean moved to the wave painting, staring at it with furrowed brows. "Connor turned up, and after that, strutted up the stairs like he lived there. Sydney opened the door and pulled him in for a kiss. It was sickening to watch, and my stomach plummeted to the ground. She was fucking him. That was the first time I truly had confirmation. I'd hidden when I saw his car and came out of hiding once they were inside and the door was closed. I'd only suspected it from the attraction they had at lunch. I think Mom had suspected it as well. But only that day, when I walked up those stairs and looked in the window next to the door, did I finally have proof that it was happening."

"The cameras?"

"I put them in after that day. They fucked again after that. A lot. After the fight."

"Did they see you?"

"Sydney did, but I ran like a jack rabbit into a neighbour's basement stairwell and hid until he went back inside. I seethed at what I'd seen. The volcano inside me was ready to blow. The woman I loved was on the floor, naked, under my uncle while he was fucking her, inside of her, the woman I wanted to be inside of."

"And how did that make you feel?"

"Like killing him."

"What did you do?"

"I walked the streets for hours. From one end of the city to the other, or at least it felt like it. And I seethed and boiled and raged." He stared at the waves in the painting and heard the crashing in his ear. "I was so damn fucking angry," he snarled through clenched teeth. "So fucking angry I could kill both of them."

A sharp as nail pain drove into the left side of his head. "Ah." He clutched at it. It fled and then came back with a one two punch left and right. "Ah." The air rushed out of him, and he squeezed his eyes tightly.

"Sean." Levinworth dumped his papers on the coffee table in front of him and moved to his patient's side. "Sean. What is it? Are you having pain? Where?" He led him to the sofa and quickly got a bottle of water from the small fridge he kept behind his desk. He handed it over. "Here. Did you take your meds? Do you need a paracetamol?" Sitting beside him, he took Sean's pulse. "It's a little fast." Watching Sean sip the water, he saw exhaustion on his face. "Do you sleep? Take your meals? What do you do all day?"

"Write, and all night. Except when I'm here, or at my publishers, or Grandpa's." Sean capped the bottle and removed his glasses. Rubbing his eyes, he felt the lump forming behind them in his brain. "I'm stressed. This happens when I'm stressed. You know that—you diagnosed me."

"I know. How often does this happen?"

Sean replaced his glasses. "When I'm stressed, when I think about being under house arrest, when I have to come here, or Alec does his spot check on me. But when I'm writing, I'm fine. Off in my own little world doing my own little thing." He deflated with a sigh. "I'm fine, doc. I just hate what happened."

"But we have to talk about it." Levinworth picked up his papers and resumed his seat. "It's still a problem so we need to rehash it. Start where you dropped off."

With another sigh, Sean leaned back on the sofa and closed his eyes. "I walked the streets for hours, burning with rage inside, until I found myself back at Sydney's." He shook his head slowly. "Never in a million years did I ever think I could hurt her, and I had no intention of doing so when I found myself back on her doorstep. I knew Connor was gone. I saw him leave with a big dopey grin on his shit-eating face." He took a breath. "And then I did it."

He banged on the vestibule door. "Down in a minute," he heard through the monitor and waited.

Sydney opened the door. "Hey, how come you're here now? It's nearly ten."

He glowered at her grimly. "Because we had a mentor session at four, Sydney. And you didn't turn up." He set his bag on the floor just inside the door. "You didn't turn up and I spoke to Michael for the hour. Which wasn't a bad thing. In fact, it was very productive, but that's not the point, is it now, Sydney?"

He hoped the heat from his glare burned her face, and his hands on hips and broad shouldered stance intimidated her even though he was only seventeen.

"I sent my apologies to Michael to pass on to you. I had a series of appointments I had to deal with, and I knew I wouldn't make it so I rang Michael. You don't actually need to see me every week. You can spend time with other people. It's part of your mentorship."

"But I wanted you to mentor me." His anger simmered barely underneath the surface, and he stepped closer. "That's why I applied for the mentorship— because you were doing it."

Sydney's brow furrowed. "And the mentorship clearly says some weeks will be sessions spent with editors, touring the printing facility, or publishing house. You even get to spend time with illustrators and cover designers, so no," she snapped. "You don't get to spend all twelve sessions with me. I'm sorry I couldn't make it this week; I rang Michael to take it. I'm assuming you got enough information out of him to help you decide what you're doing in the future. You didn't need me to be there."

"What was so important that you fobbed me off?" His hands waved in front of him. "I came to see you afterwards and saw three men leave. Who were they?"

Sydney's frown deepened. "First of all, you had no need to come here." She stepped closer and returned his anger-filled stare. "Second, how the hell do you know where I live? And third, who those men are is none of your fucking business, Sean Ryan. None of this is any of your fucking business." She thrust her finger at him. "Do you understand me?"

"No, Sydney." His tone was low and threatening and he stepped right in front of her. He towered over her five eight frame and used it to his advantage. "You understand me. I signed up for the mentorship to be mentored by you. Every week for twelve weeks. And if you can't make it on Wednesday, then you damn well better call me and arrange for us to meet another day because that is the last time you stand me up." He lowered his head, so they were eye to eye. "Do you understand me, Sydney?" He could see the terror flee through her; her brain working to do something until she stared into his eyes.

"Fuck you, you little prick!"

His dinner plate sized hand slammed across her face, making her spin around in a full circle. He watched her legs twist around themselves, and she tumbled against the stair railing. She clung to it while her feet righted themselves, and her left hand clung to the left side of her burning face.

He grabbed her left arm, and then her right in the same vice grip. He pulled her against him and slammed his lips onto hers, trying to kiss her. His tongue tried forcing its way in, but she bit it and he tore back in screaming pain. "You bitch." He forced her back against the railing and kissed her again.

She managed to grab his crotch and squeeze, her heel went down his shin, and he stumbled back in pain, doubled over. She kicked and her boot landed right where her hand had just squeezed.

He fell to his knees, screaming in pain. "You slut. You fucking slut. You fuck my uncle, but you won't even let me kiss you." He bent so far over his head touched the floor.

Sydney panted for air, her hand on her lip. "How do you know that? How do you know that?" she screamed. "Are you stalking me, Sean? What the fuck would you know about that?"

With tears streaming down his face, he sat up and glared at her. "I saw you. When I came to see you. I saw those men leave and then started for your door. Then my uncle turned up and I saw him kiss you. I knew something was happening, so I walked up to your door and that's when I heard you. That's when I saw you fucking him on the floor," he yelled.

"That was you?" Sydney asked. "I thought I saw something. I was right. But when Connor checked outside he didn't see anyone."

"I hid from both of you. But I saw you. You fucked him, you whore. You're just a whore like my mother. He fucked her before he fucked you."

"What?" Sydney shook her head. "Wait…Connor was fucking your mother before me?" She stared at his defeated expression. "Who knows that? She was cheating on your father with his brother? Why? The story. Your adult story it is about them. You denied it."

"Of course I denied it." He stumbled to his feet. "Of course it's about my parents. My stupid fucking parents. My fucking father fucks prostitutes to get off on all of his kinks, and my mother leaves her work to spend more time with him and me but ends up fucking my uncle and getting drunk." He wiped his face on the arm of his sweater.

"How long have you known about you mother and Connor?" Sydney moved slightly on the balls of her feet.

"Months." Sean sneered. "They didn't know I was home when he came over and they fucked in the kitchen multiple times." His face distorted into cruelty. "They didn't even know I was there. They didn't even know I filmed the whole thing. When they finished in the kitchen, they moved to the bedroom and fucked in my father's bed. Three times." He held up his three middle fingers. "Three fucking times they fucked in my father's bed. Three. And I filmed it all." He stepped closer. "Sydney, have you fucked Connor on the kitchen table?"

"That's none of your business. I can call your grandfather to come and pick you up. We never need mention this ever again."

"Except we are going to mention it, Sydney. Because I love you and I want you to stop fucking my uncle."

Astounded, she said, "What?"

He stepped closer and grasped her arms, noting she didn't pull away. "I love you, Sydney, don't you know that? I've loved you from the day you came to our house and took the time to come to my bedroom and talk to me. To read my stories, to listen to my thoughts and dreams." One more step and there was barely an inch between them. "I've loved you since that day, Sydney, and my love has grown exponentially since, with every meeting, every week. I love you and I want to be with you. I want you to want and love me. And I want you to fuck me like you fuck my uncle." His expression hardened. So did his grip. "But you need to stop being a whore, Sydney. You need to stop being just like my mother and stop fucking my uncle because you're mine, Sydney. Not his. Mine."

Sydney hardened, and through gritted teeth she threatened, "Don't ever call me a whore or slut again, Sean Ryan. I am a grown woman who can and will fuck whoever I want and if that's your uncle, then so be it. I'm not your issue; your father and mother are the issue. And you will not take your shit out on me. I don't love you; I don't want you, and my time as your mentor is over. Do you understand? I am no longer your mentor. You can be mentored by someone else. I'll call CC and tell her, but this is it, you won't come here, you won't see me ever again and whether or not I see Connor, is none of your fucking business."

That enraged him, and he pushed her against the wall, trying to shove his tongue into her mouth and his hand between her legs. His size held her in that position while his other hand found its way under her top to her breast.

She screamed against his lips and twisted her head sideways. "Get off me." She grabbed one of his hands, yanked his thumb back, and spun him around so his arm was behind his back. She used her whole body to push him towards the door and ran.

"Sydney," he roared, running into the kitchen. "You whore, where are you? Where are—"

He was cut off with a frypan to his face and he stumbled, spun around, bent over, his hands to his face. "You bitch, you fucking bitch." He stood up but had no time to turn before everything went black.

"I deserved it. I absolutely did. I deserved every slap, punch, and smack and crack with the frypan that she gave me. I think I knew that then, and I certainly know that now. Afterward, I was so embarrassed and humiliated by it, I knew I could never look her in the eye again. I knew my mentorship was probably lost to me if she reported me. I knew I had fucked up royally and I had no one to blame but myself. At least, I know that now. Back then, I blamed Connor, because he'd fucked my mother and was now fucking Sydney. The woman I loved. I just couldn't." Sean's eyes flew open, and he gasped. "I hated Connor so fucking much and blamed him and my dad for everything. You know, I didn't even know if Dad knew they were fucking. And if he did, he clearly didn't care. Either way, I hated them both."

"But you hurt Sydney."

"*Then* I did. I know I took it out on her, and I shouldn't have. I was so bruised and sore, I needed to see a doctor and it wasn't my mother. She didn't care at lunch. I had to take myself after leaving Connor's apartment."

"From what Sydney had done?"

"And what Connor had done."

"The two of you fight?"

"If that's what you'd call it. More, it was him being an asshole and egging me into it." He grimaced at the memory.

He groaned and came to. "Ugh, where am I?" His hand went to his head that ached with a ferociousness he'd never before experienced.

"My place." Connor threw a bag of frozen peas on his head. "Use these for the swelling. Sydney got you good with the frypan." He slumped in his chair, cocked a leg over the arm, and swigged back his beer.

"Got me with what?" Sean slowly shifted into a sitting position, holding the bag to his head. "What frypan? What happened? Ugh."

"You don't remember?" He watched his nephew rest his elbows on his knees and his head in his hands. "Maybe the frypan did some damage. I think she said she hit you twice. What were you doing at her house anyway and why were you fighting?"

"I don't know." Sean groaned. "I don't..." Memories came flooding back in patches. He'd seen Connor turn up at Sydney's, saw them fucking, stormed around the city, came back and... "Um...why did I? And why am I here?" He looked around Connor's minimalistic apartment. He was on the couch, with Connor on one of the two chairs. He could see a simple dining table and chairs, and a bed through an archway. "Why am I here?"

"You two created such a disturbance the neighbours called the cops and I turned up just as Sydney was going to call me. She said you'd gotten into a fight and to get you out of there, back here to sort you out. So, here you are."

"I don't want to be here." Sean tried standing, but the pain took him back down. "God, what did she break— my skull? Jesus fucking Christ."

"Don't let Dad and Pop hear that kind of language,

and Declan will belt you for it."

"My father loves to talk big and follows through with just as rough crap. It's not like the rest of the family stopped him from abusing Mom or me." His fingers felt the back of his head. A lump had already formed and he knew it would only grow bigger. "Fucking hell."

"Yeah, kid. I know. We've turned a blind eye, but that's how we are. Now, tell me why you were at Sydney's."

"None of your fucking business. Got a beer? I need to dull the pain." He attempted to get to his feet, but he couldn't.

"There's no way in hell I'm giving you a beer because I do not want to deal with your old man or mine. But you already smell like you've had a few. Where'd you get it from?"

"Paid a guy to buy it for me."

"Dutch courage, huh?"

"Nope. Thought it would numb the pain." Sean rubbed the spot between his eyes. It always hurt when his brain was overloaded.

"It might've until now. I think, by the look of it, you bit, or Sydney bit, your lip which is gonna look like a right mess tomorrow. And God help you at Sunday lunch. Your mother will not like how you look."

Anger bolted through Sean. "But she liked you enough to fuck you and you liked it enough to keep fucking her, making her a whore, and now you're making Sydney a whore by fucking her. Did you tell Mom you were dumping her for Sydney? Huh?" He glared at his stunned uncle. "Like the rest of the family wouldn't find out. Like I wouldn't find out. Does Dad know? Huh? That his brother is fucking his wife?"

Connor threw his beer bottle at Sean's head, hearing a resounding crack.

"Ow." Sean picked it up and threw it back, but it bounced off Connor's temple. "You fucking asshole. You're fucking my mother and now you're fucking Sydney," he yelled and threw the bag of peas at his uncle.

"You little punk-ass piece of shit," Connor spat and in one step he was grabbing Sean in a head lock and uppercutting him in the gut.

Sean heaved to the side and threw Connor face down into the side table. The lamp fell and smashed, but the statue base of Themis, Greek Goddess of Law, remained intact and Sean smashed it onto Connor's head. "You fucking asshole. You made my mother a whore and now you're making Sydney one. Oof—" He went flying backward, Connor on top in a tackle, and was being punched on both sides of his face. As he shielded his head, he managed to get his hands up to Connor's face and dig his nails into his eyes and nose.

Connor growled and leaned out of Sean's grasp, only to have a punch land on his nuts. "Ow, you little—" He reached for a decorative object on his glass coffee table and went to smash it on Sean's head, but Sean beat him to it by smashing his laptop onto Connor's.

Connor fell backwards and Sean kicked his way out from underneath his uncle. He grabbed the object and slammed it onto Connor's head.

"You fucking asshole," Sean gasped and fell onto the couch.

Connor kicked himself away. "What the fuck is wrong with you?"

"What the fuck do you think?" Sean raged, watching his uncle on the floor. "You fucked my mother behind her husband's back. Your own brother. How could you?"

Connor leaned back against the sofa. "It just happened. Neither of us meant it to. She was lonely, he wasn't home, she's still very attractive and it just happened."

"And kept happening, and kept happening and kept fucking happening," Sean yelled. "It wasn't a one-off, Connor. It was multiple times over the last year."

Connor looked up at his nephew, blood dripping from both sides of his head, and a black eye already forming. "And you clearly know a lot more than we suspected. Your mom thought you didn't know."

"I've known the whole goddamn fucking time," Sean said through gritted teeth. "Since the first. Mom keeps a diary, you know. She wrote in it every time it happened. And then she wrote how your attention had turned from her and possibly to Sydney. She knew. I knew. I'm surprised the whole fucking family don't know."

Connor spied the peas on the floor and picked up the bag, slapping it on his head. He regulated his breathing until he was calm. "Look, Sean. I'm not proud of my affair with your mom because you're right. Your dad's my brother and I wouldn't want him doing that to me, so I shouldn't have done that to him. But when Sydney came along, my God, what a woman. It's hard to not be attracted to her. She's feisty and hot and amazing and yeah, it's been happening since the night of the lunch *when the family all met her, and she's as into it as I am. But it's nothing to do with you."*

"She's my mentor," he yelled. "The one person who encouraged me to write and agreed to help me and you had to go and fuck her and ruin everything the way you ruined my mom." He grabbed his laptop and shoved it into his bag then carefully got to his feet. "That's the problem with you Ryans, you ruin everything you touch. You ruined Mom and now you've ruined Sydney. Well done, Connor." He slowly walked to the door, but heard his uncle laugh.

"Oh, my God," Connor gasped. "You've got a crush on Sydney."

Sean's hand gripped the door handle. "No, Connor, I don't have a crush on Sydney." The handle twisted and the door opened. Sean looked over his shoulder. "Unlike you, who just wanted to use her and degrade her, I love her. And now you've ruined her, too." He stepped into the hall and closed the door on his uncle's stunned laughter. "Fuck you, Connor."

He managed to find his way down to the street and hail a cab, asking the driver to drop him off at the nearest emergency department. He spent the next three hours being x-rayed and scanned and found he had a concussion and a fractured skull. They let him spend the night and he went home the next morning.

"What did your parents say when you arrived home?"

"Nothing. Dad wasn't home and Mom was passed out drunk as always."

"Did they see you that day?"

"Mom did. Later that night when I emerged from my

bedroom for food. I'd slept most of the day away. Dad didn't come home at all, that I know of."

"And you turned up to Sunday lunch looking like that? Bruised and battered."

"Yep. Mom drove me to Sunday lunch because, again, Dad wasn't home."

"Did anyone comment?"

"Oh, yeah, they did."

"Whoa," Ethan said when he saw Sean's face. "What the hell happened to you?" He reached out to touch the lump on the side of his cousin's head, but Sean pulled away.

"Don't." He peered at him through his one good eye. "Everything hurts."

"Get into a fight?" Ethan saw his father walk into the kitchen and noticed the bruising on his face. "Did you get into a fight?"

Connor and Sean glanced at each other. "Yeah, I did. Looks like Seany did, too."

"I hate that name," Sean muttered through gritted teeth.

"You got involved with what, a perp?" Ethan pointed to his father. "And Sean got involved with who?" He glanced between them.

"A guy," Sean said. "Tried to beat me up, but I fought back."

"Are you all right, Sean?" Kieran handed him the stack of plates. "Have you seen a doctor?"

"Took myself off to one," Sean said. "I'll be okay." He carried the pile of plates into the dining room and set them on the table. He took half and laid them out down

the right side, and then finished the rest off down the left side. His cousins carried in cutlery, napkins and glasses.

"That's quite an eye, Sean. Are you okay?" Douglas took his seat at the table.

Sean sat in his spot to the right of him. "I'm all right. I survived."

Lunch was served and Sean stayed quiet, not that anyone usually let him speak. They always talked over him, talked down to him, or just cut him off, or told him to stop talking.

"Sean, you've been pretty quiet all day. You okay?" Douglas asked.

"Yeah." Sean played with his food.

"Is it the bruises? Did you see a doctor?" Douglas looked at Laura, but she was glazed over with alcohol.

"I did. I have a slight concussion and a fractured skull, but I'll be fine."

Cormac stopped eating and stared at his grandson. "Is it serious? Are you okay? Do you need to see a specialist?" Cormac asked.

Sean sighed and leaned his chin on his hand. "No. I'm fine, according to the doctor."

"Then it must be something else," Douglas prompted. "School? Exams? Other kids?"

"My writing mentorship," Sean finally said, moving food back and forth on his plate.

"What about it?" Emerson asked. "Is it going well?"

"It was," Sean mumbled. "I had my fourth session this week, but Sydney didn't turn up."

Douglas frowned. "Why? She was all into it."

Sean shrugged a shoulder. "Something happened I

guess. But it's over."

Cormac and Emerson exchanged glances. "What do you mean it's over?"

"I don't know. I guess I'm not doing it anymore."

"But why? After your grandfather and I persuaded her to do it," Douglas said, looking to his son at the other end of the table.

Another shrug. "She cancelled it. I don't know why, but I guess I'm not doing it anymore."

"Probably because your stories are crap after all." Sierra smirked.

"Stop it," Ethan told her. "Sydney, her editors, and her publishing house all said Sean's stories were good, and she put you in your place over it. Just stop, it's pathetic, Sierra."

Sierra turned bright red and stared down at her food.

Sean gave Ethan a grateful smile and scored a grin in return.

"Well, in that case, I think we need to find out what's going on," Douglas said.

"And find out why Connor's face is so beat up. Connor, care to share?" Cormac sliced through his roast beef and glanced at his son. "Between you and Sean, it's like the set of The Walking Dead."

Connor chuckled and swigged his beer. "And you should see the other guy. I'd say I came out the better of the two." When no one was looking, he glanced Sean's way and saw daggers coming back at him. "How'd the other guy fare with you, Seany?"

"Asshole got what was coming to him," Sean muttered under his breath, and then choked as Declan's

hand flew up the back of his head.

"I heard that, you little asswipe," he said.

"And yet you just called me an asswipe," Sean yelled back. "How's that any different?"

"It isn't," Douglas said. "Declan, you've been warned about hitting Sean."

Declan sneered at this grandfather. "And what are you gonna do about it, old man?"

"I'll fire you," Cormac said, watching his son turn to him. "Care to apologise?"

"Don't bother, Grandpa, my asswipe of a father doesn't care if he beats his own wife and son who's got a fractured skull and a concussion." Sean managed to get out of his chair before Declan's hand found him. "I'm going. I don't want to be here." He ran out of the dining room, grabbed his bag from the hall, and slammed the front door behind him.

"And all of that led to your family on Sydney's doorstep?" Levinworth flipped through his notes. "Kieran and Sandy, then Alec and Connor, and finally Declan and your grandfather."

"But Sydney told Kieran and Sandy she hadn't cancelled, which you knew. Then Alec assumed something worse, then Connor was abusive too, which is surprising, since they were having an affair. And finally, Dad accused her of raping me."

Levinworth looked at Sean. "How the hell did he get to that?"

Sean stood up. "Walter, my father's a discussion for another day, not today. But I will say this now, I wish he were dead." He picked up his bag and silently left the room.

Chapter 10

After a week of non-stop writing and contemplation, Sean was back in his therapist's office and standing at the window.

"I want to continue on from last week. We never finished that discussion and I think we need to home in on some specifics."

Sean sighed. "Such as?"

"Such as you planting the cameras wasn't a recent thing. It was implied, by the evidence collected, that you'd only done it the last few months."

"Nope."

"When did you do it?"

"I told you last week. Once I found out she was screwing Connor."

"And how'd you get in?"

"How do you think, Walter?"

"I need you to explain it."

Sean grumbled under his breath, inhaled and said, "I come from a long line of law enforcement. How do you think? I learned to get into a house without a key, have keys made from the locks, or get a master key. And how to install teeny tiny cameras no one would suspect."

"You wrote about it in *Creeper.* Is that how you did it? Are your books autobiographical, Sean? Will I find all of the answers in your books?"

Sean shrugged a shoulder. "Maybe, Walter. Maybe."

"Why did you do it?"

"Why did I do any of it? Didn't we get to the bottom of that four years ago?"

"Certainly not the death threats you sent her."

A smirk slid across Sean's lips before he looked over his shoulder. "Not death threats."

"*Die, Bitch, Die!* isn't a death threat?"

"No. I wanted to see if I could do it. My English teacher gave us scenarios for stories, and I picked an obsessed fan sending his obsession fan mail. He was demented, ill, whatever you want to call it. And I'd seen a few movies and read a few books with the same kind of thing. Since the family's in law enforcement, I, possibly stupidly, decided to try it for real as an experiment and see how far it got me. I made it out of letters from magazine cut-outs, three simple words. I wore gloves, a face mask, hair net. I covered everything in order to not leave DNA behind, and I sent it off."

Intrigued, after not having heard this last time, Levinworth asked, "And then?"

"And then..." Sean turned from the window and faced him. "Nothing happened with the letter, and I wrote my story and essay on how I went about it, and I got a good grade for it. My teacher told me I had a dark imagination but could understand why considering who my family is. Said I could probably write crime thrillers someday. Oh…" He spread his hands in front of him and grinned. "And here I am writing crime thrillers and making a tonne of money from it."

Levinworth studied Sean's face as he walked over to his favourite painting. "Was that the only one?"

"For then. I sent one, or two, later to see what would happen."

"Do you think that led to your obsession with Sydney? Why did you pick her?"

"Because my family read her books. That made it all so easy. She was the number one thriller writer and my family of cops and lawyers read them. I certainly wasn't obsessed. I just picked her because I knew her, and Mom had a connection to her."

"When did you become obsessed?"

"I wasn't obsessed, Walter. Once I met her, I fell head over heels in love."

"*All I knew was I wanted her, I wanted to fuck her, love her, and possess her. But what the hell does a seventeen-year-old know about that. About any of that.*"

Sean's lips twitched. "You're quoting my own book at me? How gauche, Walter."

"That's an obsession, Sean. That whole passage at the beginning of *Illicit Things* shows a crush that became more. It became an obsession, and considering what you did to Sydney, you were, and still are, obsessed with her."

Sean rolled his eyes and sighed. "Not the way I see it."

"And how do you see it?"

"You read *Illicit Things*. You know."

"But I need you to tell me."

Sean gazed wearily up at the wave painting. "I had no

emotion for Sydney when I picked her to receive those letters. It was an experiment. I read some of her books and loved the way she wrote and wished I could write like that. And then I found out her best friend was Emerson Lake, and the name sounded familiar. I had seen it in Mom's college book, so I googled her and found she used to go to the same college as my mom and put two and two together and then harassed Mom into inviting them both over. Purely for the benefit of meeting Sydney in the flesh and maybe getting some help with my writing. I also wanted to see if the letter was brought up. But it wasn't. Once she encouraged me, I saw her in a whole new light and manoeuvred things so that Mom was pushed into inviting them to family lunch, *by* the family. Grandpa and Pop were huge fans, so they told Mom to invite them."

His gaze drifted away from the painting and he wandered to the next wall full of artefacts. "When Sydney was at Sunday lunch, and she stood up for me, with Dad and Sierra, and called out Mom, I just… knew…" He shook his head. "Knew I needed her in my life, not just for the encouragement and support, but because she actually saw me. She didn't look through me, she looked *at* me. And that set something off in me and maybe my crush happened, maybe it started there…no." He rubbed the bridge of his nose. "My crush did start there. But after Connor, I decided to put the cameras in. It was to not only check on what they were doing, but almost like part two of the English experiment. I had sent the letters, now let's see if I could make a key from a lock and set up cameras. But in my head it was also research. I was watching the number one thriller writer in the world do her thing and I wanted to learn about it. But I also learned about my fucking uncle." He moved on and stared at a statue. "Isn't ivory illegal in this country?"

Levinworth startled at the change of subject. "Is it? We're not talking about me. You set the cameras up after the fourth mentorship session."

"Yeah. And I saw how Connor had gone from fucking my mother to fucking Sydney."

"When did you realise you'd, in your words, fallen in love with Sydney?"

Sean huffed. "It was clearly a very short time span, Walter. Around the time of the fourth mentorship because that's when I took my anger out on her."

"Were you obsessed then?"

"No. I was madly in love and didn't want her making the same mistake my mother did. I wanted her for myself. I didn't want Connor to have her."

"Had Sydney made any inappropriate moves? Touched you, flirted with you?"

"In my head at the time, she had. But I know she didn't. She kept it incredibly professional."

"And when you were hurting her?"

Sean flashed back to Sydney's brownstone and the fight and sadness washed over him. "I didn't mean to. I just wanted her to see sense and leave Connor alone. I loved her, me, I was the one for her. But she looked so damn scared one minute, and normal the next, I thought I was getting through to her. Convincing her that Connor was no good because he'd slept with my mother behind my father's back, and that I could be the one. But

I was wrong." He walked over to the wall beside the door and stared at the paintings. "I gotta give it to her, she fought. Cracked me over the head with a frypan. But when I kissed her…"

The silence lasted a few moments, so Levinworth turned around. "When you kissed her?"

Sean faltered. "I knew my feelings were real. I knew I loved her. Knew that what I felt was love. The feeling that radiated from her lips to mine and through my entire body. Damn, I knew there would never be any other woman. I knew without a doubt and beyond all reason that I loved her, and she was the one for me."

"But she wasn't."

"Not then, no."

"Not now."

"Things have changed."

"In what way?"

"In every way."

"Why did your family go around to see her? You mentioned at lunch she'd cancelled the mentorship. Had she?"

"No. But I didn't know that. She'd said something when I was at her place. I must have taken it to mean it was cancelled."

"And did you know that Kieran and his girlfriend had gone around to see her?"

He shook his head. "No, not then."

"And Alec?"

"No. Nor Connor. I knew he went around after our fight. Sydney didn't look happy, but she let him in, and he stayed. It was after she'd talked to Alec and he must've talked to Connor, and then Connor turned up and slapped her. I sure as hell didn't know he'd done that."

"How did you feel about him slapping her?"

"I wanted to kill him."

"How do you feel about him now?"

"I still want to kill him."

"And your father. What happened to make him believe she'd raped you? You were seventeen. Of legal age to have sex. What did you say to him?"

Sean glanced at his watch. Five more minutes. "I don't think I said much of anything other than it was cancelled. Since Dad wasn't home much, he didn't know much, but Mom did ask me about it the day after. Why wasn't the mentorship still happening? Which was surprising because she didn't want me to do it in the first place. But, I think after Alec landed on Sydney's doorstep, and he accused her of things, he relayed that to Connor and Dad."

"Did you tell your parents Sydney had groomed you? Molested or raped you?"

Sean huffed. "God no, why would I do that?"

"What did you say? Did you tell them no?"

"I did. But I didn't say much of anything else."

"So, you *allowed* them to think the worst?"

"How many times do I have to say they didn't care? Mom certainly didn't, and I think Alec told Dad something he shouldn't have. I don't know what. Maybe I should ask him the next time he pays me a visit. But I sure as hell didn't know or even think Dad was going to go around to her house screaming about her being a paedophile. When I found out I was *so* embarrassed. I'd never once said we'd slept together or had sex. I don't even know what Sydney told my dad, or Connor, or Alec."

"When did the truth come out?"

"Oh, I think that's for the next session, Walter. It's time to go." Sean picked up his bag. "I did have an interesting conversation with Grandpa, though, that Sunday night. But I'll save that for next week. We're already two months into this, yet there's so much more to tell. Same time next week." He left without a backward glance.

Levinworth slowly breathed in and let it out. *Sean's obsession is still very real, but now he thinks that because things have changed, that what? He and Sydney can have a relationship? She's back in Australia, and she ratted him out to his grandfather. That's not the actions of a woman in love, but then, she had been taken in like everyone else. No one knew who Bryan Jamison was. The clothing, the disguise—everyone thought he was in his forties. Did Sydney even know? Know that he was Sean underneath? Know that she'd slept with a twenty-one-year-old boy?*

Levinworth scratched his chin in thought. *There is so much more to tell, Sean had said. What does that mean? We haven't even come close to discussing his break and enter attempt yet, or his detention. Will he reveal all by the end of our sessions?* He sighed and picked up his pen. He had a lot of notes to make.

*****

The old man was dropped off on a side street, in the pitch black of the night. He paid his cab fare, and walked down the road, stopping in an alley by an apartment building. "Are you here?"

The woman stepped forward. "Ready and waiting."

He took in her appearance. She had a white Marilyn Monroe bob, red lips, a black trench coat, and bright red stilettoes. "Good. You know what to do."

"Will you be here?" She kept her hands in her coat pockets to warm them.

"I will when you're done. Ready and waiting."

"And she's all set?"

"She is."

"Then it's my turn." She kissed him on the cheek, made her way inside the building and up to the fifth floor, knocking on the door to apartment twenty.

The door flung open. "Yeah?" He eyed the woman standing in front of him. "Who're you?"

She untied her trench and pulled it open for him to see her red lace nippleless bra, crotchless matching knickers, and a garter belt and stockings. "Declan. Care for some fun? I miss you."

He frowned, trying to remember if he knew her, and why she'd be on his doorstep in lace underwear. He scratched his nuts through his blue boxers. "Do I know you?"

She placed one hand on his chest and moved him back, closing the door with her other hand. "Extremely intimately," was all she said as the coat fell to the floor, and she grabbed his wife beater. "Let's fuck."

Five hours later, the woman emerged from the

bedroom and let another woman in. She fed her more drugs on top of the ones she'd already consumed and led her into the bedroom and tied her up. "You know what to do?" The woman nodded and sniffed. "Good. Wait until I'm gone and then go to town." She walked out of the room and closed the front door behind her. When she arrived back in the alley, she met with the old man. "All set?"

"All set," he said and took her arm as they walked off down the alley and disappeared into the darkness.

*****

Sean opened the door to his grandfather's house. "Grandpa, you home? What's so important that I had to come all the way here?" He closed the door, dropped his bag on the chair just inside the living room, and found his grandfather in the sun room at the back of the house. "Hey, what's so important? I could have come to 1PP." He saw Emerson in the kitchen doorway. "Hey, Emerson." He noticed the grim expression. "Why am I here so early? It's like eight. What's going on?"

Cormac turned to him. "Sean." He breathed in and deflated on the exhale. "I have something to tell you." Grasping his grandson by his arms, he stared him straight in the eye. "It's your father. Something happened last night."

Sean froze, his heart thundered, and he remembered to keep breathing. "What happened last night?"

Cormac took another deep breath. "At three oh two this morning, officers responded to a call about a screaming woman and kicked down the door. They found a well-known prostitute tied to the bed, high as hell, and your father forcing her to pleasure him. He thought her pimp had come for him and aimed his gun at the officers who fired three times into his chest. The bullets barely put your father down because he was so high on drugs. They handcuffed him, put some shorts on him, and hauled him outside to the waiting paramedics who took him to the hospital." He took another breath. "Unfortunately…"

"He didn't survive," Sean finished. "Did he?"

Cormac sadly shook his head. "No, Sean. I'm so sorry."

Sean breathed and stepped out of his grandfather's grasp. "He's dead? He's really dead?" His brows lowered in thought.

"Yes, Sean. He's really dead."

Sean moved over to the open French doors and stared out at the river. "What happens…now?"

"I take care of the funeral," Cormac said. "But there'll be an autopsy and investigation."

"A police funeral? Considering how he died?"

"I know." Cormac turned to the front door. "The others are here." He walked into the living room as they piled in.

"Why in God's name are we here so early?" Connor complained. He saw Emerson at the dining table and Sean in the sun room. "What's going on?"

"Yeah? Why did I have to get out of bed so early when I've got the day off?" Ethan added. "I just wanted to snuggle up and sleep."

"Is it true?" Alec came in after Kieran. "About Declan?"

Cormac addressed his remaining family. "Yes."

"What about Declan?" Connor looked from Alec to his father. "What's he done now?"

"Got himself killed," Alec said quietly, his gaze moving from his father to Sean.

"What?" the remaining Ryans said at the same time.

"How? What? When?" Connor asked.

"This morning," Cormac replied. "His apartment was raided, and he was shot when he brandished his weapon at the officers. He was taken to hospital but died on the table. I've been there all night." He looked at Sean who walked out onto the patio. "I told Sean just before you got here, He's processing it."

"Fuck. Poor kid." Connor shoved his hands into his jeans pockets and stared after his nephew. "His mom, now his dad. Fuck, Declan. How can you be so stupid?" He sat down on the couch and put his head in his hands. "How could you be so stupid?"

"What do we do?" Alec asked. "I heard there was a woman and drugs were involved."

"What?" Connor shot back up. "What woman? What drugs?"

"What was Declan involved with?" Kieran asked. "Are we going to have to cover up for him?"

"No." Cormac put his hand up. "No. We will not be covering up anything for Declan. He got himself into this mess, and the consequences will need to be dealt with. I am hoping it can be kept within 1PP and not blasted all over the news. But right now, I need a drink." He sighed and lumbered over to the drinks cabinet while everyone else stood around in shock.

"Dad," Ethan muttered, on the verge of tears. The

thought of losing his father the same way was freaking him out.

"Hey, kiddo." Connor grabbed his son in a ferocious bear hug. "It's okay, it's okay. You still got me and your mom. It's okay."

Ethan's tears poured down his cheeks and he gazed at the forlorn figure of his only living cousin out in the backyard. "But Sean hasn't."

"No kiddo, and that sucks, believe me. I feel so sorry for him right now." Connor held his son at arm's length. "Why don't you go and see Sean. He needs us now more than ever and you're the only cousin he's got left and you were always his hero. Go and see him." He watched his son nod and walk into the sun room, pause at the French doors, wipe his face, and walk over to his cousin.

"Tell us the truth," Connor demanded. "What the fuck was Declan up to?"

"His nose in coke and his dick in a hooker," Alec replied.

Connor's head spun to his older brother. "What! How could he be so fucking stupid as to get caught?"

"Sean?" Ethan slowly approached him. After the lunch at Sean's house, he hadn't spoken to him, not even at the family lunches Sean had attended since.

Sean's head turned at his name. "Ethan."

"I am so sorry." He stopped beside his cousin. "I don't know what to say other than that. I don't know what I'd do if I lost my dad." He wiped his face free of fresh tears. "I can't imagine what's going through your mind. I've certainly imagined my dad dying and what I'd go through, but actually going through it is different. I'm so sorry. We've already lost Pop, and Brandon and Sierra last month, and now Uncle Declan."

Sean's hands clenched in his pants pockets. "Do you really care, Ethan? Do you really care for me and what I'm feeling, or is it about you?" His gaze stayed steadfast on the river. "Is this all about how *you'd* feel losing your dad or is it that you're so very much a Ryan just like your dad, my dad, Alec and Kieran, Brandon and Sierra. Because, quite frankly, I don't care to be a Ryan anymore. So, what is it?" He turned and directly faced his cousin. "Are you sorry for me, or yourself?"

Ethan's head shook slightly. "You, of course. I can't imagine what you're going through."

"No one can," Sean said. "Except…" He glanced at the house. "Grandpa, or maybe Alec, of all people."

"You still don't get along with him?"

"No, and I don't plan on it, either."

"Don't see eye to eye?"

"On a lot of things, but then you know full well I don't see eye to eye with a lot of my family." Sean turned back to the river.

"*We* used to," Ethan said. "Once."

"And you were my hero. *Once*," Sean replied.

Ethan's lips curled into a small smile. "When did that change? When did any of it change?"

"When you started fucking Sydney." Sean heard the sharp intake of breath. "I was here a few weeks ago and remembered the time when I was six and had gone into the water because I wanted to see how deep it was. You pulled me out and I called you my hero. Four years later, you beat up Brandon because he was being an asshole to me. You were still my hero. The one I looked up to, the one I wanted to follow around. The only one I looked forward to seeing; the only one who actually didn't have a problem being with me and teaching me and playing with me."

"So, what happened? It can't just be about Sydney."

"Maybe not." Sean was thoughtful. "As I grew up you entered the academy, became busy, didn't spend the weekend anymore, just Sundays. And when you turned twenty-one you stayed away more often, and I missed you. I missed my hero." He looked at his cousin. "And then you became your father."

Ethan shrugged. "Is that such a bad thing?"

"When our fathers are who they are." Sean glanced at the house. "Yeah. Declan fucking Ryan had to be *my* father. Connor, *your* dad, is only reasonably better. But you've definitely turned out just like him. When you started hanging around with him you turned out the same. Drinking, women." He paused. "Sydney."

"I don't get the big deal about Sydney," Ethan said. "It didn't work out with Dad, and when I met her again a year later," another shrug, "we clicked, and it happened. She's an incredible woman."

"Sure it only clicked a year later?" Sean asked. "I definitely remember the attraction Connor *and* you had to her that first lunch she was here. And you certainly noticed your dad's attention to her."

"Yeah, I did." Ethan glanced away as memories flooded back. "It's not hard to be attracted to her, she's a beautiful woman."

"That she is. But she was my mentor and Connor fucked it up."

"That was you," Ethan snapped. "For whatever reason."

"He slapped her."

"So did you," Ethan argued. "That came out a couple of months ago at your house, just like you told Sierra to go fuck herself and then threatened me with what you supposedly know. Know what, Sean? What is it you *think* you know?"

"I know you and Sydney fucked." Sean took a step towards his cousin. "I know you did exactly what your old man did, but then she dumped you in January because this family is too damn complicated. You had the week off between Christmas and New Year and stayed at her house. You even got to try out her bed *and* the sex room *just* like Connor."

Scared, Ethan asked, "How do you know that? Did Sydney tell you?"

"Sydney told me nothing, but I know, Ethan. And I know *exactly* what you did in Sydney's name."

"Boys, come in here," Cormac called.

Sean gave Ethan a withering glance and walked towards the house.

Ethan swallowed his fear, but whispered, "He can't know, he can't know," before following his cousin into the house. "What. Ah, what's going on?"

"Because it's Tuesday, we've asked the coroner to hurry the examination along so we can bury Declan this weekend. I've decided he will receive full honours due to his time in the military and his years on the force and medals earned."

"Wasn't a decent human being, though," Sean said.

Cormac sighed and shook his head. "No, Sean. To

you and your mom he wasn't, and I'm sorry for that. But as a cop, and military vet, he will receive full honours."

"Is there a wake?" Ethan asked.

"It will be here after the funeral for family and close friends."

"Don't think he had any." Sean pulled out his grandfather's dining chair and sat down, noting Emerson was still sitting at the other end, a worried look on her face, hands clasped in front of her.

"And whoever else can celebrate him at McFinty's. I'll set up a tab and drinks will be on me," Cormac said.

"Why did Dad have an apartment when he owns a house? Who's running the house?" Sean frowned. "What happens to that now?"

Cormac gazed at his grandson. "That's something I'll help you with after the funeral. I don't know if he had a will, but the estate now passes on to you, Sean."

Sean gazed back and remained silent but gave his grandfather a nod.

"All right. I will have my team organise the funeral, Emerson has offered to organise the wake, and then, I think we should all look into therapy to try and deal with losing three members of this family within four weeks. Connor, if you and Ethan want to file for leave, feel free, I'll be handing the reins over to the deputy commissioner for the rest of the week. And now I need another drink."

Sean watched everyone. Kieran sat by the front window looking out, Alec was already on his phone, his grandfather was knocking back another drink, and Connor was hugging Ethan like a protective father should.

Mine didn't. Mine should have done that, but he didn't. Sean's brows furrowed and a sadness at never having a loving relationship with his father washed over him. His gaze moved to Emerson and saw her frowning at Cormac. He wondered what she was thinking and that in turn made him wonder what Sydney was doing.

*****

The funeral of Detective Declan Campbell Ryan was held on the Saturday after his death.

The family, those left, gathered round, along with close friends and co-workers. Cormac and Sean stood at the end of the grave watching the coffin be lowered into its final resting place.

Cormac had a pained look upon his grieving face.

Sean had a deeply furrowed brow. He didn't know *how* to feel, didn't know what he *did* feel. He just stared down at his father's coffin until Cormac threw a handful of dirt down on it. He did the same and moved over to his mother's grave, watching with one hand resting lightly on her headstone.

The rest of the family and attendees slowly walked away and left, but Sean stayed by his mother's grave watching his father's being filled up. It took two hours, and the air grew chilled in early afternoon, but he stayed.

"Mom." He sighed. "Your husband is now beside you. May you both rest in eternal hell because you now have *him* to put up with for it."

The gravediggers pushed down the last of the soil and flattened out the surface. One long rectangle of dirt was what currently remained of Declan Ryan.

"Sean."

He breathed in and turned his head towards his grandfather. "I thought you'd left."

"No. You needed to stay; so did I. My son, your father. Emerson went back with Kieran and Sandy. They'll be helping with the wake."

"And how long will that go for?"

"Until about five or six this evening." Cormac stood with his hands in his coat pockets, staring down at his son's grave. "The headstone will be erected on Monday."

Sean snorted. "Please don't tell me you had them put loving father and husband on it. I'll die laughing."

"That's not very respectful, Sean."

"He wasn't a respectful guy."

Cormac sighed. "I know. No, I just had son, brother, husband, and father put on it. Basic and simple considering the situation." He glanced around the cemetery, saw a couple of photographers off in the distance, and frowned. "We're being watched. We should go."

Sean stepped back, stared down at his mother's headstone and said, "Bye Mom," before following Cormac to Douglas's grave.

"Pop, you and Mom take care of him. He needs it." Cormac touched the stone for a few moments before pausing at his deceased wife's grave. "Alice, our son is on his way to you, if he's not there already. He's going to need lots of help." He flashed a small smile. "I love you, and Emerson makes me very happy." He walked on.

Sean touched his grandmother's grave. "Grandma, I

wish you had've been here longer; maybe you could've done something. But then again…" His fingers trailed off the headstone and he slowly followed his grandfather through the winding lanes of the cemetery to his waiting car, hands in pockets, just like him. Sombre expression, just like him.

They arrived home fifteen minutes later and found everyone still there.

Emerson rushed over and took his jacket. "I was starting to worry. Sean, I'll take your coat and pop it up in our room." She nodded to him and hurried up the stairs.

They walked into a quiet room.

"Don't stop on my account," Cormac told them as he walked through. "If there's food, eat, if there's fluid, drink, if you a have a story, tell it."

"Wouldn't want to hear mine," Sean muttered under his breath and perused the dining table laden with food. He wasn't hungry, but he picked up a quarter cut sandwich triangle and bit into it. The creamy filling was his favourite and one of Emerson's best recipes, and it worked well with the crisp cucumber and tomato. He grabbed another quarter and walked over to the doors of the sun room. They were open, allowing the mid-spring air into the house trying to cleanse it of dead spirits. He finished off his food and heard his name. Turning around, he found his three uncles and cousin. "Oh, no, I am *not* in the mood."

"Sean," Kieran said. "We just want you to know we're here for you." He got a laugh in return. "Seriously, we are."

"And where the hell were any of you when your asshole brother beat his wife and son?" Sean looked at Connor. "And we all know what you did." He crossed his arms. "There is no way in hell I need the three of you looking after me, especially you two." He waved a finger between Alec and Connor. "Kieran's done nothing wrong to me personally, and I like him, but you two can stay the hell away from me."

"Sean." Alec's voice was smooth. "We understand you're an adult and don't need help, financial or physical—"

"I did when my father beat me." Sean stared him down and saw him blanch.

"And we're very sorry we didn't do anything," Kieran said. "Especially when we could have."

"But you didn't," Sean reminded him and looked back at Alec. "I don't need anything from any of you, uncles or not. I'm just fine now that my asshole father is dead, and I can breathe a sigh of relief that the world, and especially the prostitutes of New York, don't have to deal with him ever again. So please, save your sympathies and you," he turned to Ethan, "don't bother."

"But we're the only cousins left," Ethan said. "Until our new one comes along."

"And I don't need you either," Sean told him and walked out the door towards the river.

Emerson set another platter of food on the table and walked over to them. "He's trying to comprehend what's happened; not everyone deals with death in the same way."

"No." Kieran looked at his brothers. "Guess not." He

sighed and walked off to find Sandy. They had finally told the family at Sunday lunch before Declan died. He'd been happy for them, said Kieran would make a better father than he had, and wished them well.

"Come on, kid." Connor grabbed his son by the shoulder. "Let's mingle and see if anyone else hated your uncle as much as his son did."

Alec heard them walk away, but his gaze was on Sean who stood by the river. He wandered over to him, and stood just behind. "Sean."

Sean breathed in and sighed in anger at having his silence shattered. "Alec."

"I don't know what's going on in this world that one family could lose so many members in four weeks, but we meant what we said. We will be here for you."

"I don't need you, Alec, nor Connor, nor Ethan."

"Right now, kid, you need me to keep you out of jail and on home detention."

"Ha!" Sean turned to him. "Fuck off. You have no say in any of that. I've looked over the paperwork, I've had lawyers look over that paperwork and there is nothing in that document that says you have any right to put me in jail. You have no reason to. Hell, I don't even have to wear my ankle monitor because the paperwork doesn't say I have to…or did you not realise that?"

Alec looked down at Sean's foot.

"Go ahead, have a look," Sean goaded.

Alec's eyes narrowed. "What kind of games are you playing, kid? You might think you're smart, coming first in your class and graduating in two years instead of three—"

"Which I did," Sean reminded him. "*Ahead* of you and Kieran."

"But that doesn't mean I'm going to let you get away with it." Alec stepped closer. "Your father may be dead, but we still have our weekly visits, and you will not be getting out of those." His blue eyes glared into Sean's. "I know what you did, Sean."

Sean's eyes narrowed at the threat. "And I know what my father did, what Connor's done, what Ethan's doing, and most importantly, what *you've* done, Alec. You've forgotten what *I told you*. I have so much dirt on you I could bury you and don't think I can't."

Alec flinched. "Yeah, right kid. You got dirt on me? That's a good one. You're the criminal who could go to jail."

"Been there, done that," Sean said. "But you'd go away for life." He leaned closer. "If you last that long. Look out, Alec, your career's about to implode." Sean made an explosion sound, his hands moving from fists to wide open, his fingers wiggling as if a bomb had gone off. He saw Alec's fear and laughed, walking off for the house and more sustenance. His conversations had given him an appetite and he needed more of Emerson's delicious food.

He found roast beef sandwich triangles and more of the cucumber and tomatoes. He made a plate, grabbed a beer, and went into the kitchen for some peace and quiet but he found Ethan talking to Emerson. "Hey, Emerson, amazing food, not that my dad deserved it." He sat at the kitchen table and stuffed a sandwich triangle into his mouth.

"Thank you, Sean. It was simple enough. Have you tried the desserts?"

Sean swallowed, and managed, "Not yet, but that will be my next stop. I'm starving all of a sudden."

Emerson set a plate down in front of him. "I kept one of everything for you. If you need more sandwiches, I'll make them fresh."

"Mmm, no. This'll do, thank you so much." He shoved another quarter into his mouth.

"How come he gets special treatment?" Ethan asked from his spot against the island bench.

"Because it's his father who died." Emerson cleaned up as she moved around. "When your father dies, I'll make the same for you."

Sean choked on his sandwich and his eyes grew wide. "Whoa."

"Oh, my God." Emerson covered her mouth and saw Ethan's grief-stricken face. "I didn't mean it that way, I'm so sorry." She watched him rush off into the living room.

"Wow." Sean drank some beer. "That was…beautiful."

"Oh, Sean. I wasn't thinking. I shouldn't have said it." She set down the cleaning cloth and washed her hands. "It's true, though, I'll do the same for him when Connor dies."

"With the way the Ryan boys are going that might not be long," Sean muttered and shoved his last sandwich into his mouth. "Mmm, yum."

Emerson watched his appreciation. "Glad you enjoy my food, a growing boy needs it."

"I'll say this. You treat me better than Mom ever did."

"Did you spend time with her today? I saw you walk

over to her grave."

He nodded and moved his mini desserts around the plate. "I stood there for what, two hours while they covered Dad up, and then Grandpa came over. I didn't know he'd stayed, and we stayed a little longer. Visited Pop and Grandma's graves. He told her you made him very happy."

Emerson gave a small smile. "I'm glad. He makes me happy, too."

"Does he?" Sean picked up a small lemon meringue. "Really?"

Her smile broadened. "He does." But then the smile faded. "Did." She realised what she'd said and covered it over. "I mean, of course he does, it's just been so long now. Over four years, and we're still not married and now we've lost Brandon, Sierra and Declan and I don't know if we'll ever get married. He wanted to wait until he was seventy-five and the day he retired. But with everything, I just—"

"Don't think it will happen, and if you push it to happen sooner, he may say no."

She nodded, swallowing the lump in her throat. "It's been a long time. It needs to happen, otherwise it never will."

"Yeah, I know that feeling." He saw a few people leave and sighed. "It's been a long day and it's," he glanced at the clock on the wall, "nearly six. I'm going to go."

"You sure?" Emerson reached over and squeezed his hand. "Would you like me to make you a container?"

"No, I'll be fine. Are you having lunch tomorrow?"

"Probably. But I don't know if the others will come.

We'll have plenty of leftovers."

Sean shoved a small mud cake into his mouth and rose, swigged his beer back, kissed Emerson on the cheek as he handed his dishes over, and ran upstairs for his coat. He caught his grandfather on the way down. "I'm done. I won't be around tomorrow."

"That's okay. I don't expect you for a while."

Sean dashed for the door, but turned back and hugged his grandfather. "I love you, Grandpa."

"I love you too, Sean."

Sean went home and stood staring at his wall of Sydney for a few minutes to calm his thoughts. His gaze zeroed in on the page of images of his family in the middle of the wall. He grabbed a red Sharpie and marked his father off with a cross.

When he was satisfied, he closed the wall, changed his clothes, and put on his Bryan wig and glasses. He took a moment to pop off his ankle bracelet and glitch the building's Wi-Fi and surveillance system and then caught a cab to the Upper East Side.

He hurried down the street to the brownstone and stared up at it, remembering all the times he had been there before climbing the stairs.

After opening the vestibule and front doors, and locking them against the world, he dropped his bag and coat by the door. The scent of hot roast beef permeated the air and his stomach growled as he walked into the living room to warm himself by the crackling fire in the grate.

He breathed in relief.

He was home.

Chapter 11

"Tell me how you feel."

"How do you think I feel, Walter?"

"A couple of weeks ago you said you wished your father was dead."

"That I did, and now he is."

"Tell me how you feel."

Sean's hand curled into fists in his pockets as he stood at the window. "Angry. Relieved…"

"Why?"

"Why do you think? You know what he did. I told you when I was seventeen."

"But he was still alive then. Now you're twenty-one and he's dead."

"Good riddance to bad rubbish and fucked up rubbish at that." Sean sighed. "I don't want to talk about him. Let's go back to where we left off and maybe then it will make more sense."

"Okay. Where did we leave off?"

"About my mentorship and the cancellation of it. All of my relatives turning up on Sydney's doorstep because of it. No wait…" He thought back. "Ethan didn't turn up on her doorstep. That didn't happen for another year when he started fucking her. But that's for another time. Right, the fourth mentorship session and what I did to Sydney." He deflated with a growl and bowed his head. "I still regret that so goddamn badly. Anyway…that Sunday at lunch, all I said was that she'd cancelled. I vaguely remember umming and ahhing a bit when questions were asked, but they certainly didn't ask me if she'd done anything. I was miserable. Between hurting her and fighting with Connor, then not wanting to talk about it, I think Mom was pissed that Connor showed her no attention."

"Had he mentioned being with Sydney yet?"

"He had, but not to the table. I found him before lunch." He remembered back and shuddered.

He quietly closed the bathroom door and heard murmurings in Douglas' room. A frown furrowed his brows and he inched closer to the door, trying to hear what was being said through the inch wide gap between the door and the frame. They obviously hadn't noticed it wasn't closed.

"I don't want to announce this to the whole table, but I can't help myself. I've been seeing Sydney, that hot author mentoring Sean."

"Kingston?" Alec asked. "Since when?"

"Since the time she came to lunch. She's hot as hell and sure knows how to use that sex room she's got. We've used that a lot."

"You sex starved animal," Declan declared. "How often?"

"Most weekends, some week nights. I gotta say, boys,

she's horny and wet and freaky and so easy to manipulate."

"Putty in your hands," Alec retorted.

"She certainly is. I'm just glad the two of you are married, and Kieran's got Sandy, because I am not sharing."

"Meh," Declan said. "Why do I need her when I got all the hookers I need."

"I *seethed* inside," Sean told Levinworth. "Connor bragged to Alec and my father that he was fucking Sydney *after* beating me up *over* Sydney."

"And how did that make you feel?"

"Fucking angry enough to kill."

"When you were asked at lunch, what had happened, why Sydney had cancelled the mentorship..."

Sean huffed and emotionally wrestled with himself. "All right. I might have implied that something had happened. Or maybe I said nothing and let my idiot father do the implying."

"You didn't say any of this four years ago."

"Why the hell would I admit that four years ago?"

"Did you say she touched you, kissed you, raped you?"

"I was seventeen, Walter, legal to have sex in the state of New York. As my grandfather reminded my idiot father when he turned up on Sydney's doorstep."

"How? Oh...the cameras."

Sean sent a scathing look over his shoulder. "Grandpa told us."

Levinworth momentarily closed his eyes and gave a nod. "Fair enough. So, you allowed certain members to make assumptions."

"Yep."

"Kieran didn't. But Alec did."

"He did. I know Sydney gave as good as she got when it came to the Ryan boys, as they're known. But I still don't know what Alec said to Connor or my father. I need to get that out of him this week."

"Assuming Alec spoke to Connor, and he turned up on Sydney's doorstep."

"And slapped her," Sean spat.

"And slapped her, and then Alec spoke to Declan. What made Declan think she'd groomed you?"

"We're getting ahead of ourselves, doc." Sean walked over to the wall with the wave painting, stared into it, and breathed deeply. "That night, after lunch, Grandpa turned up and said he wanted me to come and stay with him for the night. Maybe even the week. Mom argued with him, but as I was seventeen, I got final say."

"Did you *choose* to go with your grandfather?"

Sean thought back to that night. "Sort of. I didn't want to be in the house with Mom, and Dad had followed her home and berated both of us, so I packed an overnight bag and went with Grandpa."

"And?"

"And we were silent on the way. We had supper, and then he sat me down in the sun room and told me to tell him the truth. Pop had retired to bed, and Emerson had packed a bag and gone to Sydney's for the night."

"How did that conversation go?" Levinworth asked.

Sean shrugged. "Okay, I guess."

"Sean, I want you to tell me what happened." Cormac

sipped his cognac. "Between Sydney suddenly cancelling the mentorship, and you and Connor turning up with bruises and black eyes, I want to know the truth."

Sean caved in on himself and shook his head. "I don't want to talk about it."

"Do you want to talk about your mom and dad?"

He shrugged and his hands fidgeted in his lap. "No."

Cormac recalled his conversation with Sydney about not wanting to mentor a seventeen-year-old boy. "Did she do something?"

A head shake. Eyes down. "No," came out in a small voice.

"Did you do something?"

His bruised lip quivered.

"Did Connor do something to you? Did Connor do something to Sydney?"

Another head shake.

"Did you and Sydney do something to each other?" Cormac's blood surged through his veins. "Sean. Tell me. What happened to make Sydney cancel the mentorship?"

The dam finally broke and tears poured forth. "I fucked up." He covered his face with his hands and cried the hardest he had in some time. "I fucked up so badly."

Cormac kept his breathing even while waiting for Sean to calm down. "Tell me. From the beginning."

The story poured out of him. From the very first feelings of excitement to the very last feelings of love. How he hurt Sydney and then woke up in Connor's apartment and the fight that ensued. "Between him fucking Mom behind Dad's back, and Mom being an alcoholic, and Dad being a non-existent father, and an abusive one, my feelings are all over the place and my head always hurts, and I get pain behind my eyes and in my temple. It always hurts. My head, my heart, my soul." He cried harder and folded in on himself, wrapping his arms around his knees and putting his head between them. "I'm always hurting, and I hate my life, and I hate my parents, and the only good thing has been Sydney and this mentorship, and I fucked it up."

"Yes, Sean, you did. But you're not to blame for anything else. Your parents are, and I think it's high time for me to do something about it."

Sean wiped his face and nose in the sleeve of his sweater, pulling himself back up. "What are you going to do?"

Cormac sighed and his brows furrowed. "There are multiple rooms upstairs. You can pick one to move into because it's time I took charge and I'm going to help you as my youngest grandchild. We can move you in tomorrow, pack up everything you want and need and bring it here. I think you should stay for the rest of your high school year and if all goes well, your college years, unless you want to stay in a dorm."

Sean hiccupped. "Can I get a dorm room to myself?"

"Maybe." Cormac grinned. "It'll depend on the college and if they allow it."

Sean was hopeful. "I'm the grandson of the PC, and that should count for something."

"It should," Cormac agreed, watching the dark depressed cloud leave his grandson. "We'll see what we can do."

Sean sniffed. "Am I in trouble for what I did?"

"You are," Cormac replied. "And you will start your penance by starting therapy."

Sean frowned. "Oh, no, I don't want—"

"Considering what you did, you could be arrested and charged with assault," Cormac thundered. "Is that what you want?" That tone always scared the grandkids and now was no different.

Sean cowered down in his seat. "No, sir. But it's not like my dad was ever arrested and charged with assault."

"No." Cormac's lips turned into a thin line and his brows furrowed deeper. "No, but now, you need to pay for what you did, and that will be up to Sydney. I'll talk to her in a few days and see what she wants to do, and to also apologise for pushing her into it. She was right, I was wrong. But in your *defence*." He pointed a finger at his grandson. "You're a pretty messed up kid and you need help. And if therapy keeps you out of jail then you're going to damn well take it."

Sean gulped. "When will you see her?"

"Sometime this week. In the meantime, why don't you go and pick a bedroom because that's where you'll be staying for the next year or two. And it's late, so you may as well get to bed. You've got school tomorrow."

"It's a half day. I don't go in until twelve."

"Then you can keep Pop company in the morning."

Sean nodded and let out a relieved sigh. "Yeah, night, Grandpa."

"Night, Sean."

"That was Sunday night, and Kieran and Sandy had already dropped by. Alec would be next." Sean looked at Levinworth over his shoulder. "Grandpa got me in to see you and I told you my brain issues and you got me diagnosed. Did we ever thank you for that? It went a long way to understanding why I had difficulties."

"You and your grandfather did, and it was part of the service. You had mental health issues. I helped solve them."

"Yeah." Sean's head turned back, and he gazed up at the painting. "I still hear the waves, the crashing and pounding. Mainly when I'm stressed. As you saw the other time I was here."

Levinworth checked his notes. "Do you know what your grandfather did?"

"When?"

"That week. When he went to Sydney's."

"Sort of. He told me some of it and we certainly all copped it Wednesday night. That was fun. I know he went to see her and found Dad screaming down her brownstone. Threatened to demote him and threw him against his car. Dad hated him for that, but no. Grandpa spoke to her, and she confirmed what I had told him. He apologised to her and told her he'd keep the family away from her, and that's what he told us." He frowned. "Along with the other thing. But that didn't stop Ethan a year later, or my dad two years later."

"Or you a year after that."

"That's definitely for another time." Sean touched a finger to the painting. "At that family meeting Grandpa demanded to know who'd been to Sydney's. Kieran had no problem admitting he had been and told us why. However…"

"Why the hell did you do that? Did any of you do that?" Cormac demanded. "What gave any of you three."

He pointed to his first three sons. "The right to do that and be dumb enough to do it, and for God's sake, Connor, you slapped her, and Declan." He shot his third son a disgusted look. "The things you said to her were uncalled for and unwarranted."

"And you fucking demoted me," Declan yelled.

"You deserved it," Cormac roared. "I don't care what idiotic thoughts all of you had in your brainless heads, but Sydney deserved none of it. Do you understand me? All of you, all of my children, and grandchildren, will stay the hell away from her. You're all banned."

"Because of Sean?" Alec directed a glare at his nephew.

"No. Because you behaved abhorrently using the Ryan name," Cormac told him, seeing him blanch. "You made assumptions and assaulted her. She could have you arrested, especially you Connor, for assault and harassment. How the hell do you think that will look?"

"Are you sure this isn't because of Sean?" Sierra asked. "Because I'm not surprised." She glared at him across the table.

"Stop that garbage now," Douglas demanded. "This had nothing to do with Sean specifically. It's because your father and uncles fucked up and ruined everything."

Everyone looked in shock at the patriarch who never swore.

"Thanks to my idiot grandsons, Sydney won't be in our lives anymore." He directed a glare to each of them.

Cormac waved a dismissive hand. "I'm not banning you and me, just these knuckleheads." He motioned to everyone else. "Whatever your beef with Sydney is, it's misinformed and deluded, especially yours Declan, and yours Connor. Sydney didn't do anything untoward, you did. Connor did. Alec did. And because of your actions, I am banning this family, outside Pop and myself, from going near her. She wants nothing to do with any of you and I can't blame her. She wants Sean to continue with his mentorship and I will see to it that he does, because as you all learned, when you turned up on her doorstep, she hadn't cancelled the mentorship, just her part in it. She's unable to do it anymore and has advised her publisher who will organise another mentor for Sean, and I will make sure he still goes. But the rest of you need to stay the hell away." He clasped his hands together and rested them on the table. "Now, onto another matter that has to do with Sydney."

"Which would be?" Douglas asked.

Cormac sighed and looked at his father. "I looked into Sydney this week to try and find out why my grandson would have his mentorship cancelled and why my sons would be on her doorstep, and I found some interesting information."

"Like?" Connor asked. He was seated to his father's left with Ethan, Declan and Sean to his left.

"Like a redacted file out of Los Angeles where Sydney was before moving here. It was about the murder of a man who had killed ten times before. He was shot in cold blood mid-assault, in a house where two women lived. A very famous author and her assistant, turns out."

"What!" Connor stuttered in complete shock. He looked at his family members and saw they were just as shocked as he. Turning back to his father, he asked, "Sydney?"

"Yes," Cormac told him. "I rang up an old friend of mine, a retired chief out in L.A. He sent me the unredacted version. I had also received official documents about DNA and other samples that had been compared against the database in each state and all of the families were being contacted because their cases had been solved and were being closed."

"What does this have to do with us?" Alec asked.

"Or Sydney?" Sean added trying to gauge his grandfather's answer.

Cormac stared right back. "Because the man who broke into Sydney's house in L.A. and assaulted her assistant was the murdering bastard who killed your grandmother."

Gasps raced around the table, but not one person uttered a word.

Leaning back in his chair, Cormac looked from one son to the other, one grandchild to the other, and finally landed on his shocked father. "The killer of my wife has finally been murdered and it was Sydney who did it. Three shots in the back, one in the forehead, three in the crotch."

Sean tried working out the logistics. "How'd that happen?"

"I'm assuming, she shot him in the back while he was assaulting Ms Aldridge, and then grabbed him off her, rolling him onto his back and the floor, and then shot him three times in the crotch and one square between the eyes. It was never taken to trial because of the situation, and her fame and celebrity status, and the fact that DNA testing showed he was in the system as a rapist and murderer."

"Did you thank her for it?" Douglas asked.

"I most certainly did. I went there for two reasons. To thank her and to apologise. She asked that I keep you lot away from her and keep Sean on track with his mentorship. Because regardless of what happened, Sean, she believes in your talent."

Sean wanted to beam with pride, but he kept it to himself. Cormac had told him all about his conversation with Sydney earlier, and he'd never been more remorseful or stupid to think that she'd stop the mentorship altogether. But he was so embarrassed he wasn't sure if he could face the people at Pulsate ever again. He'd also have to send Sydney a big bunch of flowers and a note.

"So," Cormac addressed his family. "Your mother's murderer is dead, and Sydney Kingston killed him. While we can be grateful, you will stay away from her. Do I make myself clear?"

Connor sighed and looked at Declan, who in turn looked at Alec, almost as if silently communicating with each other.

Sean watched the interaction with interest.

"I still can't believe she did that." Sean's gaze hadn't left the painting. "She shot and killed a man. An asshole rapist and murderer, who was in the middle of assaulting Amy, and she pulled the trigger with no problem." He aimed his finger like a gun. "Bam, bam, bam, and then one in the head and three in the crotch. What do they call that?"

"Murder."

Sean spun around. "No, I mean, the head shot after

shooting multiple times. In zombie movies it's the kill shot, but she'd already shot him, rolled him over, and planted three in the dick, and one between the eyes. God." He shook his head, a huge beaming smile on his face. "What a woman!"

"Did your father and uncles stay away?"

"They did as far as I know."

"What? You couldn't tell from the cameras you planted?"

Sean gave him a filthy look. "No. They didn't turn up on her doorstep. So yeah, they stayed away until Ethan."

"Why did your father call Sydney a rapist? What did you imply?"

Sean shrugged. "Again, I ummed and aahed, but I never came out and said anything. I think Alec said something to them. Especially considering that look they all gave each other that night, and the fact Connor had boasted about Sydney to them at lunch." His mind wandered off in thought. "I really need to ask Alec. He and Connor would know."

"*If* Alec told Connor the same thing he told Declan."

"True," Sean told him. "But you know, my father had no right to be angry or upset. I'd been having sex for over a year by then and he knew all about it. I don't know why he abused Sydney the way he did."

Levinworth consulted his notes. "Refresh my memory and feel free to add anything else you left out four years ago."

Sean sniggered and flashed him a glance. "Funny. You know full well my father took me to a prostitute on my sixteenth birthday and told her to make me a man.

I'd had friends over, a cake, the usual affair that Mom bothered putting on for me. But that night, when everyone was gone and she was ten sheets to the wind, he got me in the car and said he had a huge surprise for me. Took me to an escort agency in the backend of Queens somewhere, threw a hundred at her and left me. I had no freaking clue what to do or whether she was clean, but at least we used condoms."

"How many times?"

"Twice, and one oral. He'd only given her a hundred after all."

Levinworth arched a brow. "Did it make you a man?"

Sean turned from the painting. "What does that even mean?" he asked in all seriousness. "Does it mean losing your virginity, in which case, yeah. But how else does it make you a man? I was sixteen, a *teen*ager, underage by a year, and five years away from being an adult, like now. It's five years later and I'm a legal adult."

"Did it prepare you for having sex later? Or with Sydney?"

Sean considered his next words. "Doc, it's not like I stopped having sex."

Levinworth glanced up from his notes. "You kept seeing prostitutes?"

He shrugged. "Yeah. I needed to get experience from somewhere."

"How many?"

"A few. First in Queens, at the same place, but then I found one on the Lower East Side who was amazing and knew what to do."

"And how long did you see her?"

"Until I was eighteen."

Levinworth thought back. "Weren't there killings going on back then? Pros in the Lower East Side."

"There were, and I had to be careful. But I do know my pro is still alive, so he didn't kill her. I have wondered who it was. I thought for a while it was my dad."

"Why would you think that?"

"Because he was seeing pros. Hell, he took me to the first in Queens and he was caught with his dick in the mouth of one. I don't know how long he'd been seeing them for, but it must've been awhile before my sixteenth."

"Do you have any proof that made you think that?"

"Plenty. But that's irrelevant now, isn't it?"

Levinworth stared at him. "Is it? How much did you spend?"

"A hundred and fifty a pop."

"Where did you get the money?"

"Stole it from Mom's account. A bit at a time. She was so drunk she didn't know."

"How often?"

"Once a week, so fifty-two weeks a year, two years, nearly, just over, what, fifteen thousand of Mom's money went on paying a hooker to fuck me. Just as well she had plenty left. Dad didn't know about it, of course, and was surprised to see how much there was after she died. Her will stated we got half each, and being Declan fucking Ryan, he contested it, of course, but I got my half and put it to my college tuition and paid the rest off with sales of my books a couple of years later."

"Do you think your time with the prostitutes prepared you for sex? For a relationship? Have you had a relationship?"

"No and no. It prepared me for sex with a prostitute, not a woman to love. Although, it gave me experience. As for relationships, I've been too busy writing and releasing."

"And stalking Sydney."

Sean agreed. "I did. I'll admit that now. I don't think I did then. I found out where Emerson lived. I found out where Sydney lived and took photographs of her brownstone, of her. I jumped the fence and looked in the back windows and all of that was before we'd even met, oh no," he held up a finger, "and some of it was after."

"So, your obsession started before you met?" Levinworth furiously scribbled notes.

"Again, doc, I wasn't obsessed. After that kiss, I absolutely knew I was in love."

"She was a stand-in surrogate mother. You had mommy issues."

Sean slowly walked over to the couch. "Yeah, Walter, I did. But Sydney wasn't a surrogate mother, she was the woman I wanted as my lover, and I made that happen. Not just once, but many, many times." He picked up his messenger bag and slung it over his shoulder. "The pros, my mother, my father. I wasn't obsessed, I wanted love, I wanted her to love me like I loved her."

"Do you hate your father, Sean? Did you kill him?"

"Until next time, Walter."

*****

Sean opened the door before Alec stepped out of the elevator and waited for his uncle.

Alec looked up from his phone. "Sean, you know why I'm here."

"Go for it." Sean waved him on and closed the door. He waited for his uncle to finish his inspection, crossed his arms, and blocked Alec's exist. "I need to ask you about four years ago. What you told Connor and Dad about your visit to Sydney's door."

Alec sighed and slid his phone into his pocket. "Why do you need to ask about that?"

"Because my therapist brought it up and wanted to know how Dad came to the conclusion he did. I don't know, as I never implied she'd done anything, but I do know Connor turned up *after* you, and Dad turned up *after* him. What did you say?"

Alec put his hands in his pockets. "Look, kid, I didn't say anything."

"I know you did," Sean insisted, taking a step closer. "Because *I* didn't. And *I* know what you said to her; you implied that something had happened and that my bruises were from her. She told you to check with Connor. What did you say to Connor and Dad?"

Alec pondered and realised Sean's serious expression meant business. "I didn't see your dad; I only saw Connor."

"And?" Sean frowned at the information.

"And…" Alec smoothed his jacket. "I asked him if it was true, about him and Laura, and if he was the one to beat you up."

"And?" Sean took another step closer.

Alec shrugged. "And he didn't deny any of it. I reamed him out for cheating with Laura, and told him he should've left you alone, and you were just letting off steam, and that he'd better end his affair. He said he did when he met Sydney."

"And then he goes and fucks that up by slapping Sydney," Sean said, thinking it all through. "If you didn't see dad, Connor must have, and God knows what he told him."

"You'll have to ask Connor, because your father's not here. But why are we talking about this? It was four years ago."

"Because it came out in therapy and my therapist thought I should find out." He opened the door for his uncle. "Same time next week."

"Sean." Alec paused outside the door. "Even if you speak to Connor, you may not get the answers you're looking for. Your mom and Declan are dead; maybe it's time to leave it in the past."

"Considering I have mandated weekly therapy sessions as part of my home detention, not gonna happen, Alec." Sean closed the door and looked around for his phone. He found it on the recharge stand in his office and called Connor.

"Hey, kid, how you doing?"

"I need to talk to you. Can you come over?"

"Kinda busy right now. Can you come here?"

Sean looked down at his ankle monitor. "Not really."

"I might be able to stop by tonight sometime. I was meeting Ethan for a drink."

Sean thought quickly. "Bring him. I have beer and it won't take long. You'll be out of here in about fifteen minutes."

"Then why can't we have this conversation…" After a

long pause. "Gotta go. We'll drop by around eight."

"Fine. And I'll have the beer." Sean heard the beeping and ended the call. He put the phone back on the charger. "I'll have beer all right, with a little something added so I get the truth out of both of you."

*****

That night at eight, Sean had two chilled beers waiting for them when they entered the condo. "Here we go, one beer each ready to go." He handed them out as they entered and closed the door, took a breath, and said, "How's your days been?"

He saw that Connor had already drunk half, and Ethan a quarter.

Long," Connor said and slumped onto the couch. "What'd you want us here for?"

Sean watched Ethan sit beside his father. For a long time now, he'd watched Ethan play the role of mini-Connor. Connor's twin, superglued to his hip. He always sat by his side whether on the couch or at the dinner table, unless he couldn't. He was always looking up to him, looking *to* him, taking his lead whether good or bad.

Connor finished his beer. "Got another one, kid?" He tilted his glass at Sean.

"Coming right up." Sean grabbed it and poured another beer, adding a dash of his potion. He handed it back. "I take it you're not driving."

Connor downed a quarter. "Nah, Ethan is."

Sean noticed Ethan still had half left. The good little sober driver.

"What's this about?" Connor laid his arm along the back of the sofa.

"I had a conversation with Alec this morning, and he told me to talk to you."

Connor huffed. "About what? Why would Alec say that?"

"Because, in therapy, I'm reliving my shit life at the age of seventeen and something important came up."

"You're back in therapy?" Ethan asked. "Why?"

"Some issues have arisen that have to do with my brain and how it's working," Sean said and concentrated on Connor. "But something got me thinking about how everyone landed on Sydney's doorstep." He flashed Ethan a glance. "My father and uncles, anyway. And why Dad, and you, Connor, said and did what you said and did."

"Ah, Sydney." Connor sighed. "Fucking hot chick she was. So good in the sack, too. Even better than your mother, Sean." Connor leaned back, oblivious to the stunned looks his son and nephew were giving him.

Sean slowly blinked and his eyes grew wide. "Um…" He took a breath, saw Ethan look at him and continued in confusion. "When I thought my mentorship with Sydney was cancelled, all of you turned up on her doorstep. Alec said he only talked to you, and then you turned up on Sydney's stoop, and then Dad. I never said Sydney did anything to me because she didn't. But between the three of you, lies were told, and Sydney suffered the consequences. What did you tell Dad?"

"Ah…" Connor rubbed his tired eyes. "How am I supposed to remember back that far?"

"Alec made implications that something had happened.

Sydney told him you beat me up and that you were fucking Mom, so what did he tell you and why did you lie to Dad?"

"So that he didn't find out I was fucking his wife," Connor said. "Alec came to me demanding to know if what Sydney had said was true. He got it out of me, that yeah, I'd been fucking Laura before I met Sydney. He told me I was stupid and could never tell Declan or he'd kill me. He asked if I'd gotten into a fight with you, I told him all about it. He was pissed that you knew, told me to keep it all to myself, and say nothing to Declan."

"But you did," Sean reminded him. "Because no one else spoke to him."

"Yeah." Connor put his feet on the coffee table and slumped down. "I saw him later that day and he asked if I knew what was going on with you and your mentorship since I was fucking Sydney." He finished his beer and gasped. "Ah, that's good. Got food?"

"What did you say to Dad?" Sean leaned forward from his post on the sofa arm. "What happened when you ran into him?"

"Ah, like I said. I panicked when he asked me if I knew how you'd gotten those bruises, and after Alec told me what he did, I said maybe Sydney had done something and got into a fight with you."

Sean frowned and glanced at Ethan who stared at his father's face with a pained expression. "And what else?"

"He asked what sort of fight and I said maybe she tried something with you or forced you to do something you didn't want to and fought over it, and he went berserk."

"Why would you do that?" Ethan asked him. "Why

would you lie about Sydney? A woman you were seeing, who you said you were hot for and loved fucking." He thought back. "Was that when you stopped seeing her? When you went around to her place and slapped her? Is that what she meant to you? Is that what that incredible woman meant to you?" he demanded and thrust up from his seat. Moving over to the window, he crossed his arms, and willed himself not to cry. Knowing his uncle and cousin had hurt Sydney made him sick to his gut and knowing Declan had fucked her a year after him made him sicker.

"Oh, come on, Ethan, I wasn't the only one in this family to fuck Sydney. I know you did a year later, and Declan after you. Sydney's a free spirit. We're all hot as hell, so how could she not want the Ryan boys?"

Sean brought the conversation back to his point. "You lied to my dad and implied Sydney had forced herself on me to get out of him beating you up for beating me up? So that he didn't find out you were fucking his wife. You lied about a woman who had done *nothing* to this family except fuck you and you slapped her for it." A half choke, half laugh came from him. "How could you fucking do that to such an incredible woman? I'm with Ethan on that score. How the fuck could you try and destroy a woman who did nothing to *any* of us?"

Connor sighed and rubbed his forehead. "It was four years ago. Why are you bringing this up now?"

"Because, as I've said multiple times, it came up in therapy and I told my therapist the truth. I had no idea why my dad blew up at Sydney and connected the dots to you and Alec. Alec said he only talked to you, so that means you talked to Dad and you've just admitted it. You lied." Sean got up and paced the space between his living room and the kitchen and dining areas. "How could you lie about Sydney? I get lying about me; just about everyone did. But Sydney! Fuck! Does she even know? I wonder if she figured it out."

"Again, what does it matter four, five, years on?" Connor asked. "If that was all you had to ask, then are we done? I want to get to the bar for a few drinks and a round of pool, and a good steak." He stood up and swayed a little. "Guess I'd better get that steak in me pronto. Ready, Ethan?"

"You never apologised," Ethan said quietly. "Why did you never apologise?"

Connor sighed in exasperation. "I was keeping a pretty big secret to myself and told myself I hadn't done anything wrong. Even when Emerson asked if I wanted to pass on an apology when we were here, I couldn't say anything."

"Did Dad know?" Sean asked. "Or at least, suspect that you were fucking Mom?"

"I don't know, kid. I just don't know. But he didn't try to kill me, so I'd say he didn't."

"Why did he go off his face? He knew I was having sex; he'd taken me to a prostitute for my sixteenth birthday as my present. So why the problem with Sydney if something had happened?" He watched Connor's brows rise and Ethan turned from the window. "Oh please, Connor, as if he didn't tell you and Alec. The three musketeers, the three Ryan boys who were the most dangerous. You told them you were fucking Sydney, and he must've told you after I turned sixteen."

Connor's head slowly bobbed up and down. "Yeah, he did. We thought it was hilarious. Wondered what the pro had done for a hundred bucks and if she was clean."

The comment stung Sean to the core. "Good to know my welfare was such a fucking priority and I was nothing but a fucking laughing stock in my family. *Especially* among those who were supposed to protect me."

"Sean," Connor started.

Sean waved him off and strode for the door. "I have my answer. You can leave now. I want you both to get out. Now!" He flung it open and clenched his jaw, controlling his tears until they'd gone. Not only had he been a physical punching bag for his father, but a verbal one for his uncles. "Get out."

Ethan passed in front of him, his eyes glazed with tears. "Sorry, Sean, I didn't know."

Connor came up behind him. "Sean, it wasn't—"

"Get out!" Sean's gaze remained down. He was unable to look at either of them.

Connor sighed. "Come on, Ethan, let's get to the bar."

Ethan shook his head and refused to look at his father. "No. I'm dropping you off. I need to do something tonight."

Sean slammed the door on them, threw every bolt into the locked position, then fled upstairs to his room, threw himself on the bed and cried.

*****

Cormac picked up Sean Saturday morning and took him to his parents' house. It had been empty since Laura had died because Declan had moved out and done nothing with the place.

They stood side by side on the driveway staring up at the dilapidated two-storey Hamptons style home. The white paint had greyed and chipped, the weeds were overgrown, shutters were torn off, and windows were broken.

"I had someone come around every few months," Cormac said. "Just to tidy up and do the garden. We threw some squatters out a few days ago."

"Why didn't he do anything?" Sean asked. "Once I moved out I never moved back, but once Mom died, he just left. Even though he'd already been gone. At least he'd come home on the odd occasion."

A car screeched to a halt, and they turned to see Alec get out of it. "Ah," he said and stopped. "I didn't realise you were both here." He walked up to them. "Sean's monitor went off and I came racing over. I didn't recognise it as Declan's house."

"You'd better add the address to Sean's list of places he can go. The house will need to be done up for rental," Cormac told him.

"I'm not renting it, I'm selling it," Sean said, gazing up at the house.

"Are you sure that's what you want to do?" Cormac watched his face.

Sean shrugged. "I haven't lived here in four years, almost five. Mom's been gone for nearly four, and Dad's dead. Why the hell do I need the house?" He turned his head to his grandfather. "Was Dad in debt? Do I have to pay it off?"

Cormac exchanged a glance with Alec and then looked at the house. "He was, and no you don't."

"And the money from the sale?"

"Will be yours to do with what you want."

Sean sighed. "I guess we'd better look inside and assess the damage. I take it that I'm going to have to spend thousands to fix it up so I can sell it?" He walked up the drive and paused at the front door. A lot of memories flooded back, and he didn't like any of them. He shoved the key into the lock and opened the door. The stench hit him in the face, and he covered his mouth and nose with his t-shirt. "Jesus Christ!"

Alec pulled out his silk handkerchief and held it over his face.

Cormac didn't bother and remained his same stoic self.

They walked into the entrance and entered the living room to the left. Almost four years' worth of dust, dirt, and squatters had taken its toll.

"I'm just glad I got all of my stuff out." Sean walked into the kitchen dining room and saw the carnage. "Jesus Christ."

"I'm glad we packed up your mom's belongings and your dad took his stuff." Cormac stared at the grimy mess from the floor to the walls to the ceiling. "We left nothing behind. It was all saved."

"And this is going to cost *hundreds* of thousands," Sean complained and closed his eyes. "Why did Dad not bother? We could've rented it out for money."

"I don't know why my son did the things he did,

Sean, and I am truly sorry about that." Cormac made his way through the rest of the ground floor while Sean went upstairs.

He found his parents' bedroom trashed with graffiti, and what looked to be faeces, all over the walls. "Fucking hell." The carpet was mouldy and soiled, and the windows smashed. "This is going to cost a fucking fortune."

"Good thing you're rich," Alec said, coming in behind him. "Rip it back to the studs and rebuild. It'll take a couple of months, but summer's coming, and so is warm weather. You should be able to sell it for a million or two and recoup what you spend."

Sean deflated and turned to his uncle. "That means I need to be here. Have you added it to the list?"

"I have, just like with the cemetery." Alec stepped closer and lowered his voice. "You spoke to Connor."

"He told you?" Sean eyed him wearily.

"He did. For what it's worth, Sean, I'm sorry he lied to your dad and implied Sydney had done something. Regardless of what went down, she didn't deserve Connor and Declan's abuse."

"No, she didn't. But she got it anyway and he still hasn't apologised."

"At least your dad did."

"For what that was worth." Sean moved into the hallway and remembered when Sydney had stood there. That was the only great memory of that house. When Sydney Kingston had stood in his doorway reading his stories and told him they were good, and he was talented. His heart broke at the pain that had caused and left it behind as he walked downstairs where he found his grandfather by the open front door. "Jesus, I'd better hire some contractors then."

"Do you know of any?" Cormac asked and walked out the door.

"I do and I'll get onto them now, if you don't mind waiting?"

"Not at all; make your calls."

While Sean was on the phone, Alec took his leave, and Cormac sat in his car. It was only for him to deal with his son's debt, so Sean didn't have to. He had the house to deal with. Declan had been up to his neck in credit card bills, nearing a hundred thousand across five cards. His insurance and death coverage would cover at least half, but that still left a huge chunk to pay off. He was going to have to tell the others to get rid of their debt, so it wasn't left on him.

Sean climbed into the car. "They'll be by later if you're willing to come back. Maybe we can have lunch nearby while we wait?"

Cormac smiled at his grandson and squeezed his hand. "Sure."

✱✱✱✱✱

Three hours later, Sean got the quote from the contractor. It would cost at least seventy-five thousand to remove all of the carpet and dry wall, and redo all plumbing and electricals. The costs would go higher if anything was wrong such as wood rot, termites or mould, not to mention relaying the roof and replacing the windows, floor, and walls.

Sean swore under his breath and hired them. They had added the secret door between his condos and knew they were reputable. He was going to potentially be out a hundred grand plus for this house, so it had better sell.

*****

Sean drove home after dinner with his grandfather and Emerson, and found Ethan waiting in his car in the condominium carpark. "How long have you been waiting?"

"About half an hour." Ethan followed him inside the building. "I dropped by earlier, but you weren't here, so I came back and waited."

Sean noticed his expression as he unlocked his door. "You okay? You haven't been here since the other night, and before that, Sunday lunch." He locked the door and set his bag on the coat rack. "Wanna beer?"

"Make it three." Ethan slowly walked over to the window. It gave him a wide illuminated view of the city that was off in the distance.

"Okay." Sean pulled two beers from the fridge, cracked off the tops, and walked over to his cousin. "Here. Why are you here? Is it your father?"

Ethan knocked back the whole bottle and gasped.

"Okay, guess you need this one, too." Sean handed over his bottle and took the empty one. Leaving it on the sink, he got another beer. "Something's clearly wrong."

"What the fuck is going on?" Ethan complained, waving his bottle around. "First Brandon and Sierra get blown to pieces, then your dad dies from gunshot wounds, and then Dad says what he did about Sydney." His brows furrowed in pain. "God, fuck it."

Sean watched him wander around the living room. Something was wrong and he hoped to get some information out of him. "Just spit it out. Something's clearly bothering you."

"*Everything's bothering me*," exploded Ethan. He drank another mouthful. "Sydney." Tears prickled his eyes. "Sydney's the love of my life and this family ruined it. *You* ruined it." He pointed at Sean with the bottle. "*You* and your weird, sick, whatever the fuck that was that made Dad lie to Uncle Declan. Why the fuck was he fucking your mom, 'cause that's fucking gross, man." Another swig. "Just so fucking gross. Our parents fucking. Your mom, my dad, he was inside of her. My dad was inside your mom and then he dumped her and moved on to Sydney." He finished off the beer. "Got another one?"

Sean handed over his untouched beer. What he was getting was priceless. "It was gross, but it stopped."

"It did." Ethan took a mouthful and swayed around in a circle. "But then he fucked Sydney, and he tried to destroy her."

"It didn't stop you."

"Nope." Ethan shook his head and swayed over to the window. "I was next to have her. When her house was broken into I got the call and that reignited the attraction I'd had the year before. I didn't care if Dad had fucked her, I just wanted to prove that I was the man for her and I was better than my father."

"She let you go."

Ethan sobbed and leaned against the window. "She let me go after New Year's. We spent the week between Christmas and New Year's together and just stayed at her place and fucked all the time. I love her. I loved her then and I still love her now."

"But she didn't love you enough," Sean said softly.

"No," Ethan cried, his face smearing the window with tears. "She didn't love me enough."

Sean led him over to one of the sofas and sat him down. "You need to rest, and you need to stop drinking. It's not helping things." He tried to take the bottle, but Ethan pushed his hand away.

"No, I'm not finished." He drank the last of it and belched. "You know we spent a lot of time in the sex room. She said I was as good as my father. She'd tie me up to those contraptions and whip me like she whipped him. I told her..." He clamped his hand on Sean's shoulder. "I told her to do everything to me that she did to my dad, so I could show her I was more man than him, and all the man she would ever want or need. And we recorded a lot of it. We recorded ourselves fucking in her bed and in the sex room. Even out in the backyard in the rain. That was fucking amazing. The cold drops of water hit us like tiny daggers as we fucked on the back patio. God it was hot." He slumped back onto the couch. "We took photos too. I took photos of her entire body." He waved a hand in front of him. "Every little part of her I photographed, and I took photos of us fucking so I could remember every little bit of her body. Every... little...bit." A sob caught in his throat. "I miss her so much, Sean. I miss her so much." Tears fell down his face and he slid sideways onto the couch. "I miss her so much. I want her back, especially after what Dad did. And I don't care if she fucked Declan a year later, or anyone else for that matter, I just want her back. No one comes close to her. No woman comes close…"

Sean left his cousin to sob, leaving a blanket over him, and a bottle of water and a bucket on the floor in front of him in case he was sick or dehydrated. Looking down at him, he couldn't help feeling sympathy. He knew what loving Sydney was like; he still loved her himself. He also knew what obsession was and knew Ethan at least bordered on it.

He left him and grabbed a bottle of beer on his way through to the next-door condo. He locked the door securely behind him and opened the wall to reveal all of his photos of his obsession. Sydney. He gazed upon her face and smiled. "Hi, beautiful. I haven't seen you in a while." After a few minutes of reintroduction, he booted up his laptop and sat at his desk. He connected a hard drive and pulled up a folder titled Ethan, clicked a folder labelled videos, and started a recording he'd taken from Ethan's computer. It was of him and Sydney fucking.

"Oh, God, oh, God, oh, God," was all Ethan said with Sydney groaning under him. Sean watched the way she moved and felt his penis harden over her. His body made small grunting motions until she came, and a sigh came from both of them. "God I love you, Sydney." He saw her glance at the camera and raise a brow.

"I see you," Sean said, and closed it down to click on a video he'd taken when he'd broken into Ethan's house a couple of months ago. He'd found nothing throughout the house, but when he walked down into the basement, he hit the motherlode of Ethan's obsession with Sydney. *If only Walter could see this*, he thought and chuckled. *My obsession is nothing compared to my cousin's*

He hit pause on the sleeping face of a naked woman tied to a bed. She was a woman who looked exactly like Sydney Kingston.

Chapter 12

"How are you this week, Sean?" Levinworth closed the door on their session.

"Upbeat." Sean dumped his messenger bag on the couch and walked over to his spot by the window. "But also bummed out at the same time."

"How's that?" Levinworth sat in his chair and picked up Sean's burgeoning file.

"Upbeat because I got the truth out of Alec and Connor, bummed out because of Ethan and seeing the damage to my parents' house."

"Ah, now your dad's gone you'll inherit what's left."

"Which is the house. But Grandpa's paid off his massive debt. Said I shouldn't have to. Up to his neck he was, just like he was up to his dick in a hooker when he was shot." Sean choked out a laugh. "What a way to go. I doubt he felt any of it."

"If he was high on coke, no, no he wouldn't have. And his body wouldn't know it was in shock for a while. By then, it would have been an issue of blood loss and reduction in adrenaline."

"I don't care." Sean shook his head and sighed. "Alec

told me the only person he spoke to was Connor. He didn't even see my dad. But he made implications to Sydney who told him about Connor. He told Connor to never tell my dad what he'd done."

"How did that make you feel?"

"Annoyed, in retrospect. Alec didn't do much, just made implications and pulled up Connor on his bullshit then told Connor to lie. I invited Connor over and Ethan came with him, two for one and all that. I thought it was a great idea."

"And what happened?"

"I had beers waiting for them when they arrived, with an extra ingredient to loosen their tongues. Ethan barely drank, but Connor knocked back two beers and told me a lot."

"What did you lace it with?"

"Not important, Walter." Sean kept looking at the view. "I asked Connor what Alec had said to him and what he said to my dad. He admitted he lied to Dad about Sydney so he didn't find out it was him who beat me up, or that he'd been fucking his wife. He also made implications about Sydney. Ethan, surprisingly, had the balls to have a go at his father for slapping Sydney, and getting mad at her when she'd done nothing wrong, especially after he'd bragged about fucking her. I accused him of that, too. How he, Dad, and Alec were like the three musketeers always bragging about what they'd done."

"Did your father brag about beating you?"

Sean's brows furrowed. "I don't know. But I reminded Connor that I knew dad had probably bragged that he'd taken me to a pro for my sixteenth. He made snide remarks about it. It stung like hell. That those three bragged about shit like that, even though they knew he beat me. I was Dad's physical punching bag, and their verbal punching bag. I was disgusted, so was Ethan. He apologised as he walked out the door and told his dad he couldn't hang out as he had something to do."

"How did all of that make you feel?"

Sean considered the question. "Devastated. Because I slammed and locked the door, ran upstairs, and threw myself on the bed and cried until I fell asleep from exhaustion."

"Understandable. Your uncles, Alec and Connor, knew of your, well, technically it's rape, since you were under the legal age limit, and did nothing. They all knew your dad had beaten you and your mother and did nothing."

"Yes, they did, Walter, yes they did."

"Are you angry at Connor?"

"Fuck yeah, I am. Because after he saw Dad, and Dad saw Sydney, he went off at me. Connor fucked up a lot and it had repercussions, like Sydney's black eye."

"That you originally gave her, so it wasn't just Connor who fucked up."

Sean nodded. "You're right, Walter, you're absolutely right. I did. But I did not expect to be beaten up by Connor or anything else to happened after it."

"You thought you could assault her in her own home and get away with it?"

Sean shrugged a shoulder. "I hadn't thought that far. In fact, I don't think I thought Sydney would say no. I thought I'd kiss her, and it would all work out. But she fought back and cracked me with a frypan."

"Must've hurt."

"It truly fucking did." Sean rubbed the spot on the back of his head. "Fractured my skull too. I still have a little indent where the bone healed wrong."

"Did you deserve it?"

"Abso-fucking-lutely," Sean said. "Deserved all of it and can't blame her. I couldn't then and I can't now. I was an asshole."

"You wrote about it in your books *Illicit Things* and *Creeper.* Are they autobiographical?"

"As I told you, Walter, I took some things and made up the rest. Ethan was incredibly disappointed in his father after being at my house. He came around Saturday night after I got back from Grandpa's."

"What did he want?"

"To get drunk and complain about his father. Drank three beers in quick succession. He also wanted to talk about Sydney. He still loves her. *He's* obsessed with her and believe me, I'm not, when compared to him."

"And what makes you say that?"

Sean's laughter rang around the room. "His basement walls are covered in photos of Sydney, and he has videos of them fucking. Not to mention pornographic photos of her privates, and yet people complain about me. *He's* the one who needs therapy for an obsession. I don't."

Levinworth scribbled furiously. "Do you know how long he's had that?"

"Probably since the year they hooked up, considering Sydney dumped him in January and then hooked up with my father in December of the same year. So about three to four years now."

"Do you know if Connor or your father took photos or videos?"

A shake of the head. "No, just me and Ethan by the looks of it."

"Alec or Kieran get involved with her?"

Sean laughed. "You have got to be kidding, Walter? Oh, my God, that's hilarious."

"Why would it be? She slept with Connor and his son. Slept with Declan and *his son*."

Sean's laugher continued as he walked over to the wave painting. "First off, Alec was married when we met her, so was Dad, and Kieran was dating Sandy. Once Connor and Dad…" He paused and the laughter died. "And *I* did what we did, we didn't see her again until Ethan did a year later. And then when all three turned up on her doorstep when Nora died." He sobered. "That sucked for Sydney. She liked Nora a lot."

Levinworth flicked through his notes. "Did we discuss this Nora last time?"

"No. She died after I left therapy. She was Sydney's house sitter, killed by her boyfriend on Sydney's doorstep. Sydney and Amy found her and tried to keep her alive until the paramedics came, but Dad, Connor, and Ethan all ended up responding to the call. It was after she'd dumped Ethan and before she fucked Dad."

"Did they think it was Sydney?"

"Possibly." Sean stared at the painting. "I never met Nora, but from everything I saw on TV, and everything Sydney did for her in the following year, it made me feel as if I did." He glanced over his shoulder. "She wrote *Her Last Words* about Nora, and all proceeds from the sale went to Nora's favourite animal shelter. Sydney saw to it."

Levinworth nodded. "I did see that. Rhett Rockefeller started his monthly investigative series on abuse victims and Nora's death was the first he investigated."

"Yeah, I watched that, too. They never found her killer, even though all fingers pointed to Lennie Cuzco, the boyfriend. But the judge let him go on lack of evidence."

"Your father worked that case."

"He did. That's how he and Sydney ended up together. Reminiscing about the dead and getting drunk in her kitchen. They fucked there, the first time, on the table."

"And how do you…ah…the cameras. They were still there then. Did you not capture Nora's murderer?"

"They were. They'd been there the whole time, but no, they didn't capture outside, just the inside of the front door. And yeah, I knew about Ethan and Dad."

"And how did that make you feel?"

"Do my feelings really matter anymore, Walter?"

"They do."

Sean sighed and closed his eyes. "With Ethan, it was like, he's only seven years older than me, why is she fucking him and not me? The sex was hot, and I got off on it. But when I saw her and Dad, ugh." He shivered. "It made me sick to my stomach."

"Understandable."

"Yeah, I guess it is. He'd fucked Mom, and then fucked her over, fucked God knows how many prostitutes, and then fucked the woman I loved. It made me sick to my stomach. The diseases he could have been giving her. Thank God it didn't last long." He breathed in. "I'll tell you, Walter, she came to her senses with that one and got rid of him quick smart."

"Did you hate your father for that?"

"Abso-fucking-lutely."

"Did you hate Sydney for that?"

The anger melted away and Sean felt empty. "How could I be angry at Sydney? Not by then, anyway. I still loved her, but I knew my family had cursed her. Right from the moment they met her."

"But you started that."

"Yeah, I did. But I wanted her for myself. I didn't want the family to meet her, but she'd already met Connor when some asshole left a dead rat on her doorstep."

"Was that you?"

Sean's face screwed up. "God no! I'd never do that to Sydney."

"Just send her death threats, set up cameras, break in to do it, steal her underwear, and abuse her when she turns you down."

He glared at Levinworth. "You made your point, but I didn't leave the rat."

"Did she ever find out who did?"

"Landon Security did, amongst other stalkers."

"But not you?"

"Nope, they never found me."

"What did you do after being banned from seeing Sydney?'

"Ah, haven't we already explored this?"

"Not yet."

"Well." Sean moved on from the painting. "I moved in with Grandpa, went back to the mentorship and kept on with high school. I wrote in whatever spare time I had, so I wasn't thinking about Sydney, but," he conceded, "I was writing about her, so I guess I was thinking about her. I graduated high school, had my book published, got to celebrate that and then Mom…" His brows lowered. "I'd been at college for a couple of months. People on campus knew who I was, and I managed to get a room to myself for safety reasons. I either had people ribbing me about writing young adult fiction or had them blowing smoke to see how much they could get out of me. Then there were those who hated cops and I had to deal with that. And I had girls wanting to date me because I had slimmed down and built up muscle over the year. I actually enjoyed working out and managed to fit it in around my writing."

"I know you did one year before going to Harvard Law. What did you study?"

"Drama, English, writing, psych, graphic arts. I learned how to do make-up and wigs for the plays we did. Learned how to change voices and postures."

"Came in handy for when you became Bryan Jamison."

"Or an old man, or a middle-aged man, or any other type of man. It came in handy for a lot of things, but we've jumped way too far ahead of ourselves, Walter. I started my first year of college and had people either loving me or hating me, and then my mother died."

"Do you still think your father had something to do with it?"

"Yes, I do, and I know there's proof, but that's for

next time." He hoisted his bag onto his shoulder. "You know. My family seemed like the high and mighty type with their lores and traditions, and maybe Pop and Grandpa abided by the law they promised to uphold, but my father and Connor, and Alec and then Ethan, *none* of them abided by the law they took an oath to uphold. Hell, even Brandon and Sierra weren't clean of crime. You know..." He sat on the arm of the couch closest to Levinworth. "They had absolutely no problem snorting coke, swallowing pills, and injecting all manner of things to get high. I know Sierra sucked cock like her mother had done decades before. Brandon would demand women and girls suck his, and if they didn't he'd force them. So not even those two were free from sin. They all did something illegal. Sierra was turning into quite the little hooker following in Mommy's footsteps. She even had a secret OnlyFans account with Brandon, under a combination of their names. They thought no one would find them, no one would find out; no one would recognise them. They wore wigs and heavy make-up; disguises to become someone else, just as I did. But at least I wasn't fucking my brother or sister."

Levinworth's eyes grew large. "What?"

"Oh, yeah." Sean nodded, knowing he had his full attention. "They'd do it in every video, every which way. They'd get high on some sort of drug, kiss and fuck, wearing dominatrix style clothing. Some of the scenes were close to being rape. I mean, Jesus, what Sydney did to Connor, Ethan, and Dad in her sex room was exactly what Brandon and Sierra dished out to each other on OnlyFans. Pretty damn sick and disgusting. Brother and sister fucking each other for money. But again, their mother was a whore, so they became whores too. Maybe she taught them. Maybe she was behind it all."

"Did they make money? Did no one wonder where everything they bought was coming from?"

Sean shook his head. "No. I only found out they had an account because I signed on to look at women. I recognised Sierra's tattoo she had done to cover her birthmark, and then realised it was Brandon with her. Pretty sick stuff. But once I found out, I tried to figure out a way of digging into their accounts, or how much they had. I found out they'd set up a company, off shore, if I remember correctly, and the money was being funnelled into that account. They were both over eighteen so could do it."

"What happened to the account when they died?"

Sean's lips slowly upturned into a smirk. "Alec and Sonja."

Levinworth's head tilted. "They knew?"

"I think Sonja may have helped set it up, but she needed the legal expertise of her ex-husband. I think, but I'm not sure, he got a ten percent retainer for it, and for not turning them in to the authorities. *Especially* the IRS."

"So, when they died?"

"Went to Sonja, but I think Alec's trying to get half."

"And how do you know all of this?"

"I have my sources. So, you see, doc." Sean got to his feet. "None of the Ryans were saints, except maybe Kieran who'll probably be the last one standing of the Ryan boys. As far as I know, he's done nothing illegal, so he should be fine."

"Meaning?"

"Meaning, if this house of cards is imploding, he'll be the only one to survive." He headed for the door.

"How about you?"

Sean's hand rested on the door handle. "We'll see, doc. Because I'm certainly not free from sin in all of this. Same time next week." He closed the door behind him.

Levinworth breathed slowly to calm his nerves.

Jesus, his cousins were being incestuous on OnlyFans. What the hell is wrong with that family?

He spent a half hour writing up the notes, making sure to detail everything as Sean had stated, added in his thoughts on the matter, and realised Sean hadn't mentioned if their account was still active. When he finished, he closed the file and made sure his door was locked, then opened his laptop and logged into his OnlyFans account. He also pulled up Google and started typing in Sierra and Brandon Ryan. In OnlyFans, he tried several combinations of their names, and scoured each account he came across until he found the right one. He quickly scrolled through Google to see if it came up, and then tried their combined name. There were two mentions of it, but no photos. Both links went to their account on OnlyFans. He went back to that.

"Two years," he muttered, looking at the details. "They've had the account for two years." He went to the first videos and found Sierra on her own. A few weeks later, videos of Brandon appeared on his own, and a few weeks after that, they were in them together. Things started off tamely, undressing each other, undressing in front of each other while the other masturbated, then kissing, touching, and fondling. And finally, the act of sex. Most videos were about fifteen to twenty minutes long and he watched every second or third. The sex rode the gamut from slow and romantic to rough and extreme, definitely borderline rape scenes. He looked at the date on the last video; a few days before they died. There had been a video or two per week, dependent on content. He could only guess at the dollar amount they'd made, and he wondered how long Sean had known, and if the rest of the family knew.

What the hell would Cormac do if he found out his grandchildren were fucking each other in videos on OnlyFans? And what would he do if he found out Alec and his ex-wife knew all about it and set it up and taken money for it?

"Jesus fucking Christ." Levinworth took a breath and leaned back in his chair. He stared at the last video and curiosity overtook him. He clicked on the subscribe button and paid the amount, finding triple the number of videos behind the paywall. He'd hit the motherlode.

*****

On Wednesday, Sean walked into his publisher's office. "Vincent."

"Sean, my darling boy, come, come. See what we have in store for the next release." Vincent waved him over to his desk which was laden with promotional items.

Sean dropped his bag on the velvet couch and walked over. "Oh, wow, these look great." He picked up a poster showing the next book. The cover was striking with its colours and image. "God, I love my book covers. When are these going out?"

"Everything's going out today to book stores, and TV and radio hosts all in preparation for two weeks' time," Roger said. "Then we, and they, will be prepared for the onslaught of publicity." He looked at Sean. "You doing everything by Zoom again?"

"I'll have to." Sean looked at the bookmarks with the cover on it.

"And your excuse this time will be?"

"That I'm in physiotherapy and my doctor told me to take it easy. Or that the cast's not off yet."

Vincent pursed his lips. "How long does it take an ankle to heal after being broken?"

"Don't know," Sean admitted. "I'll have to Google it. How's the standalone coming along? Is it close to being ready for its September release?"

"The interiors are coming along and we'll have the first cover by next week," Roger said. "It's quite a book, and it has to be perfect."

"Yes," Sean murmured and wandered over to the window with his hands in his pockets. He stared at the city. "It needs to be, and it needs to be released in time."

"We'll make sure of it." Vincent followed him over. "And your second book that you delivered is just as delicious. What about the third?"

"I've got a bit to go, but that'll be done in a week or two. I've also been working on two more books."

"You are prolific." Vincent swept imaginary dust from Sean's shoulder just so he could touch him. "And what are these about?"

"One is the true story of my life. A memoir."

Surprised, Vincent clasped his hands together in front of him. "Aren't you a bit young for a memoir?"

Sean raised a brow at him. "You do know who my family are, don't you?"

"Of course, and I'm sure your life is interesting to a degree, but besides publishing young adult stories at Pulsate, and thrillers with us, what else could you have to talk about?"

Sean smirked. "A lot, that you have no clue about, Vincent, unless you read my novels and read between the lines. It's a long way from being finished, and I want to release it within the year, after my novel in September. It's imperative that the timing is also right for it."

"Oh, Sean." Vincent frowned. "We're not known for memoirs, and I'm not sure we could sell enough to recoup the costs."

"I was considering taking it to Pulsate, since that's where I started. I could do the whole full circle thing, but maybe I'll follow Sydney's lead and self-publish it if you're not interested," Sean said casually, ignoring his publisher.

Roger looked at Vincent. "Why would we *not* take it? He's our number one best-selling author in the whole house."

Vincent pulled a face and hurried to his high-backed velvet chair and sat down. "Maybe so, but which name would we release it under? Sean Ryan or Bryan Jamison?"

"Has anyone done a biography on Bryan Jamison?" Sean sat on the sofa, his gaze darting back and forth between them. "There's not a lot to tell about him, and no one would have found anything out; it's only you, me, and a few select family members at this stage and they're all dropping like flies, so the secret is safe."

Roger implored Vincent. "If we don't publish this memoir, we'll be stupid. Why let Pulsate get all the glory?"

"Why let *me* get all the glory if I self-publish it?" Sean joked. "I will. And make all the money."

Vincent gave a small smile. "Oh, dear boy. I hear what you're saying, but I just don't know. We don't do memoirs because when we did, they didn't sell well."

"Maybe because we didn't know how to sell them, or because the subjects weren't as popular as we thought," Roger said.

"True," Vincent relented. "What was your timeline again?"

"After September this year. I'm thinking early next year, March at the latest. But that might change."

"Let me think about it and I'll let you know by June."

"You'd better, because once I'm out of this ankle bracelet I'm off to travel the world. I've had enough of New York and want to go and see everything while I'm still young."

"You sound as if something's going to happen to you." Vincent arched a brow. "What do you know that we don't?"

Sean stood and picked up his bag. "What I know is that my family is dropping like flies and I don't want it to happen to me. I want to see the world while I can."

"When will you go?"

"The end of July, early August. Basically, the minute I get this monitor off and *Mine* will be released and promoted. It gives me two months until the novel comes out."

"And how far are we with the memoir?"

"Halfway. I'm writing non-stop, getting help from friends with what stories to write about. I have photos, timelines, deadlines, evidence. I promise you, Vincent, it will be an explosive memoir, one to last the ages. Quite long, too. Considering." He headed for the door.

"Considering what?" Roger asked.

Sean opened the door and looked over his shoulder. "Considering who my family are and the secrets I know. Believe me when I say they are explosive. You'll be sorry you missed out if you pass on it." He grinned and closed the door behind him.

Vincent watched after him. "He's up to something."

"If he is, do we really want to miss out on it? Memoir or not, it could be explosive."

"How explosive could it be?"

"As explosive as his parents are both dead, his cousins are dead, and his former aunt by marriage used to be a pro for Madam X. We *cannot* let this go to Pulsate."

Vincent steepled his fingers under his chin in thought. "I suppose you're right. But again, he's only twenty-one. How explosive could it be?"

"If he knows family secrets, *very*. We should at least get first dibs on what he's written, and, if it's not great, then we pass."

"We could," Vincent murmured, and thought a moment before giving a nod. "We read an excerpt and we'll decide then. And it had better be explosive."

*****

Sean turned up at his parents' house to see it had been gutted of carpet and most of the walls. The windows had been replaced, and the roof repaired. It also smelt better.

"Wow, this is a lot," he said to Chip, the head of the renovation crew. "What are you working on now?"

"We're ripping off the rest of the dry wall to check for mould and rats, cleaning up the basement, making sure water and electricals are up to code and fixed. Once that's done, we'll put in new drywall, paint, and you can add the carpet. Plus, the bathrooms are being done because of the plumbing."

"So, another week for all of that?" Sean walked through to the kitchen and saw it had been ripped out and was back to bare bones. "Jesus, did it have to go?"

"Everything's been neglected for a couple of years, so yeah. But you'll get it back in the sale."

"I hope so; this is costing me a fortune." Sean walked through the rest of the house and came upon his bedroom. He'd left the walls black, and he wondered how they were going to paint over it when it had also been covered in colourful graffiti, but he saw they'd been ripped out and the room was back to the studs.

There was only one good memory associated with that room. The day Sydney had stood there. He'd been so nervous, sitting there watching her. He'd wanted so desperately to pee because of his nerves and hoped he didn't make a fool of himself in front of her. It was hard to believe that the woman he'd sent a death threat to was standing in his doorway with her head in his notebook.

Her facial expressions had showed her thoughts as her gaze dashed across the sentences, and she'd read quickly, too quickly, and it was all over, and she'd read two full stories and bits and pieces of several others, and she'd told him they were good; that he had talent.

He turned to the doorway and pictured her standing there. She'd been the only person, outside of his teachers, who'd told him they were good. That *he* was good. Who supported him with not just something that he did, but in his writing.

A sad smile barely lifted his lips. In seventeen years, that was the only good memory he had of this house, of his life in the house. Because they sure as hell didn't have any from his childhood to compete with, or his teen years. Abuse, abuse, and more abuse. He took a shaky breath and walked across the hall to his parents' bedroom.

The room that was infested with hate and anger, tears and depression. The number of nights he'd heard his mother crying was too many. And then Connor…

Maybe I should have sent that video to Dad. The one where they fucked their way through the house. Maybe Dad should have beat Connor up, then he would've laid off me. His hands rolled into fists in his pockets. *But then again, maybe not.*

He walked to where the closet had been and remembered the small door to the hidey-hole. He knew where Laura had kept her stash of evidence against his father, but there was so much more than that. Her diaries, medical reports, photos of Declan with prostitutes… He was surprised his mother had those. But he'd taken all of it when she died and then Declan had abandoned the house. After everything of his was removed, including his own private stash he kept in the wall cavity behind his bed, Sean had removed everything else with the help of Douglas and Cormac. Furniture was sold off, knick-knacks and a few personal items hidden away. All of the items they'd kept hidden built a case against Declan for abuse. But not one lawyer wanted to deal with it.

"Time and place for everything," Sean murmured. "He may be gone, but his time is coming. All of their times are coming." He sighed and went downstairs. "Hey, Chip, I'll see you next Friday," he yelled and waved when Chip stuck his head around the kitchen wall.

"We'll have the plumbing and electricals done by then, drywall too," Chip yelled back.

Sean walked into the warm May sunshine and drove to his grandfather's house for lunch. "Hey, Grandpa."

"Sean, in here," Cormac called from the sun room. "How's the house?"

"Fine." Sean dropped his bag in the living room and walked through to the back of the house. "Hey, Emerson." He gave her a peck on the cheek before giving his grandfather one.

"Hello, Sean," she greeted him warmly "How *is* the house going?"

"Pretty quick, actually. Let's hope everything else continues this quickly and I can sell it before I leave in July." He walked into the kitchen for a beer and saw a soup pot on the stove. "Smells good. Is that Sydney's beef hotpot?" He lifted the lid for a look and the aroma hit him full force. "Yum." He set the lid back on, and went into the sun room. "I didn't think you made Sydney's specialities."

"Douglas made it a lot before he passed, and I make it once a month," Emerson said. "Along with her roast chicken recipe. Now, what's this about you leaving in July?" She folded the paper and watched him settle onto the couch.

"Once I get this thing off." He lifted his left pants leg to show off the monitor. "Then I'm going exploring for two months. The last of the trilogy will be out that month, so *She Is Mine* will be done and I have some time off before the next novel comes out in September." Sean pushed his pants leg down and crossed his legs. "I'm under house arrest until then." He took a swig of beer. "Have you heard from Sydney?"

"I have and she's doing fine." Emerson took a sip of her wine. "They're coming into winter in Australia, but it's still warm where she is."

"Is she happy?" Sean asked in all seriousness.

Emerson saw his expression and nodded. "She is. Told me she's been writing."

"Will she publish?"

"She doesn't know. She's enjoying no deadlines, no publishing date. She says it's flowing just nicely."

"That's good." Sean gave a slight nod. "It's always better when it comes naturally, and we're not rushed."

"And how's your writing?" Emerson asked.

"Going well, thank you for asking. I've just finished a third book in as many months and I'm working on two more."

"Prolific." Emerson smiled. "Just like Sydney when she's in that mode. Has to go until the story stops."

"Yeah, I guess it's like that for a lot of authors." Sean

drained his beer bottle. "How much longer until lunch?"

Emerson glanced at her watch. "Oh, probably now." She dashed into the kitchen and checked the pot. "Looks like it's ready. Take your seats."

Cormac and Sean took their seats at the table as Emerson carried in the pot. She served Cormac and Sean before herself, and she hurried back for the bread fresh from the oven. She deftly sliced it up, laid it on a plate, and carried it to the table. "Here we are."

Small talk happened between mouthfuls of beef and vegetables laden on slices of baked bread.

"Amazing as always." Sean scraped up the last of his hotpot with his bread. "And I am full."

"You should be after thirds, but then you are a growing boy, you need your food," Emerson said. "Are you not feeding yourself?"

"Ah…" Sean considered his daily routine. "Breakfast," he finally said. "I work out in the morning and do my martial arts practice, then have a high protein meal. Once I sit down to write, I'm out for the count and I don't eat at all."

"Oh, Sean, you need more than breakfast. Do you want to take the leftovers home? Do you want me to bring you around some meals each week?" Emerson gathered the bowls. "I don't mind."

"No, thank you." He shook his head. "I eat when I need to and have protein bars or shakes with fruit if I need anything at night. I'm fine."

"You look as if you've lost weight. I can make you desserts…" Her voice trailed off as she walked into the kitchen and deposited the dishes on the sink.

Sean perked up. "Oooh, I'll take some of those."

Her laughter rang out. "Of course you will. Just as well I made mini versions of your favourites. But for today's dessert we have a devil cake." She carried it in and set it on the table. "And no touching while I get the plates." Emerson carried the soup pot back into the kitchen and left it on the stove. She collected the plates and dessert forks, and set them on the table. "Do I see a finger mark? Sean?"

"Hey, don't look at me?" Sean put up his hands in protest. "It's on Grandpa's side of the cake."

Emerson looked at Cormac whose grin lit up his face. "Oh, you."

"Couldn't help it," Cormac said. "Your cakes are always delicious."

With a happy sigh, Emerson cut big slices for the men in her life and a smaller one for herself.

"Mmm." Sean's eyes closed at the delicate sponge in his mouth. "Oh, my God. This is good."

"No talking with your mouth full," she playfully scolded and popped a piece into her mouth.

"I gotta agree with Sean. This is heaven, as always, my love." Cormac forked another piece into his mouth.

"It is one of my best." Emerson sipped her wine. "Oh, but I've had enough." She pushed her half-eaten piece away.

"You're not hungry?" Cormac asked.

"Not so much, these days, thanks to the dreaded menopause and old age. I have to watch everything I eat and exercise twice as much." She took another sip of wine. "I can send a chunk home with you, Sean."

"Oh, God yes." Sean shoved his last piece into his mouth and nodded. "Definitely one of my favourites."

"Okay. If everyone's finished, I'll pack it up now and leave it in the fridge for you."

"You've got an amazing woman there, Cormac," Sean said and finished off his third beer. "You better keep her happy." He gave his grandfather an arched brow and heard Emerson's laughter in the kitchen.

Chapter 13

"You still have lunch with your grandfather?"

"Of course. Sometimes it's Saturday lunch, or sometimes dinner. Sometimes Sunday dinner when the family's not there."

"Have you seen them since your conversations with Connor and Ethan?"

"No."

"No dinners or lunches with the family?"

"What family? Three are gone."

"It can't be easy."

"For who?"

"Your family. Your two cousins in one fell swoop, then your dad. Three people gone in one month."

"The table's emptier now."

Levinworth watched Sean as he stood by the window. "Does that make you happy?"

Sean looked over his shoulder. "Does what make me happy?"

"Your cousins and father being gone."

He shrugged. "Dad, yeah. I mean, why not. Sierra and Brandon, sure, they were sick fucks anyway."

"But they weren't the first you lost. Your great-grandfather last year, and your mom two years before that. Your grandmother seventeen years ago."

"Yeah, that was sick shit," Sean said, hands in pockets and staring out the window. "But Sydney killed the asshole who murdered my grandmother, so I love her for that."

"It makes six people in your life, five that have passed in three years, one seventeen years ago."

Sean thought about it. "Yeah, but Grandma was murdered, as millions of people are. Pop died from old age; Brandon and Sierra from a tampered with car valve, and my dad from gunshot wounds."

Levinworth tilted his head. "You forgot your mother."

"No, I didn't."

"What did she die of?"

Sean's hands balled into fists. "You want me to say by suicide, or natural causes. Drank herself to death or was so pissed she injured herself by falling down the stairs."

"Didn't she?"

Sean thought back. "I know she didn't."

"Mom, I'm here. You said on the phone you needed to see me." Sean let the front door close behind him and hung his bag on the coat rack peg on the wall. "Mom?" He leaned into the living room but didn't see her, so he hurried up the stairs to her room. She wasn't there. He checked his room and went downstairs to the kitchen. "Mom? You here? You said you wanted to see me? Mom?" He went outside and checked the yard and garage, but found no one. "Mom?" Locking the back door, Sean turned around, stepped across the hall, and

opened the basement door. He reached for the overhead light and flicked it on.

There, at the bottom of the stairs, lay his mother, surrounded by washing marred with her blood. His veins froze and his breath stopped.

"Mom?" His voice came out squeaky. "Mom?" His right foot went down to the next step, followed by his left. Then his right, then left. Until all of the steps between them had been covered. His gaze never left her face, frozen, wide-eyed for all time. "Mom?" His right foot hit the concrete basement floor and he leant over her. "Mom?" His hand waved in front of her face, but she remained unblinking. "Mom?"

His tongue darted out to lick his dry lips and his right hand reached down to feel her neck for a pulse. "Mom?" There was none. "Mommy?" The tears finally came, and he stumbled back onto the stairs. "Mommy," he screamed, rocking back and forth. "No." Wrapping his arms around his legs, he sobbed until he was spent.

"Mommy?" Sean stared down at the cold dead body of his mother, but finally, he pulled his phone from his pocket and called the first person he thought of. "Grandpa. Mommy's dead."

Cormac's team sped him there as it was a weekend, and he was home. Once he arrived, he took charge, got Sean out of there, dealt with his officers and the paramedics and then the coroner.

Sean sat in his room the entire time, crying, hugging himself on his bed that he'd left behind. Just his furniture remained in that room; all of his belongings he'd taken.

"Your grandfather took care of her in death. What

about your dad?"

Sean slumped onto the couch facing the window. "What about him? You knew this all last time because it happened one year into seeing you. You dealt with the fallout."

"I did. But it still affects you. You didn't mention her as a family member who died. Do you think about her?"

"Sometimes." Sean dropped his head into his hands and stared at the floor between his feet. "I try not to, but she creeps in."

"It isn't easy finding a loved one when they've died. Whether it's your parent, child, sibling, or cousin. It's hard to find them lying there, dead."

"The life gone out of them," Sean added. "Yeah, it is."

"The coroner's report said she'd fallen. At the time you told me she was murdered."

"She was."

"By whom?"

"My father. At the time, I thought it could've also been Connor."

"But you didn't have proof, and it was ruled an accident."

"I found proof in the last three years."

Levinworth looked up sharply. "You're still saying you have proof."

"I've found proof since then." Sean got to his feet and walked over to the wave painting on the wall to his left.

"What did you do with it?"

"Kept it. Hid it away. I knew that if I told my family they'd cover it up. Steal it, make sure it never saw the light of day, and he would get away scot-free as he always did." He slid his hands into his pockets. "He always did. The three Ryan boys always did."

"And you still have it safely hidden away?"

"I do. Several copies. One of them is with my lawyer." He deflated with a sigh. "I figured that if my father ever did something, to me, or someone else, but mainly to me, I'd have it as leverage, just as I've got rap sheets on all of my family members."

"How?"

"Private detectives, investigative services who can legally dig into people and find out what they're hiding. I found out what they're hiding."

"That must've been expensive?"

Sean thought about the money source for it all. "I had book money."

"Even after your college tuition? Harvard Law's not cheap."

"No, it certainly isn't, Walter. I have so much dirt on them I could bury them ten times over. But..." He shrugged. "As it turns out, karma's here for the Ryan boys."

Levinworth made a note in Sean's file. "How did your dad take your mother's death?"

"You know. I told you four years ago. He didn't care. He just didn't care."

"Who paid for her funeral?"

"Mom did. She had a will and pre-planned package already paid for."

"How did the rest of the family cope? How did they treat you?"

"I have no clue how they coped. She wasn't related to

them, and at first, they were sympathetic. Murmured sympathies, as did the others who turned up. Condolences, blah, blah, blah."

"You didn't want people's condolences?"

"No, I didn't."

"Tell me about the funeral."

Sean stood staring at his mother's body. They were in the church, had just had the service, but were now parading past the coffin. She looked okay; didn't look dead in any way, just asleep. He laid a red rose on her chest and touched her hand. Cold, frozen, almost.

"Mommy," he whispered, and allowed Cormac to lead him on.

They went back to their seat while the rest of the people paraded past showing their tears and sadness until, finally, they came and closed the coffin and carried it down the nave.

The family walked two by two behind the procession and watched the coffin being loaded into the hearse and secured. The door was closed, and they took their vehicles for the ride to the cemetery.

Sean stared out the window, unable to look at his father, or grandfather. Emerson was with them, as well as Douglas with his lady friend CC Charleston, owner of Pulsate Publishing who had just published his first young adult novel. He thought back to when he handed out copies of his book to his family. Most had been reasonably excited, except for Sierra and Brandon, and his father and mother.

"That's nice, sweetie," she'd said, and put it on the table so she could pick up her glass of wine. "I'll read it

over the weekend."

Declan slapped his down next to it. "Meh, at least something came from that mentorship."

"The one you fucked up," Sean had muttered under his breath.

Cormac and Douglas were proud as punch and had already told their friends all about it so they could support Sean.

A small smile lifted his lips as he stared out the window. At least they supported me.

They arrived at the cemetery to sodden earth and umbrellas. The rain had not let up since the night before.

"An omen," he'd said earlier that morning.

And maybe I was right, he thought as he stepped out of the car under the umbrella offered to him.

They trudged over to the family plot and stood around the hole. The soil was being held back with tarps and plywood against the downpour.

Sean stood between his father and grandfather and watched his mother being lowered into the six by three rectangular hole. The priest stood under an umbrella spewing words about God and Jesus, until, finally, the coffin stopped on the bottom.

He watched his grandfather and father grab a handful of dry dirt from a pile under a tarp and throw it into the grave and then did the same himself. He watched as everyone wandered away and kept watching as they poured the dirt back into the hole.

"Sean," Cormac said. "Time to go."

He shook his head. "No. I need to stay until it's full, until she's gone."

"We'll stay in the car," Douglas told him. "Then we'll take you back home."

"No." Sean looked up as the last fragment of his mother's coffin was covered in dirt. "You go. Don't stay for me. I can catch a cab or call an Uber."

"We can wait," Cormac said.

Sean's laugh was short and caustic. "Dad didn't. Connor didn't. Alec and Kieran didn't. My cousins didn't. Only the three of us are standing here. Look around." He waved a hand. "Everyone's gone and driving away. I'm staying until her grave is full. Go home and get warm. Seriously." He turned back to the grave. "I'm staying."

Cormac exchanged a glance with his father. "All right. Call when you're ready, and we'll come and get you." They walked through the cemetery and over to their car where Emerson and CC were waiting inside in the warmth.

"Is he staying?" Emerson asked when they got in. "It's so cold and wet. Should we stay?"

"No." Cormac sighed. "He needs to be alone with her. He needs time."

Sean stayed until the hole was filled, staring down at the grave of his mother. His dead mother. The mother he'd never see again. "You might have been a drunk, but you were still my mother." He tilted the umbrella back and turned his face to the downpour of rain. It competed with his tears, mingling until they were one and flowing down his face into the collar of his shirt and down his chest. He closed the umbrella, left it against the fence around the Ryan burial plot, and walked away.

"I hated that day," Sean murmured. "I hated the day she died. I hated the day she was buried. I hated it all. I hated the rain, my father, my family."

"What did you do once you left the cemetery?"

"Walked." Sean stared at the waves in the painting. They reminded him of the torrent of rain, rolling in waves over him as he walked. "I didn't know where I was going. I didn't know what I was doing. I just walked."

"Were you thinking?"

"About Mom, Dad, her death, how he caused it, the funeral, her coffin, her grave. It just played over and over and wouldn't stop. I just walked until *I* finally stopped."

"And where were you?"

"On Sydney's doorstep."

"Why?"

He sighed. "I don't know. At the time, you told me it was because she was the only person outside of the family who'd supported me and encouraged me, and I trusted her even though I'd hurt her. Because my mom was gone, she was the surrogate."

"You believed me then. Does it not hold true anymore?"

"It never held true, Walter. I unconsciously made my way there, for whatever reason. I knew she wasn't family, I knew I could unburden with her."

"What happened when you got there?"

"She let me in. She let me in when she didn't have to. She cared enough to help me. She'd seen the funeral on social media. Someone was posting a live video from the cemetery and using all sorts of hashtags to describe my mom. I saw them later. They were vile."

"What did Sydney do?"

"Took me in. Got me out of my sodden clothes, sat me down by the fire and filled me up with her hotpot. She fed me, dried me, and took care of me. Unlike my mother in the last ten years of my life."

"Was that all?"

"Was what all?"

"Is that all you did?"

"No. We talked. For hours. I talked about my mom and her death, that day, that year. I apologised for hitting her and told her I didn't think Mom fell of her own accord down the stairs. Sydney listened, I talked, it rained, I cried." He silently remembered the good part.

"Sit down and get warm, I'll get you a bowl of food." She scooped up a big bowl of hotpot and put it on a tray. "I'm going to have to call your grandfather. They'll be worried about you." She set the tray on his legs, and her hand brushed his. She snatched it away and rubbed the spot, frowning at him and his big blue eyes.

"I'm eighteen. An adult. it doesn't matter if I'm out. They can't stop me. Besides…" He shrugged and scooped up a spoonful of beef balls. "Considering what I've been through, I really don't want to see any of them right now. Especially Connor and my old man."

"Why?" Sydney asked, knowing full well why. "They're your family."

Sean glared up at her. "Because they killed my mother."

Stunned, Sydney could only sink into the easy chair opposite him as he told the story. "So, you think the affair did this?"

"I think my father did it."

"Not the alcohol or the depression?"

"He drove her to that. She wouldn't've done it, otherwise."

"Do you have proof?"

"I might have. But I'd need to check it out first."

"Then what will you do?" Sydney asked.

Sean stared at her, unblinking. "Make him pay. I want revenge." He dumped the tray on the floor beside the chair and stalked around the room. "I want revenge on my father and my uncle. They both fucked Mom and both fucked her over. They hurt her and me and I think Dad had something to do with Mom's death."

"Why?" Sydney watched him pace.

"Because the coroner's report said he wasn't certain whether she fell or was pushed." He watched Sydney's brows rise. "Yep. Even he couldn't tell. And I won't know until I get into my house on my own and get the cameras and recordings. I should've done that sooner. I don't know how long they're kept on her laptop for. She had a secret one you know. And I know exactly where she hid it along with her diaries and medical files of all of the abuse Dad did to us. I've seen it." He turned to Sydney. "I want revenge on my family. Will you help me?"

She sighed and got to her feet. "Sean, are you sure this is something you should be thinking of now? Your emotions are still incredibly raw. Why don't you give it some time and think about it again in a month or more?"

"No, Sydney. I want it now. I want them all gone for what they've done. To me, to you, to us, to my mom. I want them all gone now."

He finally spoke. "I unburdened my soul that night. I emptied everything I had, and she listened." A short laugh burst out of him. "She turned it into a novel after that, but then, so did I. It's hard to not use your own life as inspiration when you write."

"Did you sleep at all?"

"I did. Sydney rang Grandpa and Pop the next morning and they came and picked me up. They desperately wanted to question me on the way home and did ask if I was okay and where I'd gone. I told them the truth. That I walked until I got to Sydney's and she took care of me. When we got home, I showered and slept for half the day. I didn't realise how exhausting grief could be."

"It can be, especially when crying. It takes a lot of energy. Sean..." Levinworth watched him as he chose his words. "Did anything else happen at Sydney's? Anything you didn't tell me back then?"

"Of course, doc. There's a lot, but I'm not going to tell you."

"Ever?"

"Maybe and maybe not. Just not yet." Sean glanced at his watch. "Time's almost up, doc." He picked up his bag. "I don't think it's rained as hard since that day. It was like the heavens were crying for me, for Mom, for everyone." He took a couple of steps. "You know, doc, it's funny; that night, the night of Mom's funeral, when I turned up on her doorstep, I had no idea why I went there. Maybe you were right all along. Maybe I was looking for a mother figure, or maybe I was looking for someone to talk to that wasn't my fucked-up family. Someone who knew me, knew what I was like, knew what to say. And I told her how I felt about her. That I still loved her. I always had. Had from the moment I kissed her the year before, and I was still sorry for hitting and hurting her and I would forever feel guilt and regret. Regret for hurting her, but regret at not doing it right. Not telling her the right way."

He took another two steps towards the door. "I told her again. And I explained my reasoning, my feelings, my actions, and she just stood there staring at me as I moved towards her one step at a time. And finally, I took her by the arms and kissed her again. And next thing, we fucked against the buffet under the TV." He reached the door, his hand resting on the handle, and saw Levinworth uncross his legs and turn around in his chair. "I grabbed her and kissed her just like I did the first time and this time, I didn't let her stop me."

"Sean." Levinworth frowned. "Did you force yourself on her? Did you rape her?"

"I wouldn't call it rape." Sean smiled.

"Did she consent?"

"Well." Sean glanced up at the ceiling. "She didn't say no, verbally."

"Did she say yes?"

"She didn't say yes, verbally."

"Did you force yourself on her?"

"I was forceful in my manner, but she didn't say no."

"She didn't say yes, either."

Sean shrugged. "Not with her words, but she certainly did with her body and mouth." He opened the door. "Time to go, doc."

"She consented?" Levinworth pushed. "Sean, did she consent?"

"Not with her words, but she certainly did with her body," Sean repeated. "And it wasn't just me who was forceful. She has a sex room, remember." He walked out and closed the door behind him.

Levinworth straightened in his chair, his heart pounding against his ribcage. Sean had sex with Sydney that night, but there was no verbal consent, only physical. And force was on both sides. Sean and Sydney slept together. Jesus. He *was* eighteen but... He checked his notes. He'd been having sex since his sixteenth birthday, and he was of legal age. But was force initiated? On his part or hers?

He leaned back and took a breath. Definitely not *illegal*, but not exactly kosher age-wise. *I wonder if they've told anyone else? I wonder if Sydney knew he was Bryan three years later when they slept together again? Surely she must have? He certainly knew he was having sex with her. But did she? Jesus.*

He got up and poured himself a whiskey from his drinks cabinet. *Sean was eighteen, vulnerable, had just buried his mother, had lived with his grandfather for a year and was in the middle of therapy. Why didn't he tell me back then?* Stunned into thinking he might have missed it the first time, he quickly read through his notes from Sean's first sessions.

He mentioned going to Sydney's, but he hadn't hinted at sex. Did he omit it then or lie now? Or is he telling the truth now? Was he too embarrassed then? But not now? Is there an end game now? He's telling me things now that he didn't back then. His age could be the reason—his emotional growth could be another. So why admit it now? Is there something I need to look out for? Something he's yet to tell me? They had sex then and sex now. Did they have sex inbetween? Did they enter into a relationship? But if they did, Sydney would have known he was Sean.

He thought a few moments more and tried to remember if Sean had mentioned it in any of his novels.

What if she did know?

*****

"Bryan Jamison, you've done it again with your book *Is*. The second novel in this trilogy with *She* being the first. Strange title for a novel. Can you explain once again how you came up with it?"

"Well, Marcia." Bryan nudged his wire framed glasses up the bridge of his nose. "I wrote one very long book that I ended up dividing into three. The overall theme is about a man wanting a woman. *She Is Mine* was perfect for the title but dividing the title across three books was a marketing ploy. Just like when I didn't show my face for the first two books I released; *Illicit Things* and *Sinister Motives*. It's all about being different, and about getting eyes on your books."

"But does having eyes on your books equate to people buying those books?"

"Absolutely, if sales are anything to go by."

"And what are your sales figures, if you don't mind my asking?"

"Not at all. They're very healthy and I sell over a million copies per book."

"Print or electronic?"

"Print." Bryan gazed into the camera on his laptop.

"It's always the first stop for a book; e-books and audio will be out next month."

"You released *She* two months ago, and now comes *Is. Mine* will be released in two months' time, and then two months after that you have another standalone novel. Aren't you exhausting your fans? Aren't you demanding too much from them, buying four books from you this year?"

"My fans buy in a variety of formats, Marcia," Bryan said. "For those who want the hardcover, they go and get it. For those who prefer e-books, audio, or paperback, they wait for that format to be available. Each format has a different price point and whether or not my fans buy my books is up to them."

"And you're still home nursing a broken leg. How much longer will you be out for the count? Aren't you missing out on your own book launches?"

"I am and the cast is off, but it's still very weak and I'm using crutches or a walking stick. It's a couple of months of rehab to get it strong again, so I'm still under house arrest."

"And are you still writing? Can we expect more books from Bryan Jamison?"

"Absolutely. I've been writing like crazy and have completed two more books, plus I'm working on two more. But we'll be back to releasing one, *maybe* two books next year. Just to take a break."

"You said with the release of *She* two months ago, that we were getting one book this year originally, but then you wrote another book that you wanted out in September. You asked your publisher to speed up the publishing process. Can you tell us again, why?"

"Because the standalone coming in September will blow everyone away and I wanted it out this year. Plus, when you get a trilogy or series, do you really want to wait a full year till the next book comes out? No, you don't."

"I'm sure this will be a smash hit just like all of your others. I've read it, folks, and as the follow up to *She*, it reveals so much more of the story, and I can't wait to read *Mine* when it comes out in July. Until then, Bryan Jamison, thanks for coming on *Biblio File*."

"Thank you, Marcia." Bryan smiled until the show was out, and the Zoom window closed. He turned off the camera so nothing would be recorded. "Tell me again why I'm doing interviews a week before release?"

"Because some of the reviewers wanted to get you early before the big shows," Dexter said. "I organised for a few today so you had less to do in the next two weeks."

"But we're on all the big ones, right?" Sean had some coffee and a small lemon tart that Emerson had delivered. She'd brought two containers of mini desserts, red devil, meringues, apple pies, cupcakes. He had them as snacks with coffee.

"Rhett Rockefeller and Preston Grant are next week, along with Richard Walker from *The Book Show*. You'll do a few radio and magazine interviews tomorrow which will air and come out next week."

Sean sighed. "I thank God my visit from Alec is done and dusted for the week. I wouldn't want to be interrupted by him during an interview."

"Would he do that?" Dexter sent a quick text off.

"Oh, yeah. Get his face on screen and tell them who

he is and that he's my uncle. It would blast me right out of the water, and he wouldn't care."

"Is he that vindictive?"

"Worse." Sean drank another mouthful of coffee. "Who's next?"

Nine interviews later, they called it quits and Sean pulled off his disguise, leaving it all on the kitchen counter. "I can't wait to change into my own clothes and be me again. It's getting to be a bit too much." He opened the door. "Thanks for today, I'll see you tomorrow."

"Bye, Sean, rest up…you're looking tired."

"I know. I might actually watch some TV and have an early night."

"Yeah, right. You, have an early night?"

Sean chuckled. "I know. But books don't write themselves. See you tomorrow." He locked the door and hurried upstairs for a shower, changing into old tracksuit pants and a t-shirt. He went down to his office to clean up for the night and make sure things were ready for the following day.

After tidying his desk, he stopped at the wall of Sydney. He'd done a print out of all her book covers and next to it was a print out of his young adult and adult covers, plus a photo of Douglas with Sydney at her book singing where he'd handed on a copy of his first book. The picture showed her holding it up as she stood next to Emerson. Douglas and Cormac were either side of them holding Sydney's book *Twisted Affair*. She'd signed one for him, after Douglas had asked her. It was a sweet encouragement from an incredible woman. He still had that book, as he had all of Sydney's in hardcover; pristine and in pride of place on his shelf.

"And just like Pop, I buy the e-book and paperback to read." He chuckled. "I'm turning out just like him." He looked at her novel, the one she'd signed in the photo and flashed back to hearing an interview about it.

He turned the volume up on his laptop and listened to Preston Grant introduce his show. He'd waited for this moment for a week since it was announced.

"Coming up today, as promised, we have prolific author Sydney Kingston who writes thrillers as Cassandra Kingsley. She's here with her new one, Twisted Affair, and will be in the studio in a few minutes. But first, let's get the usual suspects out of the way."

He tuned out while Preston spoke to those in the studio and played sponsored ads. He was recording the show as he did all of Sydney's radio interviews, so he could hear them on repeat. Thanks to having a single corner room on campus, he didn't have to worry about anyone interrupting him or being there.

"And now we come to the guest of the hour…"

Sean brushed down his shirt and leaned back in his seat. He listened to the interview and when it was over, hit the stop button. It had been good, and one he'd listen to again. He picked up the copy of her book that she'd signed for him, and spent the rest of the day reading it for the fourth time.

Sean came back to the present, remembering her interview fondly, remembering his first year of college not so fondly. He sighed. "I did so much for you, Sydney. I lost weight and trained, kept myself neat and tidy, and healthy, and look at how you repay me."

Chapter 14

"Did you rape Sydney Kingston?"

"No, Walter, I did not." Sean stood at the window in his therapist's office. "I want to talk about Mom and Ethan."

"Oh, God, don't tell me that happened as well," Levinworth said in shock.

"What?" Sean looked at him, brows furrowed in confusion. "Why would you say that?"

"Oh." Levinworth shook his head. "Sorry, but since Connor slept with her…"

"Oh, no, God no!" Sean waved his hand and rubbed his eyes at the horror. "It didn't happen, that I know of. I meant; Sydney dumped Ethan just after Mom's death. They'd been off and on since September, hadn't seen each other much, since she was off travelling for *Twisted Affair*, but he got dumped after the funeral."

"Why?"

"She said our family was too fucking complicated. Who knew," he mocked.

"How do you know all of this?"

Sean finished the last of the dishes. "All done. Who's

up next?"

"We've dried." Brandon hung the towel on the rack to dry.

"And the table's cleared, napkins are in the wash, and glasses put away." Sierra closed the drinking glass cabinet.

Sean dried his hands and looked at his cousins. "Where's Ethan?"

"Scarpered. Didn't bother doing anything," Brandon said.

"I think he's on the phone." Sierra glanced into the dining and sun rooms. "Not there."

Sean hung up the hand towel and went in search of Ethan. He found him in Douglas' room, his voice barely audible. Sean put his ear to the one-inch gap at the doorway and listened in.

"I can't wait to see you," Ethan murmured. "We're almost done here and I'm hoping to get away in the next few minutes."

Puzzled, Sean kept listening.

"Yeah, I know. You haven't told anyone, have you?" Pause. "I haven't either. No one in the family knows we're seeing each other." Another pause. "I know. I don't want my dad finding out either. Imagine what he'd say if he knew." Pause. "I know. I can't wait to make love to you."

Sean's brows furrowed and he glanced down the hallway on the lookout.

"I know. I want to make love to you in your bed and fuck you every which way all over the house. And then we can go down to the sex room."

Sean's brows shot up and his eyes grew wide.

"I know. Well, then you shouldn't have introduced me to the sex room. But now that I've had a taste of it and you, I need more. I want more. I need and want you, Sydney."

Sean could barely breathe; the air had been knocked out of him. Ethan was fucking Sydney. Oh, my God.

"I'll be there soon, and we can spend the night together. I can't wait to see you. I love you, Syd."

Sean trudged down the hallway. His feet felt like hundred-pound weights. He leaned against the wall in the kitchen out of Ethan's sight. Out of everyone's sight. Ethan was fucking Sydney. Oh, my God. "Oh, my God, Sydney, how could you," he whispered. "How could you?"

Ethan walked into the living room. "Hey, we got anything else to do, 'cause I need to go."

"Not at the moment. Why, hot date?" Connor asked.

Ethan gave a sly smile. "Yeah, actually. See you next week."

Sean heard the front door open and close, and his breath whooshed out.

"That's how I found out they were seeing each other," Sean told Levinworth. "A secret call to his lover. That was September, early October. Sydney had released *Twisted Affair*, it was after the book launch because I had a copy thanks to Pop and Grandpa, and she had a break-in. Ethan was the detective, so they hooked up around that time. But as I said, it was off and on because Sydney travelled for most of October and November for the book."

"You didn't talk about this last time—why not?"

"Why would I? It would've made me look like I wasn't dealing with it. But it was a year after I stopped seeing Sydney and I didn't want to go there."

"Why now?"

"Why not? I'm older, can deal with it better. I was young and stupid and immature and confused then."

"And you're not now?"

Sean rolled his eyes at Levinworth. "Ha-ha, Walter. Very funny."

"I'm being serious."

Sean pondered the comment. "No, I'm not, I've done a lot of things in the last three to four years. Especially since my mother's death. I've matured, grown up, and faced situations not everyone gets to face."

"How do you feel about Ethan and Sydney?"

"He stopped being my hero that day." Sean stared at the pigeons on the rooftop. Three males taking turns to rut with a female. It reminded him of his mother and Connor, Sydney and Connor, Sydney and Ethan… Sydney and his father.

"Because he was seeing a woman who had also dated his father?"

"Because he was fucking the woman I loved."

"And you couldn't."

Sean smirked. "But I have. He stopped being my hero because he was fucking Sydney and then I hated him."

"Hate's a strong word."

"It's not strong enough for that situation." He breathed in and let it out in a huff. "I wanted nothing more to do with him after that. Whenever we had family lunch we all sat in our usual places. But I stayed away from him for the rest of it. He was too busy hanging out with his old man, or fucking Sydney. I wanted nothing to do with him."

"Do you regret that?"

"No." He thought back to the times Ethan had stood up for him and felt a small pang in his heart. "I regret that he grew up and moved away from the family emotionally. Once he hit twenty-one we rarely saw him. It sucked and I was sad. I was fourteen and he was gone. I only saw him at the occasional Sunday lunch. Fast forward four years and he's fucking the woman I brought into the family. Sometimes, I wish I hadn't."

Levinworth picked up on that. "You wish you hadn't made your mother contact Emerson to have lunch with her and Sydney. Bringing Sydney into the family. Why?"

"Because all of this crap wouldn't have happened."

"Neither would your writing career."

"Maybe." Sean thought about it. "Maybe not. Maybe I'd be starting now instead of at eighteen."

"So, you still would've been a writer even if you hadn't met her?"

He shrugged. "Maybe. But it's not to say everything else wouldn't have happened either. Mom and Connor were already happening. Everyone was already doing shit except me. All I'd done was send the note to Sydney. If she, *if I*, hadn't hounded Mom, she wouldn't have met the family. Connor, Ethan, my father."

"You."

Sean sent a scathing glare his way. "No need to rub it in, Walter."

Levinworth took the glare and served it right back. "I'm not. But then that means you wouldn't have met her, been mentored by her, ended up a writer."

"Ended up fucking her."

"And?"

"And what? Had the life I have now? I might've started now. I might've still applied for the mentorship. I might've gotten it."

"Might never've met Sydney."

"Might still have my mother," Sean argued. "But then again, she was already a drunk." He rubbed his forehead and walked over to his favourite painting. Taking a few breaths, he stared at the waves. "I have no clue what could've been, might've been, whatever've been, I just know everything that's happened, happened. Regardless of Sydney being in our lives."

"She wouldn't have slept with your uncle and father. Your cousin."

"Me. That's what you mean, Walter, isn't it?"

Levinworth moved on. "So, you found out Sydney was sleeping with Ethan. Did you confront him about it? Did you confront her about it?"

Sean shook his head. "No. I didn't go near Sydney, and could've killed Ethan, but only saw him at Sunday lunch. Because of Sydney's travel schedule, I knew when he was and wasn't seeing her. I had breathing space."

"And how do you know *she* dumped him?"

Sean sniggered. "The whole family knew."

"I fully understand why Sean's miserable," Cormac told the table. "But Ethan, why are you?" He looked from his youngest to his eldest grandson. It was early February

and neither cousin had attended lunch for a couple of weeks. Not even Declan was there.

Ethan shrugged a depressed shoulder and played with his beef hotpot that Emerson had made. "It's nothing."

Sean glanced up from his bowl. He knew the beef dish was one of Sydney's specialties and was savouring every morsel, but also had the feeling Ethan's funk had to do with her.

"What's going on?" Douglas asked, dipping toasted bread into his bowl. "Girl trouble?"

Ethan made a small noise and sighed. "Yeah."

Ooohs went around the table.

"Spit it out, kid," Connor told him. "I didn't even know you were seeing anyone."

"Neither did I," Cormac added. "Did anyone?"

Everyone shook their head, except for Sean who sent daggers at his cousin.

"Fess up." Connor elbowed him and picked up his beer. "Tell us."

A strangled cry came from Ethan. "There's not much to tell," he mumbled. "She…ah…doesn't want to see me anymore."

"Why not?" Douglas popped the last of his beef laden toast into his mouth.

"She uh…" Ethan cleared his throat, but he didn't look up from his bowl. "She…ah…saw Aunt Laura's funeral on social media, and in the paper, and thinks this family is too complicated and didn't want to see me anymore."

Silence settled around the table.

Sean shattered it. "But we are." He scooped up

another spoonful and slid it into his mouth, knowing every eye was on him. He ignored them.

"Yeah." Cormac nodded in agreement. "I guess we are. Did she not want to be involved with you because of us?"

"I'd been seeing her since the end of September. Our schedules conflicted so we only saw each other here and there, and then…the funeral. She realised how big we are and said it was too complicated and didn't want to see me anymore."

"Ah, don't worry, kid." Connor slapped him on the back. "Plenty more fish in the sea."

Ethan's head slowly moved side to side. "I don't want more. I want her." His lips trembled and he thrust his chair back. "Excuse me, I need to go." He rushed out of the dining room, and they all heard the front door bang.

Sean concealed his delight while luxuriating in having a part of Sydney in his mouth.

"And it's almost Valentine's too," Sierra said, reapplying her lip gloss.

"Poor kid." Connor leaned back in his chair. "I haven't seen him depressed over a girl before. Maybe I should find out who she is and have a chat."

Sean choked on a meatball and coughed, but that was quickly followed by laughter. "You are kidding, right? You want to force a woman to stay with your son? God's sake, he's a grown man, break-ups happen. Let him deal with it." He drank some water and went back to his meal.

"Sean's right," Douglas said. "Ethan's nearly twenty-six—he'll be fine. It was a four-month fling, and by his

own words, their schedules conflicted, so they didn't see much of each other."

"Yeah, but he looked so depressed," Connor said. "I don't think I've seen him that way over a woman before."

"He'll get over it." Cormac placed his cutlery in his bowl and wiped his mouth with his napkin. "He's young. He'll deal with it."

"I *still*, four years later, cannot believe Connor wanted to go around and have a chat with the woman who'd dumped his son. God knows what would've happened if he'd found out it was Sydney. But he knew anyway. I just don't know when or how he found out."

Levinworth frowned at him. "Connor knows Ethan slept with Sydney?"

"Yep. Mentioned it that night I invited them over. From the look on Ethan's face, he didn't know his father knew. It was a shock for both of us."

"Who do you think told Connor?"

Sean shrugged and walked away from the wall. "No idea. I didn't. Ethan didn't. As far as I know, when the three of them turned up on Sydney's doorstep later that year, he didn't know. So how did he find out?" Sean's eyes narrowed in thought. "No idea."

"Interesting. So, Connor told Alec and Declan he was banging Sydney, Ethan told no one. Did your father?"

"No idea. Possibly."

"And Alec and your grandfather know you slept with her back in January. I'm curious now. Do you think you could find out?"

Sean paused beside Walter's chair and looked down.

"Is that going to help me here in therapy?"

Levinworth looked up. "It might. Your family's quite the puzzle, Sean."

"Jigsaw?" Sean moved on to the other wall of artwork. "In an enigma?"

A laugh came from Levinworth, and Sean looked at him in surprise. "Maybe Sean, maybe."

Sean thought about his plans for that week. "I guess I could, but I'm going to be mighty busy."

"The new book?"

"Yep. I have a tonne of press this week. I managed to pre-tape a lot of interviews last week, but this week are the big guns."

"Rockefeller and Grant."

"Yep. TV and radio royalty. Highest rated in both fields." Sean paused. "I could call Connor—see if he'll tell me on the phone. I can't go and see him."

"Would anyone else know? Alec? Kieran?"

Sean thought about his uncles. "I think Kieran was kept out of the loop a lot, being so young."

"Kind of like you."

Sean raised a brow. "Yeah, I guess so. Alec might. But I'll call Connor first. Alec's a last resort after our fight."

"Another one?"

"No, the first one. He's up to something, the snide asshole. Do you have a copy of *Is* yet?"

"No, I'll be getting it this week and will read it over the weekend."

"Have you read *She?*"

"I have."

"As you've read all of my others since you seem to

quote my first three novels back to me."

Levinworth's lip twitched into a small smile. "I also read your young adult books when they came out, but when I found out you were Bryan Jamison I read the thrillers. Very autobiographical."

"We've had that discussion, Walter."

"We have, Sean. I'll bring it in next week. I might quote it."

"I'll sign it for you, like all the others. I did that for Pop."

Levinworth thought back to previous sessions. "You said you told Douglas on his death bed that you were Bryan Jamison."

Sean walked back to the window. "I did. He was so proud of me when I was published the first time. He and Grandpa were my biggest supporters besides Sydney. Told everyone he knew, and everyone he didn't know, that I was his great-grandson and a newly published author. As each book came out, I signed them for him and Grandpa. Something a little different each time, five in total. I told him I'd moved into adult fiction under a pen name so it wouldn't have the Ryan influence and I could do it on my own. And that I had. He was proud of me and loved the books. He was able to read all three before he died."

"And you've told no one else?"

"I hadn't at the time. But it's all coming out now."

"Your grandfather and Alec."

"I told Emerson, as you know. That was a hell of a shock, because I kept coming across Sydney at book launches and they talked about it then, and I think they've talked about it since."

"And we'll most certainly be getting to that, but our time's up for today."

"Normally it's me saying that."

"That's true," Levinworth conceded. "Until next week."

*****

That night, Sean called Connor. "Hey, I need to know how you found out about Ethan and Sydney."

"Why?" Connor sat back on his couch and flicked through the TV channels.

"Because it's important and my therapist keeps telling me to find these things out. Ethan was surprised that you knew."

"Yeah, well, Ethan doesn't know a lot of things. Just as you don't, Seany." Connor stopped on an ad with a naked woman rolling around on a sandy beach.

Sean gritted his teeth at the nickname. "How did you find out? And when?"

"I don't think it was long after it started, before Christmas, anyway. We had some conversation about dating girls, and I asked if he was seeing anyone. He was cagey and said he had to go, so I followed him, all the way to Sydney's. When I looked in the window I saw them kissing."

"Were you jealous?"

A guttural laugh came out of Connor. "That's funny, kid. In a way I was. Sydney's one hot fucker of a woman, but I ruined that, just as you did. If it was Ethan's turn, good for him. I watched them fuck on the couch just as

I'd done to her all those times."

Sean chose his next words. "Did you wonder if she thought he was better than you?"

Another laugh. "That's another good one. Sydney's not the first woman Ethan and I have shared. He just doesn't know about it. And believe me, they *all* said I was better."

Sean dry retched. "You knew in February, after my mother's funeral, that Sydney was the one Ethan was all mopey about at lunch because she'd dumped him?"

"I did, which is why I didn't say anything when you laughed and called me on what I'd said. I couldn't give away that I knew, so I went along with what you and Pop said."

"Did you ever see Sydney after that?"

"No, I didn't. Not until Nora's death. But then again, neither did Ethan."

*****

"Bryan Jamison, welcome back to Rockefeller. You're still under house arrest."

"I am, Rhett, I am. Resting the ankle as much as I can."

"Okay, let's get straight into *Is.* I've also got *She* here." He held up both books side by side for the camera. "The covers are clearly cohesive with their styling—tell us about them."

"Oh." Bryan's eyes widened. "I wanted something subtle, but significant."

"They look like Sydney Kingston's cover for *The Shape of You.*" Rhett looked at both of them. "A silk sheet or something covering a body."

"Sydney's books were an inspiration," Bryan said. "I love her books and think she's the best thriller writer around. If I can get a bit of her magic happening for my books, I'll be very happy."

"Will *Mine* have the same cover? It obviously will."

"Of course. A woman's body under a sheet, revealing each word."

"So let me get this straight. *She* had the title across the woman's breasts which are blurred out, and the sheet pulled down. *Is* has the title on her stomach and the sheet barely covering her privates. Her arm is across her chest to cover that. I guess *Mine* will have the title across her pelvis."

"Correct." Bryan nodded. "We'll also be doing a box set which will have the full title on her naked body, no sheet at all."

"Are your female readers going to be turned off by these covers, do you think?"

"It's a possibility," Bryan replied. "But considering *Game of Thrones* had a huge female audience even though there's a lot of abuse against women, they don't really have the right to complain."

"That is true," Rhett agreed and leaned back in his seat.

"Besides, the titles are placed in those positions for a reason, as you'll see once *Mine* comes out and you read the book. On the covers, her body is being claimed, but by whom?" Bryan said.

"Ah…" Rhett nodded. "I see where that's going, and now I can't wait to read the third book."

"Exactly. Don't count the covers out just yet. The covers and title placement mean something in the storyline."

"Okay. I've read both books, and as usual it's about a man wanting a woman. It's the same old trope as your first three books. Will you be changing tropes at some point?"

"It if ain't broke, Rhett." Bryan chuckled. "I've only released five books. This set is a trilogy, and I have a standalone coming in September as I've mentioned before, which will be my seventh. As long as I'm inspired by the world around me, particularly women, then why not?"

"Could your books be considered sexist in that they're always men wanting a woman? *Creeper,* and now *She* and *Is* are about a man going after a woman."

"But sometimes, my women turn the tables," Bryan said. "And *Illicit Things* was about young love and how that could become an obsession. The author in *Creeper* was a smart cookie who gave what she got, and so far, no woman has died, or been seriously assaulted, just stalked."

"What's the common theme through your books?" Rhett crossed his legs and brushed a wave of blond hair from his wide tanned forehead.

"A man who loves a woman, a man who wants a woman, and what that love and want turns into. It can turn into real love, obsession, unhealthy desire, passion. My books are an exploration of feelings at all ages, no matter who you feel them for."

"Interesting." Rhett nodded and looked at the crowd.

"How many of you have read all of Bryan's books?"

Three quarters of the crowd put their hands up.

"Keep them up if you enjoyed them."

Only a few put their hands down.

Bryan chuckled. "Now, now, Rhett, that's not fair."

Rhett laughed. "Maybe not, but the book is once again a number one bestseller. How do you do it without actually being on social media?"

"My team at Viceroy Publishing do it for me with accounts in my name. They're fantastic."

"And it seems to work. Thanks so much for joining us today, Bryan Jamison."

Bryan gave a nod. "Thank you for having me. Rhett, everyone." Zoom clicked to a producer who thanked him for his time and logged out.

Sean closed his laptop and sighed. "Only ninety-nine million interviews to go."

*****

"Welcome to the show, Bryan Jamison."

"Hello, Preston. It's good to be back on your radio show." Bryan leaned towards the camera. "We're recording this via Zoom even though it's a radio show?"

"We are. It's so the fans can see it and we can't get away with looking like slobs," Preston joked. "How have you been since the last time we spoke, which was only two months ago?"

"I've been busy, and I've been good."

"Writing more blockbuster novels?" Preston adjusted his microphone.

"I have been writing and hope they're blockbusters when they come out."

"I remember when we finally got to meet you when *Creeper* came out, and you said you'd written, like, another ten books by the time you'd signed the publishing deal. Are we seeing those books coming out, or are they on the back burner?"

"When I signed the first contract it was for the first three books that came out. The second contract was for *She Is Mine.* I have another six books that are coming across the next three or four years, and recently signed for the novel coming out in September, and another two to follow."

"That's fifteen books," Hank said. "Jesus, prolific."

"And I'm working on two at the moment. One's a memoir and it's going to be huge."

"Sales wise or size wise?" Preston asked. "And how are you famous enough, or what is it that you've done, in order to work on a memoir?"

"I have a lot of things to write about. Family history, current times, the future."

"How big's it gonna be?" Preston shifted in his seat.

"No idea. It's close to a thousand document pages. I'm sending a lot through to my editor for advice because I've not written non-fiction, especially memoir, before. And he's giving me a lot of tips and telling me what to keep and what to delete. He's even suggested making two memoirs, or two parts, because there are so many stories to tell."

"And I ask again." Preston cocked his left leg onto his right knee. "What is it, that *you've* done, in order to write a memoir? You're a forty-something college professor who writes books."

"Except I'm not a college professor." Bryan's smile was mysterious. "I really don't know where that rumour came from."

"What!" Hank gaped at the others in the studio. "You're *not* a college professor?"

"No, I'm not. I have no idea where that notion started," Bryan replied.

"Probably from your outfit," Preston said. "Plaid shirts…corduroy jacket with the patches on the elbows. That just says *college professor.*"

"They're just clothes, Preston. But I'm here to talk about my books."

"And I'm here to get information out of you. How long do you think you're going to write for? Ten years, twenty?"

Bryan's laughter was light. "Oh, that's a good one. I will type until my hands fall off, or I'm all out of ideas, or my inspiration dies."

"You type up your books?" Preston drank a mouthful of water. "Have you ever handwritten like Sydney Kingston and many other authors?"

"I used to when I was young, but quickly moved onto a laptop. I know Sydney writes by hand. I really don't know how she does it. I can only hope mine don't fall off from typing book after book month after month."

"Have you written much in the last two months?"

"I finished off the novel coming in September and the two novels after that I mentioned. I'm in the middle of two. But again, it will all depend on if my inspiration dies, and I no longer want to write."

"And what's the earning rate these days, can I ask?" Preston glanced at the wall clock and motioned to Hank.

"It's now double and a half the payments for the first twelve." Bryan sipped his lemon water and held the glass in his hand. "And that's per book."

"Hang on." Preston jumped up in his seat and put his hands up. "The standalone novels you've written just this year, have fetched over double of each trilogy?"

"No, each book in the trilogy scored two million apiece, making it six million per three books. The current books are five million apiece."

Preston grabbed his head and bounced up and down in his chair. "What the fuck! Six million for three, to five million for one. You rich fucker, Bryan Jamison."

Bryan's shy smile lifted his lips and he chuckled. "Yes, I am, Preston, yes, I am."

"How much is that in total?" Hank asked, trying to do the calculations.

"Thirty-nine million dollars in advances alone," Bryan informed them. "But understand this, I've paid my taxes and everything else. At the end of the day, I don't get to keep the whole amount paid to me."

"But you're still a rich fucker thanks to a shit tonne of royalties you'd be getting," Preston said, finally settling back in his chair. "And no one else probably comes close."

"Sydney Kingston," Bryan said. "I know that for a fact."

"I really wish we'd gotten the two of you on the show together."

"I know, it would've been fun."

"It certainly would've," Preston huffed. "But in the

meantime, go and get *Is* by Bryan Jamison."

"Thanks, Preston."

*****

The old man was dropped off on a side street, in the pitch black of the night. He paid his cab fare, and walked down the road, stopping in an alley by an apartment building. "Are you here?"

The woman stepped forward. "Ready and waiting."

He took in her appearance. Long black curls, red lips, a navy trench coat, and bright red stilettoes. "Good. You know what to do?"

"Will you be here?" She kept her hands in her coat pockets to warm them.

"I will when you're done. Ready and waiting."

She kissed him on the cheek and made her way inside the building and up to the third floor, knocking on the door to apartment eleven.

The door flung open. "Yeah?" He eyed the woman standing in front of him. "Who're you?"

She untied her trench and pulled it open for him to see her red lace nippleless bra, crotchless matching knickers, and a garter belt and stockings. "Connor. Care for some fun? I miss you."

He frowned, trying to remember if he knew her, and wondering why she'd be on his doorstep in lace underwear. He scratched his nuts through his blue boxers. "Do I know you?"

She placed her hand on his chest and moved him back, closing the door with her other hand. "Extremely intimately," was all she said as the coat fell to the floor, and she grabbed his t-shirt. "Let's fuck."

Five hours later, the woman emerged from the bedroom and closed the front door behind her. When she arrived at the alley she met with the old man. "All set."

"All set," he said and took her arm as they walked off down the alley and disappeared into the darkness.

*****

"Grandpa, where are you?" Ethan closed the front door and walked into the living room. "Have you talked to Dad? I can't seem to get in touch. He's not answering my calls. I don't know where he is. Is he on a sting, or gone undercover? Grandpa?"

"In here." Cormac stood at the sun room doors looking out at the May sunshine.

"Hey." Ethan walked up to him. "You know where Dad is?"

Cormac nodded with a heavy heart. "I do."

"Where? I wanted to talk to him about something."

Cormac turned to his grandson. "I'm afraid you can't do that."

Ethan's head tilted. "Why?"

A deep guttural sigh came from Cormac's gut. "I'm so sorry to tell you this."

Stunned, Ethan stepped back. "Then don't."

"At three oh two this morning—"

"No." A shake of his head.

"On the Lower East Side docks—"

"No." The shaking became violent.

"Connor Ryan was to be arrested for the murder of three mobsters wanted by the FBI."

"No," Ethan yelled. His eyes watered, and his mouth salivated.

"Officers found one million in coke and ten million in money in the warehouse. There was a shootout."

"No," Ethan's screams rang out, his hands covered his ears, and he fell to his knees.

"And he took five bullets."

"No." Ethan rocked forward until his forehead touched the floor.

"He didn't survive." Cormac stared down at his grieving grandson. "I'm so sorry, Ethan. Come." He slid his hands under his arms and pulled him up into his, holding him tightly. "I'm so sorry, I'm so sorry." He held him, allowing him to sob until he was done. He spied a stunned Sean in the doorway standing next to Emerson and nodded.

Emerson led Sean into the kitchen and closed the door.

"What's happened?" Sean whispered.

Emerson took a breath. "Connor was killed this morning."

Sean stepped back; his eyes went wide. "Jesus."

"I guess it's bound to happen when you're a cop." Emerson picked up the kettle and poured water into two cups with tea bags.

"Was it Connor's fault?"

She shook her head. "I don't know."

"Does Grandpa?"

A shrug. "I don't know. I think the only one to fully

know what was going on is Connor."

"And we ain't getting it out of him." Sean heard silence coming from the sun room, but the front door opened and closed.

"We're here." Alec and Kieran walked into the house and saw Ethan and Cormac on the sofa. Ethan was silent and red-faced.

"What's happened?" Alec's gaze flicked from his father. "Connor?"

Cormac nodded. "He's gone."

"Oh, my God." Kieran sank into a chair. "When?"

"This morning," Cormac replied. "I've told Ethan, and Sean and Emerson know."

"And now we do." Alec sank into the chair next to Kieran's. "What do we do now?"

"Just like with Declan. There will be an investigation and a funeral."

"When?" Kieran wiped his tears away.

"This weekend, just like with Declan."

Ethan finally spoke in a dull low voice. "Full honours?"

Cormac nodded. "Full honours."

"Can I ask something?" Sean said from the kitchen doorway.

"Sure." Cormac gave him an empty smile.

"Is the investigation into my dad finished? Or is it still ongoing?"

"Not the time, Sean," Alec said.

"Yes, Alec, it is, since there will now be one into Connor. How long will they take?" Sean looked from one to the other. "Ethan's about to go through what I've been going through. If Dad's is still ongoing, then

Connor's will take months as well."

"I have to clean out his apartment," Ethan said in a monotone.

"You can't; it's a part of the investigation now." Cormac squeezed his hand. "Declan's has just been handed back, so Sean, you and I can clean that out, but Connor's won't be available to us for a month at least."

"I can't," murmured Ethan, his breath coming in short sharp bursts. "I can't."

"I know." Cormac put his arm around him. "We'll get through this."

Ethan's tears flooded forth and he fell into his grandfather's arms.

*****

The funeral of Detective Connor Sullivan Ryan was held on the Saturday after his death.

The family, those left, gathered round, along with close friends and co-workers. Cormac and Ethan stood at the end of the grave watching the coffin being lowered into its final resting place.

Cormac had a pained look upon his grieving face.

Ethan had a deeply furrowed brow.

They both stared down at Connor's coffin until Cormac threw a handful of dirt on it. Ethan did the same.

The rest of the family and attendees slowly walked away and left, but Ethan stayed by his father's grave watching it be filled up. It took two hours, and the air grew chilled in early afternoon. But he stayed.

The gravediggers pushed down the last of the soil and

flattened out the surface. One long rectangle of dirt was what currently remained of Connor Ryan.

"Ethan."

Ethan breathed in and turned his head towards his grandfather. "I thought you'd left."

"No. You needed to stay, so did I. My son, your father. Emerson went back with Kieran and Sandy. They'll be helping with the wake."

"And how long will that go for?"

"Until about five or six this evening." Cormac stood with his hands in his coat pockets, staring down at his son's grave. Two down two left. "The headstone will be erected on Monday."

"Please tell me you had them put loving father on it."

"I had loving son, brother, and father put on it." He glanced around the cemetery, saw a couple of photographers off in the distance, and frowned. "We're being watched. We should go."

They stopped at Declan's and Laura's graves, then Douglas', Marion's, and Alice's before Ethan followed his grandfather through the winding lanes of the cemetery to his waiting car, hands in pockets just like him. Sombre expression, just like him.

They arrived home fifteen minutes later and found everyone still there.

Emerson rushed over and took his jacket. "I was starting to worry. Ethan, I'll take your coat and pop it up in our room." She nodded to him and hurried up the stairs.

They walked into a quiet room.

"Don't stop on my account," Cormac told them as he

walked through. "If there's food, eat, if there's fluid, drink, if you a have a story, tell it."

Ethan said no words, shook no hands, just stared straight ahead.

Nibbling on a quarter cut beef sandwich, Sean watched his cousin. *He's going through what I've been through for a month*, he thought. *Now he knows.* He watched Cormac lead him to the dining table and make up a plate of food. He noticed the extra girth on his grandfather—clearly from Emerson's fine food selections. He himself had gained a little weight back by eating her desserts all day. They gave him a sugar high when he needed it.

Ethan just stared blankly through everyone and wandered outside, standing on the back patio, staring out at the river.

Sean wandered over to the French doors, watching. He watched Ethan walk over to the stone wall holding the river back, watched as he climbed up onto it and stood staring out to sea. He watched as he threw himself in. *Oh, no you don't, you bastard, you're not getting away that easy.*

"Ethan," he yelled and ran across the yard to the water, jumping over the wall. He found his cousin a few metres away under the surface. Swimming out, he heaved him back and up over the wall. "You're not getting away that easily." He climbed up and hauled Ethan by his arm and leg until he slid to the ground.

Kieran came rushing over with Alec and Cormac behind him. "Ethan, Sean. Did he fall?"

"No," Sean panted and wiped water from his eyes.

"He threw himself in."

They stared down at a sobbing Ethan, curled up in a sopping ball.

"Looks as if he'll be staying here for a few days," Cormac said. "Let's get him inside." He watched Alec and Kieran help their nephew to his feet and half carry him inside. "Thank you, Sean."

Sean climbed down from the wall. "No problem. I didn't leave any clothes here, did I?"

Cormac looked at his soaked grandson. "You might have. I seem to recall Ethan did the same for you once. Pulled you out of the river."

"Yeah." Sean thought back. "He did. *Once.*"

They walked back inside, and Sean quickly found some old clothes in the room he had occupied and showered while Emerson took his clothes to be cleaned. If Ethan was staying there, he would need clothes and he wouldn't want anyone going to his house to see what was in the basement, now would he? He hurried downstairs. "I can go to Ethan's and pack him a bag."

"That's not on your list?" Alec said, but quickly closed his mouth.

Sean glanced at him. "Then put it on."

"I think that would be a good idea," Cormac said. "He shouldn't be alone and Sean's capable of going to get him his things."

Alec nodded. "I'll go and do it now." He walked out of the room.

"Thank you, Sean." Cormac squeezed his shoulder and went back to his guests.

Sean ran around looking for Ethan's keys and made

his way to the front door.

Alec met him there. "Take my car, it's the last one in the drive."

Sean looked at the keys in Alec's hand in surprise. "Ah…thanks…"

"You saved Ethan, Sean, and that means something." Alec squeezed his shoulder. "I've added Ethan's address to your list. You're good to go."

"Thanks." Sean headed out the door, desperate to get to Ethan's. When he finally returned with a bag of clothes, he stayed a while longer before heading home to his condo.

He stood staring at his wall of Sydney for a few minutes to calm his thoughts, and his gaze zeroed in on the page of images of his family in the middle of the wall. He grabbed a red Sharpie and marked his uncle off with a cross.

He changed his clothes, put on his wig and glasses, popped off his ankle bracelet and glitched the building's Wi-Fi and surveillance. He caught a cab to the Upper East Side and hurried down the street to the brownstone. He barely stared up at it because he was in such a hurry to get inside.

After opening the vestibule and front doors, and locking them against the world, he dropped his bag and coat by the door. The scent of hot roast chicken permeated the air and his stomach growled as he walked into the living room to warm himself by the crackling fire in the grate.

He breathed out in relief and chuckled.

He was home.

Chapter 15

"I don't know how many more times I'm going to say I'm sorry."

"Then don't."

Levinworth watched Sean as he stood at the window. "Do you want to talk about it?"

"About Connor? No."

"His funeral."

"No."

"How's your cousin?"

"Ethan? The bastard tried to kill himself."

Levinworth frowned. "How?"

"Threw himself in the river at Grandpa's."

"You said tried."

"I jumped in and hauled his dumb ass out. He's staying with Grandpa for the rest of the week."

"He was your hero once. How do you feel about him trying to end things?"

"I wasn't going to let him. He doesn't get away with that. With copping out just because he lost his father." Sean turned from the window. "He went into a stupefied coma after it, but Grandpa says he's okay. Staying in his dad's old room. Alec and Kieran will drop by this week to help out."

"Is your grandfather home from work?"

"He is. He took a week after Brandon and Sierra, and a week after Dad."

"And now he loses another son within a month."

Sean moved over to the wall with his favourite painting. His copy was yet to arrive, and he'd been wondering if it was lost in transit. "I guess that's what happens when you have a family of cops. You learn to deal with losing them."

"But two…in a month."

"Bad cops get caught." Sean sighed. "They both did bad things and were caught."

"I'm still sorry."

"Let's talk about something else. I'm going with Grandpa to my dad's apartment on Wednesday. We're clearing it out."

"You're allowed back in?"

"Yep. The cops are done with it, and we have to clean it out."

"And what about your parents' house? Whatever was left after your dad died is yours."

"That's nearly finished. It's going up for sale next month. God knows what we'll find in his apartment though. Grandpa paid off his debts and I get what's left."

"Do you have any idea what's there?"

"A pile of junk and his clothes, I guess. I'll have to get it cleaned up and the super will keep the rent or whatever Dad's paid up." He scratched the top of his head and then smoothed his hair. "Let's talk about something else. I've already wasted sessions on Connor and Dad."

"Talk about what?"

"Did you read *Is?*"

"I did."

"And?" Sean glanced over his shoulder.

"And it's very interesting. Very telling."

"I've already told you, doc, it's all about Sydney."

"You did. You write well. Number one on the charts again. I saw your interviews."

"All of them?"

"Many."

"And?"

"And you keep your cards to your chest. Don't give too much away. Change your voice—change your face."

"It's a pseudonym, a character, a play for the masses. I did do drama for a year."

"Learn a lot?"

"I did. Which is why I know how to become someone else."

"Do you wish you were someone else?"

"All the time."

"Why?"

"Come on, Walter." Sean rolled his eyes. "With *this* family? I *always* wish I were someone else."

"Would your life be better?"

"Absolutely."

"Then why don't you?"

Sean turned around and leaned against the sideboard. "Oh, I will be. Once I get this damn monitor off and leave you behind, I'll be leaving the family behind. Ryan is not a name I want anymore."

"Because of your father?"

"Because of all of them." Sean turned back to the painting. "I hate the name. I got it as the sacrificial lamb. I've already said that. Come July, there will be no need for it anymore."

"What will you change it to?"

The laugher bubbled up from Sean's gut and came out. "Oh, that's a good one. Probably Jamison."

"Will you change Sean to Bryan?"

"Hell no. Too close to Ryan which was the point of the name. I picked one close to my original and people still didn't figure it out. God, I made it so easy for them."

"You'd rather take on your author name. I guess you're used to it by now."

"Yeah. Jamison is Kieran's middle name. Bryan Jamison. And they *still* couldn't get it. And I'd rather be someone else, even though I'm writing a memoir."

Levinworth perked up. "Really? And under which name will that be released?"

"Sean Ryan has done a hell of a lot, but Bryan Jamison hasn't, so it will be Ryan to capitalise on some other things coming, but I have a great title for it. Guess what it is."

Levinworth looked up from his notes. "My Grandfather the PC."

"Walter." Sean's head tilted in disappointment. "Guess again."

Levinworth chuckled. "Ah, let me think. My Life In Law Enforcement. My Life—"

"Seriously, you're only halfway close. It's *My Two Lives.*"

Levinworth considered the title. "Interesting, certainly

covers who you are. Two people, two lives, two identities."

"That's what I thought. And obviously the blurb will have to mention who my family is, and how I started writing as myself and became successful before moving onto a pen name for adult thrillers. Three important factors for publicity."

"Will you change your socials? Does Bryan have socials?"

"He does under Viceroy who looks after them. But I have more. If I keep Sean, but change Ryan, that's easy enough, and then I'll do a video to promote myself with the new me. If I lose fans or followers, oh well. I have the money, I have the life, nearly. I don't care for socials if I lose followers."

"Speaking of Bryan, did the rest of your family read his books?"

"Kieran and Alec did, but as far as I know, no one else did. Dad didn't bother with books, Connor and Ethan were too busy banging women, and Brandon and Sierra were too busy banging each other."

"You didn't have to worry about them finding out the truth since the books are so autobiographical."

"I did wonder what would happen. Got a bit excited by the prospect of it. If they could figure out that they were secondary and tertiary characters in the books. That Sydney and I were always the main characters. I wish they had, but the Ryan boys aren't that smart, clearly."

"And what about Sydney's books? Did they keep reading hers?"

"Grandpa and Pop did. I think Kieran and Alec read some." He paused. "The rest of the family knew about them, and Connor admitted to reading a couple as Mom had."

"And did they read her books after the family were banned from seeing her?"

"Again, Grandpa and Pop and Kieran, although..." He frowned. "I think Ethan started when we met Sydney, at lunch, or at least when he saw her a year later, when she released *Twisted Affair*. I know he read that."

"How did you feel knowing they still read Sydney's books?"

"On one hand, I was angry because they had banned me from seeing her, and Connor had slapped her and all that shit went down, but they kept buying her books. On the other, I was proud and happy for her. I collected them myself, and Pop got *Twisted Affair* signed for me at a book signing."

"You still bought Sydney's books?" Levinworth scribbled a note in the file.

"I did. Because I had my own dorm room. I had a lockable cupboard and I kept all of them in there. I'm as bad as Pop. Kept the dust jacket hardcovers pristine and bought the e-books and paperbacks to read."

"Did anyone ever break in to your dorm, or find them?"

"No. But I made sure they knew I was the grandson of the PC and no one in my family would take kindly to me being stolen from."

"Why did you not complete college?"

"Because I applied to Harvard Law and got in. I couldn't do both."

"Did you start college and then apply, or apply for

both at the same time?"

"Started college. I realised within months that it wasn't the level of learning I wanted or needed. I did a few subjects, as I've mentioned, and then decided to apply to Harvard for the fun of it."

"The fun of it?" Levinworth's brows rose. "Law school is not for the fun of it."

Sean chuckled and walked back to the window. "No, Walter, it most certainly is not. But, I got in which was a massive surprise, and because of who I was, I suppose. When they saw what I could do, they accelerated me."

"Three years in two. That's a hell of an achievement and at the very top. Number one."

"But I'm not the only one to do it. Three people before me all with a level of autism like me have done the same."

"Not so special after all."

Sean shrugged a nonchalant shoulder. "Never said I was. Time to go, doc."

"But don't you wish you were?" Levinworth watched Sean pause at the door.

When Sean finally spoke, he said, "I am to Sydney and that's all that matters."

*****

Sean met Cormac on the pavement outside Declan's apartment building. It was a warm sunny day, about to become dark, cold and depressed. "Grandpa."

"You ready for this?" Cormac asked and looked up at the building.

Sean considered it. "I am and I'm not." He saw Emerson alight from the car. "Hey, I didn't know you were coming. You most certainly don't have to do this."

Emerson pulled a bucket of supplies from the back floor well. "It's fine. I'm just helping to bag and tag. We have a cleaning crew coming this afternoon."

"What are we doing with Dad's stuff?" Sean took the bucket from Emerson.

"Donating what we can and throwing out everything else. Ready?" Cormac asked.

Sean nodded and they went up to the apartment where the super let them in.

"The investigation team took all they wanted, and left the rest behind," Cormac said, and they walked into the apartment.

"Whew, that's ripe." Sean waved a hand in front of his face and watched Emerson start throwing windows open. "Can't wait for the cleaning crew."

"Let's make a start on his clothes," Cormac suggested. "His suits can be donated if they're still good."

They made their way into the bedroom and donned masks and gloves, Finding Declan's clothes still in good condition, they were bagged and tagged for the local op shop. The bed linen was thrown into a bag for rubbish, along with clothes in the hamper, and the rotting food from the fridge. Bins were emptied, and anything else lying around was dumped in garbage bags.

The removalists came and carried the bed away to be thrown out, and took the lounge suite, dining table and chairs, and the TV and cabinet to be donated. All that was left was the cleaning crew to vacuum and mop.

Sean stood in the empty bedroom. They had found nothing personal besides passport, wallet, and rental agreement. No evidence of his crimes or liaisons. He'd even tapped walls and looked for loose floorboards, much to his grandfather's amusement, and the closet held no surprises either. He sighed and slid his hands into his pockets.

This was where his father had been up to his nose in coke and his dick in a whore and where he'd been shot three times and handcuffed.

"He was a tough son of a bitch."

A small laugh came from Sean. "Yeah, he was. Shot three times and kept on going."

"The coke in his system." Cormac stepped into the room. "And where he spent his last night."

"Doing what he had done for so long." Sean stared at the bloodstain on the floor. "And now he's gone."

"Now he's gone." A deep depressive sigh came from Cormac. "I'm sorry, Sean."

"You've already apologised. A million times."

"I'm sorry for not teaching him how to be a better man so that he, in turn, could be a good father. I'm sorry for not stepping in. I'm sorry that you and your mom suffered."

"Do you think he did, in the end?" Sean's brows furrowed as he stared at the stain. "Suffered, I mean. Or would the drugs have made him inhibited?"

"He would've had no clue what was happening, too much adrenaline, too high, no pain from the bullets, but he would've crashed at the hospital."

"Do *you* think he suffered in the end? Do you think

he knew the end was coming?"

Cormac stepped closer and laid his hand on Sean's shoulder. "No, to both."

"Too much adrenaline, too high?" Sean's gaze never left the bloodstain.

"Too much of everything."

"Too much arrogance, too much entitlement, too much anger, too much narcissism. *Ryans don't get shot. Ryans don't die, on the job or otherwise. Isn't that the motto?*"

"Yeah." Cormac nodded wearily. "That *was* the motto. Time to go."

"Will you do this with Ethan in a month?"

"Probably."

"How is he?"

"Out of it. The doc gave him something to keep him drowsy. Alec's with him today."

"How long will he stay?"

"I'll keep him a week and see how he goes."

"Do you think he'll be okay?"

"I don't know. They were incredibly close."

Sean looked up as Emerson came to the door. "Cleaning crew's here. The super will stay and supervise, so we can go."

Cormac gave her a weary smile. "I need some fresh air. We might take the long way home. Coming, Sean?"

"Lunch?" he asked.

"Late lunch," Emerson replied. "I just need to heat it."

They walked into the living room, saw the crew preparing, and left them to it. Down on the pavement Sean looked up at the apartment. *Bye, Dad, you asshole.*

Goodbye and good riddance, he thought before saying, "I'll see you there."

"Okay, if you get there before us, it's in the pan in the fridge. Put it in the oven on two-fifty for thirty minutes. We should be home by then," Emerson told him through the back seat window.

"I'm not taking the long way round, so I'll put it on. See you later." Sean waved them off and finally climbed into his own car, leaving his father behind. He made it to his grandfather's house and put the dish in the oven.

"Sean."

He looked up and brushed off his hands. "Alec. Grandpa and Emerson are taking the long way home. How's Ethan?"

"Drowsy, but that's the pills Dad's got him on." He glanced at his phone. "I need to make some calls—can you check on him?"

"Sure. I want to see how he is." Sean watched Alec walk into the sun room and headed up to Connor's old room. He found Ethan curled up in a ball in the bed. "Hey."

Ethan didn't look up, didn't acknowledge him.

Sean closed the door and walked around the bed to the window. "I've put lunch on. Grandpa and Emerson are on their way home from Dad's old apartment. They're taking the long route because Grandpa needed air. It's a nice day." He opened the window more. "Beautiful breeze, beautiful sunshine. It needs to come in. It's way too stuffy in here, like Dad's place. Stank to high heaven. Emerson opened every window and we bagged up all of his stuff. It either went in the bin or to an op shop. When we left, the cleaning crew were coming in. You'll have to do that in a couple of weeks with your dad's place. It's depressing, especially the bloodstain, but your dad wasn't shot at his apartment, so you won't have to deal with that."

He saw Ethan's gaze flicker to him. "Because your dad was shot elsewhere. You know, I'm surprised you haven't gone raging over there to conduct your own investigation. I'm surprised you tried killing yourself instead. What a waste, especially when you have so much to live for. So much to do; a house to keep clean. I mean, your basement is *full* of stuff you really need to clean out."

Ethan frowned and slowly unfurled until he was sitting. "What did you say?"

Sean arched a brow. "Your basement is full of stuff you really should clean out. Because if anything ever happens to you, Grandpa will be cleaning it out, and imagine what the CSIs are going to think of all that."

"You were in my basement?" Ethan's voice rose. "When? You're not invited to my house. How did you get in?"

"I used your keys to get in because *someone* needed to get you a bag of clothes for your stay here at Grandpa's." Sean walked back around the bed, hands in pockets. "Who knew you had such kinks. Just like your old man. Tsk, tsk, and this family thinks *I* have an obsession with Sydney Kingston. If *only* they knew. If *only* they could see what I saw."

"Sean, what did you see?" Ethan threw back the covers and stood up. "Sean?"

"Don't worry, Ethan." Sean smirked. "I won't tell anyone.

Why would I?"

"You saw nothing," Ethan desperately told him. "Just a, a, a basement full of junk. Nothing else."

"*Nothing* else?" Sean tilted his head in thought. "Don't you mean *nobody* else?" He opened the door and stepped into the hallway, turning back to say, "You might want to get your dumb ass out of here to deal with your housework, and the death of your father." He closed the door on Ethan's stunned expression and held back laughter as he walked downstairs. He met up with his grandfather and Emerson as they came in the door. "Just going to check on lunch."

"Oh, I'll do it." Emerson rushed into the kitchen and a few seconds later declared, "Lunch is ready."

Sean and Alec took their seats at the table with Cormac following their lead. Emerson carried the tray to the table and a fully dressed Ethan strode into the room.

"Hey, ah, I'm gonna go. I need to get home," he told three stunned faces.

Sean just smirked.

"Do you want lunch before you go?" Emerson asked. "You've barely eaten the last few days."

"Are you okay to leave?" Cormac asked.

Alec followed up with. "Who put a firecracker up your ass?"

"Sean." Ethan looked at his cousin. "Reminded me that I have a life to live and my own investigation into Dad's shooting to conduct. I really need to get home."

The others stared from him to Sean.

"Someone had to." Sean shrugged. "Let's eat, I'm starving."

"Ethan?" Cormac motioned to the chair beside him. "Eat before you go."

"And I'll drive you," Alec added. "Since your car's not here."

Ethan looked from one to the other until his gaze rested on Sean who arched a brow. His jaw set and he sat down.

What the hell does Sean know and has he really gone into the basement?

Chapter 16

"Happy birthday, Sean."

"Thank you, Walter."

"This year you're celebrating without your dad."

"Like most years. And Brandon and Sierra and Connor."

"Without four members of your family."

"Six if you include Pop and Mom. Pop's been gone a year, Mom four years. Hard to believe we're in June already."

"Halfway through the year."

"And summer. I love summer."

"How did you celebrate your twenty-first?"

Sean looked over his shoulder at his therapist. "You know I'm twenty-two, Walter."

"I know. I just wondered how you celebrated last year since this year you wouldn't be having a celebration."

"I'm actually doing that tonight. No fanfare, at Grandpa's, for anyone who wants to come. Attendance isn't mandatory."

"How have you celebrated every other year?"

"As you know, my sixteenth was with my friends

during the day and a prostitute during the night. My seventeenth was at Grandpa's, my eighteenth was at Grandpa's, my nineteenth was at Grandpa's, my twentieth was at Grandpa's. How do you think I celebrated my twenty-first?"

"You spent every year at your grandfather's. Why?"

Surprised, Sean turned from the window. "Ah, I didn't have friends past high school, and once Mom died, I didn't want to celebrate at all. And, as usual, Declan Ryan didn't give a shit about his son. His only child. But Pulsate did get me a cake so I did have other people to celebrate with. That happened for my eighteenth and nineteenth. Otherwise, it was Grandpa and Pop and whoever wanted to come."

"Was your eighteenth special?"

"Meh, sort of. I was going to be a published author. A few more months and the first book would be out."

"And your twenty-first?"

"Viceroy threw me an incognito after-hours party in Vincent's office. But at home, completely different story."

"You're an orphan."

Silence settled over the room.

Sean's eyes prickled with tears, and he slowly nodded. "Yeah, Walter. I am. I became one at twenty-one, so I've been one for a while."

"I see your eyes are watering. It upsets you."

Sean walked over to the wave painting. "Yeah. Barely an adult, and I've lost both parents. One at eighteen, one at twenty-one. How the hell am I supposed to feel?"

"Like every other person who loses a parent when they're young."

"Or just every other person," Sean replied. "Don't we all lose parents?"

"We do."

"Have you lost yours?"

"My dad."

Sean looked over his shoulder. "How old were you when he died?"

"Forty."

"So, you had forty years with him?"

"I did."

"Good years?"

"Yes."

"Good for you." Sean turned back to the painting and heard the crashing of the waves.

"I'm sorry."

"For what?"

"Losing your parents so young."

"Walter, at the rate my family's going, I'll be losing all of them so young. I see that Sierra and Brandon's OnlyFans has disappeared. Sonja or Alec must've shut it down. Their socials are still up though."

"Did anyone else have socials besides you? Did you ever say?" Levinworth flicked through his notes.

"Nope. None of the rest of them have it. Grandpa made it a rule for the family. No member with a gun or law degree could have one. But us kids…" He shrugged. "Ethan has it, but barely uses it. And I have a law degree, but don't use socials except for myself, and I'm not banned."

"Will you ever practise law?"

"No. I really only wanted to do it to be the smartest

one in the family."

"Are you?"

"You know I am. You gave me an IQ test after you discovered what was wrong with me. Anyway, I don't want to talk about that now. I have a dinner to go to and a cousin to see."

"You're going to see Ethan? Are you allowed?"

"Alec put his address on my list, so yeah. I guess so. I know it's his day off."

"Does Connor dying change how you feel about Ethan?"

"Why would it?" Sean paused at the sideboard of artworks. "He still fucked Sydney. I still hate him for it, and he's done things just as bad as my dad and Connor."

"But you could be close now, if you wanted to?"

Sean shook his head. "No, Walter, the time for that is over. It was over when I was eighteen. Four long years."

"You can't forgive him?"

"What's to forgive? He did the dirty and he's still doing the dirty. Are we just going to talk about this? Do we have nothing else to talk about this session?"

"Have you finished replaying your life?"

He shrugged. "There's not much more to go, Walter. Two months, eight sessions. We haven't even got to my jobs and my publishing deal. Finding out that Dad was banging Sydney."

"We can do that today."

Sean sighed and stared at an artwork. "I'm bored, Walter. Maybe I'm down in the dumps with everything that's happened. Everything that's going on. There's nothing to talk about. It's my birthday, everything's just…" He waved a hand while looking for the right word. "I don't even know."

"You're in a funk, and that's understandable. Maybe everything's catching up with you. Are you writing?"

"Not as much as I have been."

"Your brain's had more time to digest it all. A funk is normal when family dies. You need time to get used to it."

"What if more family dies?" Sean walked to the other wall and stared blankly at it. "What if Ethan's next? He's a cop. He's gone off the rails with his dad's death. He could get himself killed. Or what about Alec or Kieran? Lawyers are shot by the assholes they serve all the time."

"It's entirely possible," Levinworth said. "That's the problem with having a family of cops and lawyers. It's always possible. Just as firemen could be killed in a fire, or a paramedic could be killed trying to save someone's life."

"Get your life taken while trying to save one. Rough job."

"They all are. They're all incredibly dangerous jobs and become more so every day."

"Because the population has gone berserk, and we don't have much of a death penalty anymore." Sean picked up his bag. "I know. Dad and Connor would always talk about the number of perps they'd caught each week at dinner. They had a weekly tally going. Ethan tried to be the interloper and outdo them. Alec and Kieran would let them back out on the street. It pissed Dad off. A lot."

"It would. The law's a thankless job."

"Especially when so many believe they have a right to take life when they want. It's just entitled, arrogant, narcissistic. Those assholes need to be gunned down."

Levinworth closed Sean's file. "Well…that's an opinion."

"What? You can't say that because you're a therapist?" Sean asked. "Interesting concept, Walter. I thought you'd be all over it with your psychoanalytical opinions."

Levinworth laughed. "Yeah, so did I, but we're all entitled to an opinion."

"And what's your opinion of me?" Sean stood beside his chair.

Levinworth looked up at him. "That there is so much more to come."

A grin lit up Sean's face. "Oh, there certainly is, Walter. There certainly is."

*****

From his therapist's office, Sean headed to Ethan's house, knocking on the door a half hour later. He knew it was Ethan's day off, but that didn't mean he was home. He knocked again and the door swung open.

"Sean?" Ethan frowned. "What are you doing here?" Guarded, he stood in the doorway, one foot behind the door to prevent Sean from entering.

"Hey. Just thought I'd stop by to see if you're coming to dinner at Grandpa's house tonight?"

"Ah, it's Monday, not Sunday."

"Yeah, and it's my birthday, and since half the family's gone, I was hoping the other half would be there." Sean noted the panic on his cousin's face. "You okay?"

"Ah, yeah." Ethan swallowed the lump in his throat and shoved his hands into his jeans pockets. "I ah, forgot it was your birthday. Sorry."

"I won't be surprised if Alec and Kieran have as well, but I know Emerson and Grandpa will definitely be celebrating since it's at his house."

"Ah, what time?" Ethan glanced up and down the street.

"Seven, like every other dinner. You okay?"

"I told you, yeah." Ethan inched the door closed. "I gotta go, I'm busy."

"Cleaning up the basement?"

The door swung back open, and Ethan shoved his finger in Sean's face. "Look, Sean. Whatever you think you know, you don't. There's nothing going on in the basement. You must've gone to the wrong house."

"And seen a shrine to Sydney Kingston?" Sean's brows rose in amusement. "Yeah, good one, Ethan. No, it was definitely this house, and I definitely know what I saw."

"You saw nothing," Ethan yelled, taking a step closer. "You saw nothing and don't even breathe a word of this to the family because I will bring you down, do you understand me?"

"If you've done nothing, and I saw nothing, why are you telling me not to breathe a word of it?" Sean asked. "Seriously, people only say that when they have something to hide."

"I have *nothing* to hide," Ethan spat. "And don't you dare say so."

"Then come to my birthday dinner," Sean said, unfazed. He'd dealt with Declan his whole life. Ethan wasn't a problem. "Or I'll know you really *do* have something to hide." He walked down the stairs and hailed the cab that happened to be passing by.

Ethan went to close the door, but he did a double take at the driver. Sydney? The driver glanced out the window before taking off. It wasn't Sydney, so why the hell had he thought it was?

*****

"Did you want a present for your birthday, Sean?" Emerson asked. "I think we all know by now that you can buy whatever you want for yourself."

Sean chuckled. "Yes, Emerson, I can. No, I don't want anything. I mean, I do, but it's not going to happen yet. I'll just have to wait another eight weeks." He sipped his beer and looked at her sitting next to Cormac. "You're pretty much all I have left now, and Grandpa. You're retiring *and* turning seventy-five soon."

"Oh, if I make it that far." Cormac sighed. "With the way my family's deteriorating I don't know if I'll cope long enough."

"Are you and Emerson still getting married on that day? It's been so long now."

"It has," Cormac said. He smiled at his fiancée and took her hand. "But little did I know I'd start losing my family. Dad, Brandon and Sierra, Declan and Connor."

Sean glanced around the sun room, devoid of the Ryan family except for them. The French doors were open for the summer breeze and he could hear the faint hum of traffic on the bridge.

"Hey, we're here," Kieran called, and he and Sandy appeared. "Hey. Happy birthday, Sean. We didn't get you anything because we didn't know what to get you."

"That's okay, we were just talking about it." He watched Sandy sit on the couch opposite and rub her almost six-month pregnant belly. "Not long now, huh."

"Oh," She rolled her eyes. "I wish it were over, but I know it's about to get worse."

Kieran sat beside her and slid his arm around her shoulders. "I wish I could make it easier."

"You can give me more massages and do more of the housework," she said.

"Or I could pay for a cleaner," Kieran countered.

"That'll help." Sandy laughed and rubbed her stomach.

"What's for dinner?" Kieran took the beer Emerson gave him while Sandy scored a bottle of chilled water.

"Steak, on the grill. Something I have learned to cook to perfection," Sean said. "I'll get started in a minute, and Emerson has provided three very tasty salads, and dessert is my favourite mixed treat plate, also from Emerson."

"Why a mixed plate of desserts?" Sandy sipped her water. It slid down her parched throat.

"Because I love all of Emerson's desserts and couldn't pick one," he said. "How many steaks should I cook?"

"Hey, has dinner started yet?" Alec called from the hallway.

"May as well make it seven," Cormac said. "And if Ethan doesn't show…"

"I'll eat his." Sean got to his feet. "I'll get the grill going, and if someone can bring me the steak in five minutes, I'll get them on." He left the family to chat and walked outside, breathing in the Brooklyn air, and kick-started the grill by the light of the summer evening.

It was roaring when Emerson carried out the tray of steaks. "All ready to go. You said they've marinated since last night. I can't wait to taste one. I didn't realise you could cook."

"Is grilling really cooking?" Sean picked one up with the tongs and set it across the bars. The juice dripped onto the charcoal beads making it sizzle. He laid them out until he picked up the last. "I'm really just laying it on the grill and the grill's doing the cooking."

"That is true," she said. "How long?"

"About twenty minutes to get a good moist well done." Sean closed the lid and adapted the temperature. "I have the same grill at home, so I've been practising."

"How do you have a massive barbecue in your condo?" Emerson asked.

"Ah, I have my ways." Sean chuckled. "It's out in the garage and I wheel it into the common area to cook."

"Ah, handy." She went inside and he saw her wash the tray in the kitchen.

The front door slammed shut and someone said, "Hey, I'm here."

"Oh, he's here all right," Sean muttered. "Wasn't about to *not* turn up after what I said this afternoon." He set his watch timer to ten minutes so he wouldn't forget to turn the steaks over, and wandered to the French doors. "Hey, Ethan, you made it. Finish cleaning out your basement?"

Startled, Ethan glared at Sean. "Ah, yeah. I have."

"You've been cleaning out your house?" Emerson

asked as she walked into the sun room and handed him a beer. "Need some help?"

He paused, jaw hanging open. "Ah, no, thank you. It's all done."

"What made you get into summer cleaning?" she continued. "I can put some rubber gloves on and get stuck in. I cleaned up this place."

"More of a late spring cleaning," he said, sucking back a mouthful of his favourite brew. "With Sierra and Brandon, then Declan, and…Dad…" He sighed. "Everything got away from me and if anything happens to me, I don't want Grandpa to have to clean out my garbage like we'll have to do with Dad, at some point."

"And how are you coping?" Cormac asked him.

"Coping." Ethan nodded. "Just…coping. I ah, went to the warehouse where it happened. I just… I don't know why. How? What was he thinking?" He shook his head and threw his hands up in disbelief.

"No idea," Cormac murmured. "I have no idea."

Sean's gaze flicked between his family members. He knew several were keeping secrets, and he knew it was possible they knew each other's. His watch timer went off. "Time to turn those steaks, ten minutes, everyone." He turned seven sizzling steaks over on the grill and the scent wafted up in curlicues of white steam. "Ooohhh." His stomach grumbled. "I cannot wait."

"Need help?" Ethan pulled up beside him.

"Nope. Ten more minutes and they are done to perfection." Sean closed the lid and reset his timer.

"I ah…wanted to ask you about today," Ethan said. "And when you came around to get my clothes. My basement is always locked. How would you know what's in it?"

Sean slid his hands into his pockets and studied his cousin. "Are you *sure* it's always locked? Because the door was wide open when I went there. I felt that I should check it in case someone had broken into the basement window and stolen something. Your laptop, TV, and stereo were all there, but I didn't know what you had in the basement, so I checked. Very interesting, Ethan. But have you *really* cleaned it up?"

Ethan stared silently at Sean, battling to keep his temper under control.

"Steaks nearly ready?" Alec yelled out the door.

Sean checked his watch. "Three more minutes. I need a clean plate, though."

"Coming up." Emerson carried two large plates to the counter beside the barbecue. "Yell out if you need help, or maybe Ethan can help you carry them." She went back inside.

"Oh, but Ethan might drop the plate," Sean murmured, looking at his cousin. "Have you anything else to say?"

Ethan hadn't stopped glaring at Sean. "Yeah, stay the fuck away from my house." He turned tail and strode inside.

"Oh, I have no need to go now. But Grandpa will." Sean stared out at the skyline until his alarm went off. He pulled the steaks from the grill, laid them onto the plates, and carried them inside. "Here they are. My Sean Ryan steaks coming right up." He laid a plate either end, and everyone took one. Salads were passed around, wine and beer opened or poured, grace was said, and they all tried

Sean's steaks for the first time.

"Oh, my God, Sean." Emerson held her hand in front of her mouth. "This is amazing."

"Thank you. There are a few things I know how to cook, and this is one of them."

"I have to agree." Kieran sliced off another piece. "Best I've tasted in a while."

Sean gave him a nod and kept eating.

Once the main meal was over and dessert was served, the toasts were made.

"Sean, you've had a bumpy road these last four years, or maybe I should say twenty-two years, you've lost both your parents, gained a successful career, and have proved you can grow and mature and be an adult," Cormac said. "Happy birthday."

"Thanks, Grandpa." Sean sipped his beer. "I ah, know that this year has been tough on the whole family. We lost Brandon and Sierra." He glanced at Alec who stared down at his plate. "Then my dad, then Connor." He looked to his right at his cousin. "And it's not just tough for me, but everyone at this table. We can only hope that Grandma and Great-Grandma and Mom were all there for them when they passed so they weren't alone. And I hope that being in law enforcement doesn't take the rest of you. Grandpa, you're retiring and getting married this year. I hope that still goes ahead. And Kieran and Sandy are having their baby, so another Ryan or two or three will be coming along."

"Let me have this one first." Sandy laughed and slid a lock of hair behind her ear.

"And maybe one day, I'll be a dad and have kids and

do a better job than the way I was raised." He looked down wistfully. "I guess I have time for that."

"As the youngest, you do," Alec said glaring at him. "If you don't keep getting yourself into trouble."

"I'm not the only one." Sean glared right back. "But either way, thank you to everyone for coming. I really appreciate it." He held up his beer and the rest followed suit.

*****

On Wednesday, Sean stopped by his publisher.

"Oh, happy birthday, my darling boy." Vincent clapped his hands three times in quick succession.

"It was two days ago…but thank you." Sean dropped his bag on the couch and sat down. "And what do you have for me for my birthday?"

"Millions of dollars in royalties," Roger said. "Once *Is* came out, people went and bought *She.* We've also seen a rise in sales of your first three books, so we think they've been reading the two new ones and then buying the rest."

"At least more people are reading them, that means more sales, more money. What about libraries? Are they buying them?" Sean asked.

"Those sales are very healthy as well," Vincent said. "Seems to be the same deal."

"Great. More people reading my books. But while it's my birthday week, what do you think of the memoir pages I've sent through?"

"Alarming, in an exhilarating way," Roger said. "It

will make the book a bestseller."

"Is it that good?" Vincent rested his elbow on the chair arm and placed his chin on his fingers. "Really? That good?"

"Extremely," Roger said. "The information he has, the life he's lived, the details he's laid out…" He looked from Vincent to Sean. "All of that had better be provable otherwise your family may sue."

"They won't," Sean said confidently. "There won't be enough of them left, and yes, I have proof. There are also a few other things in the works, not that I'm doing, but I know about them."

"Like what?" Roger leaned forward in interest. "Will it affect your memoir?"

"I hope not. I think it will boost it." Sean crossed his legs and leaned back. "I can't wait to take a break from everything."

"When were you thinking?" Vincent asked. "You do look run ragged."

"Besides the holiday after *Mine* comes out, I'll also be going on one for Christmas after *Her* comes out. Before the memoir comes out. My family's dropping like flies. More will go, this city, this state, even this country. I'm packing my bags and going on holiday."

"Are you still writing?" Roger asked.

"Not as much. Just the memoir and the other book, but I don't even know what that is yet, and the memoir's becoming so long we might have to break it into two."

"We could, if it's juicy enough," Vincent said. "But what's the other book? A new novel?"

"No, so far it's just a book of essays on my life. Much

like the memoir, but different. More personal, intimate, about me and what I saw, felt, experienced—not just about my family as the memoir is."

"A book of essays," Roger murmured. "Could be an interesting companion piece to the memoir."

"Yeah." Sean sighed. "Could be, but so far, no novels because they're done." He pulled a manuscript from his bag. "Number three. And I am done for a while. I just want to work on my non-fiction. I find it interesting."

"Writing about yourself?" Vincent held the stack of paper bound by a bull clip. "Is this your last novel for a while?"

"For a while," Sean replied. "You've got fifteen out of me. It's time for something else, like my memoir. I'm finding the writing process for it interesting because it's non-fiction and there's a pattern to writing that just like with fiction."

"So, we're buying the memoir are we?" Vincent asked Roger. "Do you think we can make money out of it?"

"Considering he's Sean Ryan, grandson of the New York Police Commissioner and a two-time successful author as himself *and* Bryan Jamison, hell yeah. Some of the stories I've read. Whoa."

"Yeah, that's my family. They're connected to Madam X, as you know. Grandpa raided her brownstone about fifteen, sixteen years ago. Alec, Connor and Declan were involved, and we happen to know about her little black book thanks to Sydney doing her biography on her."

"And since you know Sydney, when she first mentored you, have you been in the brownstone?" Vincent fanned through the manuscript.

"I have, but not for a while." Sean grabbed his bag and got to his feet. "I can write about it. I know some personal details myself, thanks to Pop. But considering the amount of trouble Sydney had when she wrote them, I don't want to get into trouble. She postponed the release date for years."

"Yeah, I remember," Roger murmured. "And you're right. But from what I've seen so far, your memoir's explosive."

Sean smirked. "Just you wait."

Chapter 17

"Is there anything specific you want to talk about this week?"

"Is there anything specific *you* want to talk about this week?"

"I asked first."

"I asked second."

Levinworth laughed. "Okay. I don't think there's too much else to cover."

"Oh, that's where you're so wrong, Walter. So wrong."

Levinworth arched a brow and looked at Sean. "Do tell."

Sean sniggered. "It was during my time at school, college, and Harvard to be exact. In order to afford everything, I had to pool resources. The money from Mom's will paid for the first year of Harvard, and the money from my books paid for the second, as well as other things. I still had to make money elsewhere and because I wanted the experience. I got myself a part-time job during my year at college, and there was no way I could do a full-time job and go full-time to Harvard Law."

"How'd you manage it?"

"At first, I didn't know I wanted to go to Harvard, as I've mentioned. I did a year at college and got myself an internship at a publishing house."

"Which one?"

"Bellamy Publishing."

"Not Pulsate or Viceroy?"

"No. I mean, I could have maybe scored one at Pulsate, I guess, and I learned a lot from being published by them, but it was before I was published by Viceroy. I wanted to learn the ins and outs with someone different."

"How did you manage that as Sean Ryan?"

"I didn't. I became someone else." Sean turned from the window. "I managed to get a job with a fake card. They weren't very security driven, so they let me go to work. I managed to make enough to cover costs at college and enough to live on."

"Did you wear a disguise?"

"I did. A wig and brown contacts. I guess that gave me inspiration later. But they didn't recognise me when the books came out."

"What did you learn?"

"I spent two weeks in each department, mail, sales, slush pile. We learned from the bottom up."

"We?"

"There were two others. We moved up the ranks together as part-timers."

"What was the most interesting part?"

"Reading the submissions in the slush pile. And we were the ones who had to make the decisions whether they were good or bad, to pass them up the chain, or trash them in the bin. I felt so sorry for the authors because some of them were really good."

"And the others?"

He grimaced. "Really bad. I actually started sending them emails thanking them for their submissions and suggesting various places they could improve their writing skills."

Levinworth's brows rose in surprise. "That was very considerate of you."

"Yeah." Sean walked towards his favourite painting. "I made up an email reply I could copy into the email and send off. Some of them thanked me for the suggestions."

"And the ones who made it up the chain?"

"Several made it to publication. Most didn't. Politics of publishing, I guess. I wish I could have helped them, too, but I have no idea what happened to the submissions once they moved on."

"Did you ever keep track of those you sent rejection letters to?"

"I did at first. Some of them self-published. I bought their books to support them, and found some of them were greatly improved, and others had been slapped up the way they had been. Some people took my advice, others did not."

"At least you tried to help them. How long did you work there for?"

"It ended up being for my first year of college. It was only meant to be for six months, but they asked me to stay for another six months because I was attentive and wanted to learn. I even got to work in the art department as they made covers and I gave my opinion. Some suggestions made it into production."

"Congratulations. What did they say when you left?"

"They wished me well, were sad that I was leaving, all the usual niceties, and were surprised that I was going to law school."

"Did you tell your family you were going to law school?"

"Not until I had to, and even then it was only Pop and Grandpa."

"Why did you have to?"

"Because I quit college after one year and started Harvard. I wasn't living on campus anymore, so I managed to get an off-campus apartment. I had to tell them when they contacted the school after not hearing from me."

"How'd they take it?"

"Well. They were upset that I hadn't told them I'd left college, but they were glad I was still doing something, and was in the family business in some way."

"Is Harvard all you did?"

Sean glanced over his shoulder. "Meaning what?"

Levinworth shrugged. "Got another job, volunteer somewhere, or was it just Harvard all day every day?"

"Ah…sneaky, Walter. I didn't get another job. I had enough money to manage week to week if I budgeted, which I did. I volunteered at the local theatre doing backstage stuff for anyone who needed it."

"Because of your year of drama at college?"

"That's what I went with. Told them I could work Friday nights and weekends. So, I helped out. I learned even more about wigs and disguises, and how to put them together."

"Is that where you concocted Bryan?"

"No, but both my year in college and working backstage at local theatres helped my knowledge considerably."

"How did you come up with Bryan?"

"That, Walter, is another conversation. We've talked about my schooling before. I also did psychology in college so I could learn some things, and Media and IT."

"Has all of that helped you?"

"It has. Obviously, Media and IT has helped with my social media and how to manipulate it, and I know how to set up the backend of websites."

"And your two years at Harvard?"

"That taught me the law, Walter. Which I already had a grasp on. Growing up a Ryan had its perks, I guess."

"How did your professors cope with another Ryan in their midst?"

"They were surprised, like so many people seem to be when they see me, considering my applications showed a highly knowledgeable brain. They took me on. They had taught Alec and Kieran, but I blew them out of the water."

"Good for you."

Sean flashed a bright smile. "I thought so. But they also thought I was cheating. I had to take my exams alone and with three people in the room. They couldn't believe I knew so much already."

"What about your graduation from Harvard?"

"Grandpa, Emerson, and Pop attended. But I didn't want anyone else."

"Why?"

"Why would I?" He cast a glance at Levinworth as he walked on to the cupboard of artefacts. "Alec's an arrogant ass, Connor and Declan…" He paused. "My dad wouldn't've believed I could graduate, let alone from law school."

"Ethan's your hero, what about him?"

"Was," he spat and clenched his jaw. "And certainly not then. All of them had been with Sydney by the time I graduated. I wanted none of them near me to spoil my day."

"Even though you graduated in two years instead of three? That's an achievement to be proud of."

"For me, sure. Grandpa and Pop were astounded. They bought me a nice watch as a graduation gift."

"That was nice of them."

"It was, and I thanked them by dedicating the last two books to them."

"You also dedicated the first three."

"I did." Sean walked past Levinworth to the second wall of paintings and thought about the dedication pages. "Book one had to go to Sydney for believing in me. Without her, none of that would've happened."

"And the second."

"Well." He sighed. "I wasn't sure about it, as she had already died, and maybe that's why she was pissed off when she saw the first book, and saw that I had dedicated it to Sydney, but book two is dedicated to Mom."

"That's right, you said the first came out before she died. You opened a box for the family."

"We were around the table at Grandpa's. I didn't

mention Sydney by name—just as the woman who believed in me enough to encourage my creativity and help me get the deal."

"Did anyone know?"

"I think the smart ones figured it out." Sean walked back to the window. "But Mom didn't see the word *mom* so knew it wasn't for her."

"But you dedicated the second novel."

"To the woman who gave me life, and who then tried to take it away, but is now gone herself."

"Cryptic. Did anyone in the family get it?"

"I think they realised, considering I'd said, *who gave me life.*"

"Did they ask why you wrote that?"

"No. But I think Grandpa and Pop understood. By then, Dad wasn't impressed, Sierra and Brandon were milking my success, but they all got autographed copies. Ethan asked for one."

"He cares about you. Does he know you hate him?"

"I…" Sean paused in thought. "I don't think I've told him that. But he knows I know about Sydney."

"How's he holding up with his father's death?"

"I went to his place, and he wasn't happy to see me. But I got the firecracker up his ass to get out of bed at Grandpa's and get back to his own. Did you figure out who I dedicated my books to? You read them."

"I could figure out the first two, and obviously the last two. Did your grandfather and Douglas enjoy having books dedicated to them?"

"Pleased as punch. Showed them to all their friends and made them go and buy copies. But the third?"

"I couldn't figure out the third." Levinworth checked his notes. *"To the sweetest Honey on the block, who made a new man out of this kid."*

Sean's giggle rolled into a belly laugh. "She couldn't believe I'd dedicated it to her, or who I actually was."

"You told her? Who is she?"

"The prostitute I found on the Lower East Side. Remember how I told you my father had taken me to one in Queens for my sixteenth? Honey's the one I found myself and went to for a year after meeting Sydney."

Levinworth flicked through his recent notes. "Right. You said you found your own. It was around the time of the prostitute killings on the Lower East Side."

"It was, so I was always worried that Honey wouldn't be there when I turned up."

"Was she?"

"She was. Safe and sound."

"But she didn't know who you were?"

"No. I always wore a mask and gloves. With the deaths I didn't want my DNA left behind, so I always wore condoms, which is a given. I covered up in a hoodie so she didn't see my face."

Levinworth frowned. "But you just said—"

"I know. When I finally decided to stop seeing her, after getting into Harvard, and then the third book came out, I picked her up as I always did and finally showed my face and gave her the book. She was surprised by everything and took the book."

"And all these years on?"

A sigh came from deep in his gut. "Ravaged by her years on the street. I tried to help her get off it. I gave her money every couple of weeks, and I put her up in my apartment. She tried to get a normal job, but just went back to her ways."

"She's still on the street?"

"Went back to it. She's always on the same street."

A silence settled in the room before Levinworth broke it. "You can't always help everyone. And some don't want to be helped."

"Mom." Sean's head shook sadly. "She didn't want to be helped."

"No, sometimes they don't." Levinworth closed the file in his lap. "Do you want to be helped?"

"You did help me, Walter." Sean gave him the piercing blue-eyed stare of the Ryans.

Levinworth didn't flinch. "Do you want to be helped?"

"I was. You helped me for two years. You cured me. I moved on."

"Except you didn't. Here you are now, two years later, with the exact same problem. Sydney Kingston."

"Sydney's not a problem. She's a woman."

"That you supposedly love."

"That I *do* love."

"Do you want to be helped, Sean?"

"I have been, Walter." Hands in pockets stance, Sean stared down his therapist.

"When did you buy your condo?"

"With the first three novels."

"Why didn't you tell anyone?"

"That is another story for another day, Walter. Have we finished for the day?"

"Levinworth looked at the time. "I guess we have."

*****

Sean met the real estate agent at his parents' house. "Hey, have you sold it yet?"

"Hello, Sean, good to see you again." Nathaniel Brown shook his hand. "We've had several viewings, and many were interested, but none at full price or over yet."

"Why?" Sean stared up at the Hamptons style home. "It's worth two point two million. This area is a hotspot in Brooklyn. And it's summer."

"It is and I'm working on getting those potential buyers to up their price, but it's only been a few weeks."

"I'd like to get it offloaded by the end of July. I'll be leaving New York for a holiday and would like it dealt with."

Nathaniel nodded. "Okay. I'll get some agents to put it out to see who bites. It's an amazing house, a little bit of the Hamptons in New York."

"It is. And was a great house to be in. We even had it blessed by a priest."

Nathaniel's head spun in Sean's direction. "What?"

Sean chuckled. "My family was not a happy one, and once it went to rack and ruin, I wanted its aura cleansed, so I had a priest bless it. No need to tell potential buyers that though."

"Ah, no." Nathaniel's phone beeped, and he checked it. "I'll get back to advertising the house and let you know if we have a buyer."

"Great…and thank you." Sean shook his hand and stood staring up at the house. While it held mostly bad memories, and only one real good one, the house was no longer his home. He no longer belonged there, and no longer needed it.

*****

On Tuesday, Alec stopped by for his weekly visit.

"Alec."

"Sean."

Sean opened the door to let him in and watched him stroll around the condo, walking upstairs and coming back down, going into the adjacent condo and coming back out. "How've you been, Alec?"

Alec looked up from his phone in surprise. "Coping, Sean. You?"

"Living my best life," he said. "It must suck for you, though. Two kids; two brothers."

Alec frowned. "What's that supposed to mean?"

"Nothing. We've lost four family members in three months; I'm just saying it must suck for you."

Alec stepped closer to Sean. "It does. I loved my children; I loved my brothers. But they were cops and it's what happens, we all know that."

"Yeah, but they went about it the wrong way. I mean, how many cops went out after being shot for fucking a hooker like Dad? Connor, I understand; he was crooked, and had clearly been doing the wrong thing. Drugs, mob bosses, money, tsk, tsk. The law caught up to him."

"Meaning what? And why Brandon and Sierra? Their car exploded."

"Do you know why?" Sean asked. "Did the forensic examiner find out why the car exploded? Was it the fault of the manufacturer?"

Alec processed Sean's words. "What are you up to, Sean? It was a faulty valve and the oil mixed with petrol and overheated."

"Ah." Sean nodded. "That's what caused it. No one told me."

"We didn't need to. Dad, Sonja, and I closed the files and kept them secret."

"Ah, it would have been nice to know as a family. I've wondered, considering it was a fairly new car, and an expensive one at that. But the manufacturer had recalled some for faulty valves. Are you suing them?"

Alec pursed his lips. "Not yet. We're still getting evidence together that the valve was installed by them or the car dealership when she took it in for a check-up."

"You'd think being such an expensive car it wouldn't have problems. Was it in Sierra's name or yours or Sonja's?"

"Why?"

"Just wondering who gets to file the lawsuit. Who gets the settlement. Will you and Sonja split it? I take it you both bought it. It's a lot of money. But then again, Sienna could afford it herself unless she and Brandon *shared* it."

"What's that supposed to mean?" Alec's eyes narrowed and he stepped closer to Sean. "What does the cost of the car have to do with anything?"

Sean shrugged. "You wouldn't think it would have problems for that price. But I also wondered who bought it since Sierra seemed to be spending a lot lately."

"And how would you know?"

Sean noticed he and Alec were now the same height

and the extra muscle he'd added had broadened his shoulders. "She showed it all on social media. Have you shut that down yet? Isn't it a bit strange that you were on at them, mainly Brandon, about getting a job, and yet he and Sierra were showing off all this stuff on social media? They must've been getting their money from somewhere. Did they have other accounts? Were they being paid to be influencers? They always seemed to have new clothes."

"I don't know what you're implying, Sean." Alec took another step towards him and thrust a warning finger at him. "But I don't like it."

"I'm not implying anything, Alec. Just asking questions because there's a lot of them. Like who do you leave your estate to when you die? Who do you give your money and possessions to when you die? I have a will. I had to ask myself all those questions, so I just wondered who Sierra and Brandon left everything to. Did they have wills? What happens when adult children die? The law says next of kin, which would be you and Sonja."

"Yes, yes it would." Alec calmed down and moved back. "Sonja and I deal with everything equally. What money they had…their social accounts. We had to contact all of the companies they worked with to let them know it wouldn't be happening anymore."

"They would've known that from the video that circulated fifty million times." Sean made a sympathetic expression. "That must have been rough."

"It was." Alec smoothed his tie and blazer. "Very."

"And they'd clearly earned a lot, buying that car and all. It always pissed me off that all of that happened because they milked my publishing success on socials. The companies didn't want them before that, and they barely had followers. But the moment I became famous they just couldn't help themselves. They had to flog our relationship for all it was worth."

Alec's head tilted in suspicion. "They were your cousins, Sean. They were happy for you."

Sean's laugh dripped in toxic sarcasm. "No, they weren't. Sierra thought my writing was crap until she was pulled up by Sydney at Grandpa's that day, and Brandon used to beat me up. Which you did nothing about, just like you did nothing about my dad beating me and Mom. Hell, even Ethan had to beat the crap out of him to make him stop. But you didn't care to. Just as you didn't care if they made money out of me. It makes no sense that you'd have an argument about him getting a real job at lunch that day when you would have known exactly how much money he and Sierra raked in each year. *Especially* from their OnlyFans account."

The blood drained from Alec's face, and he went marble white. "What?"

Sean smirked. "I know all about their social media, but who knew they had an OnlyFans account where they did things like *that?* Oh wait." He pointed at his uncle. "You and Sonja. Seriously, Alec, allowing your children to do *that?*" He watched Alec's expressions range from shock, disbelief, horror, and finally, denial.

He composed himself. "I have no idea what you're talking about, Sean. Spreading vile and despicable lies like that. How dare you! What? Do you think that because Declan's gone you can go even further off the rails—"

"I'm not the one off the rails, Alec. Your children were, and only you and Sonja knew. You kept it very well hidden, but let me tell you, anyone who knew them would've been able to find that account. I did. Who else has, do you think? They had over ten million subscribers. *Paying* subscribers. And I know you and Sonja had a hand in setting it up and you took a cut. What did you get upon their deaths, huh?" His hand flew straight up, stopping Alec's from slapping him. He stepped closer to his stunned uncle. "Martial arts taught me how to react. Don't think I can't hurt you, because I can, and you know that. And I know way too much about what Brandon and Sierra did and what Sonja *used* to do for you to get on your fucking high horse about *my* behaviour. You had better start checking yours at the door, Alec, before someone calls you on it." He shoved his hand away. "I can see that a sickness runs in the Ryan family. Maybe it started with Pop, or maybe Grandpa, but it definitely infected the first three born and their children. I have six more weeks of this bullshit. Let's see which one of us survives that long, shall we?" He grabbed the handle and opened the door. "Time to go and clean house, Alec. Before I do."

Terrified of Sean's knowledge, Alec slowly walked into the metallic grey hallway to be left with a slamming door on his tail. There was no way Sean could know all of that. Any of that. How the hell?

I warned Brandon and Sierra it would get them into trouble, but they just didn't listen. They just didn't heed my warnings. Goddamn. Now I have to call Sonja and find out if she blabbed to anyone and I need to make sure there's no paper trail, no electronic trail.

He took the lift down to the ground floor, texting the whole time. He strode out of the building and over to his car, texting the whole time. He heard back from Sonja.

We set everything up securely. No one can track us or Brandon and Sierra to it. We have the money. The accounts are closed.

But someone knows, he texted back. *And they've threatened to reveal all.* He climbed into his car and started the engine. *I just can't eliminate them.*

Alec backed his car out of the space and saw Sean waving from the window. His phone beeped and he checked it.

Why can't you eliminate them?

Driving out of the lot, he didn't see the truck coming his way. It ploughed into the side of his car and his phone tumbled to the floor.

"Bye, Alec," Sean muttered. "Talk about karma."

*****

"I'm fine, Dad, seriously. The air bags saved my life."

"Thank God for that." Cormac sat on the chair beside his son's hospital bed while the rest of the family gathered round. "What the hell happened?"

Alec glanced at Sean's smirk. "I was just coming from Sean's and didn't look to my right. I, unfortunately, was doing what I'd told Brandon and Sierra to not do a million times. Checking my phone for texts."

"God, Alec!" Kieran complained. "Are you serious?"

Alec could only half shrug one shoulder as his other

was in a sling. "What can I say, little brother? A momentary lapse of judgement. It was important business. I had it on that car stand thingy."

"How long are you in for?" Emerson asked. She stood behind Cormac, her hands resting on his shoulders.

"Until the weekend, which pisses me off," Alec replied. "I'm the fucking District Attorney; I need to be at work."

"Is anything broken?" Ethan looked him up and down. "No plaster cast to sign or decorate?"

Alec chuckled. "No, kid, no plaster cast. I'll be home on Saturday. They just want to be sure my concussion heals well, as does my fractured shoulder. I'm on meds for blood clots, as well."

"Will you be coming for Sunday lunch, so I know whether to make less?" Emerson asked.

"I'm not sure at this stage, Emerson. I'll wait and see how I feel," he replied.

"Okay. Anyone else not turning up so I know now?" she asked the group and received head shakes in return.

"As long as you're okay." Cormac hauled himself up. "We'll let you get some rest. Anything you need?"

"My phone. Did anyone find it in my car?"

"Not that we know of, but I'll contact the CSIs and see if they have it." Cormac rested his hand on his son's arm. "Until then, we'll let you rest."

"Thanks, Dad." Alec watched Kieran and Sandy walk out followed by Ethan. "Ah, Sean, can you stay a minute?" He saw his nephew's brow arch and the smirk grow.

"Sure." Sean waited for Emerson to escort Cormac out of the room. "What'chya wanna know, smart Alec?"

Alec sneered at the name. "Where's my phone?"

"How the hell would I know? You were in the car. What did you do with it? And Grandpa's right, the CSIs would have it."

"And I think you have it." Alec leaned forward and winced at the pain in his shoulder.

"And why would I have it?" Sean slid his hands into his pants pockets. "You know I was in my condo looking straight at you. You know you drove out of the lot and didn't bother looking to your right. Where would your phone be?"

"With you. How are you here? The only way you'd be here is if it's on the list and it isn't. So, where's my phone?"

"I don't have it, Alec. I have no reason to have it. But your behaviour puzzles me." Sean stepped away from the bed. "What's on that phone that you don't want people to see? It can't just be names of clients." He watched his uncle for any kind of tell. "It must be texts. You were texting the whole way downstairs weren't you? You were when you got into your car, and you kept going as you drove out of the lot. What would those texts possibly be? Or who could they be to." He tapped his chin thoughtfully. "I couldn't possibly know, but I could certainly guess. They wouldn't have been to your ex-wife perchance? Were you texting Sonja about Brandon and Sierra's OnlyFans account?" Sean saw the flash of recognition in Alec's eyes. "Ah-ha. I don't have your phone, Alec, so it must still be in the car unless the CSIs have it. Besides, don't you have a lock on it or something? Don't you have safety measures for it, in case something happens, just like this—"

"Alec!" Sonja flew into the room, but she stopped in her tracks when she saw Sean. "Oh, hello."

"Sonja," Sean greeted her with a smile. "We were just talking about you."

"Oh, really?" Sonja glanced from him to Alec who gave a slight shake of the head. She looked like a deer in a headlight and Sean sniggered.

"Yes. How he was texting you when the crash happened. I saw it all the way from my window and rushed to help, calling for the paramedics to come and aid my apparently not dying uncle."

Sonja's brows dipped. "Oh, did you think he was?"

"In this family, lately, who the hell knows when the next one will go? But I can see that the two of you need to talk about whatever it is you desperately need to talk about, so I'll leave you both. Alec. Sonja." He gave them both a side-eye as he walked out the door.

Of all the gall, he thought, walking away from the room. *As if I'd steal his phone for those texts, or to get proof of what he does. I just let my phone cloner do that job, I don't even have to lift a finger.*

*****

On Friday, Sean turned up at Connor's apartment and met Cormac, Emerson and Ethan.

"The coroner's office has handed your dad's apartment back," Cormac told Ethan. "We can clean it up and empty it out, like we did with Declan's."

Tears prickled Ethan's eyes and he gave a small nod, producing a spare set of his father's keys. "Let's go. I want to get this over with as fast as possible."

Cormac nodded and led the way up to his son's apartment where Ethan opened the door to silence.

Sean stood with Emerson, carrying buckets of bags and tags and folded boxes for what was being donated and what was being thrown out. It was the same routine as with Declan's apartment.

Ethan stepped through the doorway and stood in the living room.

Sean and Emerson hurried around opening windows and making note of the mess they were about to clean up. Coming back from the bedroom, they found Ethan sobbing in Cormac's arms, and with a silent nod to each other, they started with the food in the kitchen. By the time they'd removed all of it, Ethan had moved into his father's bedroom with his grandfather.

Sean started on the living room, boxing up the record collection, and the few books lying around, including a couple of Sydney's. He opened the cover of one and saw an inscription. *To Hot Ryan #2, hot as fuck, hot as hell, hot as sin, I cannot tell. My lips are sealed. Sydney.* The burning started in his gut and quickly rose to his throat.

"Sean?" Emerson came to his side. "Are you all right?"

He silently showed her the inscription and watched her eyes widen.

"Oh," she said as her brows rose. "Guess he read some after all."

"He said he had at lunch that day." Sean snapped the book closed and placed it in the box with the records. He placed the other books with them and found the one he'd signed. His first YA book. "He kept it."

"Yeah, he did," Ethan said from the doorway. "Why wouldn't he? We all did." He dropped an armful of leather jackets on top of a box and dropped two full garbage bags on the floor. "These are for the Goodwill."

Emerson quickly tagged them.

Ethan walked over to Sean. "I want all of this." He waved a hand over the boxes and what was left on the cupboard. "I want all of it."

"I'll keep boxing." Sean put his book in the box and kept packing. "Where's Grandpa?"

"Right here." Cormac came into the room with another bag. "These are his suits. They're still in excellent condition and can be for the back-to-work program I support."

"To help out those getting back on their feet after a hardship?" Sean asked, sealing up a box.

"Exactly. The same place your father's suits went to."

"Only three bags of clothing. Is that it?" Emerson asked. "Do we need to get anything else?"

"Just the bed linen," Cormac replied. "Along with the rest of it." He saw Ethan pick up a photo from the bookshelf. It was of him and Connor at Ethan's graduation from the academy. He walked over to his grandson. "He was proud of you."

A small, sad smile moved Ethan's lips. "Yeah. I know. He told me. Especially after Brandon and Sierra died. Told me every time I saw him, told me he loved me and wanted the best for me and was so glad I was in his life. I told him the same. That he'd been a great father and I didn't know what I'd do without him." He stuttered to a stop as the tears overflowed and leaned into his grandfather's arms.

Sean silently moved away to give them a moment and sneaked into Connor's room. He quickly checked the floor and closet for any hiding spots, or something Cormac and Ethan had left behind.

Emerson came in with a bag. "We may as well do the linen and give them some space."

Sean nodded and helped strip the bed. He checked under the top mattress and found a small brass key which he slid into his pocket. They folded and bagged the linen and Sean got down on all fours and looked under the bed. Nothing.

Ethan and Cormac finished boxing the items he wanted. "I'm taking all of this." He motioned to the five boxes. "And his TV and stereo system. I'll need help carrying it all down to my truck."

"That's what we're here for," Cormac told him and saw the cleaners in the open doorway. "Have we finished with everything? The cleaning crew is here."

They had a last look around and found they had everything Ethan needed.

"I'll take the bags down to your car, Grandpa. Are you dropping them off?" Sean gathered five bags of clothing and linen.

"I am. My detail will help you load them. We'll dump the rest in the trash before we leave."

Sean gave a nod and hurried downstairs, hefting the bags into the back of his grandfather's four-wheel-drive. He went back in but found them coming out of the lift with all of the boxes, the TV, and stereo. "Is that everything else?"

"It is." Ethan carried the TV out. "Just need help loading the truck."

Sean picked up the stereo system and followed his cousin, while Cormac and Emerson shifted the boxes out of the lift and into the lobby. Once Sean dropped off the stereo, he loaded two boxes, as did Ethan, and Cormac loaded the last.

"Do you need help unloading at home?" Cormac leaned heavily against Ethan's truck.

"No, Grandpa, thanks. I got what I wanted of Dad's…" He took a breath and blinked away the tears. "I got his favourite jackets and personal items. I can unload it all. Thanks anyway."

"Okay." Cormac gave a nod. "I won't expect you at lunch on Sunday; but know we're there if you need us."

"Thanks, Grandpa." Ethan gave him a hug. "I love you."

"I love you too. Take care." Cormac shifted his weight and walked away with Emerson and Sean. They waved as Ethan passed them, the key burning a hole in Sean's pocket.

*****

Sean went straight home and pulled out the key. It had to be to a safety deposit or a warehouse, like the one where he was found. He called the private detective he'd used for a few other things. "I have a key and need you to find what it fits. Can you come over?"

An hour later, the detective arrived, took the key and his instructions from Sean and left, leaving Sean to ponder what he was about to find.

I wonder if my dad left any bank deposits, or Brandon and Sierra. Property in their names, bank accounts. He paced his office, shuffling a deck of cards, an activity he did when he was trying to figure something out. *Does that mean everyone's got one? And what about lawyers? Alec would have been Brandon and Sierra's lawyer, but did Dad and Connor have one?* He turned and walked the other way. *If the key fits a safety deposit box, what would be in it? Money, drugs? Considering what he was arrested for, what could it be? Wait…* He paused his pacing. *What if it's not his key and not his box?*

Okay, just breathe, Sean. You don't know and won't know until the PI comes back with the information. Okay. He shook himself off. *Okay what now?*

He paused in front of the wall of Sydney. "What would Sydney Kingston do?" he murmured. "Sydney," he replied to himself. "Would keep digging to get the dirt on Connor." He flashed back to the inscribed book. *I cannot tell my lips are sealed. Sealed about what, Sydney? What did you know about Connor before you fell apart and stopped seeing each other? And did you ever go to his apartment? Even Emerson was shocked.* His phone rang. "Speak of the devil… Emerson. What's going on?"

"Nothing," she said quietly. "Your grandfather is taking a nap and I just got off the phone with Sydney. She remembers inscribing the book for Connor. It was a joke. He'd said something about how even the Ryans have secrets and lots of them, but he never told her anything specific. Just implied it a few times and asked her to keep it to herself."

"Does she know anything about a safety deposit key, or box?"

"She didn't say anything, but then I didn't ask."

"Can you?"

"Sure. I'll get back to you."

Sean waited by pacing. Connor had admitted to secrets but didn't tell Sydney, yet Sydney knew of them. The phone rang. "Yeah?"

"All Connor said, was that he had them hidden away where no one would ever find them and told her not to worry her pretty little head about it."

"Did Sydney ever go to his place?"

"Not that I know of. Sean, why did you mention a key? Did you see one?"

"I did and managed to pocket it."

She gasped. "Oh, Sean, what if it leads to danger?"

"That's why I'm having it looked into."

"But it would go to Ethan. What are you going to do with it?"

"I don't know—but pretend you didn't hear anything from me."

"A bit late for that."

*****

"Who do you think will win, Sean?" Cormac asked, comfortable in his easy chair in the sun room. The family was there for Sunday lunch, but Ethan was yet to show.

"I don't know. You know I hate sport." Sean looked

at the two teams battling it out on the TV.

"I know." Cormac grinned. "But it's all we've got left as a family. Sunday sports and lunch."

"Not that we've got much of a family left," Kieran said softly. "Half of us are gone."

Sean replied, "Four years ago we had fourteen, and now we have seven."

"Let's not talk about that." Cormac grimaced. "I'm trying to deal with all of our losses in a healthy way so I can make my retirement age."

"Only a couple of months to go," Sandy said. "Are you still getting married on the same day? I know we keep asking."

"It is, and then we'll be travelling the world." Emerson set down a tray of nibblies. "Is Ethan coming?"

"I don't know." Cormac gave her a bright smile. "Thank you, my love."

"At least Alec made it." Emerson handed him a drink. "How do you feel?"

"Exhausted." Alec thanked her. "But in need of a good meal which is why I'm here."

"And that meal will be ready in half an hour. It's roast beef and vegetables."

"And I'll have a full plate, thank you very much," Alec said. "That hospital food was goddamn awful. I need sustenance."

"Hey, everybody." Ethan banged through the door. "Are we eating?"

"Half an hour. Come and watch the game," Cormac called.

Sean watched Ethan take the beer from Emerson and

sit down next to Kieran. He looked okay, not a weeping mess like he had been.

Half an hour later, they were at the table making small talk when Sean decided to bring up a particular conversation.

"Can I ask a question about wills? I have one, but did Dad? Does anyone know? Alec, Kieran, did Dad get a will with you?"

"No." Kieran shook his head and looked at Sandy. "Do you know?"

"No, not me," she replied.

"Why do you ask?" Cormac set his cutlery down.

"With everything happening in this family, it's just making me wonder. Mom had one. She left half to me, and half to Dad. But did Dad have one? I didn't find any papers at his apartment. You took care of the bills he left behind. I took care of the house. And what about Connor? Did he leave something behind for Ethan but never told him?" His cousin looked sharply at him. "And what about Brandon and Sierra? Young people don't think about these things. I did, but did they?" He looked to Alec, who was simmering. "I guess you would have taken care of their belongings, being next of kin and all."

Alec sipped his beer and exhaled. "Yes, Sonja and I did as their parents and next of kin as I told you the other day. But as far as I know, Declan and Connor didn't have one, unless one pops up, or another lawyer pops up in the future."

Sean was thoughtful. "Grandpa, do you have one? Did Pop?"

"Ah, yeah, my father had one and I saw to it that it

was executed. He wanted his money to go to the officer charities he supported to help those coming off the force. Apart from that, he had only his belongings which are still in his room."

"And you?" Kieran asked his father. "Who gets the house and passes it down now that there's only two of us kids left?"

Cormac gave him a brief smile. "It's to be divided equally between my sons, depending on how many were left. If there were none, amongst my grandchildren. The money would go to the same charities as Dad's."

"But which one of us will get it?" Kieran pushed. "You've got the eldest and the youngest left. Declan and Connor are gone."

"You can have it, Kieran," Alec said, making everyone look at him. "You and Sandy are starting your life with your future children. Mine are gone and I have a penthouse, so you can have the house. And you all heard it here first, folks. On the record." He looked around the table and finished off his beer.

"While we're on the record," Sean said. "I don't want it either. I love the garden, don't get me wrong, but I don't want the house."

Ethan agreed. "Neither do I. I only spent weekends here as a kid. I've got Mom and her home still, and I've spent a lot of time with her in the last few weeks, so I don't need the house."

"Kieran," Cormac said. "On the record, the house is yours and Sandy's and may you raise many children here in the years to come."

"Um." Sandy blushed and tucked her hair behind her

ears in embarrassment. She glanced at the remaining family members. "Thanks."

Kieran leaned back and sighed. "You sure, Dad?"

"I'm sure. The house is yours."

His son nodded his thanks, hugged his wife, and slapped his brother on the back.

"So that brings me back to my original question," Sean said. "How do I find out if Dad had one, or a safety deposit box, and do you guys have wills?"

"I do," Kieran said. "Got it done when I graduated law school and updated it when we got married."

"I have, but it's pointless now," Alec said. "I guess I'll need to change it, especially in light of everything that's happened *and* my accident."

"Why is it pointless?" Emerson asked.

"Because my children are gone and I have no wife, so no one to pass it all onto," he told her. "I'll have to donate it now and I...get the feeling that needs to be sooner rather than later."

Sean turned to his cousin who sat to his right. "Ethan, how 'bout you?"

"How 'bout me?" Ethan swigged back his beer and leant on the table.

"Do you have a will? Who will your belongings go to? Did your dad have one?"

"Not that I know of and neither do I, and as for my belongings..." He shrugged. "They will go the way of Goodwill like Dad's stuff."

"You should've had a will drawn up after graduation." Cormac frowned. "In fact, I remember telling both your fathers to get one done and I was a signatory. Sean, thanks for reminding me." He nodded at his grandson. "I think I have copies somewhere. I'll have to check my paperwork. They'll be filled under W."

"So, Dad did have one," Sean said excitedly. "Let me know what it says when you find it. Would it still be viable?"

"Did you not learn that in law school?" Alec sniped.

Sean arched a brow at his uncle. "I didn't specialise in wills and estates, Alec."

"What did you specialise in, Sean?" Alec pushed.

"Writing," Sean returned. "And made a shit load of money out of it."

Alec's expression turned sour, and he pushed back from the table. "I need another beer." He stormed into the kitchen.

"Sean?" Cormac said.

"I didn't do anything." Sean shrugged. "And also, for the record, my will says my money goes to charities, too. It's to be divided up, as will be the money from the sales of my properties if I don't sell them first."

"That reminds me, what are you doing with your parents' house?" Kieran asked.

"After spending a hundred thousand on renovations I'm selling it."

Alec walked back into the dining room. "Any buyers yet?"

"Lots of offers, but they're below asking price, so no deal."

"Ah, tough luck." Alec sneered and swilled his beer.

Sean glanced at Cormac and gave another shrug. "What do you think my dad had?"

"Not much." Cormac drank the last of his wine. "He didn't care about the house, obviously, was in debt, and owned no property outside of the house except his car which we sold off. I doubt it will say anything we don't already know about."

"It will be interesting, very interesting," Sean agreed and turned to Emerson. "And last but not least. Emerson, do you have a will and what are you doing with your possessions?"

She smiled at him. "Same as you. Everything will be sold off and the money given to charities. My personal belongings will be given away."

"What about your IP for the TV shows?" Sean asked. "I had to figure out what I'm doing with my book rights and who gets them."

"Yes, I had to think about that as well," she told him. "I decided to sell off those rights as part of the estate, but they must go to a company that does the same thing. Investigates crimes."

"Like the crime network?" Ethan asked.

"Something like that. I've told the executor it has to be someone, or a company, with good morals and principles, and not just someone or a company to grab a quick buck off me and my name and hard work." She laid her hand on Sean's arm. "Who did you leave your rights too?"

"I had mine set up in trust to protect my rights and then the money will pay for mentorships for students and adults to learn to read and write and who might be the next best-selling thriller author."

Murmurs went around the table.

"That's very noble of you, Sean," she said. "Helping those with dreams and ambitions to better themselves through education, English, and writing. Good for you."

"I thought so," he said, and the conversation continued.

*****

The old man was dropped off on a side street, in the pitch black of the night. He paid his cab fare and walked down the road. He reached the small laneway between two houses and entered the darkness. "Are you here?"

The woman stepped forward. "Ready and waiting."

He took in her appearance. A red shoulder length Farrah Fawcett flip hairstyle, red lips, a forest green trench coat, and bright red stilettoes. "Good. You know what to do."

"Will you be here?" She kept her hands in her coat pockets to warm them.

"I will when you're done. Ready and waiting."

"And it's all set?"

"It is."

"Then it's my turn." She kissed him on the cheek, made her way down the street to the third house on the left, ascended the stairs, and knocked on the door.

The door flung open. "Yeah?" He eyed the woman standing in front of him. "Who're you?"

She untied her trench and pulled it open for him to see her red lace nippleless bra, crotchless matching knickers, and a garter belt and stockings. "Ethan. Care for some fun? I miss you."

He frowned, trying to remember if he knew her, and

why she'd be on his doorstep in lace underwear. He scratched his nuts through his blue boxers and then he realised and perked up. "Sydney?"

She placed her hand on his chest and moved him back, closing the door with her other hand. "Yes, my darling," was all she said as the coat fell to the floor, and she grabbed his t-shirt. "Let's fuck."

Five hours later, the woman emerged from the basement and walked out the front door. She descended the stairs and walked back towards the lane. Removing a burner phone from her pocket, she called the police. When she arrived back in the alley, she met with the old man. "All set."

"All set," he said and took her arm as they walked off down the alley and disappeared into the darkness.

*****

At six a.m. on Monday, the family stumbled into Cormac's living room.

"What's going on?" Sean yawed. "Why did you drag us out of bed so early?"

Cormac sat stony-faced in his easy chair. His fingers tapped the cushioned arms. He watched Alec, Kieran and Sandy walk in and waved at the couch. "Take a seat, I have bad news."

"We're not waiting for Ethan?" Sean asked, covering another yawn.

"It's about Ethan."

All four of them looked at Cormac.

"Oh no." Alec shook his head.

"At two fifty-two this morning a call came through that a woman was being held prisoner in a basement. She had been beaten and raped. At three oh two, police raided the home. It was the home of Detective Ethan Ryan. They found a woman tied to a bed in the basement, and a shrine to Sydney Kingston on one wall. Officers first thought the woman on the bed was the woman in the photos. Explicit photos. Ethan was found on the bed next to her, and upon waking up, panicked, protested his innocence, pulled the *don't you know who I am* card, and the *don't you know who my grandfather is* card, and when the officers were distracted, stupidly made a run for it and grabbed his gun and fired. He was shot in the process, and as he lay dying, as seen on body cam, said, *I did it for you, Sydney, I did it for you, I love you.* He didn't survive." Cormac inhaled a shaky breath. "Crime scene investigators found countless files on murders, namely Lennie Cuzco's file. If you remember, he killed young Nora, Sydney's house sitter. The files he kept suggest he was the one who killed Lennie, which would make sense with him saying I did it for you Sydney. There were other files, but they will be examined." He tapped his fingers on the chair arm. "I have no idea what the hell to say to this. To any of this. My grandson, my sons, cops, detectives, where the hell did they go wrong? Where the hell did *I* go wrong? What didn't I see? What didn't I do?" He heaved himself up and wandered through to the sun room leaving four stunned Ryans in his wake.

"Fucking hell," Sean whispered. "What the fuck?"

Kieran shook his head sadly and looked down at the floor, while Sandy sat stunned.

Alec exhaled and looked after his father. "Like father like son." His phone buzzed and he pulled it from his pocket.

"Found your phone, I see." Sean smirked.

Alec looked at him. "Yes, I did." He walked into the hallway to make a call.

"What do we do now?" Sandy whispered.

"Deal with it," Sean replied and looked at his grandfather standing by the French doors. Emerson was beside him, rubbing his back and murmuring.

"Are you and Alec next?" Sandy asked Kieran. "The detectives in your family are gone. Three grandkids, two sons. Alec had his accident, but next time he may not be so lucky. Are you next, Kieran?"

"No, baby, no." He slid his arms around his wife and rubbed her back. "No. We are not next. No, this is just…"

"Just what?" she asked, fear all over her face.

"Incredibly bad luck," he replied.

"We're cursed," Sean said and stood up. "A big family in law enforcement. Karma is real. We're cursed." He flashed a sad smile and walked over to his grandfather. "Grandpa, do you need us to stay? Is there anything to do?"

Cormac shook his head. "There's nothing to do except plan the funeral. The coroner and investigators will need time." He glanced at his grandson. "You go home and keep safe, Sean. This family…" Sighing, he turned back to the window.

"Yeah," Sean replied. "This family." He hugged his grandfather. "I love you, Grandpa. You mean the world to me."

Cormac gave him a half smile and made the hug fiercer. "I love you too, Sean. You're my only grandchild left."

"Until Kieran's baby comes into the world," Sean said and let go. "Let me know when the funeral is." He flashed a small smile at Emerson and walked past Alec in the hallway still on a call. He slipped out the door and drove home. Once he was there, he called the private detective. "Have you found what that key belongs to?"

"We have, and we were going to call you at a reasonable time."

"Sorry, something's happened with my family. What does it belong to?"

"A safety deposit box at Mercantile Mutual in Queens."

Sean thought about it. "That's interesting. What's it going to take to get into it?"

"Ah, ID, a death certificate, and the key."

"Great, bring it over with the address and I'll get to it later."

"Nine-thirty?"

"That's fine." Sean hung up and paced his office. Ethan had been gunned down in an attempt to flee the crime scene. He was now dead, along with his father and uncle. Three Ryan detectives in two months. Too coincidental. *I find a key under Connor's mattress but nothing under Dad's. Both are supposed to have wills, but may not, same as Ethan.* He paused and looked out the window. *Does Ethan have a key? And why didn't the police find the key at Connor's? The bed looked somewhat intact. Did the cops not search it? They normally pull everything apart, but his bed was still made. How… Could this be a trap? Did the police leave it there on purpose? But they released the crime scene to Grandpa. The Police Commissioner. Are they setting us up to see who found it? Jesus.*

He rushed over to the bookcase and consulted his law books. "Once a crime scene is released whatever is found is free for possession regardless of who found it." A few thoughts flew through his mind. *I need a second opinion.* After dialling up his old law professor, he posed the question and got a similar answer. They chatted a few moments then Sean thanked him and hung up. "Let's hope I can pull this off."

The bell rang and he let the investigator up, opening the door a few moments later. "Do you have it?"

"I do." He handed the package over. "You sure about this?"

"No, and I have a question. In your research, did the feds, or cops come up?"

The PI frowned. "No, why?"

"I've been wondering if this was left there deliberately. I found it under the top mattress of his bed. The bed was still made, albeit messy. Why didn't the CSIs find the key or strip the bed? Isn't that what they do?"

The PI nodded. "Are you suggesting they planted it?"

"To see who did something with it. What if I, or my grandpa, walked into the bank to see what was in there and then we were arrested?"

"Interesting theory. But the law states once the property is handed back, anything found by them and not by the cops or feds, is theirs."

"Yeah." Sean eagerly nodded. "I consulted my law

books and my old professor for clarity. But I'm still worried and wondered if I could send you, or a lawyer friend of mine instead."

The PI considered it. "You'd still need ID, proof he's dead, and you have the authority."

"A lawyer friend." Sean rubbed his hands together and paced his condo. "Yeah. That'll have to be it. Thank you so much. You didn't find anything else out about Connor, or my dad, did you?"

"They have wills, same lawyer, no changes, and your grandfather was signatory."

"Yeah, okay, makes sense with what Grandpa said. How about the rest of the family?"

"Same deal. All the same."

"Great, won't be too much trouble then." Sean checked the time and thanked him for his service. He needed to see Walter.

Chapter 18

After walking into his therapist's office, Sean wearily sat in the middle of the couch facing the window.

Levinworth stared at him in surprise. "No window view today?"

"Ethan's dead."

Levinworth's jaw dropped. "What? When? Oh, my God, is that what I saw on the news this morning?"

"Probably." Sean sighed. "Haven't seen the news, even though the family has basically *been* the news and *lived* the news for the last few months."

"Ah…damn." Levinworth took a breath. "How's the family coping? When did you find out? What happened?"

"Six this morning. Those of us left turned up at Grandpa's. He told us and we're coping, although I think Grandpa's headed for a heart attack."

"The shock alone." Levinworth nodded in thought. "Five dead, three grandchildren, and two sons. Jesus."

"He ain't helping," Sean scoffed. "As for what happened, doc. I told you, he was the one who was obsessed with Sydney. He had a whole wall full of explicit photos of her. He had files on the person he'd killed for her, Lennie Cuzco, Nora's boyfriend. *And* he had a naked woman who looked just like Sydney tied to a bed in the basement. He'd held her prisoner for some time and abused her a lot, in a lot of vile ways. *He* was the obsessed one. *I* never kidnapped women and held them hostage for sexual deviance. That was Ethan."

Levinworth considered the comments. "I saw on the news a cop had been shot in his own house and that a woman had been found tied to a bed." He breathed in deeply. "You're right. That is a sign of obsession. A sick, vile manifestation of manipulation and torture."

"Bet it's a case file you'd love to delve into." Sean smirked. "Actually, my whole family would be a hell of a case file."

"That's true," Levinworth agreed. "What happens now?"

"Ha! Who the hell knows?" Sean shook his head slowly. "Another funeral, another investigation, another house clean out. We helped Ethan clean out Connor's apartment last week. It had been released."

"Anything in particular?"

"Ethan kept his stuff, and donated most of his clothes. Now what he kept will have to be cleaned out a second time along with his stuff."

"Will you help your grandfather do that?"

Sean thought about it and frowned. "No. His mom is still alive and technically she's next of kin. I guess it goes to her and I guess Grandpa will offer his services as he's planning the funeral. But she might not want to."

"Have you met Ethan's mom?"

"On occasion. She came around for Fourth of July or Thanksgiving and Christmas dinner when he was young.

She and Connor were amicable for Ethan and got along."

"How old was Ethan?"

"Twenty-eight, nearly twenty-nine."

"Jesus," Levinworth muttered. "Sierra and Brandon?"

"Twenty-four and twenty-six."

Levinworth shook his head and uncrossed his legs. "I'm sorry."

"I think you said last time you don't know how many more times you'd have to keep saying it," Sean said. "It's kind of pointless at this stage."

"How's Alec holding up? I saw he'd been in an accident."

Sean chuckled and it turned into a laugh. "Serves him right. He came to check up on me for my visit, and he had his head in his phone the whole time except when we fought. He was still texting out to his car, and when he got in the car, and then he didn't look where he was going and was smashed into by a truck. I rang the paramedics and they got him to the hospital. He was fine. Just busted up. Talk about karma."

"What'd you fight over?"

Sean looked at Walter. "What do you think? His kids. Told him I knew about their OnlyFans account and the look that came over him, priceless." He made a chef's kiss motion with his hand. "That's more than likely what he was texting Sonja about. At the hospital he demanded his phone back from me. I told him I didn't have it, that the CSIs probably had it as Grandpa said, but he insisted I had it."

"And did you?"

Sean chuckled. "No, because he had it this morning."

"Was he shocked that you knew about the OnlyFans account?"

"He was, but as I reminded him, they had over ten million paid subscribers. So over ten million people knew them. Wasn't just me who would or could figure it out."

Levinworth took a sip of water. "Did he say anything?"

"Denied it, but Sonja flew into his room just then, so I figured I was right about him texting her while driving."

"At least he's okay."

"For now."

"What's that supposed to mean?"

"Come on, doc," Sean scoffed. "My family's like the *Final Destination* movies. You may escape death at first, but death comes back for you and gets you in the end. Death came for Alec, and he escaped it, but it'll get him. It's a given in this family."

Levinworth made a note on his pad. "And Kieran?"

"Who knows? At this rate, we could all be dead by the end of the year. One a month. We've got six months left. There's five of us, six with the baby, seven with Emerson if she marries Grandpa. She'll be a Ryan by then like Sandy."

"Do you really think all of your family's going to die?"

"Yeah." Sean's head bobbed vigorously. "Yeah, I fucking do." He finally got up and walked over to the window. "What the hell man? Seriously. What the fucking hell?"

"It's a lot to process."

"And I could lose Grandpa to a stroke or heart attack. If Alec and Kieran goes, he'll die, I can almost guarantee it. Three grandkids, two sons, on top of his father and daughter-in-law. Jesus."

"Do you love your grandfather?"

"Yeah, of course I do."

"I sense a but. And because I know what you said four years ago."

"But." Sean's hands slid into his pockets. "He didn't stop Dad or Brandon or Sierra or anyone from doing what they did."

"Resentful? Angry? Hateful?"

"A little bit of everything."

"How do you feel about Ethan's death?"

"A little sad."

"He was your hero."

"*Was* being the operative word."

"Did your feelings change completely?"

Sean considered his emotions and shrugged a shoulder. "Not completely, maybe ninety-nine percent."

"And the final one percent?"

Silence, until Sean sighed. "Is horribly sad."

"Are you going to miss him?"

"The old him."

"Had he changed that much?"

"Oh, hell yeah."

"Stopped spending time with you. Stopped being your hero when he slept with Sydney."

"Yep."

"What about when he became obsessed with Sydney?"

"Oh…now there's a word I know," Sean mocked. "I certainly didn't know the extent of that until a few months ago."

"And how'd you find out?"

"How'd you think? I broke and entered." Sean made air quotes around those two words. "I had a key because Ethan's not…" He paused. "*Wasn't* very smart."

"And what did you find?"

"Exactly what the cops found. A shrine to Sydney Kingston in his basement."

"Was the woman there?"

"Not at the time."

"When was that?"

Sean looked over his shoulder. "Last year, a few months ago, I don't know."

"Did you say anything to anyone?"

"No. Why bother? He'd deny it, and he'd get rid of everything in case someone went around. What would be the point?"

"The point would've been he could've gotten help and that woman wouldn't've been kidnapped and held hostage."

"We don't know that, doc. How many people in therapy are still doing what they're in therapy to break? He could have kept on going."

"He could have had the same help you're getting."

"Is this stopping me from doing bad things?" Sean faced him. "You don't know what I get up to, and neither does Alec. You don't know if I'm doing bad things in my condo or not."

Levinworth's head tilted. "True. Are you?"

"Of course I am. Good one, doc." Sean sighed and walked over to the wall painting. "Considering the sickness in this family, I'm wondering if Kieran managed to not be infected, and in turn, his baby."

"What about you?"

"As I told Alec last week, the illness affected the first three born and their children. Alec with Brandon and Sierra, Connor with Ethan, and Declan with me. I'm no psychologist, but I'd say there's something to genetic illnesses and the way assholes turn out."

"Had any of your family been diagnosed with anything?"

"Greed," Sean suggested. "Drug dependence, sex dependence, alcohol dependence."

Levinworth conceded. "It's entirely probable they were inebriated by the drugs and alcohol. Those chemicals do change the way the brain works over time. I meant mentally, like you. Do any of them have a disorder?"

"No idea, doc. Is it possible considering their behaviours?"

"Very." Levinworth checked his notes. "There are several issues they could've had that affected the way they did things, saw the law, defied it."

"Ego, arrogance, entitlement. *Don't you know who my father and grandfather are.*" Sean scoffed. "All of the above."

"It's entirely possible they were, and maybe, in Alec's case, are narcissistic personality types."

"Wife beater, child abuser."

"In your father's case, yes. Not in Connor's or Alec's."

"No, funnily enough." Sean turned around. "They let Declan get away with beating his wife and kid, and didn't do a thing to stop it, but they didn't beat their own. I never saw a bruise or mark on my cousins. Ever."

Levinworth said softly, "But they saw it on you."

"A lot." Sean's lips pursed before he exploded. "And none of the fucking assholes did anything to stop it. Stop the sickness, stop the illness, stop the disease, and they all wondered why I turned out so fucked up. Did I tell you that? After Dad's death at the wake, the three of them, plus Ethan, approached me and told me it was now their job to look out for me. And, as I reminded them, they hadn't fucking done it when he was alive, so don't bother now. What fucking hypocrites!" He stormed across the room, fists clenched by his sides, nostrils flared.

"It's very hypocritical," Levinworth agreed. "Very. I have to say, Sean, I really don't understand your family. Law enforcement, all four sons, plus your grandfather and great-grandfather, and yet all they did was make excuses for not stopping their son, grandson and brother from beating his wife and child. From domestic violence, from abusing. I'm so very sorry."

The tears Sean had been holding onto poured forth and he made small noises while trying to stop the flow.

Levinworth picked up the box of tissues on the coffee table and moved to Sean's side, offering them to him. "I'm so very sorry because I can *still* see how your life has affected you and affected you deeply."

Sean pulled multiple tissues from the box and held them to his eyes in wads.

"And I have a feeling it's going to affect you deeply for many years to come. Once the mandated therapy is over, I want you to continue. I want you to continue getting help."

"And how many years is that going to take?" Sean

stuttered, wiping his face.

"I don't know." Levinworth sighed. "But I know you also need time away from your family. Space. Distance."

"I'm planning on that when this is all over." Sean blew his nose and threw the tissues in the bin. "That's exactly what I'm planning to do come August. I'm off on holiday and I don't know how long I'll be gone for or where I'll go, or how long I'll stay in each place. But I will be gone." He picked up his bag. "But right now, I need to head home and just…" He sighed. "Be."

"Okay. I'll see you next week," Levinworth said.

"Bye, doc." Sean left and caught a cab home. Upon his arrival he called the lawyer friend he'd had go to Connor's safety deposit box.

Within half an hour, he was handing a legal envelope to Sean. "That's all of it and the account's closed."

"Thank you so much." Sean handed him an envelope of money. "Hope this helps."

His friend looked at the cash. "Certainly does."

Sean closed the door and went into his office, pulled on rubber gloves and opened the envelope, spilling the contents over his desk. He looked at them and computed what they were. "Fucking hell!"

*****

On Wednesday, Sean walked into Cormac's house. "Grandpa. You home?" He closed the door and walked into the living room, but he didn't see him.

Emerson came bustling down the stairs. "He's in the office. I'm just popping out. I'll be back later."

"Okay." Sean waited for her to leave before going down the hall and around the corner. The office was opposite Douglas' room. "Hey, Grandpa. You wanted to see me."

"I did, close the door." He motioned to Sean and leaned back in his black leather office chair and tapped the mahogany desk. "You reminded me about wills the other day, and I've gone through my files. I have copies of Connor's and your dad's, plus Alec's and Kieran's. I called Alec; he's getting his changed this week. But…" He looked out the window. "But…"

"What?" Sean sat in the chair opposite him. "Are they still good?"

"Connor left everything to Ethan, which we dealt with, but I don't have a copy of Ethan's because he didn't have one. Your dad's said everything was left to your mom, but in the case of that, it all goes to you anyway."

"And we've dealt with that."

"We have." Cormac turned back and leant on his desk. "I've contacted the law firm and they're processing both wills. The problem is, Ethan."

"He didn't have one, so it all goes to his mom."

"Yep." Cormac tapped the desk. "He'll get his funeral with honours, as he technically didn't disgrace the uniform. And his mother and her family will be at the funeral, obviously, but she refused to be at the wake. She blamed us, especially Connor, for Ethan's behaviour the last few years, so she wants nothing to do with us."

"Understandable," Sean said. "I don't want anything to do with this family either, but she did have him all week as a kid. He only saw us on weekends, so technically she raised him. Once he turned eighteen he was seen as an adult, that's not all on us." He watched his grandfather and the range of emotions sweeping across his face. "Who's cleaning up the house?"

"The police will release it to next of kin. That is Kelly, his mother."

"Bet she can't wait for that mess." Sean's brows rose. "That's going to be a doozy."

"Yeah, it is. I offered to help. Told her to let me know if she needs it."

"Without a will, she'll get the house as well as the contents. I bet she'll sell that as fast as she can. If she can. Mom and Dad's house is still for sale. No one wants to pay the price we're offering. My agent said we might have to lower it if we want a sale. He may have trouble selling off a house with a tragic basement story."

"Yeah." Cormac nodded. "I thought of buying it to knock it down."

"And then what?" Sean asked. "Selling the land to a developer?"

"Something like that." Cormac turned back to the window.

"If Alec goes, who does his stuff go to? Did he say?"

"No, but I'll guess he'll put that in the new will."

"And Dad's? Was it just basic?"

"See for yourself." Cormac pushed the copy of the will across the desk.

Sean quickly went over it, and it was the most basic kind of will you could get. Whatever he had would be sold off and debts would be paid for. "No bank accounts? No savings? You paid off his debt. What did he have if I get to keep the house?"

"Just his car, which went towards back rent and credit cards, but yeah, he'd racked up a lot of that."

"Jesus." Sean let the paper float onto the desk. "Glad I got mine sorted out. Bet Emerson's glad she got hers sorted. Oh, she popped out, by the way."

"Did she say what for?"

"No. Probably for ingredients to make all of that delicious food I love. I'm gaining weight, you know."

Cormac chuckled. "Yeah, yeah, so am I. And yet she stays as sexy as ever."

"Whoa, Grandpa, make it legal already."

"Yeah." Cormac grew silent.

Sean noticed the silence. "Do you not want to make it legal anymore?"

Cormac tapped the desk with his finger. "I do. It's just lost its sheen."

"You were waiting for the day you retired, your seventy-fifth to get married. That's a couple of months away."

"Yeah, and most of the family is gone. My two middle sons, my three grandchildren."

"You still have four of us."

Cormac gave a small smile. "The thought of it just…"

"Seems too much to bear given the circumstances. You don't have to do it, you know. I know you had a big day planned, but with the family going the way it is…"

Cormac lumbered to his feet and swept up the wills. "Yeah, I know. But I'm a man of my word and I made the commitment when I put the ring on her finger."

"I'm sure she'll understand with everything happening."

"I'm not sure *I* understand everything happening." Cormac closed his filing cabinet. "This has just…I don't know."

"Exhausted you," Sean supplied. "Emotionally, psychologically. Yeah, I know the feeling."

"Oh, you do, do you?" Cormac grinned. "And how's that? Let's go into the sun room for a drink." He led Sean into the kitchen, grabbed two beers, and continued to his easy chair. The French doors were open, giving them a lovely summer breeze. "How do you know the feeling?" He clinked his bottle to Sean's before swigging back a couple of mouthfuls.

"I just…" Sean shrugged and took a sip. "I told my therapist Ethan had died, and we talked about it, and all the other deaths, and what it all means and what's happening in our family. I broke down and he actually apologised, or should I say, he offered his sympathies and told me my family had fucked me up worse than he first thought. I write all day when I'm home. I don't eat much and I don't sleep much, but it's all taken its toll. He wants me to continue therapy when the mandate is over."

Cormac tilted his head in thought and watched his grandson. "Do you think that would be a good idea?"

Sean drank another mouthful. "I think that would be a good idea for *anyone* left in this family. Especially you."

"Yeah, your grandpa has always had the weight of the world on his shoulders, and I will carry that until my last breath."

"Two sons, three grandchildren. It's aged you."

"What do you expect? The last few months have

seemed to age you as well, and not just physically. You've matured."

"Guess I had to. Turning twenty-two and Dad dying. I'm an orphan now." He gazed out at the view. "I need to grow up and be an adult, and once this is over, I'll be taking off and touring the world. I want to see it before it's too late."

"Yeah, that was the plan for retirement. Emerson and I were leaving the day after the wedding, and we weren't coming back for a year."

"You could still do that."

"Yeah." Cormac considered the option. "I don't think so."

Sean watched his grandfather's face and wondered what other plans he was changing his mind about.

*****

The funeral of Detective Ethan William Ryan was held on the Saturday after his death.

The Ryan family, those left, gathered on one side of his grave, while his mother and her family and friends gathered on the other. Close friends and co-workers were also in attendance.

Cormac, and Kelly O'Connell, Ethan's mother, stood at the foot of the grave. She had fought to have him buried with her family, and as next of kin, had won the argument.

The priest said the words people needed to hear, and Kelly and Cormac dropped their handfuls of dirt onto the coffin.

They both stayed while the grave was refilled, as everyone else slowly filtered away. The O'Connell wake would be held at Kelly's. The Ryan wake was at Cormac's.

Sean wandered away to his parents' graves. "Another one bites the dust. Suck on that. Another Ryan is gone. I do feel sorry for his mom and her family, though. They're the first *other* family we've needed to deal with. Sonja was part of the family but has none here, so had no problem with her children being buried in the Ryan plot of the cemetery." He wandered over to their graves and stood on them. "Alec's rat bastards. May you rot in hell." He moved on to Connor's grave. "Your son wasn't even buried with you, naw," he mocked. "But you'll be waiting for him, anyway, won't you?"

And finally, Douglas' grave. "Hey, Pop, how you doin'?" Sean looked towards the funeral on the other side of the cemetery. "Grandpa's still there. So's Ethan's mom. I feel sorry for her family. They've lost him, too, whereas the rest of us we're just…*us.*" He shrugged a shoulder and watched Kelly finally walk away, and Cormac turn and walk towards him. It took a few minutes, and Sean studied his grandfather's lumbering, slow gait, downward gaze, and unreadable expression. He was stoic, in the face of death. He finally made it. "It's weird that he's so far away."

"It is." Cormac stopped at his father's grave beside Sean. "It is. Very much so."

"Guess you couldn't really argue, though. She is his mother."

"That she is." Cormac touched his father's gravestone and moved on to visit everyone before standing at Connor's. "I'm sorry your son's not here with you. But you probably knew in life that he would be buried there in death. I hope he's already with you and you're taking care of him." He rubbed the top of his son's headstone and walked away with Sean following.

They arrived home fifteen minutes later to the family that was left and a few co-workers and friends. The rest had gone to Kelly's wake.

The full news of Ethan's devastating behaviour was yet to come out, so the stories from work colleagues were light anecdotes about cases they'd worked, or jokes he'd cracked. Cormac regaled them with the selfless acts Ethan had performed, and selflessness he had displayed.

Everyone ate the food, drank the alcohol, and left by six o'clock.

At five past Cormac sat in his easy chair in the sun room and looked out the open French doors at the distant city. The family sat around him in the silence.

One patriarch, two children, one grandchild, one daughter-in-law, and one fiancée. All that was left of the Ryan family.

"Do you think they'll find out?" Sean asked, breaking the silence first.

"Find out what?" Alec asked in return.

"What Ethan did."

Another silence followed, but it was eventually broken by Cormac. "The woman he was holding prisoner killed herself yesterday."

Shocked gasps fled around the family.

"Oh, my God." Emerson's hands flew to her mouth.

"What? Why? How?" Sandy asked, clutching her pregnant belly.

Cormac deflated into his chair. "The tests showed she was two months pregnant, and after her interview, and searching the database, she disappeared two and a half months ago. It was Ethan's. He had impregnated her." Murmurs went through the group. "She managed to get up to the roof of the hospital and threw herself off. She didn't survive."

Sean felt like shit. The woman had been saved just to be so devastated she'd decided death was the better option than life. "Jesus fucking Christ," he muttered.

"Will that get out?" Alec asked. "Do I need to do damage control?"

"Do we *all* need to do damage control?" Kieran added. "Brandon and Sierra were one thing, but Declan, Connor, and now Ethan. The behaviour just gets worse."

"I know," Cormac said. "And I know it means my retirement may come sooner rather than later. The mayor has been calling for my resignation considering my sons' behaviour, and now that Ethan has been found to be a kidnapper and rapist, it's only going to get worse."

"Can they really blame you for their behaviour?" Sandy asked. "It's not your fault."

Sean's brows rose, but he stayed silent.

"It's very likely," Cormac replied. "Not only were Declan and Connor my sons, and Ethan my grandson, but they were cops under my watch. Their behaviour happened under my watch, so yeah, I'm being blamed. I'm the one who said we weren't covering for them. They were going to get whatever was coming, but since they're gone, it's not really going to matter too much now, is it? They died under suspicion, and there have been investigations and Connor's and Ethan's are ongoing."

"And God knows what they'll find," Sean said. "What happened with my dad's?"

"Your dad's wasn't that bad. It was only to do with drugs, which he's not the first cop to get involved with, and prostitutes, again, not the first cop to get involved with. But Connor was a different story." Cormac waved a hand then pounded it on the arm of his chair. "Mafia, drugs, money. Jesus. And Ethan, that will last a while."

Sean remembered what had been found in Connor's safety deposit box. *A lot more than that,* he thought. *I wonder what the investigators are finding in Ethan's house.* "Did Kelly say anything to you about Ethan's house?"

"No, no she didn't. But I do wonder if she'll even want to tackle that clean up job."

"I'm sure she'll let you know if she doesn't want to do it." Emerson laid her hand on his arm. "We'll clean it out for her."

Cormac covered her hand with his and smiled sadly. "We will if she asks. But she has her own family, and they may offer instead."

"Ooohhh." Sandy rubbed her stomach. "That was a kick."

Kieran laid his hand over hers and she slid hers out. "She's a kicking."

"She?" Sean asked. "You know the sex?"

"Ah." Kieran and Sandy blushed. "Yeah, we do."

"Hey, another granddaughter." Cormac's smile lost its sadness. "Congratulations."

"Thank you. We weren't going to say anything, with everything that's happened," Sandy said. "But we found out the sex in our fourth month."

"That's wonderful," Emerson said. "Will you be having a shower?"

"Oh…" Sandy froze. "That's another thing. We weren't sure about whether we should go ahead with it."

"Of course you should," Cormac told them. "Don't let what's happening in this family stop you."

"My family want to put it on just as they did with my bridal shower. But I wasn't sure," Sandy fretted.

"The rest of the world doesn't stop because my family is tearing itself apart," Cormac said. "You do whatever you want; it's your baby, your choice. Don't worry about us."

*****

When Sean arrived home, he stood staring at his wall of Sydney for a few minutes to calm his thoughts. He saw the page of images of his family on the wall, grabbed a red Sharpie, and marked his cousin off with a thick cross.

Seven crosses now adorned the family photos as he'd also crossed out his mother and great-grandfather. But there were more yet to cross off.

He quickly changed his clothes, put on his wig and glasses, popped off his ankle bracelet, and glitched the building's Wi-Fi and surveillance system. He caught a cab to the Upper East Side and raced down the street to the brownstone and up the stairs.

After opening the vestibule and front doors, and

locking them against the world, he sighed and dropped his bag by the door. The scent of hot roast beef salad permeated the air and his stomach growled as he walked into the living room to cool himself under the air conditioner on such a warm day.

He breathed out and relaxed into himself.

He was home.

Chapter 19

"How was the funeral?"

"Weird."

"How so?"

"It wasn't at the family plot."

"Why not?"

"Ethan's mom, Kelly, demanded that Ethan be buried with her family, even though none of hers are dead. They're all alive. He's buried with strangers."

"Because she's next of kin."

"Yeah, something like that. Buried with people he has no fucking clue about and on the other side of the cemetery to his father, uncle, great-grandparents, grandma."

"I didn't think you cared about Ethan anymore?"

Sean stared out the window, the distant grey clouds billowing for a summer shower. They heat radiated off the rooftops in shimmering waves. "One percent."

"You still cared about Ethan one percent?"

Sean shrugged. "I guess I did. But I guess what really irks me is the fact he's not with his dad. Not with the family. He's with people he doesn't know. Can you imagine that? Being buried at twenty-eight with people you don't know? People you've never met…he won't see his grandparents for God knows how long, or his mother. Meanwhile, his family's all there together. I think it's selfish on her part and she didn't care what we, Grandpa, or even Connor or Ethan wanted. Did she even know if Ethan wanted to be buried on the other side of the cemetery? No, she didn't. She did it to piss off the family, not to respect her son."

"Sounds like you care more than one percent."

Sean looked over his shoulder. "Would you like to be buried in another person's plot when you didn't know them? It's disrespectful."

"Did your cousin have a will?"

"No, sadly. She gets everything as next of kin."

"Including the house."

"Yep. Grandpa offered to clean it up. She refused him. But after the conversation we had after the funeral, it's entirely possible she wouldn't want to do that either."

"Considering what was in the basement, no." Levinworth crossed his legs and took a sip of water. "How are you holding up other than that?"

Sean sighed, something he'd been doing a lot these last few months, and he tried to find the right words. "I'm…*doing.* I'm slowing down with my writing, not going all night. I'm watching some movies, some TV, trying to get my mind off of everything."

"Want to talk about your writing? Is it still your memoir?"

"Yeah, it's a doozy. I hand on ten pages at a time to my editor and get his notes back. There's a lot to talk about."

"You said once before you weren't sure if you would make one or two volumes."

"Yeah." Sean stretched his arms above his head and cracked his back. A yawn followed. "Mind if I have a water?"

"Help yourself. The fridge is behind the desk."

Sean opened the door to see a selection of drinks. "Well stocked fridge, Walter." He grabbed a lemon lime water and cracked it open. "I think the city heat's getting to me." He gulped back four mouthfuls and capped the bottle. "But it's probably just my life."

"Definitely your family life. I'd suggest you're becoming depressed, but you'd probably fight me on it."

Sean thought about it. "No, I wouldn't fight you. I'd agree to a degree. It's hard going, though. Death's hard at the best of times, but I've dealt with five in three months and God knows how many more I'll deal with this year and we're only June." He had another drink.

"Do you think there will be more deaths?"

"Yeah, I do." Sean stood in front of the wave painting. "Alec, for sure. Karma's coming for him, and sadly, I don't think Grandpa's going to last until retirement."

"Because of the stress?"

"That, and because the mayor's trying to get him to resign because of Declan, Connor, and Ethan."

"Can't be good for Cormac's reputation."

"Nope. I'm sure people are asking why he allowed his sons and grandson to get away with everything they got away with."

"Anyone else in your family going to go?"

"We'll all go one day, Walter."

"This year?"

"Who knows, but I have no plans to."

"That's right, you're travelling in the second half of the year."

"I certainly am. Once I'm out of this straightjacket I'm off to see the world."

"The wonderful wizard of Oz?"

Sean chuckled. "Cute. But we have other things to talk about."

"Such as?"

"Did you know the woman Ethan had kidnapped killed herself on Friday?" He watched Walter for his reaction.

Levinworth's jaw slowly dropped. "You're kidding?"

"Nope. Grandpa told us on Saturday after the wake. The doctor had told her she was two months pregnant. It was Ethan's. He *and* his baby are gone. That would have been four generations of Ryans again. But I can't say I blame her."

"No. That kind of treatment can make people do all sorts. Poor girl." Levinworth made a note in Sean's file. "I don't blame her either."

"No. Everyone blames my cousin, his behaviour, and his alone. Although, again, the mayor's blaming Grandpa, and I'm pretty sure somewhere inside of Grandpa he's blaming himself."

"I can see why he would be. He's the patriarch of a law enforcement family *and* the Police Commissioner of New York City."

"Yeah." Sean finished off his water and let out a slow breath. "Yeah. As for everything else, I think in the storyline we're up to finding out how my father was sleeping with Sydney."

"That's a jump in topic."

"Kinda." Sean turned around. "We're talking death. Ethan died. He killed Lennie who killed his girlfriend Nora, who was Sydney's house sitter and my dad, Connor, and Ethan all turned up to the crime scene. It's all connected, see, Walter. Ethan killed Lennie, Lennie killed Nora, and Dad was the investigating detective which is how he got involved with Sydney. But, at the same time I found that out, I also found out he had something to do with Mom's death." He spread his hands. "All connected. It really is like one big dot-to-dot puzzle, and by the end, it spells the word Ryan." Sean sighed and took a seat on the couch facing the window. "A big fat flashing red sign that *screams* Ryan. Red for danger, red for beware, red for go back. Just flashing, flashing, flashing." He made a flashing motions with his hands. "And it just won't fucking stop." He removed his glasses and rubbed his eyes. "Do you know what it's like to have a neon sign screaming your name, flashing in your eyes all the damn time?"

"No, I don't."

"It's fucking exhausting. And it blinds you to everything else happening. But…" He slid his glasses on. "Back to the dot-to-dot puzzle of my fucking father. It was family lunch, Christmas, or coming up to, three years ago. Sydney had gone into hibernation after it happened, even though her novel, *The Shape of You,* had come out. She couldn't cope, and so Pulsate cancelled all publicity involving her personally. Still sold a couple of million copies, though. And all three Ryan boys turned up on her doorstep. Declan got the case and started spending more time there. After a while, they got drunk and fucked on the kitchen table. It lasted a month, no more than six weeks, and was over at Christmas or soon after. But he definitely didn't want anyone knowing."

"How did you find out?"

"He made a call at lunch."

Sean came out of the bathroom, saw his great-grandfather's door close and heard murmurings. He stepped closer to listen through the gap.

"Yeah, hey, Syd, listen, I'm just at family lunch. I'll be around tonight to talk about the case." Pause. "Yeah, yeah, I will be." Low laughter. "Yeah, I'll get my ass whipped in the sex room if I don't have any new information about Nora. Do I get tied up?" Pause. "Ah-huh. Oh yeah, do I get to tie you up?" Pause. "That's too bad. But I do like a dominatrix. Will you wear that little red lace set I like with the crotchless panties and nippleless bra?" A pause and a dirty chuckle. "Yeah, okay. I'll be around later, bye, Syd. Gotta go."

Sean stepped away, seething, but his father's phone rang. He stepped back.

"Hello? Hey, Rico. Why you callin'?"

Sean leaned back and glanced over his shoulder. The doors to the hall and kitchen were shut.

"What about Laura? Yeah… Yeah… Yeah, well you got rid of that, didn't you?"

Sean's ears pricked up.

"Look…" Declan's voice lowered. "All I know is, I can't have it known that I was there that day and fought

with my wife… I can't have anyone know that I pushed her down the stairs." Pause. "Yeah well, I'm just glad the coroner couldn't detect that I helped her along by holding her mouth and nose." Pause. "I wanted my wife gone, Rico. I did what I needed to do."

"And *that*, Walter, is how I know my dad killed my mom." Sean left the empty bottle on the coffee table in front of him and stood up. "But I'm done talking for now. Next time will be even more interesting." He picked up his bag, patted a very stunned Walter Levinworth, PsyD, on his shoulder, and left the office for another week.

*****

"Now this is abysmal," Sean said, looking around the table. "There's only six of us left." Everyone looked at him but kept on eating. "Not that I mean to poop the party, or anything, but geez."

"You pooped the party," Kieran told him, his face not cracking a smile.

"What do we do?" Sean asked. "How do we keep this family going?"

"We do exactly what we're doing." Cormac set down his knife to pick up his glass. "We keep working, and we keep having Sunday lunch." He took a sip of wine before going back to his meal.

Sean gave a nod and went back to his food.

"Have you found a buyer for the house yet, Sean?" Alec asked.

"No, but we've dropped the price and hope that will

help." Sean wiped up the remnants of his gravy with thick crusty bread still warm from the oven.

"It's a great home. I'm surprised there's no buyers," Kieran said. "What's the asking?"

"Two, down from two point two, and that's what the property was valued at."

"That's pretty reasonable for that area." Alec laid his cutlery on his plate and picked up his napkin. "I'm surprised people haven't grabbed it."

"So's my agent," Sean replied. "We'll see how it goes now. Oh, Grandpa said you were doing your will. Dad's didn't say much."

"You found them?" Kieran asked his father. "You should have a copy of mine, too."

"I did, and I do. Alec, do you want your old one back?" Cormac finished his meal and poured another glass of wine.

"No, just attach my new one to it, and I've informed my lawyer that you'll have a copy." Alec pulled it from his blazer pocket and handed it to his father. He was sitting in Connor's old spot so the four of them were evenly placed down the sides of the table. "Everything I have left, the apartment, savings, stocks and bonds, investments, are all to be sold off to pay off any debt and then the rest given to charity." He looked around the table, held his hands out and shrugged. "I have no children to pass it onto, no wife, so…"

"Would Sonja contest it?" Sean asked.

"Entirely possible, but my lawyer and I made it ironclad so she couldn't." Alec drank some beer. "I wouldn't put it past her, but I've warned her that it would take all of her money to contest it and then she'd get nothing anyway."

"I wonder what Kelly will do with Ethan's stuff. He kept a lot of Connor's stuff, too." Sean laid his napkin over his cutlery on his plate. "It's weird to think about who gets your stuff and where it'll go to if you die. I mean, my furniture is just furniture. Clothes are just clothes. They don't really have any meaning to me. But Ethan took Connor's jackets, his TV and stereo, records, books, pictures. It's weird and will be weirder still if Kelly throws it all out. She'll be throwing out Connor's stuff that was important to Ethan and will be throwing out Ethan's stuff that was important to him. It's weird."

"When you put it like that, yes, it is." Emerson sipped her wine. "I feel the same way about my things. They're just clothes or shoes for me to wear. Items I use. I have a few personal things I'd like to go to someone, but I've had to deal with the fact I have no children to pass it along to if anything happens to me. It will go to Sydney if she's still alive as well. But I guess Kelly won't want anything owned by Connor, even if Ethan wanted it because it was his father's."

"Sydney's inscribed books, my inscribed book, his clothes, records, they were all classics too; I'll give him that. He had good taste in music." Sean reached for Emerson's plate and stacked it on top of his. "What's for dessert?"

"Did you just pay Connor a compliment?" Alec took his father's plate and handed them to Sean.

Sean shrugged and stacked the plates. "He had good taste in classic rock, but now all of that will go to Goodwill or the dump."

"Maybe we can get it from her," Kieran suggested. "We could ask her. The worst she could say is no."

"Go to hell," Sean said.

"Fuck right off," Alec added.

"Drop dead," Emerson replied.

"I hope all of your family dies and you're left a sad old man," Cormac said.

All heads turned to him in shock.

"Do *not* tell me she said that to you," Sean said.

He looked at his grandson. "Oh, yeah."

Murmurings of *oh my God* went around the table.

"I know she's pissed off, but Ethan was his own man who did his own thing. We're not to blame for what he ended up doing or being," Alec argued.

"No, but I don't think she cares." Cormac leaned back in his seat. "She's lost her son. Her eldest child. She had three more with her current husband of twenty-four years. That's probably why she wanted him there, so all of her children would be together when they die, and she'll be there, too."

A few moments of silence was followed by Kieran saying, "Doesn't mean we can't ask."

"Maybe we could ask legally," Alec suggested. "We have three Harvard lawyers at this table. Connor was our brother, and your uncle." He motioned from Kieran to Sean. "And Dad's son. We could ask for his belongings back and something of Ethan's to remember him by."

Kieran and Sean exchanged glances and nodded.

"We most certainly could," Sean said. "Would there be any way we could get them now regardless of her being next of kin?"

"Probably not, unless Ethan had a will somewhere." Cormac lightly tapped his fingers on the table.

"Could we have an independent cleaner sort out Ethan's things under the guidance of an independent legal representative, so she doesn't throw out paperwork, wills, etcetera?" Sean asked.

Alec nodded and pointed his finger at Sean. "It's possible, but will depend how long the investigation takes, especially considering there was another person involved. We may actually be able to get Connor's items back at least. I can get that started tomorrow. Dad?"

Cormac's head slowly shook. "Do we really want to do that to a grieving mother?"

"We're grieving, too. You're a grieving grandfather just like *her* father," Sean said.

"That is true," Cormac agreed. "I'll call her in the morning, and see if I can visit her and broach the subject regarding Connor's items if she doesn't want them."

"And if she's not interested, tell her I'll get the paperwork rolling for reclamation." Alec finished off his beer. "What *is* for dessert?"

Chapter 20

On Monday morning, Sean was back in Levinworth's office.

"How are we today, Walter?"

"Still in shock over that bomb drop, Sean. And you'll be finishing that story today."

"Ha!" Sean took his spot by the window. "There is so much more to tell."

"Then let's get started."

"Such an eager beaver, Walter. Well…" Sean crossed his arms and looked out the window. "There was way more to that phone call from Rico."

"Look, I know. It was bad enough she fucked my brother, not that I really cared." Pause. "Yeah, can you believe it? It was two years ago, before he hooked up with that author who was mentoring my dumbass son." Pause. "I can't blame Connor—blood's thicker than whores." Pause. "Yeah, yeah, he was stupid and the whore is dead which is why I don't want anyone finding out." Pause. "Okay, great. I'll get it from you tomorrow. Bye, Rico."

Sean hurried into the kitchen, glad to see it was

empty and opened the fridge to cool down his simmering temperature after what he'd heard.

"You getting a beer? Get me one?"

Sean looked past the door and handed a bottle over, then picked up another and wanted to smash it over his father's head.

"So, in the one conversation, he called Mom a whore, me a dumbass, and admitted to knowing Connor had fucked his wife. Nice family, huh?"

Levinworth held his breath a few moments before slowly letting it out. "Fucking hell."

Sean spun around in shock and saw his therapist's stunned expression. "Walter Levinworth, did you just say the f word?"

Walter slowly nodded. "Yeah, Sean, I did, and I'll say it again. *Fucking hell*, your family."

"Now you know why I'm so screwed up." Sean leaned against the window, his forehead touching the glass. He couldn't even see down to the street.

"Okay, so at this Sunday lunch, you found out your father was fucking Sydney, and then heard him admit to this Rico that he killed your mother *and* knew that she'd slept with Connor. All in two phone calls. Jesus."

"And I have that proof in a secret file," Sean said. "I hired a private detective to track it all down. Call logo, paperwork—I've got it all."

"What are you going to do with it?"

"Use it," Sean said. "You know, at that lunch, he almost gave away that he was fucking Sydney. You should've seen Connor's and Ethan's faces when they figured it out.

"We're coming up to Christmas; what's everyone doing apart from being here on Christmas Day?" Cormac asked. "Only three weeks left. Sean, are you still doing promotion for your novel?"

"I am, but it's petering out. I should be done by next week and then it's Christmas break."

"And how much money did you get for this one?" Sierra asked. "And what are you buying us for Christmas since we made you famous?"

Sean's brow arched. "I have twice as many followers than you. You didn't make me famous but milking your connection to me helped you out a lot. And no, I'm not getting most of you anything for Christmas and how much I got is none of your business."

"Are any of us getting presents?" Ethan asked. He was sitting between Declan and his father. "You said most of us."

"You received my third novel." Sean sipped his lemon water, which had gone warm and watery from the ice melting. "But Pop and Grandpa will definitely be getting presents."

"There's no need to do that, Sean. Your book is enough," Cormac said. "It's not every day I get to tell people I'm related to an international best-selling author. I get plenty of kudos from the boys at work."

"Did you tell them all to buy it?" Douglas asked him.

"I did." Cormac grinned. "Did you?"

"I most certainly did." Douglas beamed. "All of my old buddies from the 35. They love to tell everyone they meet that I'm the great-grandfather of the international best-selling young adult author, Sean Ryan."

Sean's smile lit up the room. "And that is why my two biggest supporters are getting presents for Christmas and no one else is."

"Yeah, well, maybe you should spread that wealth around and help your old man out." Declan barely finished his mouthful of food before he swigged it back with beer.

"You're an adult, why should I help you out?" Sean shook his head in disgust. "Besides, most of my money's gone on my college tuition because it's not like you're paying for it."

Declan glared at his son while running his tongue around his teeth and making gross noises. "You can't even help your old man out?"

"You're not helping me out," Sean retorted. "You told me last year that now I'm a hotshot author I can pay my own way through college, so that's what I'm doing. Besides, you own a two-storey house. Why can't you rent it out for money, or sell it off?"

Declan finally closed his mouth and realised his words had come back to bite him on the ass. "I can't be bothered." He went back to eating.

Sean raised his brows at his grandfather and let out a weary sigh.

"Ah, speaking of international best-selling authors," Ethan said and looked at Sean. "Sydney Kingston." Silence fell around the table. "What's happening with the court case? Did that judge seriously let Lennie Cuzco go?"

"Yeah," Declan complained, stabbing at his potatoes. "Said there wasn't enough evidence to prove he did it.

We couldn't keep him locked up. It's fucking bullshit. I'm seeing Syd tonight, so I'll tell her then."

Sean's head popped around and he saw the looks on Ethan's and Connor's faces. Connor leaned back in his seat and stared at his brother.

Ethan stared at Declan and said, "You're seeing her tonight? Why?"

Declan looked at his nephew and saw the arch of his brother's brow. "Ah, I need to ah, keep her informed of the case and it just happened on Friday, so someone's gotta tell her."

"You could've told her on Friday," Ethan continued. "Why tonight?"

Sean watched the exchange with silent interest and could see Cormac and Emerson were interested too.

"I was busy chasing a crook on Friday and had to deal with it yesterday. Today's my only free time, so I'll see her tonight." Declan quickly shoved a potato into his mouth.

"And is talking all you'll do, Declan?" Connor asked, his arm casually across the back of his son's chair.

Declan refused to look up. "Yes, Connor, that's all we'll do."

Sean saw Emerson's expression change from surprise to puzzlement. Ooohhh, she doesn't know, he thought. But clearly Connor and Ethan are just realising it.

A shell-shocked Ethan swallowed the lump in his throat and leaned back in his chair.

Douglas spoke up. "Speaking of Sydney, Emerson, how are she and Amy doing?"

Emerson set her fork down and turned her attention

to him. "She's still in her self-imposed hibernation, taking her time to grieve, as is Amy. It only happened back in September, so it's still very fresh and raw. And they were the ones who found her and tried to save her. They're coping."

"Must be rough," Douglas said. "A horrible thing to do and to go through. But if I can lighten the mood a little, who read The Shape of You? That was definitely a different type of style for Sydney."

"Not her usual thriller, no," Emerson said. "But she always goes where the inspiration takes her."

"And not exactly my style, either," Douglas replied. "But still captivating, all the same. I'll never say no to a Sydney Kingston or Cassandra Kingsley novel."

"Even if she does end up putting out her novel on Madam X?" Sean asked. "Is that more your style, Pop?"

Douglas grumbled under his breath. "I hope she never puts it out and God help everyone who's on that list and still alive."

"That was an interesting lunch, that day," Sean told Levinworth. "The looks on Connor's and Ethan's faces when they realised Declan was seeing Sydney. The look on Emerson's face when she tried to figure it out. It was all so beautiful, as were the looks on Sierra's face and Dad's when I told them they weren't getting anything out of me. Sucked in." He slid his hand into his pants pockets. "I know Sierra had been tagging me for months on social media every time she posted something she liked, but why the hell would I spend my hard-earned money on her?" He pulled a face. "Ugh, or my dad? I can't believe he had the gall to ask me for money when he owned a house and told me to pay my way through college. Little did he know I was in Harvard Law, so he could suck it. How rude!"

"Very." Levinworth scribbled a few notes. "How did finding out your dad was sleeping with Sydney make you feel?"

"Mad enough to go and smash shit up," Sean replied. "I kept my cool for as long as I could, until I got the hell out of there and made it back to my apartment. I was on my own, thank God; it was a small three-room apartment near the school. A bed, a bath, and a kitchen diner, and it was still a struggle to pay the bills. But I got home, locked the door, dropped my bag on the floor, grabbed a pillow and yelled into it. And I yelled, and I yelled some more until I was spent. Then I cried, and cried some more until I was angry again, and then I smashed shit up—statues and stupid oddities I'd bought from a thrift store for decoration. When I was spent, I cried again and kept crying until I formulated a plan. I'd given up my job at the publishing house. I was in my first year at Harvard, and I knew I had to do something else. *Be* someone else, and somehow make all of them pay for what they'd done."

"And what did you do?"

Sean looked over his shoulder with a sly smile on his lips. "I became Bryan Jamison. But back to my dad for a moment. As I said before. I was sick to my stomach. It disgusted me so much because I knew something was happening."

"What about the cameras? You would've seen it. You would've known."

"Yeah, you'd think I would have, but starting Harvard kept me up all night, and I worked on my writing on the weekends. It took me a few months to realise I hadn't looked at the recordings for a while. By the time I got through them it was that Sunday, and I'd missed seeing Dad completely until I went back and looked again, and there they were, fucking on the kitchen table like wild animals. It sickened me even more."

"You actually stopped watching Sydney for a while?" Levinworth's brows rose in surprise. "That sounds like a breakthrough. You could actually survive without stalking her from afar."

"Apparently, I could, Walter," Sean mocked and walked over to the wave painting. "I didn't realise how much I was going to be doing between law and my writing. But I also knew Sydney was promoting *The Shape of You*, so she was gone a lot, which is why Nora was there and I didn't need to watch, so not bothering during September and October was of no consequence. There was no proof to help Sydney with Nora's death, and it didn't happen with Dad until November or December." He shrugged. "I basically played catch-up with the videos, putting it on high speed to get through them faster."

"You were busy with your YA books, from what you've said, and you then signed on for four and five, you started Harvard, and still wrote. Just YA?"

"Oh, God no. I had my first three novels on the go. My books were follow-ups to Sydney's, so they were being written after hers. But I could belt out a fifty-thousand-word YA in a week, and a novel in a month, if that was all I was doing. Just as well I had a stock of stories ready to go. But four and five were done and being edited. I just hadn't found Viceroy yet."

"Pulsate didn't want your novels?"

"No, but again, we're a bit ahead of ourselves. Back to the night of Dad's confession. As I lay bawling my eyes out, hating who I was and who I was related to, my books came to mind. I had a publisher, had worked at a publisher, but also had a whole load of adult novels ready to go and I desperately wanted to be someone else in that moment. And revenge comes to mind. Revenge on Dad, revenge on Sydney, and Connor and Ethan, and Brandon and Sierra, and I realised I needed to do something bigger and better. So, I created Bryan Jamison." Sean walked onto the next wall and stared at a new artefact. "Where did this little thing come from?" He bent down to look at the tiny carving.

Levinworth homed in on it. "An ancient Himalayan tribe."

"New?"

"For me, yes."

"Interesting."

"So is your story. Keep going."

"The thought was, I'd get revenge on everyone by being wildly successful and using my writing to get back at everyone, so I wrote extensive CVs on each family member and created characters around them. My starring roles always went to Sydney and myself, of course, while everyone else were villains. I offered the first novel to Pulsate. Michael, the adult fiction editor I'd worked with, encouraged the owner, CC Charleston, to take me on. But she ummed and aahed even though I had my YA with them. I submitted my adult novel to the next five biggest publishing houses and Viceroy was interested. They asked if I had other books and I submitted the next two. They loved them so much they snapped me up for two mill a pop. *They* knew I was going to be their biggest thriller writer because they understood how good my adult fiction was. When we met and I explained my need for privacy, and a pen name, they agreed."

"What was the paperwork signed under?"

"My company, which I had set up months before. Starting Harvard made me realise I needed to have something for my books. I set it up and the contract was signed under that name."

"You were going to Harvard, writing, and getting a new deal?"

"Yeah. Once I started at Harvard I left my job, so I didn't have that stress anymore. And when I got six million dollars and another publishing contract, I paid Harvard off, but had to be careful. Taxes needed to be paid and I didn't want to start spending too soon. It would give the game away, so my company paid me a small wage each week to pay my bills and other costs. The novels wouldn't start coming out for another year, I needed to concentrate on Harvard and writing."

"You got six mill up front?"

"I did because all three were written and submitted and bought. And I had another three written, and three on the go."

"So, *She, Is* and *Mine* were written years ago?"

"Yep."

"Hang on." Levinworth uncrossed his legs and sat straighter. "From what I've heard you say when you signed the deal you had those three, another three, and six more, and you said that in your interviews with *Creeper.* You had twelve books picked up by the time your first three were published two years ago?"

Sean chuckled. "Yes, Walter. I was prolific through my first year of college. At Harvard Law, not so much. A year later, when *Illicit Things* came out, I, along with Viceroy, had created a strategy of my pen name, image, and how we'd release the books. I was in my second year at Harvard, and I was still only twenty years old, so we decided not to show my face because hey," he pointed at himself, "it's me. We pulled it off with him not doing any publicity. We did a lot of other press. Posters, ads, all sorts, and the book was a raging success because of it. Six months later out came *Sinister Motives,* with the same thing. I was still at Harvard. Six months later, I graduated top of my class, and it was finally time to show my face, but a different version of it. And it all worked perfectly."

"It certainly did. Everyone thought you were a forty-something college professor."

"The plan was to be someone entirely different. I know how to put on a wig, and a beard. I use contacts and glasses, and I *did* get my clothes from a thrift store as Sydney once accused me. By that time, I had money from the next six books. I got out of that apartment and moved into my condo. I had the apartment in the city, I had my cars, and stuff. I was set for life."

"And Pulsate. Did they know?"

"When the sales of books four and five didn't do well, they told me they wouldn't be renewing my contract. I told them they didn't need to, I was taking my thrillers elsewhere and Michael, God bless him; he and Victor were in the meeting and told CC it would be the biggest mistake of the publishing house's life. And that's when CC said she had to cut me loose for Sydney's sake."

Levinworth's head popped up. "What? What did she mean by that?"

Sean shook his head. "I have no idea, but that was just before *Illicit Things* came out and YA number five had sunk in sales, so it didn't matter. I thanked her for the two publishing deals she had given me, and I told her my novels had been snapped up by another company."

"Did Michael know it was you as Bryan Jamison?"

"I doubt it. I haven't published the stuff he read. All of that was about my parents, and all of the novels are about Sydney, so they're completely different." He looked at his watch. "Walter, that's the story of how Bryan Jamison came to be."

"And you picked the name because Ryan with a B, and Jamison is Kieran's middle name."

"I think I've mentioned that before, doc." Sean grabbed his bag. "Next time, we'll go into how my publicity tour went and ooh boy, the stuff Sydney said about me. Bye, doc."

"Bye, Sean."

*****

"We finally have *Mine* coming out in two weeks. The

books and AI Packs have been sent out. You have publicity lined up, oh…" Roger snapped his fingers. "What's your excuse this month for not being in studio for the interviews?"

Sean set down a promotional poster on Vincent's desk. "I don't actually have one. I guess I could say I damaged it or sprained it because it was still weak."

"Or you have flu." Vincent sipped his tea from a delicate green and white China teacup.

"But I don't sound sick," Sean said.

"But you do look exhausted," Vincent replied. "Maybe something like exhaustion and you're now on bed rest."

"Do I look that bad?" Sean asked. "I saw the dark circles in the mirror this morning."

"You look like death warmed over, my darling boy." Vincent patted Sean's cheek. "You need more sleep."

Sean picked up the bookmarks with all three book covers on them. They were being given away with each book. "I'll get more next month when this is all over."

"We're sorry about your cousin," Roger said. "It's all over the press."

"It is, and Ethan was a bad boy who was exiled to the other side of the cemetery by his mother who buried him with her family. He's not even with ours."

"What!" Vincent's cup paused in mid-air. "You didn't bury him with your family?"

"It's up to his mom as next of kin. She took him away from us."

"What a bitch!" Vincent murmured. "Nose to spite face."

"What? I don't think that has anything to do with it." Sean wandered over to the couch and slumped down onto it. "But as much as I hated my cousin, I hate that he's not with the family. It's not fair. Neither is what she said to Grandpa at the funeral. Way to diss your son's grandfather." When he saw their puzzled expressions he quickly told them about the funeral. "She gets the house and all his stuff. We're trying to get Connor's stuff back, and have an independent contractor clear out his house, but Grandpa's talking to her this week."

"What a shame families have to be such assholes." Vincent sat back on his velvet throne. "But back to your book. What do you think of the cover of your next release."

Sean picked up a paperback and hardcover from the coffee table in front of him and looked at them closely, turned them over, opened them, and flipped through the pages. "They're fantastic. Exactly what I wanted. And they've been proofed?"

"They have by multiple editors. We got a couple printed off to see what they would be like and there you go," Roger said. "*Her* is ready to go for September."

Sean held up the trade paperback. The cover was simple; a cityscape of New York, a female silhouette, and the title emblazoned across the middle with his name under it. He nodded. "Perfect."

"But until September, we have *Mine* to deal with. The books are ready to go and we're aiming for another number one." Vincent finished his tea and set it on the coffee table. "But we're still considering the memoir of yours. And what about that other book you mentioned?"

"A book of essays, yeah. I'm not sure about that now. I mean, my memoir has a thousand and one stories about my life, so why a book of essays? They may as well be in the memoir. I don't know." Sean crossed his legs and slid down on the sofa, resting his head on the back of it. "I think I just needed to write it to get the thoughts out of my head to clear it out. I've written so much in such a short amount of time that the exhaustion is catching up with me. After three years of college, a part-time job, and all of my books, I just need to stop for a while and sleep." He covered a yawn.

"We have six more books that we're publishing after *Her*, so you don't need to submit for a couple of years. Have a break," Roger suggested. "Just finish that memoir first."

A tired grin lifted the corners of Sean's lips. "Yeah, unfortunately that's something that will be ongoing for a while, up until Christmas I'd say. But we can get the photographs for the cover done now and I can keep handing on what I've done. What I do need to know is what stories would be interesting, but then, after September that could all change and you might want more. What if there are enough stories for two memoirs?"

"I guess it would depend on what we'd concentrate on concerning your life." Vincent carefully crossed his delicate legs. "What's the theme?"

"Being a Ryan in the Ryan family dynasty of New York. What happened in my life with my parents and family. How I was treated, what my dad did, becoming an author with Pulsate and then Viceroy. But as I said, they might change come September."

"And what's going to happen in September, apart from your next book being released?" Roger asked.

"Something explosive," Sean rambled tiredly. "Something that will send ripples throughout New York's law enforcement. That is, if it happens. We're counting on something else to happen first, but if it doesn't, then we'll have to wait until it does. *Then* my memoir can wait."

"So, we're not publishing it now?" Vincent frowned. "I'm confused."

Sean gave a weary chuckle. "I'm writing it about my life in my family. We have a tentative date for something else to happen, but only if a certain person isn't around anymore. If he is, it won't happen. It he isn't, it will." He saw their confusion.

"It has to do with the family, so don't worry, but if the other project I, and several others, are working on goes live in September, so will my memoir six months after it. If it doesn't go live the memoir will wait. I know it sounds complicated, it's not."

"You sure about that?" Roger asked. "It sounds as if you're confused about it. But so far a lot of the stories are definitely worthy of being in it."

"Thank you, Roger. But let's concentrate on *Mine* for the next few weeks. I need an excuse."

"Tell them you've become a recluse," Roger said.

"Tell them you have a stalker," Vincent offered.

"Ha! That would be hilarious. *Me* have a stalker. After all the ones I've written about," Sean said.

"What you suggested before. You've sprained your other ankle," Roger added.

"You have the flu." Vincent whipped his silk handkerchief from his pocket and covered his mouth.

"Or maybe I just didn't feel like it," Sean replied. "I could say I'm exhausted and wasn't watching where I was going and sprained my other ankle. I've been accident prone because of being overtired. That might work. I've been in the wars this year. Which I literally have been."

"Well, there you go," Vincent said. "Problem solved. Now, we've lined up a Zoom session as a book launch which we really should have done for the last two books. But this will be a special session for those readers that have read all three books and want to ask questions about them. It will happen the week after *Mine* is released."

"My last week in therapy, yay. I don't know…guys please don't set that up. I really can't say if I'd even be available for it at this stage. With everything going on in my family."

"Ah, I hadn't thought of that," Vincent said and looked at Roger.

"We could do a pre-recorded interview of you talking about the books for people to watch instead. Maybe get fans to send in questions and film them at your home, when the other interviews are happening, and you're in your Bryan disguise."

Sean considered it. "Could we do it next week? Get in early? Because the week after could be hectic."

"We could," Vincent agreed, and the deal was done.

*****

"Did you speak to Kelly about getting Connor's stuff

back and having something of Ethan's?" Alec asked his father at Sunday lunch.

"I did. I spoke to her on Wednesday, and she was almost as hostile as she had been at the funeral before she walked out," Cormac replied. "Can't blame her. What Ethan did was a disgrace and we've scored the blame."

"Because it's not like she wasn't a bad parent," Sean muttered. "She apparently did nothing wrong raising him."

"Considering how his father went down, she *can* blame us," Cormac said. "But I told her if she didn't want us to help clean up, and didn't want any of Ethan's stuff, or what he took of his dad's, then we would like it back as it belonged to Connor. I suggested an independent cleaner, so important papers could be put aside, and everything could be laid out in piles for us to decide on. She refused on all levels."

"Oh, that's not right," Emerson said. "She's hurting, but it doesn't mean she needs to deny her son's paternal side."

"She did," Cormac replied. "I asked politely, and she refused. I suggested it's best we work this out with mediation, and she told me to go to hell. I said I'll be bringing in the lawyers, and she went quiet. I told her having the court decide was the last resort, but we'd like Connor's items back if she was just going to throw them out."

"What happened?" Sean asked before putting a forkful of chicken into his mouth.

"She told me she'd see me in court." Cormac sighed and went back to eating.

"As far as I know, Ethan's house will be a crime scene for a while. I can file the papers," Alec said. "All we're asking for is Connor's belongings back. You didn't ask for the house, did you?"

"Of course not. I just offered to clean it up for her, so she didn't have to worry about the horror in the basement."

"How could she refuse that?" Kieran asked. "We'd take on the work and she'd reap the rewards of the sale."

"I have no idea, but she stormed out of the office, so…" Cormac shrugged and kept on eating.

"Any idea when his house will be released?" Sean asked.

"Probably not for another two weeks at least, but it could be sooner if the CSIs have combed their way through and released it," Cormac said.

"Couldn't we go in without anyone knowing?" Sean asked.

Alec looked at him. "And you call yourself a lawyer."

Sean shrugged. "I call myself a writer. I know the law and it doesn't say anything about not sneaking into a house that's a crime scene. Grandpa's the PC, and we're lawyers, so surely we'd be allowed as family?"

"Nice try, kid," Alec scoffed. "But you came top of your class, so you know we can't."

"*I* know, but what *they* don't know…" Sean cheekily suggested.

"No," Cormac said firmly. "We're not doing that. We'll apply for it the proper way."

"I'll file the papers first thing," Alec said. "I know a judge who could push it through. He'll see we're reasonable in what we're after. Our family's belongings back."

"I don't like it, but I guess it will have to be that way." Cormac rested his elbows on the table and clasped his hands in front of his face. "I just want my son's belongings back."

Chapter 21

"We're up to you coming out as Bryan Jamison."

Sean chuckled. "Cute, doc, cute. But there's a lot to talk about today, as we only have two more visits to go."

"We do," Levinworth said. "Let's see how much we can talk about today."

"Okay, two years ago, Jesus, can you believe it's two years ago already, I released *Illicit Things*. I didn't show my face, and I didn't do interviews—nothing. I created a sensation and sold two million books. While I was being talked about, Sydney released *Her Last Words*, the book she wrote about Nora. While she was doing her interviews, some of them brought up my name and my books. She didn't like that one bit. The things she said about me, hoo boy. I mean, I get it. I was her competition. I had a smash hit novel, I was new on the scene, everyone who interviewed her was comparing us, and I could tell she was pissed." He chuckled again. "But then, so was I."

"Why?"

"Because she was saying shitty stuff about me, and it hurt. And yeah." He waved a dismissive hand. "I get it, she didn't know it was me, thought I was some upstart, and I wasn't the first author she'd ripped into. But because it was me, it hurt. She mentioned me and I love her, so the words cut deep. I had listened to every radio interview she'd done since meeting her, and even rang into one as Bryan before even thinking of becoming Bryan, and watched every TV show interview, and even though most of that interview was taken up with talk of Nora, still, words cut deep."

"They certainly do. Did you see her at all?"

"As Bryan or myself?"

"You'd still be yourself at that stage as you were still in Harvard and not in disguise."

"Look at you, keeping up," Sean congratulated him. "And you're right. I was myself, and it was at a book launch."

He entered the rooftop restaurant and quickly looked around for Sydney, seeing her on the other side talking to someone. He walked over to his left, away from the crowd, until he was opposite her. She was facing his direction with a woman who looked to be Emerson between them along with a dozen other people. He watched her—watched how the sun dazzled off her sequinned clothing, highlighting the gold in her brunette hair. He watched her pay attention to what Emerson was saying. A soft smile lifted his lips, and she looked his way and did a double take. She stared, but people moved between them, and he moved with them so she couldn't see him.

He stood in the shadows for the next few hours until he saw her heading his way and stepped in front of her.

He saw her face freeze in shock. "Sydney, congratulations on the new book. It's amazing like all of your others."

Sydney stared into his sapphire blue eyes. "Sean… what…"

"I needed to see you. I wanted to see you."

"I can't…wait…" She frowned and her face dropped. "Are you…Bryan Jamison?"

Sean leaned in close. "You've read my writing, Sydney, you know how I write."

A realisation hit her, and she ran.

"So, she knew?"

Sean shrugged. "I have no idea. I didn't admit it, but I think her brain was connecting dots, or maybe numbers, and coming up with the wrong answer. But she looked amazing and so was her book."

"Is that the only time you went out of your way to see her?"

"Out of my way? Yes. See her? No. I knew where she lived, remember. It also wasn't the first time I'd seen her. I'd managed to win a ticket to the launch of *The Shape of You* and went in a disguise. But it was the first time in public as myself."

"And she ran away from you?"

"She left," Sean corrected. "I seriously don't think she was running away. The look on her face was unreadable."

"That was two years ago. A year on you released *Creeper.* What happened then?"

"Nothing, I wasn't sure whether to be surprised or not, that a year from the release of *Illicit Things* and *Her Last Words,* we were in battle again. We released the book early to get to number one before her and I finally showed my face." He chuckled. "Or should I say, Bryan's face, on TV. My debut was on Rhett Rockefeller with *Creeper.* I was number one for three weeks."

"How did it feel? Finally being free from Harvard, finally being able to get out there, albeit in disguise, and finally get to number one before Sydney."

Sean's brows rose and he shook his head in amazement. "Absolutely fucking amazing on all counts. But a little weird, putting on a disguise. Long hair, a beard, contacts, *and* my glasses. I wasn't being me. I was being someone else. It was freeing, but also annoying at what I had to go through to put it on. Everything. And then…" His excitement fell away.

"And then?"

A slow, sly grin slid across Sean's lips. "And then she released *Madam X.*"

"Ah." Levinworth nodded. "She did."

"Oh, *she did*, and blasted me and everyone else out of the water. That book was freaking amazing." He shook his head and walked around the office. "Have you read it yet? You said you'd only read the bio."

"I have and I agree. It's an incredible novel."

"And she got the idea from me at that very first family lunch."

"I'd say her buying the property because of its history had something to do with it."

"Yeah." Sean waved him off. "That too. But so much happened that I've skipped over. You know, after she released *Her Last Words*, and I released *Illicit Things*, Lennie Cuzco was murdered and Dad, Connor, and Ethan turned up at Sydney's to tell her. Well," he huffed.

"How the hell were we to know it was Ethan who'd done it? And if *his* last words were anything to go by, he did it all for Sydney because he loved her. He did it on the first anniversary of Nora's death, almost like some weird love kill." He shuddered. "I know people say *I'd kill for you*, but he *literally* did. He *killed* for Sydney, and you say I'm obsessed. I haven't killed people yet."

"That I know of."

"Oh, funny, Walter," Sean said. "I haven't. That's not to say I wouldn't for Sydney. Because I probably would depending on the circumstances. I haven't, though. But I know someone who has died, and he died in October last year when Sydney was promoting *Madam X*. She'd given personal copies…" He looked up at the ceiling and realised where the list had come from. "Ohhh, that's just…or was it when she came over." Distracted, Sean turned away. "Oh, it had to be one of those times."

"Care to fill me in?"

Sean came back from his thoughts. "In October last year, a month after Sydney released *Madam X*, and she'd sent personal copies to Grandpa and Pop. Pop was sick after a long bout with pneumonia and he was…" Sean took a breath and slowly let it out, unable to say the word dying. "He was *leaving* us, and he wanted to see Sydney. She was rushed over. Ethan answered the door, she saw me and tripped over herself, and saw everyone else, and then Emerson came and got her. She spent about fifteen minutes with Pop, but she didn't tell us what he wanted to see her for. Alec attacked her over it, Connor and Dad defended her, as did Grandpa who came out to announce Pop's passing."

He breathed out and closed his eyes against the prickling tears. "After she came out, Grandpa went back in, and Ethan and I were standing in the living room staring down the hallway at her. Ethan was all lovey dovey mopey, and I just took in her beauty. She'd come from a photo shoot and looked amazing, but she looked amazing regardless. Emerson waved us away, and after she gave her condolences, she left." He stopped talking and stared out the window.

"Did Cormac say why Douglas had wanted to see her?"

"No. But considering what I found in Pop's bible, I think I know and it just occurred to me."

"When you started talking to yourself?" Levinworth chuckled.

"Wouldn't be the first time, doc. But yeah, you know about Madam X's client list. Sydney said there was one thousand names on it and three quarters were dead."

Levinworth nodded. "I remember those interviews. It's also in the biography, but she doesn't name them."

"No, for legal reasons, obviously." Sean walked over to the other wall. "Grandpa raided Madam X's, and Connor, Declan, and Alec were involved."

"I remember you mentioned that, but I'm not connecting the dots here."

"Sydney must've been giving him redemption for something, because he'd read the two books and then died after she walked out. But, just a few months ago, I got nosy and searched Pop's room. It wasn't until I found his bible, which was usually on his bedside table, down between the bed leg and the wall, and put it back on the bedside table, that I hit the jackpot. The covers didn't sit flush against the book and when I looked at the inside covers, I found there was something that had been stuck under the endpaper of the back cover."

Excitement bubbled up in Levinworth's chest. "What? What was it?"

Sean's grin was ear to ear. "It was a list of one thousand names of *very* rich and *very* powerful people and seven hundred and fifty-one names were crossed off in red."

Levinworth's jaw slowly dropped. "No…it couldn't…"

"Oh, yeah." Sean nodded excitedly. "That's what I believe it is, and now, after talking about Madam X and the list, I connected the dots. Either Sydney put it in his copy of his book, or she gave it to him when she turned up."

Levinworth's brows furrowed. "But how or why would she have it on her? She wouldn't know he was about to die, or that she'd be called to see him."

Sean put his hands up. "As I said, doc, it had to be one of those times. How else would he know…" He cut himself off. "Oh, hang on…damn! It was in his own handwriting. Maybe she didn't give it to him after all. Damn."

"Hang on. It's in his own handwriting?"

"Yes."

"That would suggest he knew exactly who was on that list. How old was the paper?"

"Ah…" Sean thought about the list. "I don't think it was new, but I don't think it was that old, either."

"So, he's seen the list and copied it, or he somehow

knew exactly who was on it and had been to Madam X. Do *you* know if it's the actual list?"

"No." Sean sat on the couch and faced his therapist. "Sydney mentioned nothing specific and neither did her books. I doubt there's a record of the list anywhere other than in the book."

"And it's in your great-grandfather's handwriting? He saw it, or he knew exactly who was on it."

"Damn!" Sean slapped his knee. "Pop, you old dog. But I'm not surprised since his name was on the list and it was crossed off."

"What?" Levinworth's eyes widened. "Douglas's name is on that list?"

"Oh yeah." Sean chuckled and his lips turned up into a wide grin. "And he's not the only Ryan on that list."

"Oh, no."

"Oh, yeah."

"Oh, damn!"

"Got that right."

"Jesus, Sean, your family."

"Yep, Walter. What do you think I keep telling you?"

"The two that are gone?"

"Yep, those two along with Pop, but there's two more."

Levinworth's left brow rose. "Cormac and Alec?"

Sean's smile grew grim. "I've crossed off the next two Ryans, and there are two more to go. Plus, a whole lot of other *very* rich and *very* powerful men still around. Some are still in their jobs, and some not. But they're all still in the state of New York."

"Jesus."

"Yep."

"So, Douglas might have wanted to know from Sydney if she knew the names on it."

"He full well might have, but I don't know much about it. Just what's in the book."

"I've read a few other bios on Madam X, and while well researched, Sydney's is the only one with photos of the black book and legers. That suggests to me she know who owns them."

A light bulb went off above Sean's head and his eyes widened. "Oh…or *she owns them.*"

Levinworth paused a moment before saying, "Yeah, you could be right."

"Holy cow, Sydney," Sean crowed. "You have Madam X's books. That thought never occurred to me."

"She has the brownstone. Why couldn't she have the books?"

"Because Grandpa raided the place years ago. The cops ripped the place apart looking for those books. They took all of the sex room contraptions, confiscated them, and took photos with it. Grandpa was pissed at his officers for doing that, but not one of them found the books. And I vaguely remember Sydney saying the owners had found nothing when they gutted the place and rebuilt it, because the cops had destroyed walls, floors, ceilings, everything. They got it bargain basement price."

"Interesting. So, we think Sydney has the books, and Douglas had a list in his own handwriting with five Ryans on it as they were clients of Madam X. I remember you mentioning your ex-aunt had decorated the building, and was possibly associated with it on a professional basis. There are *six* Ryans associated with Madam X."

"Yeah, we are a puzzle in an enigma," Sean said. "But alas, our time is up, and I have no way of knowing how or why Pop wrote up a list of the names."

"It would be interesting to know," Levinworth replied. "Because I'm really damn curious about your family history now."

Sean laughed. "Oh, doc, you ain't seen nothing yet. Wait until next week."

*****

"Bryan Jamison, welcome back to *Biblio File*. We have you here once again to talk about the third and final book in your trilogy, *Mine*."

"Thank you for having me, Marcia."

"Okay, let's get straight into it. I read this book and was surprised by the ending which resonates with the title. That was a twist I did not see coming."

"I doubt most people did," Bryan said. "As I said two months ago when *Is* came out and I was on a certain TV show, the placement of the title is connected to the storyline. While it may seem strange, the titles worked out well. And the ending was a twist even I didn't see coming."

"Oh, so you don't always know the end of your books?"

"Not always. Sometimes. I usually have an outline. I know where I'm starting, and I know where I'm going, but every now and then I'll have my muse give me a little twist which works out so much better."

"And was this a muse twist?"

"It was, and it worked out so much better than the thought I'd had for it."

"Interesting," Marcia said. "And I fully understand the placement of the titles now. I fully understand everything about these books, because even though each book is its own reveal, it really does help to read all three books back-to-back so you can absorb the full picture."

"That's because I wrote it as a full novel and it ended up too large to publish, so we cut it down to three novels and they work really well."

"All three books are out now, and your fans have a variety of formats to buy. Are you glad all three are out now?"

"Absolutely. The fans and readers can read the story in its entirety, see the whole picture of the story, and know what I meant with it."

"It also means your fans are free for the next novel coming out in September. Do we have a name for that yet?"

"We do and we're keeping it close to the chest because we're concentrating on this book and the trilogy right now."

"And are you still at home, not out from under house arrest?"

"Unfortunately, no. One of my therapists brought the flu in with her and now I have a sore throat, and don't feel well enough to be out and about. I figured I'd stay home and not pass the germs along."

"What do you think your fans will think of this book?"

"I think, like you, they'll understand the concept behind all three books, see the whole picture, and love them as much as I do. There will always be fans who like one book, but not the next, and that's okay. I'm the same with most authors I read, or most singers I listen to. I won't always love each album."

"Very true, it is a lot like that. But as all of your others, it's been a massive success and may you continue to have many more."

"Thank you very much, Marcia." He clicked off from Zoom, took a breath, and clicked onto another interview.

Three hours later, Sean was done for the day. "Don't tell me I have to do this again tomorrow," he groaned. "I'm actually really sick and tired of this now."

Dexter looked up from his phone. "You do, but then you know that."

"Yeah, I know. I really don't know his much longer I can take it. I don't even know if I'll do publicity for *Her* when it comes out."

"Why? It's two months away. Where will you be in September?"

"I don't know, but what if I'm incommunicado and can't get on Zoom?"

"Then you'll have to fly back and do your interviews."

"Blech!" Sean mumbled and pulled off his beard and wig. "Back to the grindstone tomorrow."

*****

"What's happening with Connor's stuff? Did the judge go for it?" Sean asked the family at Sunday lunch.

"He did and has allowed the hiring of an independent contractor to come in and organise paperwork and belongings to which we, and Ethan's mother, will go in and take what we want. We are allowed all of Connor's possession, plus something of Ethan's each," Alec told them. "The paperwork has been sent to Kelly."

"Bet she didn't like that," Sean said before putting a slice of roast beef into his mouth and melting at the succulence of it.

"Her lawyer contacted me and no they did not. I told them that my father had asked politely if we could have Connor's items back and she'd rudely refused, so it left us with no choice but to file an injunction. She denied us, so we made it legal."

"Did her lawyer say anything else?" Kieran asked, spooning more vegetables onto his plate.

"That *we* were being unreasonable even though we don't want the house but offered to clean it up for her. We didn't want Ethan's belongings except one token apiece. I called their bluff when I said the judge had found *her* to be unreasonable when all we were doing was trying to take the burden off her and help her out."

"Lawyer sounds as nasty as her," Sean said. "I never took her for the nasty type."

"No, neither did I," Cormac said. "But grief can do things to people."

Sean studied his grandfather. "Like age them."

"Oh, yeah." Cormac nodded in agreement. "Oh, yeah."

Sean exchanged a quick glance with Emerson. It had aged her too.

"But why does grief have to make you unreasonable to help?" Sandy asked. "All you want to do is help her deal with everything Ethan left behind."

"Probably because Ethan left a hell of a mess behind and got himself shot because of it," Alec replied. "The kid created his own mess, and he died because of it."

The mood shifted and they went back to eating for a few minutes before Sean broke the silence. "I've been wondering something, and it may bring the mood down even more, which I don't mean to do, but I need to talk about it."

"About?" Cormac sliced through his potato and wrapped a slice of beef around it.

"Ethan."

"We were talking about him," Cormac said, before putting his food in his mouth.

"Yeah, I know, but…" Sean played with his vegetables. "It's just…after Connor's funeral he tried to end it all by throwing himself in the river, and then when the cops find him he does the stupid thing of running away. I was wondering if he was still trying to kill himself. Death by cop. I mean, what was that point of me saving him if he just wanted to die anyway? I don't get it."

Silence fell over the table and awkward glances were exchanged.

"I don't get it either," Cormac finally said. "I don't get why he'd try and kill himself and why he'd run from the cops. I just…" He laid his cutlery down, rested his elbows on the table, and clasped his hands in front of his face. "I don't get it."

"Ethan was clearly sick with grief," Alec offered. "We don't know what was going through his mind after Connor died. He seemed to rally there for a few days, but then it all went to shit."

"Maybe he couldn't stand being without Connor," Kieran suggested. "We've lost a lot of family in the last year. We've all reacted differently." He glanced between Alec and Sean.

"We have," Alec agreed. "We've lost brothers, fathers, a nephew, cousins."

"A son and daughter." Kieran stared at his brother. "We've all coped differently."

"We have." Alec went back to his food, unfazed by Kieran's stare.

"So…does that mean Ethan would've tried to kill himself again?" Sean asked. "Was me saving him worth it considering what he had in the basement? Maybe we could have saved her sooner."

"But she also took her own life," Cormac said quietly. "And I don't blame her. I clearly did not know my grandson the way I thought I did. *Or* my sons."

"I'm going to bring us down even further," Kieran said. "Sean, do you know why Ethan had images of Sydney all over his walls? Emerson, do you?"

Startled, Emerson looked up from her plate. "What? Me? Why would I know? I've never been to Ethan's house. Have you?"

"No," Kieran conceded. "Alec?"

"Not me. Dad?"

"Not I," Cormac replied. "Seems like none of us knew."

"But why Sydney?" Kieran pushed, looking between Sean and Emerson. "From the looks on your faces, you two know something."

Sean looked at Kieran then back at Emerson. "Should I tell them?"

She relented. "May as well."

"Tell us what?" Cormac asked. "What do you two know that we don't?"

Sean sighed and rubbed his lips together. "The year after Connor and I did…our…" He glanced at the ceiling, looking for the right word. "*Damage* and you banned us, she released *Twisted Affair* and had that break-in. Ethan attended it. Jump forward to February when he was all depressed at the table about how a woman he'd been seeing had dumped him after seeing my mom's funeral on TV and socials and…" He glanced at Emerson who nodded. "He was talking about Sydney. It was her he'd been seeing off and on since the end of September. They reconnected with the break-in."

The three remaining Ryans stared at him, jaws hanging.

"Yeah." Sean motioned at their stunned expressions. "And Connor wanted to go around and have a chat with her which is why I laughed."

"How did you find out?" Alec asked. "Did Connor know?"

"He found out, but neither Ethan nor I knew how, until I called him, and he admitted it."

"How did you find out Connor knew?" Cormac asked.

"When I invited them over a couple of months ago to ask Connor about how Dad ended up on Sydney's doorstep." He glanced at Alec. "He let us both know he knew about Ethan sleeping with Sydney. And that was also when Ethan went off at him for slapping her the year before at her house. I called him not long before he died and asked him how he knew."

"He certainly didn't tell me that." Alec leaned back in

his seat and sighed. "All the lies."

"That you three Ryan boys kept and told," Sean snarked. "Don't play so innocent, Alec."

Alec blanched. "Yeah, I know."

"Wait." Kieran shook his head. "I'm confused. Was this back when she cancelled your mentorship, Sean?"

"Yeah. But so much more happened," he said.

"Then it's time you told us." Cormac sighed. "Clearly I covered up way too much."

"It wasn't you, Grandpa, it was us," Sean said, and told them the story he'd wanted them to know from the beginning. "From what I can piece together, Ethan fell head over heels in love with Sydney, unlike Connor and my dad, who just used her. He got angry at my dad, decided to kill Lennie in Sydney's name, and his obsessions with her grew."

"Until he kidnapped a woman that looked just like her," Alec said. "Jesus…Ethan."

Kieran shook his head. "What the hell is wrong with this family?"

"And that's not even everything," Sean said. "But some of that's for another day." He scraped up the rest of his food and felt the burning hole in the side of his head from Alec's steely gaze.

Sandy, who'd been relatively quiet, spoke up. "What are we meant to do as parents?"

"How do you mean?" Kieran slid his arm around her shoulders.

She motioned to everyone left. "Ryans are dropping like flies, and I'm seven months pregnant. I have crooked cops for brothers-in-law, and one for a nephew-in-law.

There are only six of us left until this baby comes and quite frankly, I don't know if I'll cope. I don't know if I can cope with the rest of the pregnancy, and the rest of the year. I just…" She pushed back from the table and rushed out of the room.

"She's not wrong," Sean said and watched Kieran follow.

"No, she's not," Cormac agreed.

Chapter 22

"Bryan Jamison, welcome back to Rockefeller and you've done it again for the sixth consecutive time. *Mine*, another number one bestseller."

"Thank you for having me back, Rhett. Sorry I can't be there this time, either. I've come down with a bug and don't want to make anyone sick by passing it on."

"Oh, that's unfortunate," Rhett said, leaning back in his seat. "We were hoping to get you into the studio this time."

"And I was hoping to be there, but after being under house arrest for so long, I ended up sick from a bug one of my therapists brought in."

"That's too bad, but here we are and still talking about it. *Mine* is out today, a certified number one and boy, oh boy, you weren't wrong two months ago when you said the title would make sense because it tied into the story. I completely get it now. I reread the first two before this one, and you really do have to read all three together, folks. It's so much easier to understand that way. Not that I'm saying they aren't easy to understand on their own, but it helps. Now, Bryan, tell us again about all three."

"It's about a man who wants a woman, as most of my books are, and he'll go out of his way to get her and make her his. But the twist at the end doesn't make it all that clear what he gets."

"And what I love about your books, and Sydney Kingston's, is that there's always a twist ending, and the *placement* of the title on the books leans into the story as you stated. Where the titles are positioned is beautifully done, Bryan. Was it your idea?" He held up all three books for the camera, but the director popped images of all three covers side by side onto the screen for viewers at home.

"It was." Bryan nodded. "It's a marketing ploy, it's a plot ploy, it's a story ploy. And it all works beautifully. There have been criticisms online about the covers, but I hope with this one they all make sense, especially when you read them."

"Fascinating idea, Bryan. You've obviously scored the number one slot with all three books, but then you haven't had Sydney to compete with. It must be nice knowing the reigning queen's thrillers are out of the running this year."

Bryan nudged his glasses up his nose and pondered the question. "It's nice to have number ones, it's nice knowing I didn't have to compete with my main competition, but Sydney hasn't published since last year. She's been silent on social for a while. I hope she's all right. She normally publishes something for her fans in between novels, but there's been radio silence."

"I hope she's okay, too," Rhett said. "She gave me the

idea for my investigation program that I still do once a month. It's incredibly successful and has been very rewarding, so I hope she's doing okay. I might have to do an episode on Sydney, the missing author." Chuckles came from the audience. "Won't you also be publishing another novel in two months on *her* publishing date? Are you hopeful she won't publish?"

Bryan's left brow had risen at the word *her.* "I am. As much as I love Sydney's books, I'd like to keep my run of consecutive number ones. I don't know what I'll do if I have to compete with her."

"Have you heard whether she's publishing or not?"

"No, I haven't, not for certain. Just that she's taking life easy back in Australia."

"Yes, and she should after what happened to her." Rhett looked at the books on his lap. "Okay, so *She Is Mine* are all out now, folks. The covers all make sense once you see them and read all three books. It's a compelling story, and once again, an absolute must read if you are a Bryan Jamison lover. And Bryan, if you don't mind, can you take some questions from the audience?"

"Sure, Rhett, let's do this." Bryan leaned closer to the camera.

Rhett ran into the audience and held the microphone up to a young lady. "What's your name and what's your question?"

The young woman tossed back her hair and said, "My name's Melody, and my question is, is Bryan still single. He said last year he was, and I'm hoping he still is because I want to date him." She shimmied in her skin-tight red bandeau dress.

Rhett looked her up and down and whistled. "How can any sane man say no to that."

"Don't be sexist, Rhett," Bryan said. "I am single, technically, but there is someone."

Disappointed mumbles went around the audience.

"Okay, moving on." Rhett ran to another aisle. "Yes, sir, your name and question."

"Ah yeah, hi, my name's George and my question is, is Sydney Kingston the author in *Creeper?*"

"Ah, good question and I think I asked that when the book came out," Rhett said. "Bryan?"

"She helped inspire it. I changed out thriller writer for romance writer and my character is feisty, just like Sydney."

"Thank you, George, and we have time for one more." Rhett dashed across the audience and came to another man. "Your name and question, sir."

"My name's Michael and my question to Bryan is, what happened to all of those stories I read when I mentored you? You haven't published them yet."

Bryan flew back in shock, having recognised his adult fiction editor from the Pulsate mentorship program.

"Wait, what?" Rhett looked from Michael to Bryan, and back to Michael. "Wait, wait, wait. What is going on?"

Michael calmly stared down the barrel of the camera. "I mentored Bryan early in his career and had read some interesting stories that haven't seen the light of day. I just wondered if they ever would?"

"What!" Rhett flapped a hand in excitement. "Was he any good? And you mean there are more stories out there from his early days? Oh, my God. Bryan."

"Ah, Rhett." Bryan composed himself and took a breath. "Hello, Michael, good to see you again. Ah, no, those stories will probably not see the light of day as they were a way of getting practice, of learning the craft, plotting, outline, characters, and so on."

"Tell us about Bryan in his early days." Rhett shoved the microphone in front of Michael.

"He was dedicated to learning, studious, a quick learner, and already wrote incredibly well when I came across him. He wanted to learn everything else there was to know about writing."

Bryan breathed slowly to calm his racing heart and hoped Michael didn't give it away.

"So, you won't be publishing those stories, Bryan?" Rhett asked.

"Ah, no." He shook his head a couple of times. "They were just practice to learn the craft."

"That's a pity," Rhett said and walked down the stairs as he talked to the camera. "Thanks for coming on today, Bryan. *She Is Mine*, the trilogy by Bryan Jamison is all out now, so go and read the books back-to-back to get the complete story. Will we be seeing you in studio in two months with the new novel?"

"I don't know, Rhett. I could be off seeing the world when it comes out. My house arrest will be over."

"We hope to see you next time. Bryan Jamison, folks. Roll to break." He made two circles with his arm and then pointed at the camera.

A producer popped onto the screen and thanked Bryan for his time before ending the Zoom.

Sean slammed his laptop lid down and blew out air. "Oh, my God. How the hell did he get to ask a question?"

"Problem?" Dexter asked. "Was this guy your mentor?"

"He was, at Pulsate. He was the adult fiction editor. Sydney first introduced me to him to read a piece I'd written. He and Victor continued the mentorship after Sydney stopped. Jesus Christ." He got up and paced around the condo. "He must've finally recognised my writing style, but why after all these years? And has he said anything to anyone." Biting his thumbnail, he walked back and forth in front of the wall of Sydney trying to figure it out, but couldn't.

"There's not much point worrying now. You have Preston Grant's show to do."

"Ah, yeah, yeah." Sean shook it off and took a bathroom break, made himself coffee, and grabbed two mini apple pies from the fridge. Emerson was still feeding him desserts. "Okay, I'm ready." He sat back down at his desk, checked himself in the small mirror next to him, and opened his laptop. Five minutes later he was zooming into Preston Grant's radio show.

"Welcome back, Bryan Jamison." The crowd in the studio cheered and whistled.

"Thank you, thank you." Bryan blushed and reset his glasses. "Thank you for having me back again."

"Having you back? I feel like you live here," Preston joked. "It's the third interview in four months. We're here for the final instalment of your trilogy. *Mine.* The follow up to *She* and *Is.* The whole title is a great title, and I've heard you say it was the title you had for the novel but decided to cut up the story into three so they got a word each. Great publicity, but is all of this overkill?"

"Probably," Bryan replied. "I've said with many interviews in the last four months, I fully understand that three novels in four months is a lot. But I also know there are some fans out there who will read the new release and then demand more. Readers are voracious, and they don't just want one book every year, or every two years, anymore. They want a constant stream of them, so this time, they've got it."

"But you also wanted those books out of the way and published in order to get the next book out in September. Would the books have had a normal publishing schedule otherwise?"

"It was going to be a year, originally, but I fought that and said let's keep it to every six months since you have a lot of my books. And they agreed so the public didn't forget about me. Then I wrote this other book early in the year and just knew it had to get out as soon as possible. But my publishing schedule had those three other books, so I went back to my publisher and asked for everything to be changed and again, they agreed. All three books of *She Is Mine* are out now. My readers can read them back to back and get the whole picture."

"And the book coming next?"

"Nothing to do with any of the books. It's a standalone, aside from the other two I wrote, but they may be pushed to the back of the line as there are more waiting in the wings."

"That's right." Preston slapped his forehead. "I forgot you had twelve books. Can you tell us about any of them? We now have your first six. What about the next six?"

"They're all standalone, but of the same theme. It seems to be my thing that I write best."

"A man wanting a woman," Hank said.

"Exactly. Whether it's from the viewpoint *of* the man, the woman, or a voyeur."

"A voyeur," Preston repeated. "Is that out, or is that coming?"

"Oh, that one's coming. It was intriguing for me to write as the person on the outside looking in. The voyeur is always outside looking in. My editor had to help me get that in proper publishing order."

"But you're this writing genius, so why did you need help?"

"Because it was from a third person point of view, someone's watching them, narrating the story, and my POV got a little confused. I needed clarification on *how* to write it from that view, and it takes a bit to get it right."

"Okay, so it's good to know even someone as prolific as Bryan Jamison, who writes incredible novels, needs help from his editor."

Bryan laughed. "I certainly do."

"And once again, sales have blasted through the roof," Preston said. "Early stats say it's reached one million already."

"So I've been told, which is great because it says to me that the readers and fans who bought the last two, which also sold a million apiece in the first week, are buying this one to find out what happens."

"Have many of your books sold past the million mark?" Hank asked.

"They all have. The first three sold over two million apiece within a month, so I'm hoping these three head that way as well."

"And the next novel?"

"I'm hoping it blasts past Sydney Kingston's record for *Madam X*. Almost, if not more than, six million copies."

"Wait, what?" Preston held his hands out to quieten everyone. "You want to sell more than *Madam X* with your next book? What's it called?"

"I can't say yet, and yes I do, Preston."

"We'll have to get you into the studio for that one. I can't wait to hear all about it."

"I'll be doing a massive press push for it, but I won't be here. I'm off on holiday next month and don't know where I'll be."

"I'm extremely envious. Bryan Jamison, thanks again for your time. Again, the new book, *Mine*, is out now so you can read *She Is Mine* in order. Go and get it folks."

*****

"Oh, my God, Sean, did I see right on TV this morning? Your uncle's been arrested?"

"Yeah, Walter, I keep telling you. They keep dropping like flies."

"I'm so—"

"Don't say it. I can't hear it anymore." Sean slid his hands into his pockets. "Did you read *Mine* yet?"

Levinworth studied him a few moments. "Do you not want to talk about it?"

Sean shrugged an uncaring shoulder. "What's there to talk about? He's been arrested on a thousand and one charges from conspiracy, to felonies, to blackmail and fraud. He's the fucking District Attorney of New York City and he was dumb enough to think no one would find out."

"But they did."

"The case has been happening for some time all in secret. Several bureaus were in on it. They all wanted him for something."

Levinworth held his breath a moment before letting it out. "Jesus, Sean."

"Again, don't say it."

"Yeah, ah, how's your grandfather holding up?"

"Not well. But so far, this son is still alive. So, there's that."

"Is that a good thing?"

"I don't know. I have a feeling death is coming. Just like the car accident. He survived that; he won't survive this."

"I'll keep everything crossed that he will, for your grandfather's sake."

"Can we get to lighter stuff, please? The story wasn't finished yet and besides, Alec's in jail. They won't let him out on bail and are keeping him in isolation."

"For his safety?"

"Yeah, I guess."

"What do you want to talk about?"

"It's time to move onto the last encounter with Sydney. Last year."

"Okay. Let's go. She released *Madam X,* you released

Creeper, so what happened next?"

Sean laughed. "You're eager today, Walter. Okay, after I officially showed my face as Bryan Jamison, I was invited to multiple book launches for other Viceroy authors, and those from other houses. Sydney was also invited, and I finally got the chance to meet her, but she wasn't interested in meeting me. We would do the dance—you know the one. We'd make little comments to each other, snide remarks, compliments, well, I would. Her remarks were always insults, barbs, digs, but I enjoyed it and quite a few people told us there was a clear attraction. Obviously on my part there was. But she would get pissed, and the look in her eye. Whoo, she had hatred for Bryan, and I never knew why. She took a dig at my clothes, my hair, my age… I have no idea how or why everyone thought I was a forty-something college professor. Preston Grant told me it was because of the clothes. I said, but they're just clothes. Still, I have no idea where that rumour came from, but Sydney and I would get digs in about clothes, hair, books, everything. It was exciting."

"Why?"

"Because she had no idea who I was, but I knew who she was, and it was my little secret and made it all titillating."

"Were you aroused by it?"

"Walter!" Sean admonished and frowned at him.

"It's a valid question if it excited and titillated you."

Sean pondered the question. "And the answer to that would be, of course it did. Sydney saw me as a threat to her reign of queen of thrillers. She saw me as an imbecile, but I knew, and playing those games did arouse me."

"How many times did you come across each other?"

"Multiple book launches and Rhett Rockefeller's Christmas party and then his new year launch which was the last time in January."

"So, you and Sydney came across each other multiple times until the launch and that was when you slept together."

"It was."

"How did it happen?"

"Walter, did your parents not teach you about the birds and the bees?" Sean raised his brows in amusement and walked over to the wave painting.

"Hardy ha-ha." Levinworth chuckled. "How did you and Sydney happen?"

"Well, as we did, we had a spat. A to-and-fro of words and thoughts and she always called me Byron. Did it on purpose, she did, and when she opened the door she was wearing a silk robe. Just…ugh," he growled. "I got her so riled up by following her home, that she opened the door to argue more. I told her I wanted to fuck her. That I'd fallen in love with her, and she finally ran out of breath *and* insults. I repeated my words, and I told her I was attracted to her. You should have seen her face."

"I could if you showed me the footage. You know, cameras and all."

"Ouch! Walter." Sean turned around at the snark. "Doc's fighting back."

Levinworth grinned. "Keep going."

"I kept telling her I loved her, that I was attracted to her, just give me one night. I kept repeating myself over and over, edging her into the house from the vestibule until the inner door finally shut and we fucked against it."

"Just like Connor and Ethan."

Sean's eyes narrowed. "Don't ruin my moment, Walter. Anyway, after that I carried her upstairs and we made love all night."

"Come morning?"

"I wish."

"Ugh, Sean."

"I'm joking." Sean shrugged and walked around the room. "She kicked me out. Told me in no uncertain terms it was a one-night stand and wouldn't be happening again. I tried to convince her otherwise, but all to no avail."

"Did you see her again after that?"

"You know I didn't. She left the next day and didn't tell me."

"Why would she tell you?"

Sean leaned over Levinworth's shoulder. "Because I had the keys to her basement, remember. I had her permission to come and go. I *came* all the time." He moved over to the window. "But little did I know she was going to pull that stunt on me."

"And what stunt would that be?"

"That stunt with her lawyer walking into Grandpa's office and handing over illegally gained information."

"Which would be?"

"Photos of the inside of my condo, for a start. Copies of my company's paperwork; the fact I'm Bryan Jamison. Three files thick, but then you've seen them. Did you find anything interesting in them? Because so much was left out."

Levinworth perked up. "And what was left out?"

"Oh, so much." Sean tapped his fingers together in evil glee. "So many things, let me count them all. But all of that is for another time and speaking of, we only have one more visit left together, Walter. Will you miss me when this is all over?"

"Actually, I will," Levinworth said. "I've found our sessions to be fairly light hearted, interesting, humorous, intriguing, sometimes hard, and very revealing."

"Are, there's a good one, especially since I've been *revealing* little bits and pieces for the last five months and really, we only have my detention period left to talk about, but we'll save that for next week as it will bring us full circle. Now, what did you think of *Mine?*"

"Definitely wrapped up the story."

"It was supposed to."

"Also very revealing, as you pointed out. Loved the twist at the end, you spun the story on its head. And that's why you're in here on a Friday and not a Monday."

"I was busy all week," Sean said. "Rhett, Preston, and a dozen other shows. I'm exhausted."

"Will you be doing any more press?"

"A few things next week. Mainly magazines and more radio. Some website interviews for bloggers and ugh, influencers. God, I should cancel those.

"Why? It all helps, doesn't it?"

"I hate influencers because of the leeches called my cousins."

"Ah, milked you for all you were worth."

"And then some. So, you enjoyed all three?"

"I did. Not as much as your first three, *Illicit Things*

and *Creeper* especially, also very revealing."

"There's that word again," Sean said. "Maybe I should get it tattooed somewhere."

"Or use it for a book title."

Sean snapped his fingers. "Now you're getting it, Walter. Good idea. Either way, I need to go and see Grandpa. See what I can do about Alec."

"Are you practising law? I know you graduated but—"

"Yeah, I have practised it, by giving advice in jail and then dealing with my contracts per my company. So yeah, I can do things."

"Will you and Kieran work together?"

"Maybe. I don't know if Kieran will be allowed to, being his brother."

"Won't know till you find out." Levinworth closed Sean's file. "We'll wrap this up next week. When are you getting the monitor off?"

"With Alec in jail, who knows."

*****

Sean left Levinworth's office and took an Uber to 1PP. He was allowed in by his grandfather's assistant and saw Kieran, Sandy, and Emerson in the office, along with his grandfather's team.

"Well damn well do something," Cormac yelled into the phone before smashing it into its cradle. "Goddamn lawyers."

Sean and Kieran raised a brow at each other. "What's happening?" Sean asked.

"It's bad," Kieran replied. "Really bad."

"They have him in protective custody, but won't tell me, *his father*, where the hell he is." Cormac heaved to his feet and lumbered over to the window. "They won't let me see him to know he's all right. Won't let me talk to him. Won't tell me if he's seen a lawyer. Considering I've lost two sons and three grandchildren, I don't want to lose another one, but they have no sympathy and no compassion. His dealings were wrong and they're out to punish him for it."

"He should be released on bail, but they might see him as a flight risk," Kieran said. "His children are dead; no wife, a change of will—they might think he'll run even though he still has family here."

"I do not want to lose another son," Cormac roared. "Not another one."

"I've been told to stay out of it." Kieran reached over and grasped Sandy's hand. "Our boss at the law firm said unequivocally not to get involved."

"Or what?" Sean asked.

Kieran looked at him. "Or we'd be fired."

Stunned, Emerson said, "Both of you?" She got nods in return.

"They can't fire Sandy; she's pregnant, and they can't fire you for wanting to defend your brother. *They* know that's against the law," Sean argued. "Sue them."

"Nothing to sue over," Kieran said. "We still have our jobs."

"What in God's name is wrong with this family?" Cormac finally turned from the window, his hands clasped behind his back. "With the way we're going, we'll end up on Emerson's *Twisted Minds* TV show."

Startled, Emerson exchanged a guilty glance with Sean. "Ugh, why would you say that?" she asked nervously.

"I don't know." Cormac sighed and paced in front of the window. "Isn't there anything we can do?"

"Keep going through the official channels; keep hounding them," Kieran said.

"Hasn't got us anywhere so far," Cormac replied. "How much longer do we need to wait?"

Two hours of phone calls, lawyers, the FBI, CIA, ATF, DEA, ICE and all the other acronymous bureaus later, Cormac received a call.

"Yes?" His face froze and the blood drained from it.

"Oh, no," Sean said, watching his grandfather.

Cormac put the phone down. "We need to get to the hospital now."

Fifteen minutes later, they were escorted into the morgue to see the body of Alec Ryan on a slab.

"What happened to my son?" Cormac yelled to all attending. "You're FBI, CIA, ATF, and all the fucking rest, and the prison, and yet you allowed *my son* to be killed."

"We did what we could," the prison warden said. "We didn't even know it had happened. He was being moved from one room to another."

"All of you assholes arrested him and took him to that prison. You'll keep him in solitary, you said. He'll be fine, you said. My son died without his family, just like all my others." He finally cracked and grabbed the table. "My son is dead because of you bastards."

Kieran and Sean stood on either side of him and looked down at the body; white, already cold and drained of blood. His death had been registered at three oh two.

Chapter 23

Levinworth made notes in his file. It had been fifteen minutes since Sean had showed up and stood in front of the window, but he was yet to speak. "Sean?"

"Walter."

"How are you?"

"Devastated."

"Understandable. Your family?"

"What's left of it."

"How are they?" He heard a deep depressive sigh.

"How do you think, Walter?"

"Do you think your grandfather will survive this?"

"No."

"Do you want to talk about your detention? That's where we're up to in the story."

"Seems a bit pointless now."

"You won't get your final visit from Alec."

"Don't need it anyway. It was all fake as shit, like his life."

Levinworth cocked his head and honed in. "Fake as shit?"

"The monitor wasn't even a real one. I figured it out

when they put it on me. Alec made a big deal out of having some guy in a cop uniform put it on. Such a show. He didn't even know I knew how to tell a fake from a real one."

"And how do you?"

"There's a small hole, big enough for a pin to fit in on the top. Real ones have that hole on the side, but they all work the same way. He really thought he had me dead to rites with his phoney-ass contract and his monitor. What a joke. I knew full well what the contract said, and it was all bullshit. Just like my family."

Levinworth pursued that line of questioning. "Why do you say that?"

"Take a look around, Walter. My family are all dead." Sean flung his arms out wide and turned around. "There's three of us left and Grandpa won't make it past next week."

"You don't know that."

"He cracked in the morgue. For the first time he *actually* cracked. Kieran and I had to physically support him. He won't last long. Certainly not to his seventy-fifth and retirement. He and Emerson were meant to get married that day, but that won't be happening either."

"Don't count him out just yet. He's been strong so far. He might rally and make it."

"No." Sean shook his head. "The marriage held no excitement for either of them anymore. And with the family gone, there's only two of us to attend. It won't be joyous, and it won't happen."

"You seem sure that's a fact."

"If you saw my grandfather, you would be, too."

Levinworth gave a nod of his head. "I guess you're right."

"I don't want to be."

"Your detention."

"You were there. You came every day. You saw how I adapted quickly when they learned I was a lawyer. I taught them things; they taught me things."

"Such as?"

"They taught me how to get out of an ankle bracelet without setting it off. And then I wrote it into my novel in code and sent it in an email so they wouldn't know."

Levinworth looked at him. "The pinhole."

"Well done, Walter. How'd you know?"

"You're not the first I've seen with a monitor, so I'm not surprised. You're smart. Stick a pin in and it opens and stays green."

"It worked well, when I need it to be on most of the time. I took it off this morning because it's not like Alec was doing it. Or some phoney cop."

"Where have you been going without it?"

"Lots of places, but I cannot tell. Maybe I'll put it in a book."

"Do you know why you're here, Sean?"

"Yes, Walter. I do, but you don't, and neither did Alec or my grandfather."

Puzzled, Levinworth tried to figure out his words. "I know exactly why you're here."

"No, you don't, and only two people do and I'm one of them. Haven't you been listening to anything I've said? You record each session." Sean walked over to the wave painting. He didn't hear it as loudly as he had when he started. Now it was just a soft distant sound.

"I have been, and I've made extensive notes. You went into detention for stalking Sydney, and putting cameras in her house, amongst other things."

"*Not* breaking and entering," Sean said. "I wasn't the only one with cameras, you know."

"And what's that supposed to mean?"

"Figure it out, Walter. You have my voice recordings, so go back over them. Find the clues and *believe* them this time. It's all there, all the pieces are there just like a jigsaw."

"In an enigma?"

"You have no idea, Walter. I gave you the answers, I gave you everything, and now it's our last visit that didn't even need to happen. But it was all a game. The detention, the monitor, the five months of house arrest. Everything that's happened in the last six months, since January, since five years ago, all the way back to the beginning has been nothing but a game." He walked back to the window. "At least, on our part. What we found along the way only added to it. It added to the bomb we'll one day bring down that's been five years in the making, and those who made it are done with it. Isn't it ironic, don't you think?"

"Not really," Walter disagreed. "And that song wasn't ironic, either."

"Poor Alanis," Sean mocked. "But what's ironic is, that this will not be our last visit, Walter. My mandated time maybe up, but I'm taking you up on your offer of therapy. It's just a matter of where and when. I'm still your patient, and you cannot tell, by law. You have to keep that all to yourself."

"I do." Levinworth nodded. "I cannot reveal anything."

"Ah, there's that word again. But alas I must go. We'll talk again soon, Walter. My mandated therapy is now over, as is my family."

"You know, Sean, you're about to walk out that door for your last visit for God knows how long, and I still don't know what all of this was about. According to you."

Sean flung his messenger bag over his head and shoulder and sat on the sofa arm closest to his therapist. "Irony, Walter. Love, passion, desire. It was about best-selling novels. That's how it started when Sydney moved to New York. She wanted inspiration, and she found it. *In us.* The Ryans of the NYPD. The Ryan family. And she set it up. *We* set it up. It was all about best-selling novels. First her and then me. That's why I write about all of it. What my family did, what Sydney and I did, it's all in there, Walter. Read between the lines, as you started doing. It's all in there. The whole truth and nothing but, and thanks to my family being full of fuck ups, Sydney got a lot out of us and so did I. She wanted to know what it was like to fuck fathers and sons, and brothers and cousins, and I wanted to know what it was like to fuck the woman I loved. This was never an obsession, Walter. That was Ethan. This was about best-selling novels and making money and doing things out of our comfort zone. Sydney knew all about the cameras and photos because those cameras were hers that she had set up. I just adjusted them which is why you saw me on them. But she recorded it all. We would watch her fucking Connor and Dad and Ethan and then fuck. It was pure porn. Pure revenge. Pure hate. We got off on what we were doing, because it was out of our comfort zones and something different. How do you think I had keys to come and go as I pleased? Because we love each other, Walter. We were lovers from the night of my mother's funeral onwards. I'm the reason she dumped Ethan and then lied to him about it. It was never an obsession, it was all a game, and then she changed the rules and I've been here in detention for something we're both in on. Because it's all a game. But as I said, it's time to go, Walter. I have to bury another uncle and possibly a grandfather."

Fear fled through Levinworth. "How much of it was a game?"

Sean paused with his hand on the door. "Most of it."

"And your family?"

"You see now, Walter, that would be called revenge. And I might talk about that another time."

Levinworth heard the door shut and let out a guttural sigh. "Oh, Sean, what the hell have you done?"

*****

The funeral of District Attorney Alec Clayton Ryan was held on the Thursday after his death.

The family, those left, gathered round, along with close friends and co-workers who still believed in him.

Cormac and Sonja stood at the end of the grave watching the coffin be lowered into its final resting place beside his children.

Cormac had a pained look upon his grieving face.

Sonja had a deeply furrowed brow. She'd insisted on

being there, she was his ex-wife of more than twenty years, and mother of his two children. She stared down at the grave until Cormac threw a handful of dirt down on it. She did the same and walked over to her children's graves and stood watching, one hand resting lightly on her daughter's headstone.

Attendees slowly walked away and left, but Kieran stayed by Cormac's side.

So did Sean.

They watched Alec's grave being filled in. It took two hours, and the air grew chilled in early afternoon. But they stayed.

The gravediggers pushed down the last of the soil and flattened out the surface. One long rectangle of dirt was what currently remained of Alec Ryan.

There would be no wake at the Ryan house; just a sombre reminder of how corruption could destroy a family.

When Sean finally arrived home later that night, he sighed in relief. It was almost over. The heavy weight of multiple funerals had lifted, and he strode into his office and opened the wall of Sydney, crossing off Alec's picture on the A4 page of family images. Eight down, how many to go?

With luck, no more and he was done.

He strode over to the cupboard that held his Bryan Jamison disguise, and he reached for his wig and glasses before realising he didn't need them anymore. Nor did he need to use a burner phone to call a cab, or the frequency jammer to glitch the surveillance system of the building so he could leave without being seen, or a pin to keep his ankle monitor open. Smiling, he picked up the ankle monitor and dumped it in the bin. He wouldn't be needing that anymore, and nor would he need to wait for someone to come and take it off. It was fake. He had known it. Alec had known it. He quickly showered and changed, grabbed his bag, and left out the front door.

Twenty minutes later, he parked his car outside a brownstone in the Upper East Side. He stared up at it, remembering all the times he had been there before, and a smile curled his lips as he ascended the stairs.

After opening the vestibule and front doors, and locking them against the world, he dropped his bag by the door. The scent of hot roast chicken salad permeated the air, and his stomach growled as he walked into the living room and cooled himself under the air-conditioning vent.

He breathed a sigh of immense relief.

He was home, and this time he wasn't leaving.

*****

On Friday morning, Cormac got a call from Kelly's lawyer. Due to the current circumstances surrounding Alec, and Ethan's house being released to her, she would allow them into the house to clean up along with an independent auditor to catalogue everything left. Her only term was it be done on the weekend.

And so, on Saturday, the family stood on the sidewalk outside Ethan's house; a small, two-storey brick and wood home in Queens. They were waiting for the independent auditors and couldn't enter until they had arrived.

"I can't believe we're here," Sean said, turning around to look at the houses on the street. He did a full turn.

"This is weird."

"It is," Kieran agreed, his arm firmly around Sandy's waist. "What are we supposed to be doing?"

"Taking Connor's things back while helping the contractors sort out Ethan's belongings. We're not to touch anything else unless it's been photographed and catalogued," Cormac told them.

"That will take hours," Kieran complained.

"Is her lawyer coming?" Sean asked. "He probably wants to make sure we don't steal anything."

"He will be." Cormac sighed and leaned against the car and crossed his arms. "I don't know if I can do this."

Emerson leant against him and rubbed his back. "You don't have to. We'll do it. And there's a cleaning crew that's going to take the furniture and rubbish."

"You could stay in the car," Sean suggested, and stood against the car next to him. "View from afar, so you don't have to face it."

"The cleaning crew may not even let us help," Sandy said. "None of us might end up doing anything."

"That's okay, we'll find something," Emerson said. "Maybe cleaning out the fridge."

"Women's work." Sandy smirked.

A car and a van pulled up to the curb and a truck backed into the driveway.

"Mr Ryan, I'm William Cordon, the independent auditor." The man held his hand out and shook hands with all of them.

"My son Kieran and his wife Sandy, my grandson Sean, and my fiancée Emerson."

Cordon nodded at each one. "Hello. My job today is

to gather everything together, take photos, and have it packed up for both you and Ms O'Connell. Her lawyer has already stipulated they don't want any furniture, they just want his clothes and belongings that weren't his father's. Everything else is to go to the dump."

"Of course," Cormac said. "How long will that take?"

"Depending on how much stuff Mr Ryan had, we could just be a few hours."

"So where do we start and how can we help?" Cormac asked.

"My people and I will do a walkthrough to see what there is and film it for Ms O'Connell, and then we'll get started. The crew will remove the furniture, and we'll get into his belongings." He waved to the van and ten people piled out. "We'll get started and come and get you when we're done."

"Of course." Cormac felt Emerson's grip on his arm tighten and squeezed her hand in return.

Thirty minutes later, Cordon leaned out of the front door and waved them in. "Okay. It looks as if he didn't have a lot of furniture, only three pieces in the basement, five in his bedroom, and those in the living and dining rooms. If you want any of that, grab it as it goes out the door, because it's going to the dump." He stepped aside as the crew carried the bed from the basement past them.

"They didn't take it?" Sean watched them carry it out. "It's evidence."

"If the item's too big they don't take it," Cormac muttered. "The storage facility can't fit everything. Photos have to do."

"Okay. My people are packing the items from the

living room. Please point out anything that belonged to your son, and while the crew cleans out the kitchen, I'll head upstairs with helpers to start on his bedroom. We'll lay it out on the bed and the floor. When you're ready, come up." He went upstairs with two cleaners.

"That box of photos and books, and the records were Connor's. I packed them myself." Sean pointed to the two boxes and looked inside. "He didn't even unpack them."

"And that one over there." Cormac pointed. "I helped him pack that." He turned and looked at the bookshelf along the wall next to the door. "He put the photos up though. They were Connor's." He motioned to the three on a shelf and watched a staff member pack them with the boxes.

"Do we care about the knick-knacks?" Sean asked. "I didn't see any of these at Connor's."

"His TV and stereo." Emerson looked around. "The stereo's here, but not the TV."

"He's got more pictures here." Kieran stood at the matching bookcase on the other side of the door. "Pictures of him and his mom, with his family, with us, and his dad."

"We'll take the ones with us and his father. Kelly won't want them," Cormac told the crew. They stepped out of the way for the furniture to be carried out.

Not that he had much. A dining table and chairs in the dining room, a lounge suite in the living room, a few paintings and prints on the wall.

"Does anyone need any help?" Emerson asked. "I could help clean up the kitchen, or the laundry…" She got a no thank you in return. "I feel quite useless standing here. Are we able to look around?"

"Of course," one of the crew said.

She patted Cormac's arm and took Sandy's hand. "Let's have a look." She led her through the dining into the kitchen. "Nice for an old house. Do you need help?" she asked again. "I can hold the garbage bags, or maybe clean out the fridge." Getting a head shake, they walked over to the back sliding doors and looked into the garden. "Hasn't been touched in a while."

"I don't think Ethan cared about gardening," Sandy said.

Sean decided to have a look on his own and quietly slipped away to the basement. He wanted to see it in broad daylight, but all that greeted him when he got to the bottom of the stairs and turned around to the back of the room was the bare wood floors and walls. Everything was gone. The photos, the furniture, the woman. He slowly turned around in a full circle. There was no storage room, no laundry; just a bare room called a basement. With a quick look up the stairs, he hurried to the back of the room and started tapping walls and searching the cracks in the floor. If Ethan had left something behind, he wanted to find it, but sadly, there were no hidden recesses, and no clues to find. The room was completely empty.

"Not even a hidey-hole for all of those photos of Sydney," he mused. "What was it he actually cleaned up? Or did he clean up nothing?" As he walked up the stairs, he tapped on each floorboard, seeing if he could lift them. They stayed in place. There was nothing.

He quietly made his way back to the entrance and stood looking up the stairs.

Cordon came down. "Okay, we've laid out his clothes

on the bed. He had some of his father's things?"

"Five jackets, yes." Cormac walked over. "I know it may seem like a futile or frivolous thing, but we'd like Connor's belongings back."

"Of course. Have you set aside his items down here?"

"The five boxes just here." Cormac pointed them out. "We'd also like Ethan's other photos of him with our family and his father. I doubt his mother would want them."

"She did say anything to do with your family, you could have," Cordon said. "Now, about those jackets. Do you know which ones?"

"I do. I can pick them out. I helped him with Connor's belongings." Cormac trudged up the stairs behind Cordon as Emerson and Sandy came back into the living room.

"A bit of a minimalist, wasn't he," Emerson said, looking around at the almost empty room. "Didn't do anything with the yard."

"I guess his mom gets his car," Sean said. "There won't actually be much left."

"No, he doesn't seem to have much," Kieran said. "Unless it's all upstairs."

"The only rooms back here are the bathroom and laundry," Emerson said.

"And probably only two bedrooms upstairs," Sean added. "I'm going to have a look." He dashed upstairs before anyone could object and ducked into the empty bedroom, having a quick look before walking into Ethan's room. "Need help?"

"He took five of Connor's jackets." Cormac waved a hand at them. "He donated everything else. Can you take these downstairs?"

"Sure." Sean gazed over the clothing piles on the bed. "He had the basics. Wasn't a clothes horse, either. He didn't seem to have a lot of stuff."

"No, we noticed that," Cordon said. "It makes it easier for us. We'll bag up the rest and then remove the furniture."

"His toiletries?" Sean asked.

"We'll get those."

"No photos?" Sean glanced at the bedside table.

"Just two, one of each family." Cordon handed the Ryan family photo over. "You can have this one."

Sean placed it on the pile of jackets and carefully picked it up. "Grandpa."

"I'll be down in a moment," Cormac said gravely. "I just need a minute."

Sean nodded and made his way downstairs. "We're taking these as well." He handed Kieran the photo and set the jackets on top of one of the boxes. "Five boxes and five jackets. Are we taking the stereo?"

"We are, but I still don't know where the TV is. Was there one upstairs?" Emerson asked.

"I didn't see one." Sean dusted off his hands. "It may have been in the basement."

The four of them looked at each other. "They may have taken it."

"Or he may have gotten rid of it," Kieran suggested.

Sean frowned. "You don't just get rid of a TV. I'll go back up and check." He hurried back up. "Hey, is there a TV here? We can't find Connor's."

"The only one up here is over there." Cordon pointed to the corner of the room.

"No, that wasn't Connor's," Sean said. "His was huge and it's not the one in the living room."

"A TV doesn't matter." Cormac sighed. "I'm going downstairs." He lumbered out of the room.

Sean watched after him before turning to Cordon. "Did you find his paperwork? Passport, will, the house deed, utilities? They all need to be taken care of."

"We found his bills in the kitchen and will pass them onto his mother." Cordon checked his watch. "Her lawyer should be here, but we haven't found any other paperwork."

"Not even a filing cabinet?" Sean shook his head in surprise. "I'm shocked that he didn't have any paperwork. Grandpa took care of Dad's and Connor's, and now Alec's." He became sombre. "But Kelly gets to sort out Ethan's. If there's any. Mind if I look around?"

"Go for it." Cordon studied Sean's face, seeing pain, shock and denial.

Sean took a breath and wandered into the bathroom, opened every drawer and cupboard, then moved onto the closet. He tapped on walls and checked the floor and ceiling.

"Having fun?" Cordon asked.

"Wondering if he had a hidden safe," Sean said. "He must have had paperwork somewhere. And where did he keep his gun?"

"Bedside table, and you could be right about a safe. We'll have to get our x-ray gun out and look around."

"And the garden?" Sean walked back into the bedroom. "What about it?"

"Hidden doors, cellars, sheds, anything?" Sean stood at the window. "My cousin was a very secretive person;

we had no clue."

Cordon glanced out the window. "We'll do a sweep of the house and garden once the furniture is gone."

"Don't forget the garage." Sean sighed and turned to the room. "What the hell was he doing?"

"From what I hear, some pretty bad things," Cordon said. "But I've got work to finish."

Sean nodded and left him to it, walking back down to the living room. "Hey, where's Grandpa?" The three of them shrugged. "He came down ages ago." A dull thud drew his attention, his head turned to the right, and he stepped backwards into the hall. "Did you hear that? It sounded like something in the basement."

Kelly's lawyer walked in the door and said, "I'm here for Ethan's belongings for Ms O'Connell."

"Join the queue," Sean said and hurried down the hall to the basement staircase. He peered down and saw Cormac lying on the floor. "Oh, my God, Grandpa!" he yelled. "Call 911. Kieran." He pounded down the stairs with multiple people behind him. "Grandpa, Grandpa." Sean fell to his side, feeling his neck for a pulse. It was barely there. "Grandpa."

Kieran got on his knees. "Dad, Dad. Hang in there. Don't let this get to you."

Emerson was beside Sean. "Cormac, oh, my darling, hang in there. I love you."

Sandy was standing on the landing looking down, the phone to the 911 operator at her ear.

Kelly's lawyer, Cordon, and several crew members worked to save him.

"Grandpa," Sean said. "Don't you dare leave me, too."

Chapter 24

The funeral of New York Police Commissioner Cormac Donovan Ryan was held a week after his death, one month shy of his seventy-fifth birthday, his retirement, and his marriage to Emerson Lake. The service was held at St Patrick's cathedral and lasted two hours. His only surviving son, Kieran, and only surviving grandson, Sean, were in attendance, along with Sandy and her family, and Emerson and hers, plus every officer who had worked under him and those who didn't.

When the service was over, his coffin was driven to the cemetery and carried to the Ryan family plot to be buried alongside his wife, his parents, three sons, and two grandchildren.

Kieran and Sean stood at the foot of his grave watching it be filled. Emerson and Sandy stood either side.

Outside the fenced in plot stood over five hundred officers, friends, and colleagues to pay their respects. All working officers were in full uniform; those not wore suits. Sandy's family stood under the tree, as did Emerson's, which consisted of CC Charleston, Amy Aldridge, Olivia Sutton, Gemma Madison, and Sydney Kingston.

The coffin laid, Sean, Kieran, Sandy, and Emerson threw handfuls of dirt in. The folded flag was passed to Kieran who held it to his chest.

Everyone stood silent as the priest said his words. They held little comfort for Sean. The family's Catholicism meant nothing to him anymore. It had meant nothing as his grandfather died in his arms, unable to be resuscitated. It had meant nothing when they identified the body in the morgue. It had meant nothing when the coroner handed in his report. Fatal heart attack.

Sean stared down at the coffin, hands in pockets, knowing that his life was incomplete. While he might have a future, his past was all but gone. Especially with his grandfather now gone from his life.

When the grave was full, the officers gave a final salute and filed away one by one in a simple, silent line.

Sandy's family moved forward for her, taking her back to the Ryan house for the wake.

A man stepped forward. He'd been keeping his distance from the grave, not wanting to disturb proceedings, but now he wanted to show his respects. He stopped beside a line of women and glanced at the one closest. He did a double take. "Ms Kingston?"

Sydney turned her head and moved her black lace parasol out of the way to see who had spoken. "Ah, Mr Levinworth. You're Sean's therapist. How nice of you to pay your respects."

Walter stared at her in shock. "You know who I am?"

"Of course. I've heard all about you." She turned back to the grave. "What a horrid day to have a funeral. It's so stiflingly hot. I felt sorry for those officers, standing there in the heat. They must've sweltered. I know I have. Haven't you?"

Walter looked down at her black knee length dress with the matching short sleeved blazer over it. She'd added stockings, black pumps, and lace gloves to match the parasol. Her brown hair was in a stylish bun. He found himself aroused and hot and smoothed his blazer. "It is just a bit." His brain quickly tried to work, and questions exploded out of him. "Why are you here, Ms Kingston? Is it to support Emerson, or Sean?"

Sydney's left brow rose. "Both, Mr Levinworth. Emerson's my best friend. I thought it high time I came and supported her. And Sean deserves support as well. As do Kieran and Sandy as the only remaining Ryans."

"Has he had your support the whole time? Or is what he said true? This was all a game?"

Sydney smirked. "Isn't it all fun and games…until it's not?"

"And people get hurt," he said, watching her for signs.

"Until revenge is served on a cold hard slab," she replied and gave him a sly smile and a nod. "Walter." She stepped towards Emerson who moved into her arms. They hugged fiercely. "Oh, Em, I'm so sorry."

"So am I," Emerson sobbed.

Kieran and Sean finally turned and walked out of the plot.

"Sydney," Kieran said. "Thank you for coming."

"Of course." She hugged him. "Your father was always kind to me, and he loved my best friend." She squeezed Emerson's hand. "Are you heading back for the wake?"

"Yes, Sandy's already there. Are you coming?"

"I am. I need to support my girl and those who are left." She gazed up at Sean. "You holding up?"

"Barely," Sean said and told Kieran to go on ahead. "I need to chat to someone."

"All right, I'll see you at home." Kieran slapped him on the shoulder and escorted Emerson and the Pulsate ladies to their car.

"Sydney." Sean moved into her waiting arms and sobbed on her shoulder.

She held him tightly, stroking the back of his head until he finished. "Walter's here," she whispered.

Sean raised his head and wiped his face. "Walter." He dried his hands on his pants legs and shook Walter's hand. "I didn't know you'd be here."

"I'm paying my respects," Walter said and pointed to the family plot. "She's almost full."

Sean sadly looked at all of the graves. "That she is. Thank you for paying your respects. As you can see, it's just me and Kieran left."

"Let's hope he won't be here next," Walter said.

"He won't be here for a very long time." Sean shook his head. "I'd say death has had his fill. More than enough to last a lifetime. Thank you, Walter, for all you've done. You really have helped me." He held out his hand.

Walter gave a nod and shook it again. "I'll just pay my respects to everyone."

"Thank you, Walter, that's sweet. Meanwhile, we have a wake to get to and all of those officers that were here are coming. We'd better get going. Sydney." He turned to her. "Have you met Walter?"

"I did and thanked him for his help with you. It was

nice to finally meet you, Mr Levinworth."

"And you, Ms Kingston. I didn't know you were back in New York."

"Oh." Sydney gave him a mysterious smile. "Who said I ever left?" She and Sean slid their arms around each other and walked away.

Levinworth's brows lowered. Sean's last words from his last session bounced around in his head. *It's all there, I've told you the whole time, you just needed to listen. This was all a game to get bestsellers.* Sydney's words spoken just moments ago joined in, *Isn't it all fun and games…until it's not,* and *until revenge is served on a cold hard slab.* He went back to Sean's words, *You see now, Walter, that would be called revenge.* To Sydney's, *who said I ever left.*

He slowly followed until he saw them climb into their car and leave. Together. Smiling. Happy. "Jesus fucking Christ!"

*****

Two days after the funeral, Emerson, Kieran, Sandy, and Sean stood in the dining room of Cormac's house.

"Uncle Kieran, she's all yours now." Sean held onto the back of his grandfather's chair. "You're the last man standing, so you get the house and everything in it."

"But it does not feel good," he said, listening out for his father's voice. "He's not here."

"Unlike Pop who did pass here… Grandpa passed at Ethan's home. Ethan was in his home, so maybe his spirit is with Grandpa's. Alec was in a jail, Connor in a warehouse, my dad in the hospital, and my cousins in their car. None of them are here, but they are in your heart, and this was their home, *your* home growing up, so now it's up to you to raise a new brood of Ryan's into law enforcement and be the head of your own clan."

Kieran snorted. "Yeah, sounds great."

"It can be," Sean replied. "It *has* to be. For everyone's sake. You and I are all that's left until your daughter comes along and I don't know how much longer I can stand using the Ryan name. I need to run from it, hide from it, just…" He shook his head and heaved a sigh. "Find *myself.* Find *me.* Like Emerson." He reached for her hand, and when she took it, he squeezed. "You'll be okay. He treated you like a queen."

She gave a small smile. "He did. And I loved him, but now he's gone, and I didn't get to be his wife."

"You were for all intents and purposes," Kieran said. "He loved you, we know he did, and had no problem with you being his new wife."

"Thank you." She wiped away a few tears. "I know everything now goes to you, and I've packed up all of my belongings, but…" She withdrew her hand from Sean's and looked at the square cut diamond engagement ring. "I'd like to keep this, if you don't mind."

"He gave it to you, so it's not mine," Kieran said with a shake of his head. "It's yours."

Her smile was tight to keep the tears at bay. "I loved him. I did. I truly did. But even we knew times were getting strained. We both doubted we'd even make it, and now look. They're all gone."

The doorbell rang out in the silence.

"That's for me," Emerson said, and brushed the tears from her face. "I'm leaving New York and going to Australia with Sydney. I need to get away from everything and give myself time to heal and grieve. But let me know when the baby arrives and I'll send a present." She waved Sandy over. "Come, let's hug it out. This is probably the last time I'll see you." They hugged and cried before she turned to Sean. "You. Come here, my almost grandson-in-law. You've been an absolute delight to watch grow into the mature *and* successful man you've become."

Sean caught her in a bear hug and lifted her off her feet. "Thank you for being in Grandpa's life. You made him happy in his final years."

"He made me happy." She settled on her feet and swept her mane of black curls off her face. "It's time for me to go, and the three of you to talk. I wish you good luck, and good times, and I'll see you when I see you."

The doorbell rang out a second time.

"Better go." She hurried to the door and opened it to see Amy, Sydney's assistant.

"Ready to go?" Amy asked.

"I am." Emerson rolled two suitcases with two matching bags attached out the door to her and rolled another two sets out to the porch.

"You need help?" Sean grabbed the last two sets. "I'll take these out to the car for you. Why do you even have six cases and bags?"

She laughed as he rolled them out and turned to Kieran and Sandy. "I really hope you take this house. I know the next few years will be hard with all of the court cases and lawsuits that *are* happening and *will* happen. But Douglas and Cormac would love for you to start your family here." She grasped Sandy's hand. "I know it will be hard, but the two of you can do it."

"Ready?" Amy popped up on the doorstep and grabbed another case.

Emerson gave Sandy and Kieran a last smile. "Take care, you two. It's been a hell of a ride and it's not over yet." She let go of Sandy's hand and reached for Amy's. "I am, so let's go." She grabbed her other case and they hurried out to the car.

Sean stepped inside and waved as they left. "One down, one to go." He closed the door and walked back into the living room, before pulling an envelope from his pants pocket and handing it to Sandy. "Now it's my turn. For the two of you and your growing family."

"What is it?" Puzzled, Sandy opened the envelope and looked in it. "Oh, Sean no." She pulled out a cheque for two million dollars. "No, we can't accept this." She showed it to Kieran. "We can't."

"You *can*," Sean said. "If you don't want it personally, put it in trust for the kids to pay for their educations. Tell them it's from Cousin Sean."

"What's this from?" Kieran took the check and studied it.

"Your brother's house."

Kieran's head shot up. "What?"

Sean gave them a sad smile. "I sold the house. That's the lot. I didn't want it. The house, that is, but I also don't need the money. It's yours to help with your future, 'cause you may need it with what's going on."

"Ah, Sean, we can't." Kieran looked at his wife.

"You *can* and you will," Sean argued. "It's for your future and your children's future. Now, let's sit down because I have a few other things to tell you."

Chapter 25

Two weeks after his last visit, Sean turned up in Walter's office.

"Sean," Levinworth said in surprise and closed the door after him. "I wasn't sure if I'd see you again, least of all so soon."

Sean sank onto the couch, tears already filling his eyes. "It's been rough."

"I'm sure." Levinworth sat in his easy chair and waited for him.

Sean's head shook in despair and the tears rolled forth. "I really am damaged, aren't I?" He looked at Levinworth. "I'm so fucking broken, but I shouldn't be because I have a future to go to and yet here I am on my therapist's couch crying like a fucking baby."

Levinworth took a breath. "What's happened?"

Sean sniffed and wiped his face with the backs of his hands before grabbing the box of tissues on the coffee table in front of him. He wiped his face and nose. "I need to confess. It's time for confessions, final admissions, and you can't tell anyone."

"I'm under oath to not reveal any information,"

Levinworth said.

"Okay." Sean brushed a wavy lock of hair from his eyes. "Emerson went home with Sydney, and I feel like I've lost a grandma, too. She's gone. She's been a rock these last few years, just like Grandpa. And I sat Kieran and Sandy down and told them everything." He paused. "Well, not everything, everything. But mostly concerning me. That I'm Bryan Jamison, etcetera. I sold my condos and my apartment, and my parents' house. I gave them the two million from that for the kids' futures. Told them if they ever needed help or money to let me know and I'll help in anyway. I told them the whole story about Sydney, Connor, and Dad from five years ago. I'd only told them briefly about Ethan's involvement with her just after his death because Kieran asked about his obsession with Sydney. Can I have some water?"

"Help yourself."

Sean picked a bottle of lemon lime sparkling water from the fridge and swallowed half before he continued. "We had to deal with Grandpa's will. Kieran and Sandy get the house, and his money went to veterans' services, as per his request. Emerson kept her ring. Kieran had no problem with that. We also had to deal with interviews from the FBI, CIA, ATF, and God knows how many other agencies. Kieran's filed a lawsuit against them for Alec's death, and I asked my lawyer to help them out. They also have a few lawyer friends helping them deal with it all, so that's good." He finally sat back down. "I don't know how much longer it will go on for, but we've been told that between Grandpa, Declan, Connor, Ethan, and Alec, there will be investigations that last years. That means lawyers and bills and fees. Grandpa had money, but it goes to the services, as per Pop's will. And they don't have a lot of money saved, so the money I gave them may disappear."

"Will that be a problem?"

"Meh." Sean shrugged. "They didn't want it, so I said set it aside for the kids. I won't be too happy if it goes on lawyers. I'd rather help out with that, and they keep the money for the kids."

"If it's ongoing it will cost a fortune."

"It will." Sean drank another mouthful. "I ah…also need to confess to a crime."

Levinworth's brows rose. "What would that be?"

Sean kept his gaze on the bottle in his hand. "Grave robbing."

Levinworth's head jerked back. "What?"

Sean's gaze moved to his therapist, and he blurted out, "I knew he'd be lonely there on his own for eternity, so I hired a gravedigging crew to dig up Ethan and then Connor and we pulled out Ethan's body and rolled him over to Connor's coffin and buried them together. We then filled up the graves and made out it was just maintenance on the grass. Their equipment was really quiet, I paid well, and we did it once the cemetery closed. It was weird and awful, and they stank and were embalmed, and I had to move Connor's body to the side, so I could put his son in his arms, kinda, and then I had an engraver put Ethan's name and his birth and death dates on Connor's headstone." He sat there gasping. "I know what I did was illegal, but I didn't think it was right that he was there on his own. He needed to be with his family."

Levinworth could only stare at Sean as he cried over his cousin. "So, you actually cared more than one percent?"

Sean tearfully nodded. "Yeah."

"Oh, Sean." He sighed. "I really don't know what to say anymore. The tragedy of your family this year beggars belief, and all I can suggest is you do take that time off and see the world and come back when you're ready."

"Can we do it via Zoom?"

"Sure." Levinworth nodded. "Whatever you need I'll accommodate you, because all of this, all of your family… Ah." He rubbed his eyes and crossed his legs before stretching his arms over his head and cracking his back. He slumped in relief and sighed. "I looked at your family plot and felt the trauma and the sadness myself. Gravestone after gravestone after gravestone lined up with military precision. I finally see how your family was *and is* a burden. Even after everything you told me, and I've gone over your file from then and now and I see it *and* you *and* the family in a whole new light."

"Good or bad?"

Levinworth sighed. "Most definitely bad. And I am so sorry you had to live that. I can see why you want to change your last name."

"Yeah, but that's not going to happen for a while. Not with Kieran taking on the whole world and trying to reclaim the Ryan name. He wants to make it stand for good again in Grandpa's name. Regardless of how crooked and vile his three older brothers were, *and* his nephews and niece."

"Does he know about Brandon and Sierra?"

"He does. I told him because it could come out in the

case against Alec. I told him about Sonja, how she was a pro for Madam X, and back in Russia, and that Brandon and Sierra weren't even Ryans by blood, and not even related to each other. Sonja had Brandon, but he wasn't Alec's, and they stole Sierra from an adoption agency, after Sonja lost the baby she *was* having. I bet the two of them found that out, and that's why they were fucking and making a shit tonne of money out of it, and Sonja and Alec did nothing but milk them *for* that money."

"Whoa, wait." Levinworth put his hand up. "You what now?"

Sean gave a short laugh. "Yeah, that's just one more secret they all kept. It's no wonder Alec was never overly emotional after their death. Hell, I don't think he got emotional at all, because they weren't his and he knew it."

Levinworth leaned his head back to stare at the ceiling. "Jesus fucking Christ."

"Yep. I also told them what I knew about my dad and his fucking of all those prostitutes on the Lower East Side. He *was* the prostitute killer from years back. He fucked them and then killed them." He saw Levinworth's jaw drop. "Yeah, Walter. I have proof. And I told them he killed Mom and have *that* proof. And then there's Connor. When we cleared out his apartment I found a small brass key hidden in his bed. It was to a safety deposit box which contained different passports under aliases, foreign money, and a couple of flash drives with all kinds of files on the crooks he was dealing with and stealing from, and some other bizarro shit he was involved with." He sighed and leaned back on the couch. "Everything will more than likely come out in the next few years. Kieran's not sure how much he can keep quiet and out of the press."

"Fuck," Levinworth said. "How did he take all of that?"

"Sandy nearly went into labour, and he was disgusted and shocked. He asked me how I knew. I told him what I knew and had found out on my own. I told him there was something we could do and to not be angry because it may be a good thing when it was all over. Especially if he wanted to tackle the family's crimes and clear our name."

"You said *our.*"

Sean shrugged. "For now, it is. I was the sacrifice, remember. I'll have it until the memoir, until the finale of my life, so another year or two at least."

"I thought you meant your death for a moment."

Sean managed a smile. "I hope that won't be for a very long time. Do you have any questions, Walter? This is our last visit for a while." He studied his therapist's face. "I know you're dying to ask. Go on." He finished off his water.

Levinworth couldn't wait any longer. "You and Sydney. It's true, isn't it?"

"What's true?"

"Everything you told me. Everything I thought was a lie, or a delusion. It's true."

"It is, Walter. All for shits and giggles, and best-selling novels."

"And the deaths of your family? You mentioned revenge."

Sean grinned and said in a sing-song voice, "Now *that's* what's come to pass, revenge is best served cold on a morgue slab, and all of it will come to light, what the Ryan family did in the dead of the night."

"Poetry, cute." Levinworth couldn't help grinning.

"The lies they told, the pleasures they took, from all and every, child, brother, wife and crook. The evidence is piled high, and Vesuvius is about to blow, but for me, Walter, it's time to reap the seeds I planted years ago."

"And we're still going." Levinworth nodded.

"Are you not listening, Walter?" Sean asked. "I'm telling you and you're not listening to the words I speak; it's been all fun and games and the shit's about to peak." He put the bottle on the table and settled back on the couch. "It's been fun, Walter, most visits, 'cause that's all this ever was. Telling my therapist that I was screwed up thanks to my family, which I am, and what screw-ups they were, which they were. It was never about obsession; it was about a game to end all games. To bring down one of the most entitled, arrogant, law enforcement families on this planet, and to write best-selling novels and fuck like wild animals while doing it. And now, Walter, because I booked a two-hour appointment, you might want to get my file and take note, because the confessions I'm about to tell, you *will* be able to quote."

He watched his therapist quickly pull his file out of the cabinet and get his recorder.

"Just like you quoted my books to me, you quoted the truth, something I have told you all along, Walter. You just didn't listen." He moved along the couch until he was as close to Walter as he could get. "Now, click record and I'll confess; you won't be bored, because this family's such a mess."

PART THREE

Chapter 26

She flew out of her bedroom, along the hall, down the grand staircase to the ground floor, and made her way into her office. Her heart thundered in excitement as she booted up her laptop from stealth mode. Once the document was up, she pounded on the keyboard, the final scene she'd been waiting to come to her, and she knew it was how the book was meant to end.

An hour later, she typed *The End* and scrolled quickly to the top to type in the title of the yet unknown novel. Her fingers hesitated. The title she had no longer felt right and the one that had fleeted through her mind in excitement was fast forgotten and no more.

"Damn," she whispered, and sat staring at the blinking curser. For how long, she didn't know, but until the perfect title came to her.

She typed three letters just before the security buzzer rang out in the cold dead silence.

She startled. "Who? What the hell?" She glanced at the clock on the laptop. Five a.m. She'd been there since three when she'd woken with her idea.

She hurried along the hallway to the door, checked

the security camera to see who it was, clicked the gate button, and opened the door. She let her long awaited visitor in.

Sean flew into her arms and kissed her passionately. "God, I've missed you, I love you. Let's go to bed."

"Emerson and Amy are in their own wing, and we have ours." Sydney locked the door and gate and led him upstairs to make mad passionate love.

In her office, as the laptop powered down, the cursor blinked at the last of the three letters.

HIM

PART FOUR

Chapter 27

Two months later, on September eighteenth, Walter received a package. He opened it and found the hardcover of *Her* by Bryan Jamison, and *Him* by Cassandra Kingsley, Sydney's pen name. A letter accompanied them.

Dear Walter,

Here is the real story of our love. It was never an obsession, and was always real, and even though I told you on our last visit the truth behind most of it, here's our love story in our own words.

Sean and Sydney.

Walter Levinworth, PsyD, couldn't help laughing. He'd be getting his own book out of this.

PART FIVE

Chapter 28

One year later, on September eighteenth, Walter received another package. He opened it and found the hardcover of Sean's memoir, *My Two Lives*, and Sydney's memoir, *The Women I Am*. He also found a DVD box set of Emerson Lake's sixth and final season of *Twisted Minds*. A letter accompanied them.

Dear Walter,

Here are all of our secrets laid bare, in all their glorious detail in our memoirs. You might find Emerson's series also incredibly informative. It debuts around the world tomorrow with our books.

Sean and Sydney.

Walter popped the first DVD disc into his laptop and pressed play.

"Hello and welcome to the sixth and final season of Twisted Minds, I am your host, writer, director, and producer, Emerson Lake. This series has been years in the making due to the complexities of the people

involved. The Ryans of New York. From Commissioner Douglas Ryan, to his son, Police Commissioner Cormac Ryan, to sons Alec, Connor, and Declan, and grandchildren Ethan, Brandon, and Sierra. This series details all of the criminal activity and ill-gotten gains of the most famous family in law enforcement. From visits to the infamous Madam X, to being drug lords, prostitute killers, and kidnappers. Threats and violence against perps, and partners, to stolen children. All of the lies, the secrets, and the scandals are laid bare. And now, youngest son, Kieran Ryan, is desperately trying to bring his family name back into good repute while dealing with the downfall of his famous family. He's one man determined to lead by example and put the deaths and illegal dealings of his family behind to forge a better life for his wife, children, and all future Ryans. This is their story, in the Rise and Fall of The Ryans of New York."

About the Author

L.J. has been writing since 2006, when her first of many novels, ***The Road To Vegas,*** was born. In 2016 she created the ***Porn Star Brothers*** series about three sizzlingly hot Australian born Greek Island raised brothers who became the hottest porn stars in '70s America.

L.J. lives in Australia, loves '80s music, disaster movies, and collecting Jackie Collins books as Jackie is her inspiration and mentor.

L.J. Diva is the adult pen name for author Tiara King. You can find more about Tiara on her website; follow her on social media, or visit her publishing house, Royal Star Publishing.

Socials

tiaraking.com.au/ljdiva

royalstarpublishing.com.au

Sign up for *Tiara's* Newsletter...

Make sure you're always in the know and never miss free exclusives, the latest news, book updates, and so much more with newsletters from...

tiaraking.com.au

Have you read these?

The Porn Star Brothers Series

Porn Star Brothers
Forever
Love Never Dies
Stefan: The New Generation
DeLuca
Spiros & Jenny
And Always

The Illicit Things Series

Her
Him
Madam X

A Novel Investigations Series

Designs in Crime
A Killer Plot
Murder on the Set
A Novel Investigation (omnibus)

Or these?

NOVELS

Burning Desires
Anything for You
Falling for London
The Road to Vegas
Hollywood Dreams
The Billionaire's Dirty Little Secret

SHORT STORIES

The Body
The Perfect Plot
The Star of Your Own Crime Scene